MIKE CAREY
THICKER THAN WATER

MIKE CAREY
THICKER THAN WATER

orbit

www.orbitbooks.net

ORBIT

First published in Great Britain in 2009 by Orbit
This paperback edition published in 2009 by Orbit
Reprinted 2009

A CIP catalogue record for this book
is available from the British Library.

ISBN 978-1-84149-656-6

Typeset in Garamond by Palimpsest Book Production Limited,
Grangemouth, Stirlingshire

Printed and bound in Great Britain by
CPI Mackays, Chatham, ME5 8TD

Papers used by Orbit are natural, renewable and recyclable
products sourced from well-managed forests and certified
in accordance with the rules of the Forest Stewardship Council.

Mixed Sources
Product group from well-managed
forests and other controlled sources
www.fsc.org Cert no. SGS-COC-004081
© 1996 Forest Stewardship Council

Orbit
An imprint of
Little, Brown Book Group
100 Victoria Embankment
London EC4Y 0DY

An Hachette UK Company
www.hachette.co.uk

www.orbitbooks.net

Acknowledgements

I'd like to thank my brother, Dave, who went back to Liverpool with me so I could check my memories against what's left of the reality. It was a strange time, and it would have been a lot harder without him. Thanks also to A, who wrote the original on which Mark's poem is based, and taught me what little I know about how it feels to be in that place.

To Barbara and Eric, with love

1

This is kind of how it would have looked, if you were watching from the outside – and this is how the papers reported it when they finally got hold of the story.

Ten minutes shy of midnight on 3 July, a van pulled off Coppetts Road into the front drive of the Charles Stanger Care Facility in Muswell Hill, North London. It was just a plain white Bedford van, unmarked and with very high sides, but it parked right in front of the doors in the bay marked AMBULANCES ONLY.

One woman and two men got out of the van – the woman in an immaculate black two-piece, the men in pale blue medical scrubs. The woman was wearing large, severe spectacles which gave her a stern schoolteacherly appearance – although she was unsettlingly beautiful, too, and she carried herself in a way that made the sternness seem to be an ironic – almost a provocative – pose. She checked her reflection in the nearside mirror, tilting her head to the left and then to the right while staring at herself critically out of the corners of her eyes.

'You look lovely,' said one of the two men.

The woman shot him a look and he threw up his hands in ironic apology. *I was only saying.*

The night was almost oppressively warm, and very quiet. The Stanger itself, normally the source of many unsettling sounds at night – screams, sobs, curses, prophetic rants

— was unusually still. There were crickets, though, despite the paltriness of the Stanger's grass verges, which seemed too meagre to support an ecosystem. But this was London, after all: maybe the crickets had to commute like everyone else.

The three went in through the swing doors, the woman leading the way.

The nurse on duty at the reception desk had seen them pull up and now watched them enter. She had to buzz them in through a second set of doors that had been installed very recently to enhance the Stanger's security. She did so without waiting for them to announce themselves, because she was expecting them: strictly speaking, that was a breach of security right there.

She noticed that the two men didn't look entirely convincing as hospital orderlies. One was a slender Asian man with a certain resemblance to Bruce Lee and an air that you could — if you wanted to be polite — call piratical. The other wore his scrubs as though they were pyjamas that he'd been sleeping in for three nights, and had a sardonic self-assured cast to his features that she instinctively mistrusted. His mid-brown hair was unkempt and his mouth subtly asymmetrical, hanging down slightly more on one side than on the other so that when his features were at rest they seemed to wear either a wry smile or a leer.

But these things she noted in passing, because most of her attention had immediately switched to the woman. It wasn't just that she obviously outranked the two men: it was something magnetic about her face and figure that made it an unmixed and startling delight just to look at her.

The woman's appearance, to be fair, was both striking and out of the ordinary. Her hair and eyes were black, her skin white — the undiluted white of snow or bone rather than the muddy pink-beige mix that passes for white according to normal labelling conventions. Since she was dressed in black, relieved only by the occasional hint of dark grey, she could have been a monochrome photograph.

The woman gave the nurse a civil nod as she walked up to the desk. 'Doctor Powell,' she said, in a voice that was as deep as a man's but infinitely richer in tone and nuance. 'From the Metamorphic Ontology Unit in Paddington. We're here to collect your patient.' She laid four sheets of A4 paper on the countertop: a transfer form from the local authority, a court document granting temporary power of attorney and two copies of a signed and notarised letter from Queen Mary's Hospital in Paddington acknowledging the receipt of one Rafael Ditko into the Hospital's care and jurisdiction. The letter was signed *Jenna-Jane Mulbridge*.

The nurse at the desk gave these documents the most cursory examination possible. She was secretly admiring Doctor Powell's easy self-assurance, Doctor Powell's very impressive outfit and, to be blunt, Doctor Powell's magnificent body. The nurse herself was only five foot three, so she envied this other woman's height and long legs. She noticed, too, how well the doctor's black hair, shoulder-length but pulled back quite severely, framed her pale, exquisite face. And she noticed that the blouse was buttoned all the way up to the top, giving no hint of cleavage: perhaps this was because the doctor's curves were ample, her nipples large and obviously erect, and there was no line or ridge in the blouse's hang to indicate the presence of a brassiere. Any further display would tip over from arousing to indecent.

An incongruous image rose into the nurse's mind, making her blush. She imagined herself unbuttoning that blouse, pulling it open on one side or the other and planting a kiss on one of the doctor's breasts. She wasn't gay – had never even had a passing crush on another woman – but the black, bottomless eyes behind the big spectacles seemed to invite such intimacies and promise reciprocal explorations. Or perhaps it was the doctor's perfume, which was even more striking than her appearance. At first it had seemed almost harsh, with sweat and earth mixed up in it, but now it had an aching sweetness.

'You need to stamp the bottom copy of the letter,' the doctor said in that same thrilling voice. The nurse, flustered, pulled herself together and did what she'd been asked, although the outline of the doctor's face and upper body remained on her eyes like an after-image as she fumbled for the stamp and applied it with trembling fingers.

'And sign,' said the doctor.

The nurse obeyed.

'I believe Mister Ditko has already been prepared for transfer,' the doctor said, folding and pocketing the letter. 'I'm sorry to rush you, but we have another call to make tonight and we're already late.'

In point of fact they were fifteen minutes earlier than their scheduled arrival time, but the nurse wasn't going to spoil the moment by arguing. She was fond of the music of Nick Cave, and a line from one of his songs went through her head right then. *A beauty impossible to endure.*

She paged the duty manager, since she wasn't allowed to leave her station, but she only paged once and she hoped he'd take his time in coming. In the meantime she engaged the doctor in conversation, ignoring the two men as if they didn't even exist. Later she was unable to describe a single thing about them: she wasn't even sure whether they were black or white. They could have been fluorescent green for all she cared.

The duty officer arrived all too soon, introduced himself unctuously to the distinguished visitors and took them away along the main corridor, out of sight. Forlornly, the nurse watched them go. She should have asked for a phone number, at least. But then, what would she have done with it? She was straight. Straight and married. A momentary madness had overtaken her, and now she struggled to fit the memory of it into her definition of herself. What did a woman's breasts taste of? Why had it never occurred to her to find out?

The duty manager had much the same experience, complicated in his case by the painful erection he got when he had been walking alongside the doctor for only a few paces.

'Mister Ditko is in the annexe,' he explained, adjusting his walk a little to de-emphasise the bulge. 'In a purpose-built room. The engineering was quite complicated – and very expensive – but your Professor Mulbridge seemed confident that she could duplicate it.'

'We have very extensive resources at the MOU,' said the doctor, sounding cool and detached and giving no sign at all of noticing the duty manager's crisis of etiquette. 'Our annual budget is eighty million, and that's supplemented by donations from various sources. Mister Ditko's cell is already built and waiting for him.'

The duty manager winced. 'We don't like to use the word "cell" . . .' he began. But they'd reached their destination by this time, and the massive steel door, like the door of a bank vault, made the mouthful of euphemisms that he was about to utter taste a little sour, so he let the remark tail off.

A burly male nurse was waiting for them at the door, and on the duty manager's nod he now unbolted it. Three large bolts, at top, midpoint and bottom, and a formidable-looking mortice lock – another recent addition – at which one of the two orderlies (not the pirate, but his colleague) stared with undisguised fascination.

'I would have expected Professor Mulbridge to supervise this transfer herself,' the duty manager remarked conversationally. 'She's been trying for so long to make it happen.'

'She's got a lot on her plate right now,' said the man who'd been ogling the mortice lock. 'Saving the world, one ghost at a time.'

The remark struck the manager as surprisingly irreverent, and so it stuck in his mind. Like the nurse on reception, though, he was finding that the unfeasibly gorgeous doctor was acting like a kind of lodestone to his mind, pulling his attention inwards towards her whenever he tried to think of anything else. God, she smelled like – what? What was it? Whatever it was, you wanted to eat the smell, in shovelled handfuls.

The door swung open, revealing a room that was basically a featureless cube, without furniture or ornament.

A sourceless white radiance, harsh and even, filled it. The walls, ceiling and floor were also white.

In the centre of the room – the only thing it held – was a steel frame, about seven feet high by four wide. It was just a rectangle of steel: two uprights joined by two horizontal struts, to the bottom of which three sets of rubber-rimmed wheels had been fitted on cross-axles which had been set very wide to give the whole structure some much-needed stability.

Around the inside edges of the frame there were twenty or more steel loops to which thick elasticated cables had been attached. A man hung in the centre of the frame, dressed in an all-over-body straitjacket to which the free ends of the cables had been fitted. The overall impression was of a fly in a spiderweb. The man in the frame thrashed and squirmed, but his movements were absorbed by the cables so that he never moved more than an inch or so in any direction.

And his movements were sluggish and uncoordinated in any case. He seemed to have been drugged. His eyes were unnaturally wide, the over-enlarged pupils filling them to the point where no whites showed. His mouth was slack, and a little gluey liquid had collected at its corners.

'OPG,' said the duty manager, as if any confirmation of that was needed. 'Thirty micrograms, intramuscular. If you need any to take with you, we've got some doses made up already – and it's not likely we'll need them any more once Ditko is—'

'We're good,' said the man who'd spoken before. 'Thanks. We've got our own ways of calming Mister Ditko down.'

The duty manager shrugged. 'Fair enough. Now, this thing is heavy.'

'We've got it,' said the doctor, stepping into the cell. She turned the frame around one-handed – a feat which made the manager's eyes widen, because he knew exactly how much it weighed.

The man hanging in the frame twisted his head around to look at her. He said something that the duty manager couldn't make out. It sounded like a single word – possibly a name – but it had a great many syllables and it certainly wasn't Powell.

'Asmodeus,' the woman answered, dipping her head in acknowledgement. 'It's been a long time.'

The man's head sagged. He was fighting a big enough dose of the drug to kill a small herd of elephants. OPG was a neurotoxin, cleared for clinical use only in a very narrow range of situations. This patient, Rafael Ditko, was explicitly one of them. 'Bitch,' he muttered thickly, sounding like a wet-brained alcoholic. 'Hell-bitch.'

'Does he know you?' the duty manager asked, curious.

'We met,' said the doctor. 'A long time ago.'

'You diagnosed him? He was your patient?'

'No.' The doctor gestured to her two attendants, who came and took the two ends of the frame. 'It was before he was confined.'

She didn't offer any further explanation, and since the context wasn't a clinical one the duty manager didn't feel as though he had any right to press the matter. He stood aside as the two men wheeled the frame out of the cell. It was noticeable that they had to lean into it and apply their weight with some determination to make the heavy structure move: the woman hadn't done any of those things. She must be scarily, thrillingly strong, the duty manager thought.

Although he wasn't needed, and his job was done, he walked in procession with the little group as they made their way back down the main corridor. He offered the opinion that this transfer ought to have been carried out years before. 'Ditko has always been a problem for us,' he said. 'We're not a specialised facility, in the way that you are. We can't afford to watch him as closely as he needs to be watched. And we're under different kinds of scrutiny.' He lowered his voice. 'It's fair to say,' he murmured, with a quick smile at the doctor, 'that you can put him to some good use, yes? I mean, that you'll be doing more than just keeping him sedated? Professor Mulbridge has some research in mind, I'm sure. Into Ditko's condition. And it really needs to be done. He's an incredible specimen. I don't mean to be cold-blooded, but seriously — incredible. With the right equipment, and the right person directing things, you could find out a lot. And if you needed some input from us here; observations and conclusions, based on . . .'

The duty manager faltered into silence as the doctor turned to face him, raising a hand to stop her two attendants in their tracks. She stared at him, and her bottomless black eyes seemed to pull him in closer to her as though she had her own personal gravity field.

'Thank you,' she said. 'That's very good of you. I'll be sure to call on you at some point. Soon. I'll come soon, and we'll work together. Just you and me. Intensively.'

She turned her back on him and walked away, the two

men resuming their efforts and pushing the steel frame after her. The duty manager remained rooted to the spot, staring after them. He no longer had an erection. Doctor Powell had brought him to climax with her voice.

The doctor gave the nurse at the reception desk a civil nod as they left, and the nurse as she buzzed them out responded with a smile, feeling the warmth of the doctor's attention sweep over her like an intimate caress. She continued to watch them as they lowered the rear ramp of the van, loaded the steel frame onto it and raised it up again. These operations took perhaps three minutes, during which time the duty manager limped past her into the gents' washroom and did not emerge again.

The van pulled away, and the driveway was empty and quiet for perhaps a further minute or two. Then another van, dark blue this time, drove up and stopped. A sleek black car rode before it, and another behind it.

A large delegation emerged from the three vehicles, assembling itself behind an imposing grey-haired woman in her early fifties, dressed in a three-quarter-length dark blue coat in an antiquated and somehow faintly reassuring style. Her face bore an expression of calm and benevolence, which contrasted with the hatchet-faced mien of the big black-suited men who flanked her.

The nurse buzzed them in, but she was puzzled. The Rafael Ditko transfer was the only note on the duty sheet for the night, and this didn't look like a casual drop-in. In fact, it looked like a formal visit from a head of state.

'Jenna-Jane Mulbridge,' said the grey-haired woman, with a smile, presenting the nurse with a set of documents that was the exact duplicate of the ones she'd just filed.

'From the MOU at Queen Mary's. We're here to collect one of your patients for formal transfer. I think you were notified.'

The nurse boggled at them, her mouth opening and closing. She looked down at the paperwork, which seemed to be all present and correct. She looked up at the woman in the long coat, whose amiable, expectant smile was starting to turn down at the edges.

She paged the duty manager, who did not emerge from the bathroom.

'Well, this is going to sound funny . . .' she said, in a quavering voice.

A long way west and a little way south, the white van pulled off the North Circular Road onto the weed-choked forecourt of a closed and derelict petrol station. Reggie Tang killed the engine and turned to look at me – quite an impressive feat, since it meant looking past Juliet. Reggie is gay, of course, but that's no defence against Juliet. Short of having your genitals surgically removed and locked away in a blind trust, there *is* no defence against Juliet.

'This is where I bail,' he said.

'I'm going across the river at Kew,' I pointed out. 'Then I'll come back around. I can take you a lot closer to home.'

Reggie gave a sour smile. 'Thanks, Castor,' he said. 'But I think I'll walk. If you get pulled over, I'd just as soon be somewhere else. You promised me a ton, right? I'd hate to think you were as big a prick-tease as your girlfriend.'

Juliet gave Reggie a thoughtful stare, then turned and looked inquiringly at me. 'Prick-tease?'

'Macho shithead obloquy,' I parsed. 'Means a girl who promises but doesn't deliver.'

'Oh. I see.' Juliet turned to look at Reggie again. 'But I *do* deliver,' she assured him, deadpan. Reggie blanched, which on his dark-hued face made a striking effect. Juliet held his gaze and licked her lips, slowly. To forestall pants-wetting and hysterics, I took out the small sheaf of tenners that was Reggie's pay-off, slapped him lightly in the face with it to break the spell, and shoved it into his hand.

'Off you go, son,' I said. 'And don't spend it all in the same shop. Remember, if the Met come rolling by, you were sat at home tonight with your dick in your hand. Or maybe Greg's dick, I'm not fussed.'

Juliet looked away, letting him off the hook. There hadn't been any real malice in the show of strength – except that even a faint whiff of misogyny pushes a lot of her buttons – and I know for a fact that she's on the wagon these days as far as devouring men's souls is concerned. Still, she can get inside your head and vandalise the furniture with frightening ease. And Reggie had been a real help tonight, even though he really didn't owe me any favours, so I'd have hated to see him leave with bits of his psyche hanging loose.

He muttered some kind of goodnight and scrambled out of the van. I took it out of neutral and started to turn the wheel, but Juliet put a restraining hand on my arm.

'I'm getting out here too, Castor,' she said.

'Seriously?' I was surprised. 'I can drop you off right outside your door.'

She smiled – or at any rate showed her teeth. 'And then the thing in the back would know where I live.'

'The thing in the back,' I said, a little grimly, 'is my best friend.'

Juliet shook her head. 'Not really,' she said. 'Not any more. There's a little of Rafael Ditko left, still, but mostly he's Asmodeus now. There's a kind of progressive deterioration that comes from being possessed by a demon — a deterioration of the human host, I mean. And because I know what Asmodeus is, and how he takes his pleasure, I'd prefer to keep him as far away from my private life as I can.'

I thought about that in silence for a moment. 'And yet you agreed to help me tonight,' I pointed out cautiously.

'Yes.' Juliet's tone was thoughtful. 'It's something I've been discussing with Susan. The idea that you can experience pleasure in helping someone else even when there's no direct advantage to be gained from doing it.'

'Altruism,' I hazarded.

'Yes, exactly. Altruism. I decided to be altruistic tonight, to see how it felt.'

Susan is Juliet's lover and more recently her civil partner — a union that's already done a lot for Juliet in terms of taking some of the rough edges off her and making her less likely to rip people's heads off in the course of casual interactions. But it's a steep learning curve, in some respects. Steep, and bumpy, and filled with sudden, unexpected potholes.

The reason why it's all those things is because Juliet is a succubus, which is to say a demon whose specific modality is sex. She feeds by arousing men's desires and then consuming them, body and soul — the guy's lust functioning in some indefinable way as a necessary ingredient in the feast. I mean, maybe she could still bring herself to devour a man who was thinking about his tax returns, but it would be like eating plain boiled rice or pasta without sauce.

To describe Juliet's physical attributes is just a waste of words. She's tall and slender with narrow hips but full breasts. She has the pale skin, the dark eyes and hair and yada yada that I mentioned earlier on. But these things are accidents: she could be any colour, any size, any shape. The point is that Juliet does something to your brain. It's a combination of her scent – which is fox-rank on the first breath, ineffable perfume on the second – and her hypnotic gaze. Two seconds after you look at her you can't remember the face of any other woman you ever met, and you don't want to. She rewires your perceptions, painlessly, effort-lessly: she becomes your Eve, your Helen, your long-lost and looked-for harbour.

Which until recently was an exquisite adaptation to a predatory lifestyle – as brutally functional as a tiger's claws or a shark's teeth. Now, as I think I already said, she's taken the pledge and wouldn't rend and eat you if you asked her to. It would just get her in trouble with her missus.

'Well, how was it for you?' I asked, clearing my throat which felt a little dry. 'The altruism, I mean?'

'Interesting,' said Juliet. 'And not unpleasant. But I think a little of it may go a long way, Castor.'

'Meaning . . . ?'

'Meaning I've got a full caseload, and if you need any more favours in the days or weeks to come don't hesitate to ask someone else. And conversely, if I should need a second gun on anything I attempt I expect you to drop your own affairs and be available to me at any moment of the day or night.'

'Nothing would make me happier,' I said, deadpan. 'Day or night.'

Juliet studied my face for smutty double meanings, but all the meanings were right there on the surface. If she asked, I was there. She knew that. Unfortunately, it was true of most of the people she met so it didn't mean all that much.

'When Professor Mulbridge finds out that you stole her prize specimen from under her nose,' she observed, 'it will make her very angry. She'll want to get back at you. She'll think of ways to do it that you won't see coming.'

I acknowledged this with a vague shrug. 'She's been angry at me ever since I turned down her job offer,' I said. 'Let her come. I'll be ready for her.'

Juliet looked as though she was reserving her own opinions on that one, but she let the point go. 'Bind Asmodeus well,' she said, getting out of the van. 'If he gets loose — really loose, with no anchor in your friend's flesh to hold him back — you can't imagine the harm he could do.'

But on that point she was wrong. My imagination is just fine, and I know what will happen if Rafi's passenger ever finds a way to step off the bus.

'I'll be careful,' I promised.

'Yes,' she agreed, with no hint of sarcasm in her face or voice. 'I know you take no unnecessary risks, Castor. Not by your own definition.'

'Thank you.'

'Shall I tell you now how flawed your definitions are?'

'Give Sue a kiss from me,' I said. 'Platonic. On the cheek. Nothing threatening.'

'She has *my* kisses.'

'Then I guess she's doing okay.'

Juliet smiled with real and sudden warmth. 'Oh yes,' she agreed. With a final wave she stalked off into the darkness, and was gone more suddenly than the darkness itself could fully explain.

There was a Judas window in the back of the cab that let me look into the rear of the van. I slid it open and peeped through, although there was really nothing to see. Nothing to hear, either: the silence was absolute.

'You okay, Rafi?' I ventured, after a few moments.

No answer. Well, better nobody home than Asmodeus taking Rafi's calls. And better that he sleep all the way to where we were going, because it would make unloading him at the other end a lot less complicated.

I wound up the window and drove away. I still had to get to Lambeth and back tonight, and I wasn't looking forward to the drive. Or to what was waiting at the other end of it.

But I did what I had to do, which – when it comes right down to it – is the epitaph to most of my days. I handed off to Imelda's people down in Elephant and Castle. There were two of them: handsome black men of few words who were ten years my junior and could have folded me backwards until I broke if the notion had come into their heads. I gave the van's keys to the taller of the two, who wore a beanie and bands in rasta colours and had a braided beard that impugned the manhood of any man he met. He waved the keys at me like a schoolteacher waving a pointer.

'Imelda wanted me to say this to you,' he rumbled. 'And she wanted me to say it slow, one word at a time.' He tapped the keys against my chest five times, once for each word. 'Don't – make – me – regret – this.'

Being on his turf and his time, I took the insult with as much good grace as I could muster. 'You ever get any snarl-ups south of the river?' I asked.

He gave me a suspicious scowl. 'What?'

'The beads,' I clarified, pointing to his beard. 'Do they get in the way when you muff-dive?'

His eyes widened and his mouth set in a tight line. 'Man, you're asking for some real—'

I nodded, making the wrap-it-up gesture used by studio floor managers. 'Tell Imelda I'm grateful,' I said. 'And tell her I'll sort this out soon. She's got my word on that.'

South Circular. Kew Bridge. North Circular. In Pen's car now, which at least didn't handle like a barge, but I was at the end of my rope, physically. Tiredness kills. Ask anyone. The only thing that kept me awake was surfing the news channels to find out if I was a wanted man.

Pen was waiting in the kitchen with all the lights on. She wanted a debriefing, which was extensive and occasionally hysterical, shading eventually into alcoholic.

When I rolled into bed at last, drunk with fatigue and spent adrenalin and a great deal of actual alcohol, I fell into sleep like a man stepping off the edge of a cliff. On the way down, I thought with a slightly numbed wonder about all the shit that was going to hit all the many and various fans when the morning came.

And decided to sleep until noon.

*   *   *

But we got through the next day without the sky falling, and then the day after that. There was nothing about Rafi in the papers or on the TV news: there weren't even any good rumours flying on the conspiracy websites, and nobody came to the door to ask me where I'd been on the night of the third. Gradually, Pen and I relaxed from our bunker mentality.

I called Imelda, who said that she'd got Rafi settled in pretty well at her place. 'Rafi?' I echoed, just to be sure. 'Not Asmodeus?'

'Rafael Ditko,' Imelda confirmed. 'In his own right mind and native disposition.'

'You're a wonder, Imelda.'

'Yes, I am. That doesn't mean I'm any happier about this, incidentally.'

'I know. This wipes out any debts between us.'

An edge came into her voice. 'No, Castor, it doesn't. It leaves the balance on my side. And when I call in that favour, you will damn well know about it.'

'Okay.' I was prepared to bend over backwards a long way to placate the Ice-Maker: not many people could have done what she'd done, and I'm not counting myself in that number.

A couple of weeks passed. Pen went down to Peckham every two or three days to visit Rafi, and every visit after the first was what you might call a conjugal one. Without going into indelicate detail, the visits required Imelda and me to pull out all the stops to make sure that Rafi's infernal other half didn't surface and try to make it into a three-some. That didn't bear thinking about.

In fact, there were a lot of aspects of the situation that

didn't bear thinking about, as Imelda was only too happy to remind me. But you can get used to anything, over time. There's no atrocity so atrocious that it can't become a routine.

We felt like we were on top of things. We'd plucked Rafi from the jaws of Jenna-Jane: we'd given him some kind of a doll's-house miniature version of a life. We were shit-hot, all things considered: so good, so sharp, so fly that we knew, even while we were congratulating ourselves, that we couldn't afford to lower our guard by a fraction of an inch. We were good with that. We were holding the door to Hell fast shut, our shoulders braced and our muscles locked.

But how much use is that when the roof falls in?

2

The sound of hammering dragged me up from uneasy dreams. Then the dreams and the noise got muddily entwined, so that for a few confused seconds I was knocking nails into a cross where one of the Bee Gees – Robin, I think – was hanging in place of Christ. I tried to apologise, but he was laying down the lead vocal riff from 'Staying Alive' and with the headphones on I don't think he even heard me.

Then I was awake, and I realised that the noise hadn't stopped. I got myself upright and threw the covers back, my head throbbing as though my brain had been set to 'vibrate' and was taking a lot of incoming calls all at the same time. Why was that?

Oh yeah. Because last night we'd been down in Peckham at the Ice-Maker's, for the third time this week, and when we got back Pen had been too wired to sleep. So we'd talked until the early hours, about old times and counterfactual worlds, until the alcohol drowned the adrenalin and we finally staggered off to our beds.

Half a bottle of Courvoisier XO on an empty stomach, and less than two hours' sleep: the perfect way to start the day, if you want it to feel as long as two days and be filled end-to-end with pain.

I don't have a dressing gown, but I am the proud owner of a Russian army greatcoat – the latest in a long lineage

– so I made that do instead. The bare boards of the stairs were cool under my feet as I trudged down from my attic roost, feeling like something simultaneously thin and fragile and flammable. What time was it, anyway? It had to be well past four o'clock; but, since the half-moon of grubby glass over the door was pitch black, it was still before dawn. Either that or I'd been woken up in the middle of a total eclipse. Someone was going to pay for this, if only in the coinage of over-the-top invective.

Pen came out of her bedroom just as I got to the first-floor landing. She was wearing a black silk kimono with a motif of cranes and floating islands. The raven on her shoulder looked like someone's sardonic comment on the twee chinoiserie, but it still set off her long red hair to good effect: no pallid bust of Pallas ever made as good a perch as incendiary Pen.

She looked spooked, though, and I knew why it was that she hadn't just rolled over in bed and ignored the door knocker's peremptory summons. 'Fix, don't answer it!' she said, her voice hoarse from sleep. 'It's got to be the police. They've found out!'

I put my hands on her shoulders to stiffen her moral fibre – not usually necessary with Pen, but these were special circumstances. 'You didn't do anything illegal,' I reminded her. 'I did, but they probably won't be able to pin it on me – and you're clean even if they do. Anyway, it's been two weeks now. If they'd had anything on us, they would have dragged us in for questioning ages ago. So whoever it is that's down there waking up the neighbours, it's not about Rafi. Why don't you go back to bed and let me deal with it?' I made my tone as emollient as

I could: I'd only become Pen's lodger again a couple of months before, and I was anxious not to spoil the warm afterglow of our reconciliation.

'Bugger that,' Pen snapped back. She was deeply rattled, but it wasn't in her nature to back away from a fight – or even to arrive late for one.

So we went down the stairs in convoy, Pen leading the way. Edgar the raven screeched and baited in protest at the jostling, raising a breeze that would have been pleasant if it hadn't smelled of raw meat.

Pen spoke a couple of words to the door, under her breath, rapid-fire, and then drew back the bolts. Most people make do with woodbine sprigs and factory-stamped magic circles to keep them safe at night, but Pen is a priestess in a pagan religion that she probably made up herself, so she handles her own security.

Because she was still in front of me, blocking my view, and because the night outside was as black as a bailiff's soul, I saw Pen's reaction before I saw the man standing in the porch. She started and took a half-step back, then got herself under control again with an effort I could see even from behind.

'Sorry, Pen,' said a voice I knew very well indeed. 'I need to talk to Fix.'

Pen stepped aside with enormous reluctance, each movement seeming like an effort, and Detective Sergeant Gary Coldwood walked in out of the night. I muttered a coarse oath, and Coldwood shrugged laconically in reply.

'Get it out of your system now,' he suggested. 'You've got a long ride ahead of you.'

Pen looked from me to him and back again. Then she

looked across at a horrendous vase — some kind of Ming-dynasty cuspidor — that she kept on the newel post at the foot of the stairs. There was a terrible strain on her face, and I could see exactly what she was thinking. I shook my head emphatically.

Coldwood conveniently assumed that I was reacting to his words. 'No arguments,' he said brusquely. 'I'll explain as we go, but this is time-sensitive. And it's not business as usual, Fix. Far fucking from it.'

'So I'm back on the books,' I summarised, for Pen's benefit more than for his or mine. 'You want me to read a crime scene for you?'

Coldwood nodded slowly, but he seemed to think the nod needed to be qualified. 'Something like that,' he allowed. Behind him, Pen sagged with relief as her nervous system stood down abruptly from Defcon One.

'I'll leave you two to it then,' she said cravenly, and she had it away on her heels. Edgar took flight at the last moment, dipping at a steep angle through the narrowing gap as Pen kicked the kitchen door closed behind her. He soared across to the shelf over the street door, where he stared down at us with beady-eyed fascination. It's hard not to see him and his brother Arthur as Pen's Hugin and Munin — spies in bird form sent abroad to gather intelligence in situations where she can't eavesdrop herself.

'Did I walk in on something?' Coldwood asked. 'Not that I give a monkey's, you understand. But your mate Rafi checked out of his digs a fortnight back, didn't he? So if you're knocking off his lady love behind his back, you'll probably wake up some day soon wearing your entrails as a bow tie.'

I gave Gary a look that might have dropped him where he stood if my hangover headache hadn't taken the edge off it.

'Leave it,' I suggested.

'Only too happy to.' He looked at his watch, rubbing the ugly scar on his right cheek absent-mindedly. 'Half past four,' he mused. 'Going to take us the best part of an hour, even at this time of night. Get some clothes on, Fix – and bring your paraphernalia.'

I could see in his face that there was no room for argument.

'What's it about?' I asked.

'You'll see. Don't worry, I'll get you back in time for breakfast.'

Edgar gave a derisive caw. I knew what he meant: I'd heard that one before too.

Coldwood was right about it being a long drive, because we ended up south of the river, crossing foul old Father Thames at Lambeth just as the sun came up. The sky was clear apart from a few wisps of cirrus dead-centred in the windscreen of Coldwood's unmarked Primera: it was going to be another scorcher. I looked between the maculate white chimneys of Battersea power station for a flying pig, but there wasn't anything moving up there. We were on our own as we tacked south by east through the rat runs of Southwark.

'How much further?' I asked Coldwood, since he didn't seem to want to tell me what it was I was going to be looking at. He didn't answer: just looked at his watch again and made a vague calming gesture, like a stern dad to a child whining 'Are we there yet?' He seemed to have forgotten his earlier promise to brief me in the car.

'Tell them we're coming,' he instructed his stolid, hatchet-faced driver. The driver nodded and muttered into a walkie-talkie. 'Got the sarge and the . . .' He hesitated and flicked a glance over his shoulder at me. 'Exorcist,' I filled in helpfully, but he decided to leave the sentence unfinished. 'We're on our way to the scene now.'

'Don't let the C2s in until we're finished,' Coldwood called out to him, and the driver relayed the instruction to whoever he was talking to. 'C2s' was an idiosyncratic abbreviation for *celebrity chefs*: it was what Coldwood and his Serious Crimes Unit muckers called their valued colleagues in the forensics division.

We drove through Newington as it was waking up: shopkeepers taking their armour plating down to greet the new day, or tipping buckets of foaming bleach on the dog turds in front of their doors; a sluggish street-cleaning van nosing its way along the gutters like a pig looking for truffles.

'You didn't seem surprised to hear that Rafi Ditko had gone walkies,' Gary commented, looking back at me from the car's front passenger seat. His face was so devoid of emotion that a passing artist might have mistaken it for a blank canvas. 'We were only officially notified about it yesterday.'

'Well, I keep my ear to the ground,' I responded in kind.

'Good way to get your face trodden on.'

'If you catch me at it, feel free to cast the first boot.'

Gary frowned. He hates being smart-mouthed in front

of his chattels and gofers, and this probably rankled all the more because he was doing me a favour: letting me know, in his own winsome way, that Rafi's disappearance from the secure care facility where he'd lived – if you wanted to call it that – for the past three years had now become a police matter. It wasn't good news, but it was coming sooner or later so there was no point in crying about it. We'd see what we'd see.

Perhaps by way of clawing back some of the points he'd just lost, Gary switched to another topic. 'So who is it that's watching you?' he asked.

I blinked, false-footed. 'Who's what?' Now this *was* news to me, and I couldn't quite get my guard up in time to hide it. 'Two-man tag team,' Gary said. 'One on the corner, one in a car a bit further down the street. Discreet operation, but they must have a budget.'

'Probably the rent man,' I said sourly. Jenna-Jane bloody Mulbridge, much more likely. Maybe this was why she'd kept Rafi out of the news: so I'd relax, get sloppy and lead her straight to him. But obviously it hadn't worked yet, or they wouldn't still be there. And now – well, fore-warned was forearmed.

Just south of Elephant and Castle we turned off the main drag onto a service road that took a slack-bellied run-up around the back of the station car park before screwing up its courage and leaping over Kennington Lane in the form of a concrete flyover. All the other traffic on the road was pulling to the left or right in two confused, jostling streams before they got onto this overpass, because directly ahead of us three more police cars had been parked so that they blocked the whole carriageway: or at least the whole carriageway apart from a single narrow gap guarded by a hard-faced WPC. Seeing us coming straight towards her she raised her hand to wave us away, but then she recognised either Coldwood or the driver and stood aside to let us through.

The road beyond had the unsettling emptiness of a school playground during the summer holidays. By this time on a weekday morning it ought to have been heaving; but there were only four vehicles that I could see, and none of them were moving. Two of them were Astras in police livery, with uniformed cops standing in inert clusters around them. A blonde woman in a black Dryzabone was talking to one of the clusters, pointing off towards the distant skyline: two boys in blue went forth to do her bidding. I thought I recognised that tall slim figure and hard handsome face, but there was no point in jumping off that bridge until I came to it.

The third vehicle was an ambulance, standing with its back doors wide open and its hoist platform down, and the last was a sprightly pillar-box red Ford Ka parked on a precariously angled concrete apron too narrow to be called a hard shoulder. Something about the sight of it gave me a sudden qualm of unease. I wasn't entirely sure, though, whether or not that response was coming from the part of my perceptual equipment I call my death-sense. I couldn't see anything dead in the vicinity – or, for that matter, anything in that badly defined and mystifying state we choose to call undead – but then we were still a hundred yards or so away. When we got closer, maybe I'd find out what it was that had set me off.

But we didn't get closer: Coldwood tapped the driver's

shoulder and we slowed to a halt at the side of the road, up against a buckled steel crash barrier that seemed to have done its job on more than one occasion.

Coldwood got out, a little awkwardly because his legs hadn't been set particularly well after being broken the year before – at certain angles they moved in a robotic, discontinuous way. I followed him because this was clearly the end of the ride. Walking around the back of the car to join him, I glanced idly over the edge of the parapet. We were high enough up that we were looking down on the mottled apron of a rooftop car park. The asphalt was bare apart from a phalanx of wheelie bins in one corner, behind which a black jacket lay like a dead bird: part of the inexplicable roadkill of the inner city.

Coldwood leaned against the flank of the car, hands in pockets, like Patience on a monument but with a more pugnacious facial expression. 'So what's the score?' I asked him when it was clear that he wasn't going to speak first.

'You tell me, Fix,' he suggested.

I waited for the other shoe to drop. For the most part I ply my trade wherever there's a profit to be made, and the Metropolitan Police's homicide division has been a lucrative source of income for me on more than one occasion. At one time, in fact, the Met had been my main client, and I'd started to take it for granted. But then, like an old married couple, we'd parted company at last because of irreconcilable differences, mostly arising out of me being arrested for murder. It had been a while since Coldwood had put any work my way, and a longer while since I'd asked him for any favours. So there was something else going on here, and I was damned if I was going to commit myself to anything, even an opinion, before I knew what it was.

But Coldwood seemed equally coy, and the staring match couldn't go on for ever. I shrugged and reached inside my greatcoat. There's a pocket there that I sewed in myself – deep but narrow, just the right size to hold a tin whistle with an inch of clearance at the top so that it's easy to hook it out in a hurry. The whistle in question is a Clarke Sweetone in the key of D. I've tried other brands and other keys, but only in the way that a compass needle tries to pull away from north. It never sticks.

Whistle in hand, I headed over towards the parked Ka. From behind me, Coldwood said, 'Fix.'

I turned and looked back at him. He hadn't moved. 'Yeah?' I demanded.

'Do it from here.'

I measured the distance to the car. 'I can't see anything from here,' I pointed out.

Coldwood held my gaze. 'How do you know until you try?'

There was a time when bullshit like that would have made me dig my heels in, when I would have turned around and walked away rather than play a command performance with a blindfold on. But at this particular time there was something like an unsettled debt between me and Coldwood, dating from an occasion – quite recently – when I'd almost got him killed: that one incident explained both the limp and the scar. And right about then, when I was more or less evenly balanced between giving him a tune and telling him exactly where and how deeply to shove it, the blonde woman came striding up to us, walking right past me without a glance to address herself to Coldwood.

'This isn't right,' she said without preamble. Her expression was grim and tight.

Coldwood nodded. It wasn't a nod of agreement: he was just acknowledging an argument he'd clearly already heard. 'You're down on record, Ruth,' he said, 'so you can stop banging the drum any time you get sick of the sound. But you don't have any seniority on me here and this is the way we're doing it.'

The blonde woman turned now and favoured me with a cold, clinical stare. She was beautiful – really beautiful – but in a hard and austere way that told you more clearly than words how little she cared about what you thought of her. She wore her hair short, and her blue eyes stared out at you pale and unframed, without the benefit of mascara. She favoured greys and blacks, with occasional concessions to blue. Maybe she thought warm colours would be provocative. Tonight she was at the darker end of her spectrum, and her subtle curves were reined in to leave as straight-edged an outline as possible.

'Hey, Basquiat,' I said to her.

'It's not even fair to *him*,' she said, which threw me for a moment until I realised that she was still carrying on her conversation with Coldwood as though I hadn't spoken – and that the 'him' in question was me. 'Or are you finessing the case before it even gets started by making sure it gets thrown out of—'

Coldwood cut in before she could finish.

'I just want Castor to read the scene,' he said. 'I've used him before, and I'll probably use him again. It's custom and practice, and there's nothing for anyone to hang an objection on. And you'll notice that we're standing way over here, not inside your perimeter. Not even close to it. You can even stick around and chaperone me, if you're worried.'

Basquiat turned her gaze back to Coldwood, her eyes narrowing.

'And that will help a lot,' she said, 'given that you came down from Turnpike Lane together.'

'With a driver,' Gary pointed out, looking away towards the rising sun. 'You're welcome to ask him what was said, on or off the record.'

'Oh, please.' Basquiat's tone was blistering. 'Any man on your squad will swear that black is pink-and-fucking-ochre-plaid if you tell him to. I want him when you've finished with him.' Those were her last words on the subject, apparently, and she was already walking away as she said them. I gathered that 'him' was back to being me.

Barely acknowledging the interruption, Coldwood looked across at me and gave a horizontal wave, inviting me to get started. This time I accepted the invitation, because it was pretty damn obvious that I wasn't going to find out what this was all about until I did. Not business as usual, Gary had said. Yeah, that was for damn sure — although anything that had him and Basquiat at each other's throats was bound to have a familiar ring to it.

I put the whistle to my lips, looking towards the parked car because that was where Basquiat and the uniformed cops were and it was obviously the epicentre for whatever had happened here.

I started to play. Not an exorcism, because those take time to plan and prepare: this was more like an echo-sounding, sending my attention out along the filaments of the music to see what I could see.

This is what I do for a living, and if I say so myself I do it pretty damn well. If you're an exorcist, you're born with the knack: the extra chunk of sensory equipment that lets you see what can't be seen and touch what can't be touched. But each of us finds a unique and personal way to tap that common barrel. One might scrawl symbols in a magic circle; another might chant words in dead languages, or light candles, or deal hands of cards or any of a thousand other quaint, banal, potent rituals. I play music, and the music becomes an extension of my mind, plugging me in like the jacks of an old-fashioned telephone switchboard to the world of the dead – which, things being how they are, is usually buzzing.

It was a knack I'd discovered more or less by accident. I'd always been able to see the dead, but I never knew I could bind them until my sister Katie was run down by a truck a couple of weeks after my sixth birthday. It was in trying to dissuade Katie from coming into my bedroom at night with her blood-caked face and talking to me in the dark that I performed my first – entirely accidental – exorcism. I did it by chanting rude playground songs at her until she shut up and went away. Sounds. Patterned sounds, expressing in pitch and rhythm something that I couldn't define or perceive in any other way.

Later I discovered that music worked even better.

Later still I picked up a tin whistle, and it shaped itself to my hand as though it belonged there. Christian Barnard must have felt like that when he picked up his first scalpel. Or Osama Bin Laden when he flicked off the safety catch of his first AK-47.

This particular tune didn't have much in the way of either form or progression. It just ambled backwards and forwards through the same sequence of chords, all in the lower half of the whistle's register and sounding somewhat sullen and melancholy. But as the notes skirled around me the world darkened: or rather, my perceptions shifted a little along the spectrum that has life and death as its two poles.

I was expecting to see the road get more crowded at this point. If anyone had died in the little red car, or under its wheels, then they ought to have come sharply into focus now. In fact, I ought to have been seeing them already, because the newly dead stand out like halogen bulbs in my eyes most of the time. But my death-sense isn't infallible. The whistle is.

This time, though, and apart from the added depths and subtracted highlights, the scene before me didn't seem to have changed at all. Okay, there was a smudged-out but broadly humanoid figure standing in the air a little way out from the edge of the flyover: a suicide, maybe, or someone who'd walked the parapet on a drunken bet and then fallen off. But the elisions and imperfections in that shape – the fact that I couldn't even tell for sure whether it had been a man or a woman, or how old it had been when it shed its flesh and blood and bone and sinew to stand naked in the world – showed that it hadn't arrived there in the recent past. It had died years if not decades ago and that was probably why I hadn't seen it at first.

Over time, ghosts fade like the colours on a cheap tee-shirt. And that ghost was the only one that was haunting this section of the overpass.

Turning my attention back to the parked car, I shifted my fingers on the stops of the whistle and slowly ascended the scale. Like most tin whistles, my Sweetone only has an effective range of about two octaves: but if you're not too worried about the sensibilities of the people around you, you can make brief forays outside that range by half-holing and by varying how hard you blow. I took it as far as I could, an unmelodic shriek creeping in on the highest notes as I pressed down with all eight fingers and pursed my lips more tightly.

Nothing.

I let the last fractured notes of that shapeless abomination of a tune drop like glass splinters from between my fingers. Then I lowered the whistle, shook it twice to clear it of saliva and slid it back into my pocket.

'So tell me about it,' Coldwood suggested.

I turned to face him, looked him in the eye. 'About what, Gary?' I asked, with brittle politeness.

He nodded in the direction of the car. 'What happened here.'

I shrugged. 'I don't know what happened here,' I admitted bluntly. 'But I'll tell you what didn't happen. Nobody died. And you must have known that when you hauled me out of bed and dragged me halfway across London to watch the sun come up.'

Coldwood did the deadpan again – one of his favourite party tricks. 'This isn't about what *I* know, Fix,' he told me. 'It's about what *you* know. And it's probably a good idea if you keep your temper. Because sometimes when you lose it you say things you don't mean.'

'That's the human condition,' I observed. 'Now what the fuck am I doing here if you don't have a DOA?'

He came away from the car's flank, squaring his shoulders. 'Where were you earlier tonight?' he asked me, in the guilty-until-proven-dead tone that all cops use when they deliver that line.

'What?'

'Where were you earlier tonight?'

Well, the truth wouldn't serve so a lie would have to do. 'I was in bed, Gary. I was snogging Morpheus, tongues and tonsils and everything, until you woke me up and brought me here. Why? You got something you want to put me in the frame for?'

'Was anybody with you, Fix?'

'A squad of cheerleaders, but I didn't get any of the names.' Coldwood waited me out. 'No. There was nobody with me.'

'But Pen was in the house?'

'Yeah.'

'You two share your usual drink before bedtime?'

'No.'

'No? Then when was the last time anyone—?'

'It was a *lot* of drinks. Different kinds, but variations on a theme of thundering oblivion.'

'So when was the last time—?'

'Jesus! A bit after one o'clock. So if someone sneaked down here to the wilds of Walworth and blew someone else's brains out through their ear, then yeah, it could have been me. All I'd have had to do is avoid those roadworks around Saint George's Circus, and I'd have been laughing. Then again, if brains were flying, I think I would have got a hint of them just now. But I didn't. And you being a homicide detective, Gary, that puzzles me. It puzzles me to Hell and back again. So I repeat: what the fuck?'

It looked as though the preliminary interview was over. Gary's gaze shot off to stage left again, towards the red car with its entourage of plods. 'Okay,' he said. 'Go take a look. But don't touch anything. If you do, we'll both probably end up wishing you hadn't.'

What I was wishing was that I'd declined Coldwood's invitation in the first place. But then it hadn't been phrased in a way that left me the option. I walked over to the car, aware that he was following me at a discreet distance. Basquiat was still throwing her weight all around the uniformed division, but when the cop next to her looked in my direction she followed his gaze and our eyes met.

She gave a gesture to the uniforms that basically meant back off, and they did. As I walked around the side of the car, everyone got out of my way. That gave me a clear view of the amazingly wide bloodstain that had spilled down the embankment from the car's driver-side door. A sheet of clear plastic had been laid over the stain, its edges neatly anchored with white marker tape and annotated with esoteric symbols. Not magic symbols, I hasten to add: not the lexicon of wards and stay-nots that I know all too well. These were the marks of a different mystery, signalling trajectories, angles, identities, values, place markers for people and objects removed for forensic testing. It wasn't a world that I was particularly at home with.

Basquiat nodded towards the windscreen, but I was

sideways-on to it and whatever revelation awaited me there was still a few seconds away. I slowed and stared in through the side window, amazed at the sheer amount of blood that had splashed all over the upholstery, the dashboard, the steering column. There were even a pair of fluffy dice, gore-covered and dangling like trophies from a bullfight. And if someone had fought a bull inside this cramped little car, then maybe the volume of blood that had been spilled was reasonable after all.

Basquiat and her harem of constables were all staring at me, a certain tense expectation visible in most of the faces. Coldwood was behind me, but something told me that he was watching me too. As nonchalantly as I could, I took the final three steps that brought me to the front of the car.

There's something about your own name in someone else's handwriting that gives you an instant blip of recognition, even when you meet it in unusual circumstances. And this certainly counted as unusual in my book. For one thing, it was written backwards, from right to left: but then, that was because it had been written on the inside of the car windscreen, by someone sitting in the driver's seat. More strikingly, it was written in blood.

F, first of all: a big sprawling capital F whose elongated upright stretched all the way from the top to the bottom of the glass: presumably a sign of how copiously the poor bastard must have been bleeding. A ragged red wedge hid the rest of that first word, apart from the curve of whatever letter came next.

But 'Castor', underneath and a little to the right, stood out very legibly indeed, in spite of the problems the writer seemed to have had keeping the crossbar of the 't' and its curving upstroke separate, and in spite of a ragged tail-off on the 'r'. But then, he was probably running out of writing materials at that point.

'Jesus!' I said. Or at least my lips formed the word. I don't think any actual sound came out. The words *'Use a pen, Sideshow Bob'* flitted incongruously through my brain.

'Know anyone by that name?' Coldwood asked, standing at my shoulder.

'Jesus, Gary!'

'I know. You probably want to breathe slow and deep. If you pass out on the road it will dent your rep.'

I groped for a mental handle or key: something that would make sense of this obscenity. For a moment there wasn't one, but then the salient fact smacked me in the face like a slab of raw fish.

'He's not dead. He didn't die.'

'No. He's at the Royal, in intensive care. They're fifty-fifty as to whether he'll pull through.'

I'm used to death; and I've looked at it in the style pioneered by Judy Collins – from both sides – so maybe I get a little free and easy in my attitude. Right then, though, my stomach was pitching in slow, queasy arcs, and I suddenly felt like I was standing a couple of degrees off true vertical.

'How could he not die?' I asked, hoping my voice didn't sound as uneven to the peanut gallery as it did to me.

Coldwood's tone, by contrast, was blunt and matter-of-fact. 'He just didn't lose enough blood, amazingly. He was cut up like you wouldn't believe. His face. His throat. His upper torso. Defensive wounds on his hands, too, which is probably how he was able to write your name. Someone spent a lot of time on him and tried out a lot of different angles. Mostly pretty shallow cuts, except for one across his shoulder and into his throat. If he dies, that will be the one that killed him. Went right through the brachio-cephalic artery. Hence most of this mess: the brachio is like Old Faithful in pillar-box red.'

Gary likes to flaunt his knowledge of anatomy, picked up when he did his BTEC higher certificate in forensic medicine at Keighley College. At any other time I would have bounced back with some caustic comment about what you can learn working round the back of a Fleet Street pie shop, but right then the wellsprings of my jaunty banter seemed to have dried up. Or maybe congealed.

'Who was he?' I asked. 'I mean – who is he?'

'Local lad. Lived over there, all on his tod.' Coldwood pointed off to the east, where the horizon was dominated by one of South London's least-loved landmarks: the Salisbury estate. I'd seen it a couple of times before, so I knew what it was. Another bit of utopian city planning gone tits-up and stinking as soon as the paint dried and the real world set in.

Twelve massive tower blocks were arranged in a three-by-four formation: guardsmen standing to attention in some apocalyptic parade. They were about twenty storeys high, and the first thing you noticed when you looked at them was that each of the four rows of three had been painted in a different colour, shifting – as your gaze panned right – across the spectrum from pastel pink, through buttercup yellow and duck-egg green, to moody indigo. The second thing you noticed was the walkways that connected the towers at irregular intervals above the ground, welding them into one entity: the uber-estate.

I don't hold much with premonitions. Mostly our unconscious minds just tell us what we already know, lending a supernatural confirmation to a preformed prejudice. But as I looked across the rooftops towards the Salisbury I felt that twinge of presentiment brush my mind again like a wind-borne cobweb. So what I'd felt earlier hadn't come from the car: it had come from the distant vista behind it. There seemed to be a smudge of black like a thumbprint in the air, blurring my view of the Salisbury. It wasn't smoke, because in modern, post-industrial London there's nothing around to do the smoking: it was a psychic effluent, hanging there untouched by wind, immune to rain. It was the stain of a great sin, or a great unhappiness: or more likely, I thought, pulling my gaze away from the tombstone towers, it was the collective residue of a lot of smaller discontents and domestic tragedies, trickling together and then left to curdle.

'I don't know anybody there,' I said. A stupid thing to say, really: it was just an instinctive reaction to want to distance myself from what I was feeling – from what was coming in on Radio Death.

'You sound pretty damn sure,' said Basquiat, looming behind Coldwood's shoulder very promptly on her cue, as though she'd been waiting in earshot but out of my line of sight this whole time.

'I mean,' I amended, taking my eyes off the distant vista with an effort, 'none of my friends live around here. I'm not aware of knowing anybody on the Salisbury estate. It's something I would have remembered.'

'Why's that?' Basquiat asked, politely but with an edge.

'Because I've heard of the place. It would have stuck in my mind. Especially if I'd just popped over to stab one of the residents to death in his car before I'd even had breakfast.'

'But you stuck in *his* mind, obviously.'

'Yeah.' My eyes flicked back to 'F Castor' written arse-first in black-edged red. 'Obviously.'

'So tell me about your movements last night,' Basquiat suggested. A uniformed cop at her elbow flicked open a ring-bound notebook and held a biro at the ready. Basquiat's beautifully proportioned unadorned face stared at me expectantly.

'I already told Coldwood,' I pointed out.

'Right. And now you're telling me.'

Better to draw the line now and find out where I stood.

'If I'm under arrest,' I said, 'then Grandma Castor would turn in her grave if I said anything without benefit of legal counsel.'

'You're not under arrest,' Coldwood said. He was still looking at the skyline, keeping his back turned to his colleague as though it hurt even to look at her. At the Uxbridge Road cop shop their feud was getting to be the stuff of legend. 'Ask me why.'

'Coldwood—' Basquiat said warningly.

'Why am I not under arrest, Detective Sergeant Coldwood?'

'Because there are three sets of prints in that car – the victim's, and two sets belonging to Mister A.N. Other and his friend Nobody. There's also a straight razor, which all three of them had their mitts on at different times.

And none of them is you. There's no evidence trail, and there are seventeen other Castors in the Greater London phone book, with five more ex-directory. If we arrested you for being the only Castor we know personally, it could look awkward at the committal hearing.'

'Thank you,' said Basquiat. There was no inflection in her voice at all.

'You're welcome,' Coldwood answered, still without looking round.

Basquiat looked at me with her lips set in a tight line. 'You said you don't know the man,' she reminded me.

'Right.'

'But if I tell you his name, maybe you can have a little think about it.'

I nodded. My throat was still dry and my stomach hadn't made up its mind to settle yet. I wasn't in the mood to be coy, even if it played to my advantage. 'Sure.'

'Kenneth Seddon.'

My stomach made an instant decision. I swallowed acid bile.

'Oh,' I said, on such a dying fall that Coldwood swivelled round to stare at me. Basquiat was staring too, her eyes narrowing with a slightly indecorous eagerness.

'Rings a bell,' she said. It wasn't a question.

'Yeah,' I admitted.

'So you do know him?'

'Knew him,' I hedged. 'Once. Not recently. Not for years.'

'In what capacity were the two of you—?'

Fuck it. Save the subterfuge for stuff that you've actually got a chance of hiding.

'He tried to kill me once,' I said. 'But he messed it up.'

3

Kenny Seddon was a name from another life — and the impact of memory, hitting from such an unexpected angle, was as grating and discontinuous as a bad special effect in a cheap old movie. Zoom in tight on my face, ripple dissolve.

I live in London these days, as you probably already noticed: London was where I fetched up when I'd had my fill of moving around, and it suits me pretty well. But I was born in Liverpool and I lived there until I was eighteen, the bulk of my childhood and adolescence falling across that black hole in space and time and good sense known as the 1980s.

So I grew up in a city that was in thrall to two different kinds of decay.

The first kind was historical — dating from World War Two — and it wasn't anything that specially belonged to Liverpool or to the North-West. After all, the Luftwaffe hadn't had it in for Scousers any more than they did for anyone else. It was just that most of the rest of the country seemed to have had the money to repair some of the damage: through some mysterious combination of municipal incompetence and cheeky mop-top corruption, Liverpool never did.

By the punk era the war had been over for more than three decades, but about half the streets I knew had gaps in the rows of terraced houses where bombs had hit – and the substrate in these random spaces, underneath the burgeoning weeds and sparse earth, was shattered brick and slate. We had a word for those places: we called them *débris*, pronounced 'deb-ree'. We swam in ponds on the Walton Triangle that were not ponds at all but bomb craters, and on one memorable occasion when I was seven the whole of Breeze Hill was cordoned off for the best part of a day because an anomalous object had been found that some council functionary thought was an unexploded bomb. It turned out to be a hot-water tank of an esoteric design, but you really never knew.

The other kind of decay was different, because it moved and grew and shifted its outlines. It was a disease that we were all sick with, and didn't even know we were – the slow, inexorable decline of Liverpool's fortunes as a port and an industrial megapolis, which closed factories and shipyards, threw families out onto the street or more usually caused them to disappear without explanation, and turned my father's life, like the lives of most of the men he knew, into a complicated game of abstract strategy where the goal was to find some place where they were prepared to pay you a day's wage for a day's work before some other bastard found it first and shut you out.

As kids, we experienced both of these things – the war damage and the economic meltdown – as almost unmixed blessings. Bomb-sites and boarded-up factories were our adventure playgrounds: spaces that the adult world had abandoned in its wake and took no further interest in, so that we were free to annex and colonise. The battlefield where I clashed with Kenny Seddon was a case in point

– and so were the weapons that we chose for our duel to the death. But the reason why we became such bitter enemies was different. That came from me; from a third kind of decay that was mine and mine alone.

From as far back as I could remember, I lived in a city that was inhabited by the dead as well as the living. These communities existed side by side, and at first it was hard for me to tell them apart. Okay, some people could walk through walls and some couldn't, but there are lots of things that work like that when you're a kid: aspects of experience that you don't understand and mostly can't ask the adults around you to explain.

And there again, some people could move, the same way I could move, while some were inexplicably chained to one place. And some people grew older while some never changed at all: but the ones who stayed put and didn't change were often terrifyingly marked by violence or disease, to the point where it was hard to look at them. Strange. Very strange.

Gradually I followed these clues to a great and un-suspected truth: that the word *dead*, spoken in whispers around us children and dripping with finality, didn't denote an ending at all but a transition. What happened when you died was that you slipped away from the people you'd known and entered this other state: this state where you could look but not touch and where your appearance froze in the aspect of death as though you were a moving but unchanging photograph of what you'd been before.

I realised, too, that this was something most other people didn't know, couldn't see. In my snot-nosed inno-cence, I tried to fill in the dots for them, but that turned out to be harder than it looked. A lot of harsh language and a few smacks to the head taught me that nobody wants the mysteries of the universe explained to them by a kid with a tidemark on his neck and scabs on his knees.

Nobody ever did come up with a word that defined us for what we were – the sensitives, the dark-adapted eyes, the ones with the built-in death-sense. Later, by virtue of what we did, we were called exorcists: but back then that game hadn't got started yet, and nobody could see it coming. As for the other stuff – the zombies, the were-kin, the demons – that was more than twenty years away. We were a bunch of John the Baptists who'd turned up to the party before the balloons and streamers had even been set out.

So if we were smart we learned not to talk about it. It was a strategy that saved you a world of pain in the short run.

Kind of a shame, then, that I let my guard down and said what I said to Kenny Seddon – the last person in the world who was going to take it lying down.

Kenny was one of those scary psychopaths you just have to work around when you're a kid. His mum died when he was eight – of what my mum and dad, when they talked about it at all, called 'the big C' – and the rest of his growing-up followed a template of his own making. His dad worked at the Metal Box, then at Dunlop, then at Mother's Pride, racing ahead of the bowwave of industrial collapse and chasing the work wherever it could be found. He turned his three sons over to his elderly mother to look after when he was away, but she was too old and they were too wayward, so they did their own thing and she lied to cover their tracks.

Kenny was the toughest of a tough brood – only two

years older than me if we're talking strict chronology, but he was the kind of kid who seems to go straight from infancy to adolescence, becoming big and muscular and intractable and getting into the kind of fights that leave blood on the pavement while his peers were still making the difficult transition to lace-up shoes.

He was a bully's bully, ruthless and arbitrary to a fault, and he brought fear and pain into my life on a number of occasions. In the urban wastelands that we swept through like a swarm of grubby locusts, he was a moving hazard that none of us ever figured out how to negotiate. Once he decided he was going to write his name on all the younger kids in the street – a literal sign of his authority over us. His rough-hewn scrawl on my upper arm turned into an archipelago of bruises that lasted a good few days after the ink had faded.

Another time he pushed me out of an apple tree that we were both scrumping from, in the high-walled cider orchard behind Walton hospital. We were twenty feet or so above the ground and I would have broken a leg or maybe my back if I'd fallen the full distance. As it was, I slammed into a branch four or five feet below the one I'd fallen from and managed to cling onto it. Kenny laughed uproariously: something about the spectacle of me dangling over nothing with my legs churning the air struck him as great slapstick humour. When my brother Matt climbed down to rescue me, Kenny pelted him with apples and swore at him, threatening to push him out of the tree too if he didn't leave me to struggle back up onto the branch by myself. Matt ignored him and hauled me to safety, crab apples raining down around the pair of us.

None of this was personal, though: Kenny terrorised everyone with equal enthusiasm, including his own two kid brothers, Ronnie and Steven. He broke Ronnie's leg once with a rough tackle during a game of street football, and then made Ronnie tell their dad that he'd fallen off a wall.

But the weird thing about all these incidents was that they never made much of a difference to our day-to-day customs and practices. All the kids of Arthur Street and of neighbouring Florence Road did pretty much everything together. Whether we were taking over the street with our huge sprawling games of kick-the-can, stealing from the allotments in Walton Hall Park or making one of our frequent raids on the kids of the Bootle Grammar School, we moved en masse. At these times Kenny was *our* psychopath: he was much valued both for his ability to handle himself in a barney and for being one of the privileged few who could decide what we did next and actually make it stick.

One raw day in Whitsun week, the year I turned thirteen, he decreed an expedition to the Seven Sisters, those ponds that marked where the bombs had fallen on the railway line forty years before. It was too early in the year to swim – even in high summer the Sisters were bone-meltingly cold – but we could collect tadpoles, fish for sticklebacks, muck around on the edge of the water and pretend to push each other in, explore the surrounding grass and weeds for metal bolts that you could shoot out of a catapult and have huge, ill-defined mock battles through the bulrushes and stinking shallows. It was guaranteed entertainment, on a bank holiday when the shops were shut and there was sod-all else to do, so we were all up for it.

And if 'we all' suggests a warm and inclusive cosiness, then strike it out and put something else in its place. There were lots of ways you could be bounced out of the collective. The gang of us, if you could corral us in one place for long enough to count, probably numbered around fifty on a good day, and we ranged in age from eight to fifteen. The frequency distribution was about what you'd expect. Very few of the youngest kids had the stamina to keep up with our wilder activities, and a lot of the fifteen-year-olds had discovered other, more absorbing pastimes that kept them busy elsewhere, so the thickest concentration was in the middle of the age breakdown.

As far as gender went, we were equal-opportunity delinquents. The hardier girls ran with us and did as we did, without question or challenge. The rest, for the most part, stayed back in Arthur Street close to the home fires, understudying with scaled-down Hoovers and plastic kitchen ranges the role that society had defined for them.

Anita Yeats was one of the ones who ran with us, even though she was around the same age as Kenny and my brother Matt – the top end of our spectrum. By that age, most of the girls weren't allowed to knock about with us any more, and didn't want to. They had better things to do with their time, and parental prohibitions had kicked in, making them put aside childish things. Anita's body was in the middle of that scary, enthralling transition: she was developing adult curves, her aspect morphing mysteriously from pinch-faced gamine to shithouse rose.

So it was going to be the last year of running with the

street pack for Anita, and probably for Kenny and Matt, too. Maybe that added an edge to things, I don't know. Maybe it was part of the reason, in some indirect way, for Kenny picking an argument with Anita. And maybe, too, it was an offshoot of a broader inter-family feud, of the kind that were always breaking out whenever someone's uncle's son went to the bar and left someone's cousin's dog out of the round. But the main reason was that Kenny had been sniffing around Anita in a semi-obvious way ever since he hit puberty, and she'd never shown the slightest sign of returning his interest. It was only a question of when his arousal would finally topple over into aggression.

And it turned out to be that Whitsun morning. Kenny rounded on Anita as soon as we'd descended onto the Triangle at Breeze Hill – one of the points where the huge acreage of waste ground touched the real world.

'Sod off home,' he said brusquely. 'We don't want you, Yeats.'

'Why not?' Anita demanded reasonably. There were other girls in the party, so 'you're a girl', besides sounding lame and even potentially unmanly, just wouldn't wash. And it had to be a reason that wouldn't extend to Anita's kid brother Richard – known for the most part as Dick-Breath – who was also in the gang.

'You're too slow,' Kenny snapped. 'We'll be waiting for you all the fucking time. Go home.'

'I'll keep up.'

'You never do. And you'll argue over which way to go. We'll have to listen to you giving it this' – imitating a yammering mouth with thumb and fingers – 'all the frigging time.'

'I won't talk.'

'Well, your mam's a slag and we'll catch something off you.'

Anita flushed phone-box red. Then, as now, bringing someone's mother into the argument was moving directly to Defcon One: it was the Taunt Unendurable, and it required the Riposte Valiant. Dick-Breath kept his head down, having earned that derisory name for his willingness to do whatever was needed to curry favour with the bigger kids. But Anita was woven out of sturdier as well as more brightly coloured fabric. Mouthing off to her just wasn't safe, and anybody with less heft than Kenny would have thought twice about doing it.

'Fuck off, Kenny,' she shouted, balling her fists. 'You gobshite!'

Kenny smacked her, open-handed, across the face, hard enough to make her stagger.

'Your mam's a slag,' he repeated. 'She's knocking off Georgie Lunt.'

Anita screamed and went for him, but Kenny was a head taller than her and he fended her off with a violent shove. 'So you're probably a slag too,' he said. 'It runs in families. Who are you knocking off, Anita?'

For some reason, this was shocking to me. I'd seen boys fight girls before: there was no real room for chivalry in our rough-and-tumble code of ethics, and girls could do you some serious damage if they fought like they meant it. It was just that this was so cold-bloodedly staged, and so obviously unfair – Kenny manufacturing the argument to pay Anita back for his blue balls – that it made my blood boil. And not just mine. I saw Matt, my big brother, lean forward as though he was about to step in between Anita and Kenny and take up the challenge on her behalf. My survival instinct – like Dick-Breath's – was a bit better developed than that: Kenny had more or less the same height advantage over us as he did over Anita and, as we'd all learned on many occasions, he didn't recognise the dividing line between what was legitimate and what was inconceivable.

But I did what I could. I replied to the taunt.

'Well, your mam killed herself, Kenny,' I called out. 'It wasn't cancer – that's all my arse. She cut her throat with your dad's razor.'

There are moments in life when you know you've gone too far: you can tell them by the eerie stillness that descends around you – only half a second long in reality, but in subjective time easily long enough for you to think 'Oh Jesus, I wish I hadn't done that' and then start in on the Lord's Prayer. Kenny swivelled to stare at me, his eyes bulging out of his head in cartoon slo-mo. He opened his mouth as though he was going to say something, but no sound came out. Everyone else, including Anita and Matt, was watching him with strained, breathless curiosity. This was going to be bad.

But it was just such an easy call to make. I could tell the living from the dearly departed pretty accurately by this time, and Mrs Seddon's ghost had a huge tear in the flesh of her throat and an apron of dried blood on her faded floral dress – a bit of a dead give-away, if you'll pardon the expression. I'd seen her looking out of the window of Kenny's house so many times that I'd lost count, and a couple of times I'd seen her hanging around

Kenny himself, staring in miserable, befuddled longing at the wayward son she'd left behind along with her tired flesh. As for the razor, that was just a guess. But whatever she'd used to do herself in, it had been spectacularly effective: it hadn't been a kitchen knife, unless the Seddons kept their kitchen knives a lot sharper than we did ours.

So I threw in the razor out of a nascent sense of drama, to add to the overall effect. And on that level, it was a roaring success. Kenny's huge fists rose into my line of sight like a pair of half-bricks held up by a kung-fu master to demonstrate the cleanness of the break. Then one of them moved, and magically I was lying on my back with no understanding at all of how I'd got there. The left side of my mouth tingled unpleasantly, and there was something wet on my face.

'You little bastard,' Kenny said, and he stepped in for the inevitable follow-up, which would have been a kick to some unprotected part of my body.

But Matt stepped in too, and he caught Kenny on the side of the face with a hard jab that made him stagger and lurch before he got his balance back. A moment later the two of them were grappling like all-in wrestlers.

Kenny versus Matt wasn't as ridiculous as Kenny versus me would have been. Matt didn't have Kenny's height or anything like his weight, and as a choirboy at Saint Mary's church he was widely considered to be a pushover, but I knew from countless brotherly skirmishes that he was stronger than he looked and quick with it. None of that should have stopped it from being a foregone conclusion, though: the general consensus was that you couldn't stand against Kenny when he got going any more than you could stop a freewheeling truck by standing in front of it.

But Matt was making a good showing – seeming in the first few frenzied seconds to be giving almost as good as he got. He managed to hook a thumb into Kenny's eye socket and force his head back so that Kenny couldn't butt him, and he landed a sucker punch to Kenny's stomach when the opportunity presented itself. Kenny retaliated by slamming his fist into Matt's jaw – a solid punch with all his weight behind it that made Matt's head rock back and then forward again like one of those dogs in the backs of cars whose over-sized craniums are mounted on springs. But Matt kept his guard up and blocked the vicious low blows and crotch kicks that would have ended the fight in one go.

Then there were a few moments when the two of them were so tightly pressed together that they couldn't really punch or kick at all: they just swayed backwards and forwards, struggling for leverage. I could see a few people in the group – Kenny's brother Steven, who was my age, and his best mate Davey Barlow who was red-haired and rangy and almost as big a psychopath as Kenny – looking doubtful and unhappy, as if they weren't sure whether or not to intervene. The protocols were complicated. If Kenny invited them, they could wade in and kick the shit out of Matt with no loss of honour: if he didn't and they joined in anyway, there was always the chance that someone would say later that Kenny couldn't have won the fight on his own. In any case, I tensed to jump in on Matt's side if they intervened on Kenny's.

Then Kenny broke free, got in another devastating punch to Matt's face but jumped back, not pressing his advantage. The two of them stood panting, dishevelled, Matt's nose and Kenny's lip bleeding.

It couldn't end in a stand-off. Kenny's status in the gang, however vaguely it was defined, wouldn't allow it. I was expecting him to wade in again at once and finish what he'd started: then, when he hesitated, I thought he'd decided to throw the fight open to his brothers, to Davey, and to anyone else who wanted to earn his doubtful and short-lived favour.

But he didn't lower his head and charge, and he didn't shout 'Twat him!' He just stood for a second or two, on the balls of his feet, breathing like a bellows. And then fate intervened, in the shape of a policeman coming down the gravel bank towards us, shouting a challenge that we couldn't hear at this distance. Given how quickly all this had happened, it wasn't likely that he'd been alerted by the noise we were making: he must have seen us as we descended from the road above and decided on the balance of probabilities that we were up to mischief. The railway land was council-owned and we were trespassing, which was reason enough to send us on our way.

We scattered. We always did, when we were an all-ages mixed rabble: a few older lads on their own could have bearded a rozzer and then legged it when he gave chase, but the presence of the younger kids guaranteed that someone would be caught and brought to book. So the order of the day was to explode in all directions like a cluster bomb and hope the multiplicity of targets would slow the copper down long enough to allow us all to get away.

Matt cut off across the tracks towards the ragged borders of Walton Hall Park, with Anita almost keeping pace beside him. I retreated with a few of the smaller kids through the tunnel, which led to another railway cutting a quarter of a mile up the line behind Bedford Road. I didn't see where Kenny and his cohorts went.

So a stand-off was what we got in the end, whether we liked it or not – and for most of the gang that would be a 'not', because an unresolved fight left a sort of tension in the air like the hair-prickling feel of undischarged lightning. Better to get it over and done with, pick up any busted teeth and move on to the next big thing.

But for some reason that wasn't what happened. Everybody expected Kenny to take the first opportunity to finish the fight. Instead he let it lie, and the next few times when we all met up he gave a good impression of having forgotten that it had ever happened.

I wondered why. I considered asking Matt, but the two of us seemed to be growing apart very quickly around then. Matt still looked out for me on the street, and at home too since we were yet another one-parent family by this stage (our mum had left home the year before after a matrimonial bloodletting that I was considered too young to have fully explained to me). But cooking baked beans and sausages out of a tin and making sure I didn't get my head kicked in marked the limit of Matt's involvement with me: he had nothing to say to me any more, and since dad had always been the taciturn type there was a silence around the Castor household that had gone beyond pregnant into stillborn.

So I had to come to my own conclusions about what had happened that day on the Triangle, and my mind went back to those two seconds when Kenny had hesitated after breaking Matt's hold on him. It occurred to me, incredible as it seemed, that Kenny might actually have been afraid. Of my brother. Because Matt had taken everything that Kenny could throw at him and he hadn't gone down. Maybe Kenny wasn't certain that if he took up the fight where he'd left off, he'd be able to win it: and maybe that uncertainty kept him from doing the obvious and calling down a general *fatwa* on Matt. You did that to weak kids, where there was no question that your own alpha status was at issue. If you did it to a potential rival, people would notice. Kenny was a wily little bastard, and at fifteen he already knew what Hitler and Napoleon and Attila the Hun had learned the hard way: that the appearance of strength *is* strength.

And, by the same token, people would notice if Kenny went after me. It was Matt who was his contemporary, so it was Matt who was his legitimate target. I was protected by the bizarre unspoken gospels of the street, which were the measure of our lives and our souls right then.

It was only a matter of time, though, and I could see whenever Kenny looked at me that he hadn't forgotten my remark about his mother's suicide. I'd spoken of death to the king, and one way or another he was going to make sure I paid for it.

His opportunity came sooner than either of us expected. That summer Matt dropped out of school, immediately after taking his O levels, and transferred to Saint Joseph's Catholic seminary at Upholland, about eight miles away from Walton. It was unusual for Saint Joe's to take someone into holy orders at sixteen, but the Jesuit who ran the place had noticed Matt when he was doing a talent-spotting trawl through the parishes inside the Queen's Drive ring road, and he'd been impressed. He was prepared to stretch a point, he told our dad, and let Matt enter the college now. He'd take his A levels at the same time as he started his holy orders, rather than finishing his studies at the attached high school first. Matt would be expected to live at the college, and although he could see his family at weekends they wouldn't be encouraged to visit him and break his concentration at other times.

Dad wasn't thrilled. His plans for Matt's future involved Matt getting a job and turning up some money for his keep. But he was a good Catholic himself, and he knew better than to throw down with the Pope and his bare-knuckled posse. He bought Matt a suitcase from the second-hand shop and away my brother went without a backward glance. As far as I can remember, we didn't even say goodbye.

But at least I knew now where Matt had got the balls to fight Kenny Seddon to a standstill: he had God on his side.

So now there was nobody to run interference for me, and no strict reason according to the Walton book of etiquette why Kenny shouldn't beat me into tenderised steak. But he bided his time for a good three days after Matt left, waiting for the perfect place and time.

The place was up on the roof of the Metal Box factory – the Tinnie. It was a favourite spot for the gang that summer, now that the owners had finally given up on maintaining any kind of security over the disused site. We'd found a way in by levering out one of the uprights of the back fence and tearing the plywood sheet off a door marked AUTHORISED PERSONNEL ONLY.

With the electricity turned off and all the windows boarded up, the interior of the factory was a three-dimensional maze of absolute darkness. You brought torches, and you stuck together, because on your own in the dark you were fucked. Previous parties had mapped out routes, but you could only find them with a torch. We filed through the cavernous machine shops and silent corridors and scaled the echoing stairs like mountaineers conquering an indoor Annapurna, finally breaking out into the daylight through a hole in the roof underneath which someone had set up a precarious folding ladder dragged in from God knows where.

From the roof – since the whole of Walton is built on the side of a hill and we were close to the top of it – you could see the city set out below you. You could also swing on the flagpole over an eighty-foot drop, and collect metal offcuts which for some reason lay around the place like forgotten treasure. They were the pieces left behind when steel sheets were pressed out into box templates, and they came in a range of intriguing shapes: some like capital letter Es, others in the form of triangles (always right-angled) or diamonds with one vertex shaved off flat. They were all about two millimetres thick, and they were highly collectible because of their lethal sharpness and their resemblance to the shurikens we'd all seen or at least heard about in *Enter the Dragon*.

There was the usual horseplay as we fanned out to look for hitherto unknown shapes and sizes of offcut. Davey jostled Steven Seddon, pretending to shove him over the foot-high parapet down into the street far below, and Steven went complaining to Kenny who kicked his arse for being so pathetic. John Lunt, who was one of my millions of cousins, stationed himself over the hole in the roof so that he could gob on the stragglers as they came up the ladder. Peter Gore tried to get a game of off-ground tick going, and foundered immediately on the fact that we were all a long way off the ground already. Peter tried to establish some rules that would work in this anomalous situation, but he was shouted down.

And Kenny's other brother, Ronnie, started to tell the story of the Tinnie Ghost.

'It was the watchman, you know. These lads broke in, and the watchman went after them, but they threw him into one of the machines and he got all squashed and ripped apart, like. And that's why he's still here. On the roof. If you look into the puddles you might see his reflection, you know, and if you do then you're gonna die. Everyone who sees him dies before they get back down to the ground.'

Some of the smaller kids tried not to look at the puddles without being too obvious about it. One of them bleated to his big sister that he wanted to go home, and was coldly ignored.

'What happened to the lads?' someone asked.

'He killed them in their sleep,' said Ronnie. 'One by one, like. They dreamed he was throwing them into the machine and they had heart attacks. And the last one, when they went into the bedroom the next morning, they found him all ripped apart. Bits of him all over the room, like. Blood and bits of bone everywhere.'

This was shite on a heroic scale, and I felt it was down to me to light the beacon of truth.

'How did anyone know what they dreamed about,' I asked, sardonically, 'if they died in their bloody sleep?'

Ronnie didn't falter. 'They screamed "Get me out! I'm dying in the machine!"' he said.

But I was getting into my stride now. 'Anyway, ghosts don't have reflections. Ghosts don't even have shadows. And what's he doing haunting the frigging roof if he died down in the machines? It's bollocks.'

Ronnie bridled, and jug-eared Davey jeered from my left. 'Who asked you, Castor? How many ghosts have you seen?'

I launched into an answer, realised part-way through the sentence that I might be getting myself in too deep and began to stammer. Before I could pull back and regroup, Kenny stepped up between his kid brother and his brick-built enforcer and glared down at me.

'Castor's an expert on ghosts, isn't he?' he sneered. 'Sees them all over the place. He's got the I-Spy book and everything.'

I didn't answer. I didn't like the way this was going, not least because the mood of the gang was against me. I was being a smart-arse. A smart-arse is always lower on the pecking order than anyone except a chicken or a grass. Very few of the faces that were surrounding us were showing anything like sympathy.

'He saw our mam, didn't he?' Kenny pursued. 'With her throat cut and blood all over her. Didn't you, Castor?'

'Yeah,' I said. 'I did.'

Kenny's face set hard. 'Well, you're a lying cunt,' he said, 'because she died down in the ozzie in the cancer ward. You'd shit yourself if you saw a real ghost, you wanker.'

'*You* would,' I retorted, groping for a response that would knock him back on his heels. 'I wouldn't.'

'You're a chicken, Castor.'

'I'm not.'

Kenny shoved me in the chest, not hard enough to hurt but hard enough to reinforce the challenge.

'Prove it,' he suggested. And before I could answer he bellowed 'Gauntlet!', punching the air with his fists.

'Gauntlet! Gauntlet!' Ronnie and Steven crowed, and the shout was taken up on all sides.

The gauntlet was just a piece of casual sadism that usually looked a lot worse than it was. Everyone lined up in front of you. You ran past them, down the line, and people kicked you and punched you as you passed. It was a test of manhood, invoked when someone had allegedly brought the gang or the street into disrepute. You collected a few bumps and bruises, but you had a certain amount of control over your own vector and if you fell you could angle your fall outwards, away from the line, and take a time-out: the people making up the gauntlet weren't allowed to move until you got to the other end.

'Okay,' I said, shouting to make myself heard over the din. 'Fine. I'm not scared.'

'Over there,' said Kenny, pointing. I turned to look in the direction he was indicating, and like Gertrude Stein said on a different occasion, there wasn't any there there. The slightly pitched coping stones of the ledge were only a step away, and beyond that there was a sheer drop to the street. He couldn't mean . . . ?

Kenny's hand clamped on the back of my neck and he pushed me forward. I flailed in his grasp, thinking that he was going to push me over the edge. He didn't. He just stood me up on the narrow parapet and then stepped away, warning me with a wagging finger not to move.

'Gauntlet,' he said, pointing to left and right. 'There and back again, you little twat. Or else say you're a chicken.'

'Fuck off,' I riposted.

'Right, then,' said Kenny, with a gleam of malicious triumph in his eye.

He set Ronnie and Steven to work collecting offcuts, and then arranged the gang in a long line from end to end of the roof, about twenty feet away from the ledge where I stood and wobbled, trying to look nonchalant. The three stooges handed out the offcuts so that everyone had two or three – except that a lot of people, Anita among them, had dropped out by this stage and were refusing to play. It was a hard core of about twenty kids who faced me, their faces radiant with the thrill of the hunt.

Enough was enough. I put one foot down off the parapet.

'You come down,' Kenny snarled, 'and you're a fucking chicken. You admit you're a chicken. We don't have chickens in the gang. Ready . . . aim . . .'

The sane response would have been some pithier version of the proverb about live jackals and dead lions, but I hesitated. I didn't want to be faced down by Kenny, because at that moment his face represented everything that I hated in the world – including Matt running off and leaving me so he could look for God.

The pause was just long enough.

'Fire!' Kenny bawled, and the air was filled with whistling steel. I ran, because the alternative was to be sliced to pieces where I stood. To be fair, I was probably exaggerating the danger from the offcuts themselves. They were absolutely useless from an aerodynamic point of view because they were too thin and light to hold to a line – but there were a fuck of a lot of them, and it would only take one hit to make me flinch backwards reflexively and make the long swallow-dive onto the rutted asphalt of the factory's forecourt.

I ran head down, only looking at the stone under my feet. I got lucky. A spinning steel rhombus took a small nick out of my cheek, but it was turning in the wind and had spent most of its momentum when it hit me. Another bit into my arm, but again very shallowly and with no real force. Apart from that I reached the corner unscathed – and unopposed for the last ten yards because everyone had spent their ammo in the first few exuberant moments.

'Time out to reload!' Ronnie shouted, and Kenny nodded his imperial assent. They all went looking for their own ammo this time, and they were a bit more liberal in interpreting the rules. Some of the kids came back with lumps of shattered brick and one or two had taken out homemade catapults.

This had started out way beyond a joke, and now it was in *Lord of the Flies* territory. If I made the return journey, a single hit would knock me off the ledge.

'Fuck this,' I said, stepping down off the parapet onto safe, solid ground.

'Get back up there, you little piss-pants bastard,' Kenny commanded, striding across to me, 'or I'll throw you off my fucking self.' He grabbed a double handful of my lapels and shoved me backwards, trying to make me stand up on the ledge again. I resisted, leaning back without letting my feet leave the ground, although that exposed me to the very real danger of losing my balance and falling backwards over the edge.

'Sod off, Kenny!' I said. 'I'm not doing it. I've had enough.'

'Not yet you haven't,' Kenny said grimly. 'We're not finished yet.'

I struggled in his grasp, trying ineffectually to trip him so I could break free. His superior weight made it a forlorn gesture, but I had to try. I stumbled backwards, planting my feet on the ledge because there was nowhere else to go, but when Kenny tried to disengage I went with him, gripping his left arm tightly. He punched me in the face to loosen my grip, and once again set me up on my perch. I staggered, seeing stars.

'Now you fucking run!' he snarled, stepping back quickly. 'Ready . . . aim . . .'

I don't know what I would have done on the word 'fire': fortunately I never got to find out, because the command never came. Instead, Kenny made a really unlovely noise: a sucking gurgle that cut off before its time and ended on a terrifying silence. His mouth opened and closed and his arms spasmed, as though he was trying to get a good grip on a parcel of a peculiar shape and heft.

He turned around a hundred and eighty degrees, presenting his back to me. There was something odd about it: his shirt was gaping open, split from side to side as though he'd started to turn from Bill Bixby into Lou Ferrigno. And then from within the shirt – filling it miraculously like the endlessly rising bubbles in the plastic trim of an old-fashioned Wurlitzer – blood welled, saturating the cloth in an instant, to spill down his jeans in a lapping tide.

He hadn't turned around on purpose to show me this: he'd turned to stare at Anita, who was still standing there with a slender length of steel in her hands. It was one that we would have discarded in our hunt because it was far too long and thin to throw. As a makeshift scimitar it clearly had its drawbacks, because Anita's hands were bloody too, dark red beads sliding down her fingers onto the pale metal. She held Kenny's gaze as she let go of the steel strip so that it clattered down on the ground between them.

'Kick the can,' Anita said, in a very level, very matter-of-fact tone. In the game of the same name, it was the phrase you shouted as you freed all the kids who'd already been caught.

Kenny opened his mouth to answer and vomited a huge amount of dark red blood. Then he collapsed, and Anita fled. Ronnie and Davey made a half-hearted attempt to catch her, but their coordination was shot to hell by the shock of what they'd just seen. She got away clean, and in the mess and chaos that followed so did I.

Like I said earlier, you had to go down through the levels of the factory in convoy unless you had your own torch, so I was stuck with my former tormentors until we were back on terra firma. But the business of lowering Kenny down the ladder and then carrying him in blood-boltered relay from floor to floor occupied so much of the gang's attention that they paid none at all to me. The game was over in any case, and it had turned out to be a game of two halves with a vengeance.

The relay carried on all the way to the casualty department at Walton hospital, which was right next door to the factory. It turned out later that Anita had cut deep enough with her wild swipe to puncture Kenny's lung, which had started to deflate. She'd also hit his posterolateral artery, which supplies blood to the spine. The bumps and stresses of Kenny's forced descent hadn't helped the situation either, and he was down to four pints of blood by the time the doctors got to him.

He was away from the street for a long time — first of all in intensive care, then on a normal ward, and finally with an aunt way out in Kirkby where his dad sent him to recuperate. All of this was relayed to us by Ronnie and Steven, who without their big brother to make up the trinity were now humble rank-and-filers in the gang. Davey Barlow, the Igor to Kenny's Frankenstein, faded out around then too, so we experienced something of a renaissance. I remember the rest of that summer as a good time, marred only by the fact that Anita also abandoned the gang after that day, and by occasional letters from Matt that made me resent his absence all the more.

When Kenny did come back, he came back as someone else. His sixteenth birthday had taken place while he was still away from the street, but it was obvious when we saw him walking up Breeze Lane eight months later that he was carrying an unaccustomed weight on his shoulders. He had a job now, at Plunkett's garage, and a girlfriend out in Kirkby who he visited every Saturday night. He had a context that kept me safe in perpetuity from his vicious streak, like a Walton get-out-of-jail-free card.

Grown men didn't hit kids, unless the kids were their own.

So these were the events that passed in review before my eyes after Basquiat spoke the fateful name. They didn't come in exactly that order, as a clean and coherent sequence: they were mixed in with a lot of other things. For me, thinking about Liverpool was always like trying to take one tissue out of one of those little hotel-room boxes where the bloody things are interleaved and as thin and fragile as the Turin Shroud: one tug and you take the whole box.

So I also remembered my mum coming home to Liverpool three years later to face my dad down and move in with her former fancy man, Big Terry Lackland. I remembered Matt's finishing his holy orders and becoming Father Matthew Castor, on a spring day in torrential rain, wearing a rough-hewn but beautiful scrimshaw crucifix that Mum had bought from the pawnshop as his ordination present. I remembered – with confused emotions – my own escape, when I aced my A levels against everyone's expectations including mine and pissed off to Oxford without a backward glance: the best way to leave, in my experience, if you can make it stick.

And as the cascade reached its inevitable conclusion, I remembered the one Castor who wasn't around to see all this stuff happen. The one whose death taught me what I was and launched me on my path, bringing me by insensible degrees to this moment and this place.

I remembered Katie.

And the rest was silence, until Gary Coldwood broke it with a blunt question, pulling me by the heels back into the present day.

'So you and Mister Seddon weren't on the best of terms?' he demanded.

I shrugged, as casually as I could manage. 'It's not a Batman and Joker thing, Gary,' I said. 'It was a hell of a long time ago, and I haven't seen him since. Haven't even thought about him.'

'It's probably fair to say that he's thought about you,' Basquiat pointed out, her tone hard. 'He painted your name in his blood.'

I shrugged again. 'Maybe he was starting to write his will,' I suggested. Well, what the fuck? My conscience was clean, at least as far as attempted murders were concerned. Whatever this looked like, I knew what it wasn't: it wasn't *The Tell-Tale Heart*.

'You still want to leave this hanging?' Basquiat asked Coldwood.

Gary shook his head once, brusque and emphatic. 'No,' he said. 'We'll need to take you in for questioning, Fix, and we'll need a formal statement. I'm sorry.' That one hit me before I was ready for it.

'What about the other seventeen Castors?' I asked, aghast.

'They stopped being relevant when you told us you knew this bloke.'

'So am I being charged?'

Coldwood opened his mouth, but Basquiat's snarl cut across whatever he was going to say.

'That would look great in court, wouldn't it? Invite you down here to read the scene, then arrest you when you get here? No, Castor, you're just assisting us with our inquiries. Anything else will have to wait until we've got the forensics in.'

She was looking at Gary rather than at me as she said all this, and it was clear that there was an unspoken question between them.

'Under the circumstances, Detective Sergeant Basquiat,' Coldwood said with clipped formality, 'I think it advisable that you conduct the interview with Mister Castor. My personal and professional relationship with him probably precludes my being involved in interrogating him or taking a statement from him.'

There was a momentary silence, then Basquiat nodded, seemingly satisfied.

'But if you're thinking of having a testicle roast,' Gary added, 'then think again.'

'He's as safe as if he was in God's pocket,' Basquiat promised blandly.

She jerked her head in a way that obviously conveyed a lot of information to her entourage of bluebottles. Two of them fell in on either side of me and led me away.

4

It wasn't as bad as it could have been. Basquiat played by the rules, mostly. She was just kidding about God's pocket, but I got to keep my testicles.

She seemed mostly concerned with getting me on record about my previous relationship with Kenny, and she only cut up rough when I tried to back-pedal from the lurid story I'd sketched out on the overpass. I've had a few run-ins with the law in my time and I'm pretty good on the rules of evidence, so I knew that none of what I was saying could be used to establish just cause: but I also knew how bad it would sound in court if the Met ever did decide to charge me, so I was more careful with my phrasing than I'd been during the first rendition – and Basquiat, knowing her job, shone a torch into every area of vagueness and obscurity and tripped me up whenever I contradicted myself.

There was no malice in it, which made this a distinct improvement on the time when Basquiat had interviewed me with her fists in the course of the Abbie Torrington case. But I was still sweaty, dishevelled and exhausted by the time we were done – and, admiring the detective sergeant's lean good looks in passing, I was reminded that there are more pleasant ways of getting that way.

After the interview and the grand, formal taking of the statement they left me to cool for a while in a smaller cell at the end of a long corridor that smelled of piss and stewed cabbage. Someone told me once that the Uxbridge Road cop shop used to be a workhouse back in Victorian times, and I can believe it. There's a damp, miserable effluvium about the place that you'd need a Jamaican steel band and a flame-thrower to disperse. There are also a fair number of ghosts, and I got to meet three of them: two broadly human in appearance, the third an amorphous nightmare that had forgotten what it was long ago and now only held itself together by some inchoate impulse that kept it moving like a shark around and around the lower storeys of the building.

I was doing the same thing, only on the inside: prowling my own memories in pointless circles that always seemed to bring me out in more or less the same place.

Eventually Basquiat came back in and told me I was free to go.

'What swung it?' I asked her, knowing that she'd mainly been keeping me around while she made her mind up.

She looked at me hard for a second before answering: I had no right to ask, of course, and if they did end up charging me they wouldn't want me in a position to second-guess the evidence. On the other hand, there's never anything to lose by trying.

'The forensics are starting to come through,' she said grudgingly. 'They confirm what Coldwood said about the prints. You weren't one of the people who held that razor. There are also a few . . . anomalies about the wounds themselves. Things we'll have to look at again.' Her eyes defocused for a moment, as if she was taking that line of reasoning a little further inside her head. Then she recollected herself and became brisk. 'So we won't be charging you just yet, Castor. But you should probably keep yourself available in case we need to talk to you again. Tell us if you're going anywhere.'

'What about if I go to the Salisbury?' I asked.

Her expression soured. 'I've got two gorillas on my team,' she said. 'They were transferred out of Lambeth for questionable use of force. If I see you anywhere near my crime scene I'm going to get the pair of them to give you a Swedish massage in the back of a slam van. My sacred, solemn word.'

'I've had promises like that before,' I said, accepting the little bag with my belongings in it. 'I always end up getting my heart broken.'

'Don't worry about your heart, worry about your neck,' Basquiat suggested as she walked out.

Sometimes it's best to let events take their course. As Taoists say, the best direction is *wu wei* – with the course of the water. You abandon the illusions of will and control and drift freely in the currents of life letting chance or fate choose your direction.

I'm not a Taoist. For the most part, when it comes to the river of life I sink to the bottom and then I start walking. Against the current.

So now, being a free man again and loosed onto the streets in the dazzling, over-emphatic sunshine, instead of declaring a goof-off day and making a beeline to the nearest pub to meditate on my misspent youth I found my thoughts drifting to the Salisbury – and to that stubborn stain of psychic effluent that I'd seen from afar. Was that what Kenny had been trying to tell me about?

Could it hurt to take a look?

The answer was yes, of course. It's always yes. But I went anyway.

Back in the nineteenth century, when London was basically a big pile of crap with some buildings floating in it, and when a cholera epidemic was raging through the city like a drunk with a Gatling gun, they had this theory about what they were dying of. Nobody had made the link yet to infected water – not until John Snow came along in the 1850s with his epidemiological version of the New Testament. So the best idea they could come up with in the meantime was the miasma: a vast cloud of bad air, the exhaled breath of a million diseased and dying people, that drifted over London and infected you if you breathed it in.

That turned out to be bollocks, and Snow saved tens of thousands of lives when he tore the handles off the Soho pumps to prove his point. In the twenty-first century most people laugh at miasmas.

Not exorcists, though. We know better than anyone that things can gather in the air, unseen, and that you can breathe them in without knowing it. Most places have emotional resonances: random echoes of the emotions felt by the people who live in those places or walk through them. Mostly they stay at a low level because – to use a crude metaphor – the peaks and troughs don't match up. It's like ripples in a pond cancelling each other out as their wave fronts intersect. Occasionally, though, if a lot of people are feeling the same thing, then instead of cancelling each other out the emotions reinforce each other, etch themselves deeper and deeper into what we flippantly call reality. When that happens you can get a very strong emotional residue hanging over a particular place and enduring over time. Schools, prisons, death camps, brothels, army barracks, even churches: they have their own psychic flavour, which exorcists pick up on the same wavelength that allows us to see the dead. We're like dogs in that way, pricking up our ears at a whistle that nobody else can hear.

The Salisbury Estate had an aura of this kind. I could feel it from a long way away, when I got off the bus at Burgess Park and started to walk north towards it. The closest of the towers was a good half a mile off, but already there was a thickening in the air that you could almost taste. The people around me – mothers with pushchairs, mainly, along with the occasional homeless guy and truanting kid, because this was the dead waste and middle of the day – didn't seem to notice anything wrong. They kept right on walking, didn't even look over their shoulders at the great grey towers looming behind them. So I knew it was my tuning-fork soul, resonating on a frequency that the rest of the world was deaf to.

The miasma intensified as I got closer, but although the individual towers of the Salisbury separated themselves out in my field of vision the feeling didn't attach itself to any one of them.

The contradiction between those two impressions – the vividness of the sensation and the vagueness of its source – came as something of a surprise. I've learned the hard way that the physics of the material world don't apply to my chosen field all that much: if they did, an enraged geist wouldn't be able to pick me up and slam me into a wall because his massless form wouldn't allow him any leverage. And zombies wouldn't be able to move without a working heart to oxygenate their putrefying tissues.

But it's a reliable rule that most hauntings have a fixed physical locus, an anchor point, where something that no longer belongs in this world has somehow got stuck and failed to move on. Finding the anchor is one of the first steps in any exorcism, because it means you can apply your leverage to the point where it's going to have the biggest impact. It's like aiming your fire extinguisher at the base of the fire, not at the flames.

This field of buzzing emotional energy wasn't playing by the rules. It remained diffuse, impossible to pinpoint: my psychic compass wobbled and spun, looking for a true north that seemed not to be there.

The emotional weight that the miasma carried became more and more vivid as I approached: intensified, without narrowing down. What I was tasting in the air was a tension, a restless alertness, together with a sort of shift in my vision that made everything I was seeing subtly different – as though I was seeing it through a window that had been misted with somebody else's breath.

I walked between the first of the Salisbury's towers as I came off Freemantle Street, passing a primary school on my left. Kids are like dogs, too, and the two hundred or so toddlers swarming around in the playground seemed unusually subdued and thoughtful. They were playing on the climbing frames and hopscotch grids, but silently and with a disconcerting solemnity.

I looked up as the shadow of the Salisbury's eastern-most block fell across me. The towers all had name plaques fixed to their walls at head height, the names barely visible beneath a hundred layers of granulated, half-erased graffiti: this one – the pink tower that stood at one end of the artfully arranged colour field – was Sandford Block, and its companion on my left, a slightly warmer shade of the same basic colour, was Cole. I thought of cattle brands, and of Adam naming the beasts. These hulking monsters wore their names lightly, and didn't seem to have been tamed or humanised by them to any measurable extent.

The remaining towers stretched in a colonnade ahead of me, probably about a quarter of a mile long and two hundred feet wide. Over my head were the first of the walkways, linking the towers within a rigidly geometrical spiderweb. The floor was paved with blocks of faded rose-pink and yellow, between which weeds grew in stubborn profusion: everything else was poured concrete, forty years old now and well into its mid-life crisis. There was a shopping trolley abandoned at the foot of Cole Block, lying on its side like a dead wildebeest. There was also a small cluster of boys in their early teens who were completely ignoring me as they kicked a football against the concrete wall, taking turns to hone their ball control in solo displays that clearly had a competitive edge to them.

I checked the address that Nicky Heath had given me, scribbled on a torn-out page of *Notes for Persons in Police Custody*, the Home Office pamphlet they give you these days in place of the old 'You've been nicked, me laddie.' I'd asked Coldwood for the address first, but he'd warned me off even more emphatically than Basquiat had, pointing out that if I was serious about not wanting to be arrested the best thing I could do was sod off home and stay there.

'You're forgetting one thing, Gary,' I pointed out.

'Which is?'

'I'm also serious about being innocent. I didn't take a straight razor to Kenny Seddon's throat. The last time I wanted to do that, I hadn't even started to shave.'

Coldwood shook his head. 'So?'

'So I know Kenny wasn't writing my name in blood because he wanted to tell you who'd attacked him. You're still open-minded on that subject, which is more or less where you need to be, but I'm not. It was something else – some other kind of message, and I've got to assume it was meant for me. Not "It was Castor what done it" but "Castor, take a look at this." You understand? I don't know what it's about or if it's really any of my business, but I need to find out before I can let this drop. And since you won't even tell me where Kenny lives, I don't trust you to tell me anything else you turn up. No hard feelings.'

'I'll tell you everything I think you need to know,' Coldwood promised, and the stolid emphasis told me exactly how carefully he was choosing his words.

'And I'll do the same for you,' I assured him, with a straight face. Then I walked on out of the station, found the nearest working phone box – my mobile being down on batteries again because I can never be arsed to recharge it – and called Nicky Heath, my technically dead sometime-informant. He shagged Kenny's address from the electoral roll in about ten seconds flat.

'New case?' he asked me after I'd taken the details down.

'Not exactly, Nicky,' I said. 'But it's something I'm looking into. And I'll probably be coming to you for a bit more than this as soon as I know what I'm looking for.'

'Sure. Tell me about it tonight. You're coming to the screening, right?'

I trod water mentally while I tried to work out what he meant. Then I remembered the gold-trimmed card that had dropped onto Pen's doormat three weeks before – requesting the pleasure of my company at a one-off presentation of Ridley Scott's *Blade Runner* (the original theatrical release, not the director's cut) at Nicky's formerly derelict cinema, the Walthamstow Gaumont. Strictly by invitation only, gatecrashers strongly discouraged – and since Nicky had indulged his burgeoning paranoia by turning the Gaumont into a cavernous booby-trapped fortress, that phrase hid a whole world of pain.

'The screening,' I echoed. 'Right. I'll see you there.'

And if that was what it took, that was what I'd do. But business before some implausible imitation of pleasure.

Kenny Seddon lived at 137 Weston Block, Nicky had said. I could check each tower in turn, but why not use the natural resources that were already on offer? I wandered over to the small group of boys who were still intent on their kick-about. A few of them turned to watch me as I approached, but the lad who was in possession of the ball carried on side-kicking it up into the air and then bouncing it off his chest in a metronomic rhythm.

They were younger than I'd thought, most of them probably not yet into their teens. That was welcome, because along with the broad daylight it gave me a certain assurance that they wouldn't roll me at knifepoint for my mobile phone. They didn't look threatening, it has to be said, but there was a certain edginess to their expressions. Maybe they were tense for the same reason that the kids in the schoolyard hadn't seemed to be enjoying their play-time all that much: because on some level they were aware of the psychic miasma and were responding to it. Or maybe they just thought I was the truant officer.

'Hey, guys,' I said. 'Which block is Weston?'

Most of the boys seemed happy to stare me out, but one of them pointed. 'Fourth along,' he said, flicking his flax-blond hair out of his eyes with his thumb. He was as skinny as a whippet – a whippet that's been on a low-fat diet for a while – and the nervous gesture made me notice that he had a grubby bandage wrapped around his hand. One around each hand, in fact. He was so pale that his skin looked like paper. His orange tee-shirt bore the enigmatic legend URBAN FREESTYLE.

I nodded, said thanks and turned to leave.

'Eighth floor,' the boy added, to my departing back.

I stopped and looked at him again.

'What?' I inquired.

The boy hesitated, looking confused and a little hunted. 'The – place you wanted,' he said. 'Number 137. It's on the eighth floor, right next door to where I . . .' He trailed off into silence, frowning as he tried to remember what I'd actually said.

Some of the other lads glared at him. They clearly felt that giving information to casual strangers was a bad idea on general principle. I couldn't fault their thinking on that one. 'Your turn, Bic,' one of them said pointedly. He threw the ball hard at the blond kid, who just got his hands up in time to catch it. The conversation was over, and there was no point in pushing the point. I walked on across the pastel-coloured pavement, heading for the tower that he'd indicated.

When I looked back, twenty seconds or so later, the boys still hadn't resumed their game: they were watching me out of sight, except for the blond boy who was staring down at the ball as he rubbed his bandaged hand against its surface. He still looked unhappy about what had just happened. He'd clearly heard the number 137: I just hadn't said it.

The miasma stabbed against the inside of my temples, suddenly agonisingly acute, then faded again just as abruptly into the background rasp that it had now become.

Up close, Weston Block was an impressive if unlovely structure, its coat of duck-egg green doing nothing to bring it into harmony with its surroundings. There was a broad stairwell going up its side, leading to the first of the walkways a few storeys above my head. There were also double doors leading into a foyer with three lifts side by side, marked like the outer walls with many overlays of spray-painted graffiti. As it turned out, none of the lifts worked. There were interior stairs too, but they smelled heavily of mildew cut through with the sharper stink of urine.

So I went back outside and ascended into the sky on Shanks's pony.

The first walkway was three floors up. It was wider than it looked from the ground – almost as wide as a street. And like a street it had its own lighting: octagonal grey lamp-posts supported art-deco globes that didn't sort well with anything else I could see. There was a chest-high stone parapet on either side of the walkway to stop people tumbling down onto the pavement below, and a trellised arch at the end furthest from me that looked as though it had been put there for the benefit of climbing plants. But nothing decorated the walkway except for some broken glass tastefully strewn around and a few overfilled black plastic bin bags spilling out their freight of tea leaves and tin cans into my path. The parapet was cracked at a couple of points, as though the walkway had suffered a little from subsidence and never been repaired.

This seemed to be where the older kids hung out – school apparently not being an option that anyone around here took very seriously. A group of them were sitting on the parapet, smoking. One of them looked at me with unfriendly interest as I hove into view, then looked away and spat casually over the edge of the walkway.

I slogged on up the stairs. A lean guy in his thirties, with slicked black hair, a piercing above his right eye and an acrid stench of body odour fighting an olfactory ground war with some cheap cologne, jostled my shoulder as he passed me going down. Then suddenly he stopped, giving me a harder look. He was as pale as the kid, Bic: in fact, his pallor had gone beyond whiteness into the yellow sallows of nearly exposed bone, so he wasn't equipped to blanch. But his expression was one of stunned surprise, and my death-sense prickled as he stared at me. Not what he seemed, then: a zombie, most likely, but with enough animation in his face and movements to be of fairly recent vintage.

He'd been handsome once: big-eyed, long-haired, slender in face and build. In a zombie it was pathetic and obscurely indecent. You wanted to look away. *Consider Phlebas, who was once handsome and tall as you*, and used to have to beat the girls off with a shitty stick.

I waited for a moment, because he seemed to be about to speak. When he didn't, I decided to break the ice myself.

'Anything I can do for you?' I asked.

The guy grimaced and shook his head. 'You look like someone I used to know,' he said, his voice a bone-dry murmur. What was that accent? If he'd spoken again I might have placed it. But he didn't. He turned away again and went on down the stairs.

Happy to disappoint you, I thought. But brief as it was, the encounter had an oddity about it that skewed my mood. The guy had seemed not just surprised to see me but unnerved. In fact he looked a little bit like the man in the story who flees to Samara to avoid Death, only to find he's kept the appointment after all. Maybe Death and I have a family resemblance that nobody's ever pointed out to me.

Well, it would have to keep. He was already out of sight, and in this maze I'd be lucky to find him again if I started after him. Anyway, I was here to check out the lie of the land, not to chase herrings of whatever colour.

The next walkway was on the eighth floor: exactly where Bic had said I should go. I stepped back into Weston Block through a swing door that didn't swing any more on account of a broken mounting. A short corridor stretched ahead of me, with two doors on either side and one more straight ahead. The first door on my left was 137.

So Bic's directions were right on the money. Interesting. I'd had my pocket picked before, but not my mind. Or had the news of Kenny's near-death experience already filtered through to the Salisbury, making the kid guess that this was my destination? Occam's razor said yes, but when you make a living out of dealing with the yobs and malcontents of the invisible kingdom you tend to keep an open mind on a whole lot of things.

The door to 137 was identical to all the others in sight – a single piece of wood, painted more or less the same shade of green as the tower's exterior, with the number of the flat blazoned on an oval ceramic plate that was screwed onto the door at chest height, and only a Yale lock to keep the world out. I could have cracked the lock inside of a minute if I'd brought the right tools, and at some stage I might end up doing exactly that: but not in broad daylight, and not without my lockpicks. This was more in the nature of preliminary reconnaissance: you can get into a lot of trouble if you waltz at dead of night into a place you've never even seen for a spot of breaking and entering.

The walls inside the block were mostly free of daubed exhortations and expletives, but I noticed that something had been scrawled in black marker next to Kenny's door, a foot or so off the ground. I bent down to examine it, moved mostly by idle curiosity. There were no words here: only an image as simple as a cave drawing. It showed a teardrop shape with straight lines radiating outwards from it in a ragged starburst.

'He's not in,' said a voice from behind me.

I straightened and turned around. A woman was staring at me from the doorway at the end of the hall, which had opened without me hearing it. She was tall and red-haired, the red serving to set off the general lack of vivid colours anywhere else about her person. Her eyes were grey, her skin pale and freckled like the house-sparrow egg Matt had shown me once during his brief and uncharacteristically cruel foray into bird's-nesting. She wore what you might call earth colours, although the earth in question would be the margins of a desert: sand and dry topsoil blowing away in a tropical wind that never quit. She could only have been about forty, but she looked older. You immediately identified her as someone who'd had a crummy life and bent under it to keep from breaking.

She was looking at me with something like suspicion. Either for purposes of self-defence or because I'd caught her in the middle of making lunch, she held a long kitchen knife in one frail-looking hand. The smell of frying that wafted out into the hall from behind her seemed to confirm the second hypothesis.

'I'm sorry?' I asked, smiling a slightly imbecilic, wrath-deflecting smile. Not that this lady had any particular wrath to give.

'Mister Seddon. He's not in. He hasn't been in all day.' The woman's voice was very low, dipping lower still at the end of every phrase as though whenever she opened her mouth she was sticking her head up over a parapet and then reflexively ducking again in case she got shot at.

I tried to look surprised and disappointed as I ambled across the hallway towards her. 'Are you sure?' I asked. 'Miss—'

'Mrs.'

'Mrs . . . ?'

'Daniels.' She looked back over her shoulder with a distracted air, then back at me. 'I can't really talk right now,' she said, and then, as if the lapse of manners had to be balanced or atoned for in some way, she added 'Jean. Jean Daniels.'

'Of course. Mrs Daniels. Kenny said for me to call today.' That sentence hung in the air for an over-long moment, while I assembled some other lies to go along with it. 'For the books.'

The red haired woman frowned. 'The books?' she repeated.

I nodded gravely. 'I'm collecting for the rummage sale,' I said. 'At Saint Gary-le-Pauvre. The priest's a friend of mine, and I like to help out.'

'Oh.' The frown didn't disappear, despite this morally unimpeachable cover story. If anything it deepened. 'Well, I know Mister Seddon's not in because my Thomas had to take his post from the postman this morning and we've knocked six or seven times to give it to him. You'll have to come back another time.'

I didn't take the hint: this was a recon mission, after all, and that included making contact with the local citizenry. 'Kenny's a fine man,' I said, throwing out a random hook. 'But we've not seen each other in a while. I hope he's well. I'm sorry, I should have introduced myself. I'm Felix Castor.'

I held out my hand, but Jean Daniels didn't seem keen to reciprocate.

'So you're from the church?' she demanded again. Her tone was solemn and slow: the tone of someone working through a complex syllogism.

'That's right.'

'And you said "the priest", so – a *Catholic* church?'

'Well . . .' Too late to temporise. 'Not un-Catholic,' I admitted lamely. 'Definitely on the Catholic side of the equation.'

'But Mister Seddon is Protestant, isn't he? Bitter orange, was the way he put it. I remember it particularly because it was one of the first things he ever said to me.'

Bitter orange. It was a resonant phrase for anyone born and bred in the briar patch of Liverpool 9. Mrs D was right, too: I remembered now that Kenny's dad and all his uncles had been in the Lodge, marching in bright orange sashes and Moss Bros suits along County Road on the Glorious Twelfth.

Fortunately, Mrs Daniels seemed more apologetic than indignant to have caught me out in a flat lie. Or at any rate, she went on talking to cover the social embarrassment. 'The very next day after he moved in, when I met him for the first time by the lift, Mister Seddon asked me what denomination we were. And when I said we weren't anything very much he wasn't happy at all. He said we must have been brought up something, in a Christian country. So I told him my parents were Catholic, my Tom's were High Church Anglican, and he never had another word to say to us.' She shook her head in solemn wonder. 'It's a shame the uses some people put the Lord to – making hate where there should be love, and turning a good message into a bad one.'

'Well, Saint Gary's is an ecumenical mission,' I assured her, wishing I'd thought up a better cover story: she was sharper than she looked. 'But it's never been about the religion for me. I just like to do good for goodness' sake.'

'You're not a priest?'

'Not in the slightest. My *brother*'s a priest,' I offered, as though that helped to establish my own credentials.

'Like I said, I really just wanted to check in on Kenny and find out if things were going okay for him these days. We go back a long way. In case I didn't mention it before, I'm Felix. Felix Castor.' (I knew I was repeating myself but I reckoned it was time to be persistent.)

I stuck my hand out again. It would have been rude to ignore it twice, and Mrs Daniels seemed deathly afraid of giving offence. She put her own hand in mine, a little limply, and allowed it to be shaken.

Which meant that I finally got to read her. This kind of random trawling is an automatic thing with me: the same morbid sensitivity that lets me see ghosts even where others can't sometimes allows me to pick up surface thoughts and emotions from people's minds when I touch them. So I do it even in situations like this one where there probably isn't much to be gained.

What I got from Mrs Daniels was powerful, narrowly specific, and no use to me at all. She had a shallow cut on her forearm and she couldn't think how she'd done it. It was making her itch like mad but she didn't want to scratch in front of a stranger. That was also why she hadn't wanted to shake my hand, because she'd left the cut uncovered to make it scab faster and she was embarrassed to have it be seen. She was worried about someone – no names, no image, just a conceptual knot that was full of warmth and uncritical love – and worried in a different way about the time she was wasting as she stood here talking to me. She was also embarrassed about the kitchen knife, and she glanced down at it now as she disengaged her hand from my grip.

'Cooking his lunch,' she said by way of explanation as

she held up the knife for my inspection. 'I should get back, really. I can't turn the ring down all the way and the fat might catch. Things aren't.'

I thought I might have misheard those last two words, because they didn't seem to be attached to the rest of the sentence in any meaningful way. But Mrs Daniels saw my puzzled blink and went on with barely a break.

'Well, you asked me if things were going well for him – for Mister Seddon. They're not. He's going from bad to worse, really. I don't think he's ever got over it. He puts a brave face on, because you've got to, but it's not something that ever goes away, is it? You'd always wonder if there was anything you could have done.'

I was lost in this welter of restricted code. I tilted my head in polite inquiry. 'Anything you could have done to . . . ?'

'Well, to stop it,' Mrs Daniels said, looking at me with eyes that carried a full share of the world's hurt. 'I mean, you'd be thinking that if you'd seen the signs early enough you could have said something. Got some help. I know they say you can't, but I think it depends on the circumstances, doesn't it?'

It seemed safest to agree. 'What *were* the circumstances?' I asked earnestly. 'I've never felt able to ask.'

Mrs D shook her head bleakly. 'I could tell you some tales,' she said, with a lack of enthusiasm that belied the words. 'But I won't. Not now. The time to have said something was before, when it might have done some good. I blame myself. We all should blame ourselves. He deserved better. Whatever was going on at home . . .' She paused, then went on quickly, nervously, as if she'd just stepped across an unacknowledged abyss and didn't want to look down. 'He still deserved better. We've all got a responsibility, I think, don't you? To say what can't be said? A boy that age has got his whole life ahead of him. I used to see him with the girls, and there were two or three who wouldn't have said no if he'd asked. But he was lost. He never looked like he was in the same world as everyone else. And then you start to hear the stories, from the other boys. My John's the same age, but it was my Billy, my youngest, funnily enough, who knew him better than anyone. And he's said things that pulled me up short, more than once. It was there. He wasn't hiding it. A hundred people saw it, and twice as many as that knew all about it. But nobody said a thing, did they? Nobody ever does. That's what I meant when I said we were all to blame.'

She'd talked herself into a state of mild distress, her voice becoming more animated as she wrestled with her own undefined sin. Now she looked at me expectantly, but I had no idea what it was she was expecting. Commiseration? Absolution? A smack on the wrist? I struggled to find a loose thread in her tone poem that I could seize and pull at to see if it unravelled. Kenny Seddon was a bit long in the tooth to be called a boy, so presumably this 'he' was someone else. A son? Did Kenny have a family? I was nearly certain that Gary had said he lived alone. I opened my mouth to frame a question that wouldn't give away my ignorance.

A bellow with a lot of bass in it sounded from the open door at Mrs Daniels's back, drowning out whatever I was going to say. 'Jean! Jeanie! Is there a shirt in here that's been ironed?'

Mrs Daniels folded in on herself in some subtle, mostly

non-physical way. 'That's my Tom,' she said. 'I've got to go.' She stepped back over the threshold, starting to close the door. Then she stopped abruptly, her face splitting open in a radiant smile that took me completely by surprise. It wasn't for me, though: she was looking past me along the hallway, and whatever it was she was seeing made that infolding reverse itself; made her open up again, like a flower at the end of a long, dark night.

'It never fails,' she said, her voice suddenly alive with droll over-emphasis. 'Put some chips in a pan, and here he comes.'

I turned to see the blond boy, Bic, walking towards me. He gave me a puzzled glance, nodded vaguely, and then submitted to his mother's exuberant embrace. When she'd squashed him a little out of shape, she held him at arm's length for inspection. 'You're filthy,' she said. 'You can wash before you eat, you little urchin.' She took the sting out of the words by tousling his hair with the same vigour that she'd applied to the hug.

'Get off, Mum!' Bic protested, deciding that enough was enough. He ducked under her arm and past her into the flat, but only because she didn't contest it.

'Children are the treasure house of the world,' Mrs Daniels declared, favouring me with a self-conscious but sincere smile. The fact that I'd seen her in her parental role seemed to have broken the ice between us in some decisive way.

I nodded, returning the smile. 'Shouldn't he be in school?' I asked, mainly for the sake of prolonging the moment of trust and intimacy.

'Baker day,' Mrs Daniels said, with a roll of the eyes.

'In-service training. All the secondary schools are closed today. It's lucky I'm on a late shift, isn't it? God knows how other mothers cope. I'm sorry, but I've really got to go now. Nice to meet you, Mister . . .'

For a moment I considered giving her a false name, since my real one clearly hadn't stuck either time. There might possibly be some point in lying, if Basquiat came gunning for me in earnest and wanted to establish an evidence trail. But I gave the detective credit where it was due: she wouldn't stay in the dark for long if she seriously wanted to check up on me.

'Castor,' I said, making the hat trick. 'Felix Castor.'

'Good day to you, Mister Castor. I'll tell Mister Seddon you were looking for him.'

The door closed in my face – all the way, this time. Tom's needs had to be met, and clearly Mrs Daniels had no more time for small talk. I stood in the corridor for a few moments longer, trying to make sense of what she'd said. Clearly something had happened to Kenny recently. Something bad, that had left a permanent shadow – or had seemed to. Something he could perhaps have prevented, because there were signs in advance that other people had been able to see.

It was probably unrelated to the attack on him, of course – and the odds were overwhelming that it had no bearing at all on why he'd written my name in his own blood as he sank into unconsciousness and possibly into death. But I had to start somewhere, and if I couldn't cajole the truth out of the neighbours I knew someone I could buy it from at the market price.

I went back into the daylight at last, and it was welcome.

There was something oppressive about the interior of the tower that made me grateful to see the sun again, even if it was beating down like a hammer on an anvil. A wounded-ox lowing of distant traffic met my ears, audible again because I'd been out of it for ten minutes. The miasma was becoming harder to sense for the opposite reason – because it was holding steady now, and my senses were starting to tune it out.

I might as well carry on north, I thought – maybe pick up the Tube at Elephant and Castle. I headed on along the walkway, past more bin bags and a bike that had been chained to a lamp post with a D lock and then deprived of its wheels to deter theft. Unless the wheels had been stolen to deter cycling.

I saw the same sigil again – the teardrop with its corona of radiating lines, this time executed in red paint – on the parapet wall. Next to it, spray-painted on the grey cement of the walkway itself, were the words NOW IT BLEEDS. The words were also done in red, and they looked fresh and new in this faded place. I crossed to look at them, then squatted down and touched the curve of the final S. Very fresh: the paint was still wet.

From this vantage point, I noticed for the first time that the concrete slabs of the parapet wall had been set with narrow gaps in them every few feet. The gaps afforded a view of the lower walkway beneath me and then the ground, where Bic's friends – or maybe a different group of boys entirely – came briefly into view on their way to somewhere that probably wasn't any better than here.

Someone on the lower walkway was watching them, or

at least looking out in that direction. He was standing right up against the parapet, his back to me. He wore a raincoat of pure unblemished white that recalled Alec Guinness as Sidney Stratton, the Man in the Ice Cream Suit, and his sleek, possibly brilliantined black hair stood out all the more starkly against it. There was something indefinably familiar about that black-white contrast, and about the man's ramrod bearing; his refusal to lean against the parapet even though it was right there, at the perfect leaning distance and height. I had a presentiment that was nothing to do with my death-sense.

Another man walked into my severely restricted field of vision and joined him. This guy was big and rangy and looked subtly out of proportion: but then I was seeing him from an odd angle. His face was almost completely flat, as though he'd made humorous Tom-and-Jerry-style contact with a frying pan. When he spoke, his mouth opened across its full width in a way that looked strained and awkward, the lips not moving at all. It was like a ventriloquist's doll talking, the lower jaw bobbing straight up and down to convey by clumsy shorthand the full range of human articulation. His complexion was appalling, the skin piebald with blotches and roughly pitted.

The man on the lower walkway turned to face the newcomer as he approached, and a jolt of surprise went through me when I saw his face, even though I'd sub-liminally made the connection already. It was Father Gwillam, of the Anathemata Curialis.

Gwillam pointed up towards one of the higher walk-ways diagonally across from us. Flat-face spoke again, and

Gwillam sketched something with his fingertip in the air in front of his face. It looked like brackets.

Flat-face left, at a fast trot. At the other end of the walkway he was joined by a woman — tall, somewhat heavy-set, with long dark hair tied back in a ponytail. She seemed to have bandages tied around her hands, like the ones that the boy Bic had had. They headed off together towards the south end of the estate.

Time for me to book, too. I knew enough about the good father to make that particular encounter a must to avoid. But I wasn't quite quick enough. He turned and looked up, directly towards me, as though he'd known that I was there all along.

The sun was hanging over my shoulder, directly in his face. From that distance and at that angle I'd probably just be a silhouette.

Probably.

I didn't stay to find out.

5

Harrison Ford went first, sidling out onto the landing from the barely opened door of his apartment and checking out the lie of the land before he allowed Sean Young to join him. Her immaculate hair and high-gloss lips suggested the unearthly perfection of CGI, but in 1982 that wasn't even a twinkle in George Lucas's eye. She just happened to be perfect.

'You're talking through your arse,' Nicky informed me curtly, wrenching my attention away from the on-screen action. He flicked a couple of switches on the projector, unnecessarily, just to remind me who was in charge. 'There's no way Deckard is a replicant.'

Suppressing a shiver that was purely physiological – the projection booth was as cold as the inside of a refrigerator – I tapped the glass that separated us from the auditorium below. 'Just keep watching,' I instructed Nicky.

On the screen, Ford looked down. The heel of Sean Young's shoe had kicked against some small object on the floor, making it move and catch the light. He bent down and picked it up, but the focus stayed on his face for a moment or two before pulling to the thing in his hand: a tiny unicorn made out of the silvered paper and card from a cigarette packet.

After the briefest of pauses, Ford nodded – one of the most eloquent and compelling gestures in the whole of cinema, in my lowbrow opinion. He followed Young into the elevator, the door sliding closed behind him with a terminal, echoing THOOM.

I whistled and examined my fingernails through the final bit of tacked-on action, with its tacked-on voice-over, waiting until Vangelis faded up and the credits rolled. Irritably, Nicky unlocked the spool from the projector mouth and fast-forwarded it into the can. Down below us, the auditorium went from black-shot-with-silver to pure, midnight black.

'It just means the other detective – Eddie Olmos – has been inside his place,' Nicky said, shrugging in exasperation. 'Why do you have to build a whole thing on top of that?'

'Because it's the turning point of the movie,' I explained patiently. 'It throws everything up into the air – Batty's death speech, "It's a pity she won't live", the whole works – and then makes it come down again in a new pattern.'

'Yeah, well, Rutger Hauer says you're full of shit,' Nicky pointed out, fitting the lid onto the can and carefully detaching it from the projector's housing.

'Fine actor – not the sharpest tool in the box,' I summarised.

'It's left ambiguous.'

'In this version it's left ambiguous. In the director's cut, the sequence where Deckard dreams about the unicorn nails it down tight.'

Nicky put the film canister into the steel cabinet at one end of the projection booth, closed the doors and double-locked them with painstaking care. 'I prefer Deckard to be human,' he said, tugging on the handles to make sure the doors were secure. There was a slight tension, both in his voice and in the set of his shoulders.

I let it go at that point. Maybe it's a nostalgia thing, because Nicky used to be human once too. That was before he had a heart attack in his late thirties and joined the ranks of the existentially challenged. Some people come back in the spirit – as ghosts – and have an uneventful afterlife hanging around the places they remember from back when they had a pulse. Others take the low road, invading and possessing and reshaping animal flesh (the default option, if only because animal spirits are weak enough not to make a fight of it most of the time) into something broadly resembling the body they used to have. That's how werewolves are made, although the term most often used these days is the polite, non-judgemental *loup-garou*.

Nicky is a stubborn bastard, in death as he was in life. He took the third option, generally considered to combine the drawbacks of the other two – the isolation of the ghost and the flesh-management problems of the werewolf. He came back in the body, as a zombie.

For most people it's a short-term option: bodies rot, and once they pass a certain point all the will-power in the world won't make them move any more. Nicky was holding that crisis at bay with an idiosyncratic mixture of home embalming, faith healing and careful refrigeration. And to be honest he looks pretty good for a dead guy: the artificial tan he buys in by the bucketload disguises the waxy sheen of his pickled flesh, and his Mediterranean good looks still make women take a second look unless they're close enough to catch that subtle whiff of formaldehyde.

And he's a zombie of substance these days, with an impressive property portfolio including the disused cinema where he lives, so who the hell am I to knock it? He's ahead of the game, even if he's playing posthumously.

'So you bumped into this guy Gwillam,' Nicky said, changing the subject as he pocketed the keys to the film cupboard. 'The papal-backed motherfucker who tried to kill you over that Abbie Torrington business.'

'Gwillam doesn't have the blessing of the pope,' I corrected him. 'In fact his order – the Anathemata – were excommunicated by Benedict XVI in a job lot as soon as he sobered up from his launch party. They do their own thing now, and the Church tries to pretend they don't exist.'

It was a half-truth, but it would do for now. The last time I'd met Gwillam, he'd hinted strongly that the excommunication was just a way of letting the Anathemata off the leash. They were kind of like the provisional wing of the Catholic Church now: a guerrilla army of religious fanatics with a scarily open-ended brief: save humankind from the dead and the undead, in God's holy name. In the case of Abbie Torrington, that had included compounding the murder of a little girl by the extinguishing of her soul. Gwillam hadn't been happy when – with Juliet's help – I had managed to piss on that particular picnic.

Nicky didn't seem happy either. 'Don't bury me alive in the fucking details, Castor,' he said, making for the door. 'It's the same guy, right? The one who thinks people like me are the intro to Armageddon? Sees himself as God's soldier in some fucking big holy war?'

'Yeah,' I admitted. 'That's him.' I didn't bother to point

out that I'm the one who's normally inclined to skip the details in favour of a simple-minded soundbite. Ninety-nine times out of a hundred I leave the obsessive, anally retentive stuff to Nicky, because that's where he really shines.

'Great,' Nicky grunted. 'So you just say that straight out and then we know where we stand. You want me to turn over some stones? Find out what those foam-flecked holy rollers are doing down in Walworth?'

He was holding the door open for me. I took the hint and stepped out onto the landing. Nicky came out after me, locking the door behind him and setting the alarms and deadfalls. I waited until he was finished because it's a task that takes all of his attention.

'No,' I said, when he looked up at me again. 'That's not what I want.'

He tried to hide his disappointment, but fine muscle control is an early casualty for a zombie and his poker face needed work. 'How come?' he demanded.

'Because he plays dirty and he's got men with guns,' I said. 'Also, men with teeth and claws and way too much body hair. He uses *loup-garous*, Nicky. Werewolves who've been given cast-iron absolution in advance for anything they do when they're under the influence. Can you believe that? He's passing round get-out-of-Hell-free cards. And he's already got a grudge against me because I worked that switch on him with Abbie Torrington's locket. The last thing I need to be doing is giving him more reasons to want me six feet under.' Nicky opened his mouth to lodge an objection, but I kept on going. 'Anyway, I don't think Gwillam's got anything to do with this. Kenny was attacked last night. I only got there as quickly as I did because I was helping the police with their inquiries. Whatever brought Gwillam sniffing around, I'm betting it's something else.'

'Or maybe the Anathemata set up the whole thing,' Nicky suggested, 'and Gwillam wrote your name on the car windscreen to frame you.'

'I don't think he's that subtle,' I said. 'He's more of an "If thine eye offend thee, pluck it out" kind of guy. Assuming he wanted me out of the picture, he'd just snap his fingers and I'd be landfill somewhere. Then he'd go square himself with the Almighty by means of a few Hail Marys and a nice stiff flogging, and it would all be good.' Nicky was still looking at me expectantly. I shook my head. 'Makes no difference,' I said, as he opened his mouth to speak. 'Believe me, Nicky, you don't want to tangle with these boys. Or rather, I can see that you do, maybe because you're thinking Gwillam will be a big, fascinating nut to crack. But he'll see you and raise you, and you're the one that's going to end up looking like Humpty Dumpty.'

I was talking to myself as much as to Nicky, because the truth was that I really did want to know what the Anathemata were doing so close to my home turf. I just didn't think I was in a good position to find out. I was still exposed on the Rafi front, and now I was a possible suspect in an attempted murder. If ever there was a time to keep my head way down below the parapet, this was it.

We headed down the stairs towards the main auditorium.

'Humpty Dumpty was an egg,' Nicky remarked.

'Sorry?'

'He wasn't a nut, he was an egg. You mixed your metaphors.'

'Point stands.'

'Then what *do* you want from me, Castor?'

'Mainly I just want you to run some searches on Kenny Seddon,' I said. 'How long he's been at the Salisbury. Where he was before that. Anything he's done that's left a footprint, and any recent events on the estate that he might have been mixed up in.'

'What kind of events?'

I thought about Jean Daniels and her litany of hints and euphemisms: *something* had happened, but I wasn't even close to being able to define what kind of something it had been. 'I don't know,' I admitted. 'Anything at all. Cast your net as wide as you can.'

'You could do that at your fucking local library,' Nicky said acerbically. 'You getting lazy, Castor?'

'Well, there is one more thing.'

'Go on.'

I took a sheet of paper from my pocket and showed it to him. On it I'd sketched the ellipsoid shape with the radiating lines – the one I'd seen twice during my brief visit to Kenny's flat. 'Have you ever seen this before?'

'Looks like a schoolkid's drawing of a vagina,' Nicky commented. 'Last time I saw one of those, I still had a functional heart. And a functional penis. You need the first to get the second, you see, because erectile tissue—'

'What about these lines coming out in all directions?' I asked, forestalling the biology lesson.

'Evidently it's a bright, shiny vagina.'

'It was drawn on a wall at the Salisbury. The words "Now it bleeds" were written in spray paint right next to it.'

Nicky shrugged. 'The vagina hypothesis still looks robust,' he said. 'Why do you care, anyway? Is this anything to do with Kenny Seddon?'

'It might be,' I said non-committally. 'It just struck me as odd, that's all, so I thought I'd Rorschach you with it and see what it reminded you of. Now I wish I hadn't. There's a weird, poisoned atmosphere around the place, that's all. And maybe that's why Gwillam is there, now that I come to think of it. If he thought there was demonic activity in the area, he'd have his shock troops armed and ready.'

'But you said you were avoiding Gwillam.'

'I'm avoiding a head-on confrontation with him, yeah. But I'm still interested in anything that's going down at the Salisbury that's even slightly out of the ordinary. That's why I'm asking you. Your antenna is pretty sensitive when it comes to stuff like this.'

He acknowledged the compliment with a nod. By this time we were right in front of the doors to the auditorium. Nicky threw them open, brought up the main lights by tripping a big steel switch on the wall, and walked in with me following along behind him.

The rest of the audience stood up, turning to face us.

There was only one of her, but this was Juliet so one was more than enough. She smiled at us smoulderingly, her black-on-black eyes swallowing the light.

'What did you think of the movie?' Nicky asked.

Juliet thought about this for a moment. 'I enjoyed the deaths,' she said, like someone looking around your living room for something to compliment you on and finally settling on the curtains because all of the furniture is eye-wateringly bad.

'You enjoyed the deaths,' Nicky repeated, his tone pained and indignant. 'You still don't get it, do you? It's a story. It's a fucking—' His hands fluttered ineffectually for a moment as he struggled with some way of defining narrative that he hadn't already used. 'Ah, forget it.'

'A story about something that hasn't yet happened, and isn't likely to happen,' Juliet agreed. 'I understand what it is. I just don't really see what it's for.'

'It's for pleasure,' I said. 'Don't tell me you don't understand pleasure, Juliet. I won't believe you.'

'But you know the things I take pleasure in,' she countered, calmly exact. 'Blood. Sex. Blood and sex together. Simple and primal things. Things that never lose their freshness and savour.'

I tried to shut down a whole slew of mental images that were filling my mind in proliferating excess like pop-ups on an Internet browser. 'I've seen you watching the telly with Susan,' I pointed out. 'You seemed happy enough then.'

'Did you notice whether or not my eyes were in focus?'

'Pearls before swine,' Nicky muttered, crossing to the trestle table he'd set out earlier. 'Okay, the inaugural screening is over. The Nicky Heath Gaumont is open for business, and God bless all who sail in her. Which will just be me, except when I see fit to invite you plebeian scumbags. That's it for the speeches, so let's get to the alcohol.'

On the table was a bottle of 1982 Chateau Pichon-Lalande Pauillac, which Nicky had opened and decanted earlier.

He poured three glasses, held out one in each hand for me and Juliet to take. Then he raised the third glass himself, put it to his nose and inhaled deeply. That's how Nicky takes his booze these days: he drinks the wine-breath, like ghosts are supposed to do, because he lacks the digestive enzymes to deal with the stuff if he actually drinks it. The sound he makes when he breathes is harsh and dry and pained, because inflating your lungs is something else that doesn't come naturally to a corpse.

Juliet finished her glass in a single swig and licked her lips. There's something subversive about the way she does that: it makes you think of huge jungle cats tonguing gobbets of bloody tissue from between their teeth after a kill. Nicky looked away – not out of fear or distaste but because the bottle had cost him three hundred quid and he knew that she hadn't really tasted it going down. Juliet is only an epicure when it comes to flesh: anything else she sees as window dressing.

'So you did it,' I observed, clinking glasses with him. 'Congratulations.'

'Thanks.' He took another snort of the Pauillac's heady bouquet. 'I thought I might go for a double bill next time.'

'Yeah? What movies?'

'*Night of the Hunter* and *They Saved Hitler's Brain*.'

I blinked. 'I don't see the connection, Nicky.'

'Stanley Cortez cinematography. The Salisbury is a fucking dump, Castor.'

The change of topic threw me for a moment. 'Yeah,' I agreed. 'It's high up on my list of places not to go. But it was meant to be a model community, right? The estate of the future.'

Nicky nodded. 'That was the hype,' he said. 'They got Derek Winch in to consult, back when everyone still thought he was God. Some other guy built it, though — don't remember the name, but you can see the thinking. Get Winch's name on the project, then ship someone else in to do it for half the money in a quarter of the time. They were gonna have shops, restaurants, cinemas up there, fuck knows what. The idea was that you never had to touch the ground if you didn't want to — you could live your whole life up in the towers. Use the walkways like streets, come and go as you pleased, be one step closer to Heaven. Which, coincidentally, was the slogan they used when they opened it up for applications.'

'Heaven,' Juliet echoed, pouring herself another brimming glass. Her tone was heavy with sarcasm.

Nicky watched her tilt and swallow, with a slightly tragic face.

'But it all came apart,' I prompted him.

He nodded. 'Before they'd even finished building it. The usual bullshit. They went in without enough money, cut corners, raced deadlines to save political face. But some people will tell you the design was screwed to start with.'

'How do you mean?' I asked him, listening with half an ear because I was still thinking about the teardrop graffiti with its corona of radiating lines. Actually I was thinking about that and Gwillam, and I was almost making a connection, but chasing it just made it flicker and fizzle out before I could grab hold of it.

'The walkways were the main problem,' said Nicky. 'Having streets eighty feet off the ground seemed like a fantastic idea when they started out. Pure sci-fi. They were talking about a city in the air – linked estates from Peckham to Elephant and Castle. Leave your worries on the ground, take to the skies and live clean.

'Only it turned out that you left a lot of other stuff on the ground, too. Like law and order. The Salisbury was a vertical maze – and it was impossible to police the place because muggers, pushers and gang-bangers could be somewhere else before the cops ever got within spitting distance. The walkways turned into thieves' rookeries. And then people started dumping their shit out on them rather than carting it down to the ground floor. And then the damp set in because the concrete was made out of spit and bumfluff. Closer to Heaven, maybe, but you bring the weather with you.'

I took a fastidious sip of the wine: Juliet was emptying the rest of the bottle into her glass, so I figured I'd better make it last. 'That's more or less what I heard,' I said. 'Didn't Blair do a photo op there back in '97, just after he got in?'

'Shit, yeah. That's where he did his "forgotten people" speech.'

'And then—?'

Nicky sneered nastily. 'He forgot them.'

I decided I'd talked shop for long enough. We were here to celebrate, and we weren't making much of a fist of it. I toasted the echoing vault around us and the newly painted screen at the far end of it. 'To the Walthamstow Gaumont,' I said. 'Like its owner – come back from the dead with grace and style.'

Juliet drained her glass and crushed it in her hand, letting the fragments spill out between her fingers and squeezing out a few drops of blood to follow them.

'Ye'air gva aku norim, hesh te va'azor,' she said.

Nicky gave her a pained stare. 'Which is . . . ?'

'The closest thing I know to a blessing.'

'Well, thank you.'

'You're welcome.'

'And now I've got succubus blood on my carpet. Is it – like – acid or something?'

'It's like blood,' said Juliet. And then to me, 'Would you like a lift?'

'Where are you going?' I asked her.

'Home. To Susan. Our working hours haven't overlapped for the last three days. I'm starting to forget what she tastes like.'

'Then it's thanks but no thanks,' I said, resisting the urge to ask for further details that I probably didn't need to know. 'I'm going back into town.'

'To this council estate?'

I shook my head. 'To Whitechapel. The Royal London.'

'The hospital? Why?'

'That's where they took Kenny Seddon.'

'Your enemy?'

I laughed at that. 'Not my enemy, Jules. Not exactly. Nor my friend, ever, that I knew of.'

'You said you fought over a woman—'

'A girl.'

'—Who you both lusted after. Didn't that make you enemies?'

'I never lusted after Anita Yeats.'

Juliet looked me in the eyes for a long moment. 'Yes,' she said. 'You did. At some point.'

There's no point arguing with Juliet about something like that. 'Well, I never did anything about it,' I amended.

'Leaving that aside,' Nicky interjected, 'isn't this same shitbird Seddon in a coma or something?'

'Yeah. He is.'

'So, what — you want to leave some fucking flowers?'

'No. I just thought it wouldn't do any harm to take a look at him — and if I get the chance, maybe try a laying-on of hands. You know I can sometimes do the psychic wiretap thing.'

Juliet shook her head. 'This is how you approach all your cases, Castor. You wander around the edges of them until things happen to you. That's not a plan — it's the absence of a plan.'

'What would you suggest?'

'In this instance, I'd go and find Gwillam and threaten to sink my teeth into his throat if he didn't tell me what I wanted to know.'

'But I don't think he knows what I want to know,' I pointed out.

'Then you'd have the pleasure of ripping his throat out. And incidentally — notwithstanding my earlier point about not asking me for any favours — if your path and his do cross again, I want to be there. He bound me the last time we met: bound me and humiliated me. It would be pleasant to balance the books.'

Job satisfaction. It's a very important part of what we do.

'So that would count as a small favour from me to you,' I mused.

'Hypothetically, I suppose. It hasn't happened yet.'

'But in the futures market it's solid gold. Can I borrow on it?'

Juliet chastised me with narrowed eyes, but she didn't say no.

'I'd be really grateful for a second opinion,' I said. 'Whatever it was that I was sensing down there on the Salisbury, it wasn't your bog-standard haunting.'

'How do you know?'

'Because it didn't feel right. It's too big, and it doesn't have a proper focus. It's like someone tore a whole bunch of ghosts into confetti and sprinkled them over the entire estate.' I threw out my hands in an inadequate gesture, fingers spread. 'The feeling is everywhere, Juliet. I've never come across anything quite like it.'

'Couldn't it just be a lot of different ghosts? You said yourself this place is a slum. And it's old enough now for a lot of people to have died there.'

Reflexively, I touched my left hand to my chest – to where my tin whistle nestled close to my heart. 'No,' I said. 'It couldn't be that. I'd hear it differently. You know how my thing works. To me, a bunch of ghosts in the same space would be kind of like half a dozen bands jamming in the same room. This was just one impression. One thing, but spread out over a wide area. It's like – you know how they say ants and bees don't have individual minds? That they're part of a hive mind, a collective self?'

'Go on.'

'That's all. It was all around me, and it was all the same thing. Big. Broken up. Not localised. Equally strong over the whole area of the estate, which is like a quarter of a mile from end to end. Did you ever come across anything like that?'

Juliet considered this, furrows of concentration appearing

on her brow. While she thought, I put some time into just admiring her face: it never felt like time wasted.

'Possibly,' she said at last. 'But not for a long time.'

'Will you go take a look?'

She didn't answer for a moment. She was looking at me as if she was trying to read something in my face. Or maybe she was just exasperated by my inadequate verbal photofit.

'If I'm passing,' she allowed, 'I'll take a look.'

'Thanks, Juliet.'

'*If* I'm passing, Castor. You wait patiently and you don't hassle me. I'll call you as and when.'

'Thanks,' I said again.

That would have to do, for now. I thanked her for the advice about jugulars and hit the road.

6

I hadn't thought about Anita in years, and now suddenly I couldn't get her out of my head. Every time my mind went into idle, as it did while I was Tube-hopping south and west across London, old memories of her kept popping up out of nowhere – no doubt shaken and stirred from the cerebral substrate by the pants-wetting trauma of seeing my name written in Kenny Seddon's blood.

Had I fancied her? Jesus, who was I trying to kid? Of course I had. More than once, in fact. The first time had been when I was four and was dragged against my will to Northcote Road Primary School to see my brother Matt playing Joseph in the nativity play. Anita was his Mary, and I liked the way she smiled. She delivered her lines nicely, too. I committed two of them to memory, and used to repeat them to myself every once in a while for the sheer pleasure of the sounds: "Come, Joseph. I am close to my time and we must reach Bethlehem before our baby is born" and "I thank you for your gifts and for your great kindness."

But that was just a childhood infatuation. The year after she stabbed Kenny – the year she turned sixteen – Anita was the most beautiful thing that had ever walked on two legs. And she'd saved my life! So naturally I was besotted with her to the point of insomnia, and used her as the raw material for a thousand fantasies ranging from the sloppily romantic to the baldly pornographic.

It didn't help, though. She'd completed her metamorphosis by that time: she was all grown up and I was a kid. The yawning chasm of two years was way too wide to vault across – at least in that direction: if I'd been older than her it would have been a different story. She dated one of the boys who loaded the vans at Hannah's pie bakery in Arthur Street: a guy named Alan, who was eighteen and had all the advantages of a job, a car and a total absence of acne. I hated him and wished harm on him, even though he'd once given me a quid to put a bet on for him at Coral's.

But that passed. It always does. You learn to scale your desire to things within your scope, when you're fourteen. Or at least you learn to distinguish between desires you can hope to satisfy and ones that are just between yourself, your conscience, and the box of tissues on your bedside table.

By the time I finally lost my virginity – to Carole Aubrey in the car park of the Red Pepper Club on Rice Lane – I wasn't even fantasising about Anita on a regular basis. The top slots were filled with movie actresses and female vocalists, interspersed with a few comic-book characters who really belonged to an earlier stage of my adolescence.

But I still saw Anita around, because Walton was a small place. Too small for her, I thought. I always expected her to leave, because it seemed to me at that time that leaving was the prerequisite for having any kind of a life.

And we were still friends, in the way that people who've collected frogspawn and played knock-down-ginger and climbed on factory roofs together will tend to stay friends.

I bought her the occasional drink at the Breeze or the Prince Arthur, and we'd share family news. She'd ask how Matt was getting on at the seminary, and I'd lie because I didn't really know. And I'd pretend to take an interest when she told me about Dick-Breath's progress at the Prudential, from doorstep insurance salesman to team manager and all-round messiah.

Once – only once – I made a pass. It was New Year's Eve, when you can get away with a lot of indiscriminate kissing: the general rule being that you took it as far as you could and had a plausible get-out clause if the lady objected. I swung into the Breeze with a couple of mates ten minutes before the towel went up, hog-whimpering drunk, kissed my way down the length of the bar – maidens and matrons and all – until I got to Anita who was standing in the corner watching her cousin feed the one-armed bandit.

We clinched, and it was good. Deep, and intense, and lasting as long as our lungs did. But when I tried to come back for seconds she touched the tips of her fingers, very lightly to my chest, and shook her head. I saw tears rising in her eyes, and I was alarmed. Tears? For who?

'You okay, 'Nita?' I asked her, taking pains to get the consonants in the right order because being able to handle your booze was part of the measure of a man in Walton.

'I'm fine, Fix,' she said, looking away for a moment while she blinked the tears back under control. 'I was just – I was waiting for someone, and he didn't come. I'll be all right.' She looked up at me again, giving me a dazzling and almost completely convincing smile.

I bought her a Babycham, which she didn't touch.

We talked about politics and punk rock – and then, when I was really drunk, I told her about what I was and what I could do with a tin whistle. This was before the rising of the dead went from a trickle to a torrent, and long before exorcism had become an everyday profession, but Anita listened without comment. When I got to the part about my sister Katie, she pressed her hand to the back of mine where it rested on the table, willing me comfort.

I walked her home, and she gave me another kiss. On the cheek, this time: a thank-you kiss. I realised that that was as far as it was ever going to go between us, and I didn't mind because it was cool that we'd had that moment of contact rather than a grope, a hangover and a lingering sense of embarrassment.

But whoever it was that stood her up that night, he needed his fucking head examined.

I like the Royal London: it's got a bit of class, as hospitals go. Tell me it wouldn't lift your spirits to be wheeled out of an ambulance past that terrific eighteenth-century façade. 'Bloody hell,' you'd think, 'I'm going up in the world.' But the neo-brutalist nightmare they're nailing onto the back of the building is a different bucket of entrails entirely, and for my money you can keep it.

Kenny was in intensive care, Coldwood had said. I walked in off the street, striding straight ahead past the A&E reception desk and the assembled sick and lame. I was gambling on the ancient truism that people are much less likely to challenge you if you look like you know where you're going, and it seemed to work: or at least it got me a long way, through A&E and Outpatients and into the slightly dilapidated annexe where the intensive-care wards were located.

The dead watched me every step of the way. In fact, I was having to walk right through some of them, because they were as thick on the ground as leaves in autumn – and like leaves in autumn they presented a rich, mesmerising spectrum of decay. Lots of people die in hospitals, and they die from a lot of different things, all of which leave their marks on the spirit as well as the flesh.

Nobody knows why some people get up again after they've been laid in the grave and others don't: Juliet puts it down to a character flaw, a fear of taking the necessary jump head-first into another mode of existence. But she's always fought shy of explaining how that other life works or where it's situated or how much a square meal costs there.

These ghosts, anyway, were mostly afraid and mostly confused. Their deaths were variations on a theme: arbitrary, painful, early, undeserved, uncomprehended, lingering, undignified, lonely, pointless. They were exactly the type – if you can talk about the psychology of the dead with a straight face – to retain the trace of their injuries and diseases in their risen forms. So I was looking at, and stepping through, a standing exhibition of all the horrible things that can go wrong with the human body both when it's damaged from outside and when it rises against itself.

Some of them tried to talk to me, their voices thin and high and warped by a distance that wasn't purely phys-ical. I ignored them and kept on walking. There was nothing I could do for them, apart from playing them the short, sharp tune that would push them off the rim of oblivion – and I don't do that kind of thing any more unless my back is really to the wall, for the simple reason that I don't know where I'm sending them. I'm a Pied Piper who learned somewhere down the line to see the rats' point of view.

Following the signs I climbed a stone staircase enclosing the wrought-iron gridwork of a Victorian elevator, coming out onto a wide landing whose quarry-stone tiles were ancient enough to be dished in the middle.

Unfortunately there were two intensive-care wards, one to each side at the head of the stairs – and each of them was behind a set of double doors that bore a chrome lozenge at chest height on the left-hand side: a digital combination lock, known among professional thieves as a yes-or-no.

The riddle of which ward Kenny had been admitted to was solved immediately by the uniformed constable standing guard on the door to my right. That just left the two obstacles – the lock and the copper. Maybe I could use the one to fend off the other, but only if I got the timing right.

I headed right on over to the door, trying to keep the air of brisk certainty up and running and facing down Mister Plod with a stare of cold superiority.

'Evening,' I said.

'Evening, sir,' he answered. His gravelly voice matched his shoe-leather skin and brick-shithouse build. He looked like someone who'd jumped a plane out of Zimbabwe just ahead of a bunch of pitchfork-wielding farm workers.

He also looked as though he didn't like me very much, based on first appearances, and was prepared to hate me on further acquaintance. If Basquiat had stationed him here, maybe he was one of her two 'questionable use of force' gents. I looked forward cordially to never finding out.

I only locked stares with him for a moment: then I turned my attention to the lock. It was a Baring Streamline-D, which meant it had a four-digit key and three factory defaults. And I used to know what they were, right off the top of my head, but that was back in my student days when stage magic and escapology were the only things I could get serious about. These days I have to rely on the mnemonic, invented by my sensei Tom Wilke, the Banbury Bandit:

> *Old fox speaks true.*
> *'Stuffed turkey never flew.'*
> *So fuck this zoo.*

Which if you take the initial letters of each word translates into 1563, 7294 and 6530 (the z standing for zero).

Digital locks are called yes-or-nos because unless you're big on logic gates and home electronics, whether or not you can pick them comes down to a single question: did whoever put the lock in bother to change the factory default setting?

Trusting to the morally deficient saint or angel who watches over the affairs of exorcists and career criminals, I keyed in the first combination. I was already pulling on the door handle as I hit the fourth digit, and since it didn't yield I belted into the second combination without a pause.

7294 did the trick. The door came free with a metallic quack. Giving the constable an amiable nod, I walked on in. He shot me a look, as though he was only an inch or two away from asking me who the fuck I was, but common sense dictated that if I had the combo I was someone who had a right to be there. I pulled the door to behind me before he could pull on that skein of logic far enough for it to unravel.

A quick glance around me showed an empty nurses' station in a short well-lit hall with four doors leading off. The only room I could see into from where I was standing was definitely a ward, with at least one occupied bed. The incumbent was invisible except for a bony outcrop of shoulder sheathed in drab beige NHS pyjamas. The same kind, probably, that your grandad and mine wore in their dying hours.

There was a sink just beside the door, underneath a poster exhorting anyone who came in to wash their hands thoroughly with the disinfectant soap provided. I took the opportunity to have a good scrub-up, partly because it would look right if the cop was watching me through the reinforced glass but mainly because – like a surgeon – what I was hoping to do here did involve some physical contact. Kenny might have been a legendary shit when we were kids, but I didn't want to polish him off with *staphylococcus aureus* after he'd survived having his throat cut.

Then I walked to the nearest door and peered inside. There were four beds, one of which had screens around it. From behind the screens a female voice, deep and vibrant, was conducting one half of a cheerful conversation: the other half consisted of silences of varying length.

'That's right, Malcolm. Hold your bum up off the covers, just for a second. Easy. Easy. Lovely, there you go. You can rest now. And we're going to do the same on the other side, but I'll let you get your breath back. Does it hurt? No? Good. If it hurts, you tell me . . .'

The other three beds were all occupied by silent, sleeping men, one of whom had his face wrapped in bandages from hairline to chin, with only a breathing tube protruding from where his mouth ought to be. The chart beside the door told me that he wasn't a Seddon, and neither was anyone else in the room.

Or the next. Or the one after that.

It was the last room where I found Kenny, or at least his name on the door. It was there alongside another name – H. Piper – but at first glance only one bed seemed occupied. It was the nearest one, and there was no way that the man in it was Kenny. He was at least thirty years too old, for one thing, and for another he was black – as far as I could tell from the small areas of skin that were visible in between the bandages and the drip-feeds and the strips of micropore tape that were keeping all the dermal sensors in place.

I went back outside and read the list again in case either of the names had been crossed off. They hadn't. Hurriedly, conscious that the nurse could appear at any moment, I scanned the room again. This time around I realised that the bed diagonally opposite me in the far corner of the room wasn't empty at all: it was just that the guy lying in it was so skinny that he barely altered the line of the covers.

With one instinctive, pointless look over my shoulder,

I slipped back inside and crossed the room. Looking down at the figure in the bed, I almost winced.

If this was Kenny Seddon, the years had kicked the living shit out of him. He'd been a big lad, and he'd grown into a big man – but right now the bigness was wrapped around nothing but skin and bone. The shape of his skull was unmistakably visible under the sallow skin of his face – one side of his face, anyway, because the other was mostly covered by a taped-on wound dressing – and where his badly fitting pyjamas lay indiscreetly open his ribs showed in a series of yellow-white knots like clenched knuckles. He looked like a tent that had collapsed in on itself when someone kicked the ridge pole away. And his laboured, irregular breathing suggested that someone was still working away from the inside to get the tent back up again, but making no headway.

But I could see, more or less, how the man I was staring at now could have been the boy I'd grown up with half a lifetime ago. And that recognition had the eeriest feel to it of all: I mean, obviously I've never woken up to find a horse's head in my bed – yet – but as a *memento mori* Kenny had most of the competition beat cold.

I didn't bother to look at his med chart because it wouldn't have told me anything. I did look into the locker next to his bed, out of pure habit, and found nothing there except a plastic pitcher of water with a flip-close lid, a plastic tumbler still shrink-wrapped for your germ-free convenience and a Gideon Bible. If Kenny had had anything on him when they brought him in, someone had taken it away for safe keeping.

Which meant that Kenny himself was going to be my

only source of information here. Maybe he'd obligingly be dreaming about the guy who took a razor to his brachio-cephalic artery, and I could just take a psychic snapshot as I drove by. But most likely not. The little tasters and teasers I get from skin contact are seldom coherent enough for that: it's a long way from a video download.

I could have put my hand on Kenny's forehead, but I didn't want to: it had the wrong kind of overtones, somehow. Instead I pulled aside a corner of the blanket so I could touch his hand. Then I just stood there, stupidly, staring at his wrist with the blanket peeled back.

Anomalies with the interior of the car, Basquiat had said. Well, there were anomalies with Kenny, too, and I was looking at one of them. His wrist had been bandaged where he'd taken the cuts in the course of the attack, and the bandage was fairly wide. But the livid-edged furrows of older cuts, inadequately healed, showed clearly both above and below it. These weren't defence injuries – not unless he lived with a ninja and they fought for the last Jaffa cake every day of the bloody week. These were the marks of old suicide attempts, or of regular, unremitting self-harm.

I reached out and touched the tips of my fingers to his open palm. Silence. Nobody home. I stood as still as I could, eyes tight shut, trying to find Kenny's frequency through the emotional effluvia pooling all around me – the gone-but-not-erased emotions that had soaked into the hospital's walls over the course of the last century and a half and now seemed to my strained perceptions to be sweating out of the brickwork.

I was picking up something, but it wasn't much: a

dimly flickering filament of consciousness like a 25-watt light bulb left burning somewhere in the basement rooms of Kenny's mind – the psychic equivalent of a pulse. But I was getting nothing else: not memory, not emotion, not even the raw light-dark strobe of an untranslatable dream. Kenny wasn't a good sender, and the conditions were almost as bad as they could be. It seemed I'd spent a lot of effort and ingenuity to no good end.

But then, acting on an impulse I didn't consciously examine, I slid my hand across Kenny's palm until the tip of my index finger touched the line of one of his old, half-healed wounds. Instantly, that faint pulse opened up like a hot red flower and I flinched from the shock of the contact, almost pulling my hand away.

What I was feeling was a mixture of contradictory emotions that turned around and through each other without merging, like oil in water. There was pain in there, sharp and real and narrowly focused: but the pain was shot through with a restless hunger that was almost erotic in its intensity, and riding on the hunger there was a sense of urgency, a formless conviction that translated as NOW, NOW, NOW, LET IT BE NOW.

It took a real effort not to step back, not to break the contact, because the emotions were so alien and so powerful: someone else's excitement, someone else's suffering and need flooding my synapses. I felt as though I was collaborating in an assault in which I was simultaneously victim and accomplice.

Images began to surface in the flow of emotion like corpuscles in plasma or felled trees on a rolling river. I saw a small, cramped room barely big enough for a bed and a chest of drawers, the top of the chest piled high with CDs and empty CD cases; the towers and walkways of the Salisbury, by day and then by night; and a hand, probably male, touching the surface of a broken mirror in which a face was reflected in jumbled jigsaw pieces. The face was eerily familiar, but I didn't have time to reassemble that jigsaw before the ceaseless rush of thought carried it away from me again, brought me instead a razor, a bitter taste, a drumming, repetitive song.

> *I got the sword*
> *I'm good because*
> *I got the sword*
> *I'm good because*

I tried to screen the music out but it had an insane, viral insistence: it overwhelmed and effaced the other sensations one piece at a time until there was nothing else left but the pounding drumbeat.

I opened my eyes and pulled back my hand, stopping the drumbeat dead. My fingertip tingled and throbbed as though I'd touched a hot plate and a blister was starting to form.

'He's looking better than he was,' said a voice from behind me. A woman's voice: the nurse. A moment later I heard her footsteps coming towards me.

I managed not to turn.

'Yeah?' I answered. 'How do you mean?'

She walked past me, brisk and businesslike, carrying a grey plastic bowl, half full of water, which she set down on the table next to Kenny's bed. She had a towel and a flannel hung over one arm, and she laid them out too with practised, economical movements. From her pocket she took a bottle of liquid soap. She was a short brunette, broad at shoulder and hip and as formidable as her voice. She was probably about my age, but she wore it better. Most people do.

'His blood pressure is up a bit,' she said. 'Sixty over forty. And his eyes are moving in his sleep – I saw that when I came in before. That's a very good sign.'

There had to be some reason why she was talking to me like an old friend instead of asking to see my credentials or screaming for the cop on the door, and I'd figure it out sooner or later. For now I was content to gather whatever rosebuds were on offer.

'What do you make of the wounds?' I asked.

She straightened and looked round at me, looking a bit bemused. 'What do *I* make of them?'

I nodded. 'Sure.'

'Well, you're the expert.'

Okay. The penny dropped at that point. She couldn't think I was a consultant on his rounds, so she must be mistaking me for one of Coldwood's boys, stopping by to scrape up a bit more forensic evidence. It says a lot for the public perception of the Met that a guy who rolls in out of the night in a long coat with two days' worth of stubble on his chin is taken to be one of London's finest rather than a wino looking for a berth.

'Yeah,' I agreed, straight-faced. 'I am. But you know how it is with experts: *multum in parvo*.'

The nurse blinked. 'Multi what?'

'Means "deep but narrow", which defines me perfectly.

'I'm –' well I'd better not be Castor this time out, in case that name ended up on a charge sheet some time soon '– Basquiat. Rudy Basquiat. Detective Sergeant. Who are you?'

She gave me an old-fashioned look and tapped the badge she wore on her ample chest. She was *Petra Ryall, charge nurse*. Right. I bet when she lowered her head and charged she'd be something to see.

'Petra,' I said. 'What I mean is, I just look at things from one angle. And your angle is going to be different because . . .'

'Because?'

'Because I'm a tough, hard-bitten, cynical London cop and you're an angel of mercy.'

Nurse Ryall grinned at me. 'You think they'll give us our own TV series?' she asked.

'Bound to.'

'Well, I only know what I saw when I was putting the dressings on, but I was thinking the angles are all weird. Did you think that?'

'You first,' I said, 'then me. What do you mean by weird?'

She shrugged, looking away into the corner of the room as she consulted her memory. 'I just mean . . . all over the place,' she said. 'Some of them low, some of them high. Left side, right side. Daft, really. They said he was in a car when he was attacked. You wouldn't think there'd be room in a car for someone to, you know, come at him from all sides like that.'

I nodded encouragement, as though she was echoing my very thoughts. 'Say he was struggling to get away, though,' I suggested. 'Trying to get out of his seat belt, maybe. He'd be squirming around, presenting different parts of his body to the attacker. Maybe it happened like that.

'Maybe,' Petra allowed, but she sounded doubtful. 'I don't know. There was something else, you know? Well, of course you know. If I'm talking rubbish, just tell me.'

'Go on,' I said.

'Well, some of these cuts were really two cuts. The razor had hit the same place twice. You can tell because there's different lines – different incisions – that overlap each other. So it's more like he was being held still and the other bloke was going and going at him. Does that make sense?'

'Perfect sense,' I assured her. 'Evidence, inference, conclusion. You'd make a good detective.'

She seemed to appreciate the compliment. 'So are they connected?' she asked, waggling her finger to indicate Kenny and the room's other occupant.

I was momentarily thrown. 'Why would you assume that?' I asked, temporising.

My surprise must have shown on my face. Petra hesitated for a moment, maybe wondering if she'd overstepped the bounds of forensic decorum. 'Well, because of the address, I suppose,' she said. 'Same postcode. And two stabbings coming so close together. Not a razor, I know, but I thought it could still be . . .'

'No, absolutely,' I agreed as she faltered into silence. 'We haven't discounted that possibility at all. I'm just impressed that you made the connection. Were they really as close together as all that, though?'

She rounded the other bed and consulted the chart.

'Three days,' she admitted. 'I thought it was only two.'

'And the MO,' I mused, chancing my arm. 'Sometimes the differences can tell you a lot.'

Petra looked down at the frail old man lying in troubled slumber between us. 'Lots of wounds again,' she said. 'But lots of little punctures, this time. And all more or less the same depth. Creepy. You'd think someone had tied him up with barbed wire or something. But he was just lying in his bed, wasn't he? Until that priest found him and brought him in.'

Priest?

'Father Gwillam,' I said.

'Yeah, him.' She glanced up at me, her face earnest and unhappy. 'Who'd do a thing like that to a poor old man?' she demanded. 'It's horrible. Sometimes I hate this world.'

I nodded, but my mind was racing and it was all I could do to maintain a suitable poker face. Was it the differences or the similarities that were more important here? Was I looking at variations on a theme or two unconnected acts of random violence? One attack involved stab wounds, the other puncture wounds. And Kenny had been ambushed in his car while this other guy seemed to have been attacked by a burglar. But from what Petra had said, both victims were from the Salisbury estate. And the Salisbury estate was suffering from two parallel infestations: sinister graffiti and the Anathemata.

It was worth taking the temperature one more time, particularly as I didn't have anything to lose here. Without asking permission I leaned down to examine the sleeping man at closer range. The puncture marks that Petra had mentioned weren't in evidence, but three small dressings on the man's face — at forehead, cheek and chin — showed where some of them had been. I touched his cheek gently with the back of my hand, as close to the edge of the bandage as I could.

Nothing. I wasn't sure what I'd been expecting — or whether the same kind of searing, vivid newsflash I'd got from Kenny would have been welcome or not. But this man was soundly asleep and his mind and soul were folded in on themselves: there was nothing to be gleaned from them, or at least not by me.

'Thanks for taking the time to talk to me, Nurse Ryall,' I said, giving her a nod as I stepped back from the bed. She was watching me with a sort of puzzled patience. 'You've helped me to clarify some thoughts.'

'Well, you're welcome,' she said. 'Listen, I came in here to give Mister Seddon a bed bath. I'm going to have to put the screens up, and since you're not a relative . . .'

I raised my hands. 'I'll leave you to it,' I said. 'I'd love to see you in action, but I've got places to be and crimes to solve. You know how it is.'

'Yeah,' she agreed, nodding. 'I think so. Down the — what-d'you-call-it — mean streets . . .'

'A man must walk. Exactly.'

'You're dead laid-back for a detective, aren't you, Sergeant Basquiat?'

'I used to be on the drug squad,' I said. 'The ganja gets to you after a while. Cheers, Petra.'

I left her rolling Kenny carefully onto his side. Sooner her than me.

The cop on the door gave me less than half a glance as

I left. People walking out were even less in his remit than people letting themselves in with the right security code.

I looked at my watch. Still nowhere near midnight, but by the time I got over to Walworth the witching hour would be over and done with.

Good. I had things to do over there that I didn't want the daylight to look upon.

7

The Salisbury at night was if anything even less pre-possessing than it was by day. The light of a hunter's moon bleached the unresisting pastels from the faces of the towers, so that they looked like titanic ribs of bone, and shadows accreted like crusted blood under the walkways.

But the air was alive. While the residents slept, it seemed that the emotional miasma I'd felt on my first visit woke and stirred. It had been an annoying distraction when I'd been here before, setting my teeth on edge until I finally attuned to it and let it fade into the perceptual background. But it was in the foreground now with a vengeance, buzzing in my ears like an angry mosquito.

No, not angry. It wasn't anger I was feeling, it was something else – but reaching for the word made the feeling disappear, the droning whine shutting down like a mosquito does as soon as you've got the rolled-up news-paper at the ready. And it wasn't really in my head that the mosquitoes were buzzing: it was in my fingers and in the palms of my hands, as if there was something that I had to do that was getting more urgent by the moment.

Yeah, that was it, now that I thought about it. It was the same feeling of urgency and greed that I'd got when I'd touched the old wounds on Kenny's wrist.

I came in from the north this time, and because I knew my way I walked more quickly. Maybe I could be in and out before this oppressive presence gave me a headache and ruined what was left of my night.

It was getting on for one o'clock in the morning and the place seemed deserted. Most of the lights in the flats were out, too, suggesting that the good people of Walworth had called it a night and turned in early. Maybe they were afraid of werewolves, although in real life it was the dark of the moon that caused most of the problems on that front: that was when the animal flesh fought back hardest against the human spirit that was riding it, resulting in some truly scary amalgamations of man and beast.

I scanned the graffiti wherever the moon shone its torch-light on a wall or pillar. I didn't see the peculiar symbol again, but the slogan NOW IT BLEEDS was emblazoned on the wooden slats of the wheelie-bin corral, and under-neath it in a different hand – or at least a different colour – GONNA GET HURT.

I found my way back to Weston Block and up to the eighth floor. It was as silent as the grave – not that that particular simile has a whole lot of meaning these days. I was half-afraid that the external door would be locked after dark. It wasn't, but it opened with an extended, rust-stopped groan like a homage to a Boris Karloff movie. I opened it just to my own body's width and slipped inside. Then I wedged it open with an empty Silk Cut packet that was lying on the floor so that we wouldn't get the same performance again when it slid to.

Kenny's door held out against my lockpicks for about a minute and a half: it would have been less than that if I'd been able to turn on the landing light, but it seemed a better idea not to. As soon as the cylinder click-clacked its laconic surrender I slipped inside and closed the door silently behind me. I could relax now. So long as I didn't make any loud noises, I was unlikely to be disturbed.

I took the penlight I'd brought out of my pocket and flicked it on. Its strong but narrow beam showed me a dismal hallway, cluttered up with boxes and discarded shoes. Three hooks on the right-hand wall bore about sixty-three coats. The carpet, which looked to be of 1970s vintage, had a mandala pattern in a lot of vivid colours, none of which did anything for any of the others. There was the faint, sad smell of an unlived-in space ruminating on old meals, stale cigarette smoke and rising damp.

I searched the coat pockets. Since I had no idea what I was looking for, one place was as good as another. There were betting stubs in one, keys in another. The rest came up blank apart from fluff and orphaned matchsticks.

The hallway was only three strides long. At the other end of it, instead of doors leading to a living room or bedroom, there were stairs going down. I'd come across this sort of design before, when I'd lived in a council block off the Barking Relief Road: in the building trade it's called vertical herringbone. Instead of having all the rooms for each flat laid out on a given floor of the building, you tessellate them in three dimensions: so you can have your door on the eighth floor, like Kenny, and the rest of your flat on the seventh – or if you're unlucky, the seventh and eighth and ninth, depending on how awkward the space is and how ingenious the builders have been in not wasting any. Most people I know who've experienced it hate it because it means that your bedroom can be right up against someone else's den – their TV blaring away on the other side of a thin sheet of plasterboard while you're counting sheep with less and less conviction.

I went down the stairs, which led directly into Kenny's living room. I was seeing it in the light from a lamp on the walkway immediately outside the window, because the curtains were half-open. I crossed over and closed them before turning on the light.

Nothing much here, either: an ageing three-piece, an aquarium in which a rainbow fish and a few neon tetras circled, a bookcase that held only a dozen or so books, a magazine rack stuffed to bursting with old copies of *TV Quick*, and a huge widescreen TV. I searched perfunctorily, then more thoroughly, looking under cushions and down the backs of chairs. Nothing of a remotely personal nature surfaced, and *a fortiori* nothing that gave me the slightest idea of what Kenny had been trying to tell me: assuming – and I was feeling less certain of this now than I was when I'd walked out of the Uxbridge Road lock-up – that he'd been trying to tell me anything at all.

Only one other door out of the room, and it led to a second hall from which all the other rooms opened off. The first one I opened was a bathroom, decorated in light and dark blue with a striking missing-tile motif. The second was a bedroom: large double bed, unmade; wardrobe and vanity table, the latter suspiciously bare; a cross hanging on the wall over the bed, which made me think – involuntarily and with a grimace – of my mum and dad's room back in Walton, where the cruci-fied Christ stared down on all their goings and comings. More than enough to give you functional impotence, in my opinion. Like the living room, the bedroom had a window that looked out directly onto the walkway linking Weston to the block next door.

If the flat held any clues as to what Kenny had tried to tell me, this was where I was going to find them: but something made me check the last door, too. It was another bedroom, and I stared in from the doorway with a cold prickle of recognition. It was a room I felt I knew, even though I'd only ever seen it once: and the once, needless to say, had been when I'd pressed my fingertips to Kenny's wound back at the Royal.

It had all the hallmarks of a teenaged boy's room. In addition to the hi-fi tower and profusion of CDs (mostly death metal and heavy rock) there were posters of Vin Diesel and Abi Titmuss on the wall – mercifully not together – and a lamp on the bedside table bearing the Manchester United logo. There were differences, though, between this room and the one I'd glimpsed in Kenny's memories: the CDs were neatly stacked now: the general leavening of socks and boxer shorts that had graced every horizontal surface in the remembered room were gone, the bed was stripped, and the hi-fi had a thick, unblemished patina of dust on top of it. Nobody had lived here for a long while.

You'd always wonder if there was anything you could have done, Mrs Daniels had said. About what? Where was the kid who'd slept in this bed? What was it that Kenny had never got over?

I was aware that anything I touched in here was going to leave marks in the dust. Not fingerprints, because I was wearing gloves, but even so it seemed like a bad idea to advertise my visit too blatantly. I retreated with a slight feeling of unease, and went back into the main bedroom: Kenny's room and, judging from the double bed, his wife's room too. But she clearly wasn't around, and nobody had mentioned her. In fact, Coldwood had already told me that Kenny lived alone.

I started with the chest of drawers. It contained mostly socks and underwear and tee-shirts, and they were all in the left-hand drawers: the drawers on the right of the cabinet were empty. Evidence was mounting up: Kenny had had a family, and he didn't have one any more.

He didn't have any photos of them either, annoyingly: the bedroom and the living room were as void of personal memorabilia as a hotel room. I wouldn't have been surprised to find a Gideon Bible in one of the drawers.

After half an hour of methodical but unproductive rummaging, all I'd come up with was Kenny's porn stash tucked away on the top shelf of the wardrobe and a shoebox behind the porn that was full of old decks of playing cards, all apparently well used. Sometimes I can get emotional resonances from objects, too, although they tend to be more muted and tenuous than the ones I get from touching people. I took off one glove and touched the inside edge of the box, very lightly. It echoed with pulses of old excitement, anticipation, pleasure, layered very deep and very strong. Evidently Kenny had enjoyed the odd game of poker.

Thinking about the absence of photos I realised that I was ignoring the obvious. I went back through into the living room and checked the bookcase, where I'd suddenly remembered that one of the book spines was a lot bigger than the rest: yeah, there among the Jeffrey Archers and the Wilbur Smiths was a photo album bound in red leather-effect plastic. Slipping my glove back on, I drew the album out with a feeling of muted satisfaction. This might at least give me a feel for what was going on in Kenny's life: probably not a smoking pistol, but maybe something that would point me in another direction. At the very least, I'd get to meet the elusive wife and kid.

In fact, I got one out of two. The album started with baby photos of a chubby, wrinkled Winston Churchill-alike baby who progressed over the space of ten or twelve pages into a much less chubby toddler and then into an increasingly tall and gangly boy with riotously unruly brown hair and a sheepish grin that seemed to be his default option when facing a camera. I flicked a few more pages and watched him grow into an even more gangly, longer-haired teen. And in the process I found the first mutilated photo. After that there were many more.

It wasn't the boy's image that was being mutilated: it was that of a woman who was sometimes with him – holding him as a baby, cuddling him when he was older – sometimes alone and sometimes posing beside a man who was unmistakably Kenny. In every photo where she appeared, the woman's head had been excised with angular slashes from a knife or razor blade – usually *in situ*, creating holes that went right through to the other side of the page and cut out irrelevant wedges from the photos that backed onto them. It was always and only the face that was taken: usually the thick, lustrous blonde hair remained untouched, along with a micrometer-thin stretch of forehead. Kenny and the ever-growing little boy smiled and smiled, standing beside and linking arms with this woman whose eyeless absence stared out at me like an unspoken reproach.

More and more uneasy, I put the album back on the shelf. Then I went back into the bedroom to clear away any traces of my presence there. I put the shoebox back on its high shelf, then started to stack the porn mags up in front of it as they'd been stacked before. The incongruity of this struck me as I was doing it. What needed hiding more than two years' back issues of *Barely Legal*? What do you keep *behind* your porn stash?

I took the shoebox down again and gave it another look. The sides of it were decorated with geological strata of stickers: characters from some manga cartoon, band logos, football players in identical head-and-shoulders poses. It had belonged to a kid at some point, and probably for a long time.

I carefully unpacked its contents onto the bed. Underneath the fourth layer of Waddington's Number Ones there was a slender black box that was too long and thin to contain a deck of cards. It was made of plastic and bore the Lorus name and logo, so it seemed fair to assume that it was intended to hold a wristwatch. I clicked it open and found myself staring at a heterogeneous collection of objects.

The razor blades were what caught my attention first: a half-dozen or so of Wilkinson's finest, still in their wrappings and held in place with a red elastic band. Next to them were some sticking plasters and a styptic pencil, a small vial of pale yellow liquid that turned out to be cologne, and the shiny steel business end of a dart with the flight removed. There was also a single razor blade that was out of its wrapper and embedded in a wine cork: the cork in turn had been neatly spiked on one of the plastic brackets inside the box that had once held the wristwatch in place.

Everything was clean, with no trace of blood and the only smell the very faint floral-alcohol whiff of the cologne. I knew what I was looking at, though, and I knew what it was for. I touched the bare blade gently and confirmed what I'd already guessed. It wasn't the playing cards that were associated with that old and frequent feeling of joy and excitement: it was this little hurt-kit.

I closed it up again, put it back in the shoebox and the shoebox back where it belonged. I was piling up the porn barricade again when out of the corner of my eye I caught a movement from outside the window. Too late now to turn the light off, or to duck down out of sight: I'd just be advertising the fact that I didn't have any right to be here. Instead I finished what I was doing, closed the wardrobe as slowly and casually as I could, and then turned to look out into the night.

I couldn't see what had moved at first, because everything seemed still now. Then, as my gaze panned from left to right across the scene, I finally saw the small figure standing on the concrete balustrade of the walkway on the side furthest away from me. It looked like a boy, far from fully grown, with his shoulders hunched and his head down, staring at the ground sixty feet or so below. He was standing absolutely motionless, which was why he'd been so hard to spot: the movement that had alerted me at first must have been when he climbed up onto the balustrade.

Nothing in his posture suggested that he was about to jump: he might have been waiting for a friend, or for a bus, except for the insane place he'd chosen to do it.

But somehow I could see in my mind's eye how this was going to end: the shapeless, half-exploded blood-and-bone sack that had once been a human being, on the pavement below. I was seeing it as though I was remembering it, looking straight down from the spot where the kid was now standing.

Maybe that flash of false memory galvanised me. I don't remember thinking it through or reaching any kind of rational decision. I was suddenly caroming out of the bedroom, across the lounge and up the stairs, taking them three at a time. I hauled Kenny's front door open and let it slam against the wall, heedless of the noise: then I was out through the spavined swing doors and onto the walkway, in all maybe twenty seconds after I'd first sighted the kid standing there.

But once there I came to a sudden halt, uncertain what to do. The boy was still standing in exactly the same place, about fifteen feet away from me, and in exactly the same posture. There was something unnatural about his still-ness: anyone in that position, standing over a drop like that, would sway slightly as they unconsciously adjusted their balance. This kid was as rigid and immobile as a statue.

I took one step, not towards him but towards the parapet, thinking that if he looked like he was going to jump I might have a moment in which to tackle him from the side and push him back onto the walkway before he could fall. I kept my stare fixed on him the whole time, and that movement brought his face into profile so that I suddenly realised who it was: the blond boy who'd given me directions the first time I'd come here.

'Bic,' I called softly. He didn't respond, didn't seem to have heard. His eyes were wide and staring, and he didn't blink.

I took another step, and then another, trying not to make a sound. If he was in some kind of a trance, waking him up was probably the last thing I wanted to do.

When I was almost close enough to touch him, he spoke. 'Gonna get hurt,' he murmured, his tone mild and contemplative.

I didn't know if it was a warning or a complaint. I didn't much care, either. If it was a warning then I was going to ignore it: if he was lamenting his own situation, then he'd probably thank me when he woke up. *If* he woke up.

As his knees flexed, I lunged. His feet were already off the ground when I caught him around the waist, but he weighed nothing and my momentum more than made up for his. We went sideways, not out and down, and I rolled as I fell so that I didn't squash the breath out of the boy or slam him head-first into the concrete. As a result I landed awkwardly, my forearm and elbow making jarring contact with the ground so that for a moment I was focused only on my own pain. In that moment, Bic struggled free with a yell of surprise and alarm. He scrambled away from me on his arse and his elbows, his face making up for its earlier immobility by running through about a dozen expressions in as many seconds. Then he looked down at the cold concrete he was sitting on, at his hands and at the livid moon staring us down from over the shoulder of Weston Block. Something made a pat-pat-pat sound, very close, like soft applause, but there was nobody on the walkway except the two of us.

'Shit,' Bic said, in a tone of simple, stunned disbelief.

'You're okay,' I said, unnecessarily. 'You were sleep-walking.' It wasn't enough, but maybe it would cover the basics.

'I'm—' he began. 'I'm – not – where am I? Who are you? You keep the fuck away from me or I'll lamp you. What did you do to me?'

'I stopped you from jumping,' I said. It sounds a little brutal, put like that, but I'd just realised why Bic had looked at his hands – and where the muffled reports were coming from. He was bleeding: thick, sluggish liquid pooling in each palm, looking pure black in the leprous moonlight, before it overflowed and spattered down onto the concrete like oil from a leaky carburettor.

'No way,' Bic said, without conviction. 'No – no way.'

I got to my feet and walked across to where he sat, his back against the parapet and his frightened eyes raised to stare into mine. I took hold of his hand and turned it so I could see the wrist. It was unmarked: no wounds there, old or new. The blood was welling up from the centre of each palm, and it was falling like sticky red rain. He still had the bandages wrapped around his hands but they were already saturated, not even slowing the flow now.

I unwrapped the bandage, since it was doing no good in any case. I figured that if I saw the wound I could maybe decide what ought to be done before the kid passed out from loss of blood. But mainly I was acting on instinct: the prickling in my own palms was a lot stronger now, as though I was holding a mobile phone, set to vibrate, in each hand.

There was no wound in Bic's hand: there was just blood,

welling up from under the skin of his palm and wrist and fingers like water soaking and spreading through the fibres of a paper towel. I saw this in a split second, in the light from the lamp directly overhead: then he snatched his hand away and scrambled back from me, glaring.

I swallowed hard, because the sight of the non-wound had shaken me. 'How long has this been going on?' I asked Bic, as gently as I could. He didn't answer.

'I'm going home,' he muttered, looking away along the walkway. But he didn't move, and actually he was looking in the wrong direction. Weston Block was behind us.

'That sounds like a good idea,' I said. 'It's right here. Come on.'

'Okay,' Bic said automatically. He was still looking off in the same direction. I followed his gaze and saw a group of people walking towards us, just coming out from under the shadow of the next tower along.

There were seven or eight of them: still kids, technically, but a lot older and a lot bigger than Bic. Old enough to think of themselves as men. They were walking in a ragged line, spread out across the full width of the walkway. The one at front and centre was almost as skinny as Bic, but he was bracketed between two serious bruisers who might as well have had lapel badges reading ENFORCER. The rest of the gang kept a pace or two behind these three as they marched, knowing their place: it seemed like not much had changed since the days when I ran with the Arthur Street posse. Maybe some things never do.

'What are *you* up to?' the alpha puppy demanded, giving me a stone-faced stare. Then his glance went to Bic and his eyes widened in surprise. He bent down and hauled the younger boy to his feet, roughly enough that Bic staggered and almost fell again.

'I've fucking told you!' the bigger kid said severely. 'You don't go out after it gets dark. Why the fuck can you never do what you're told?'

So this was Mrs Daniels's other son: her John, whom she'd described as an IOU. He reminded me more of one of the small bomblets from a cluster munition: they're both promises, I suppose, but one's more likely to be kept than the other.

He turned his attention back to me again, and we played at staring each other out. He was dressed in a Ben Sherman I-can't-believe-it's-not-leather jacket, black jeans and the obligatory DMs, and his fists were clenching and unclenching as though he was itching to take a swing at me. His eyes didn't track together, which I took to be a bad sign. Whatever he was on, if it was taking nibbles out of his nervous system it was bound to be having an effect on his mood, too.

'Was this fucker copping a feel or something?' he demanded.

Bic shook his head emphatically, either in disagreement or just to clear it. 'I was falling, Johnno,' he said, 'over—' He finished the sentence with a graphic gesture, pointing out past the parapet wall. 'He grabbed hold of me. Pulled me back. I think I was – walking in my sleep or something.'

'In your sleep?' The alpha puppy – Johnno – repeated, incredulous.

'Yeah.'

The answer didn't seem to satisfy anyone. One of the

rank-and-filers pulled Bic away out of the line of fire as the others closed in on me, following their leader. There was something wrong with all their eyes, now that I was looking for it: they were too wide, and when the light from the lamp caught their faces at the right angle I could see that their pupils were hugely dilated. Methamphetamine? Special K? Or maybe they were just high on life.

That momentary lapse of attention took me past the point where I could have made a run for it. The gang had me enclosed in a hollow semicircle now, and a metallic *snikt* sound from waist height told me that at least one of these likely lads had a flick knife. That first insidious sound was followed by several more from the same stable, and I could see blades sliding into hands in glittering profusion. It was as if a switch had been pulled somewhere. This had just stopped being a general for-form's-sake intimidation and become something else: something more ritualised and more inevitable. If I couldn't talk these little sods down this was going to get really messy.

'What are you doing on my soil, you fucking queer?' Johnno demanded, but his voice was dreamy rather than aggressive.

'This?' I said, making a circular gesture with my raised index finger. 'This is your soil?'

'That's right.' Johnno nodded twice, slowly, almost like a genuflection.

'How far?' I asked.

'What?'

'How far is it yours? I mean, where does your soil begin and end?'

Johnno raised his hand, letting me see the knife for the

first time. The blade was long and slender, barely tapering at all towards the point because it was more or less an icepick to begin with. He tapped the point of it against my chin.

'I own the fucking blocks.'

'All of them?' I asked.

'Johnno!' Bic's voice, calling from the distant outskirts, where he was invisible behind the wall of his elders and biggers. 'He didn't touch me.'

'Shut up, Bic. Yeah. All of them.'

'So you'd be the one to ask about anything that was going down here?'

The briefest of pauses. 'You don't ask anything, cunt,' Johnno said, and again his mild tone was at odds with the words. 'I ask, and you answer. You sneak around here in the middle of the night. Touch up my fucking brother—'

He shoved me in the chest with his free hand to emphasise how pissed off this made him. My back was already to the parapet, so there was nowhere to go but down. Pity. Down was the one place where I was determined not to go.

I tried one last time. 'I was looking for some information,' I said. 'But if you'd rather I came back another time . . .'

Johnno laughed softly and suggestively. 'Come back when they take the fucking stitches out,' he suggested, and his hand drew back. In the gap between conception and execution I brought my head forward and nutted him on the bridge of the nose with all the force I could bring to it.

The decapitation technique is meant to work well in a

dictatorship, where a lack of orders from the top can paralyse a political or military organisation not used to acting on its own initiative. But the rules for a rumble are simple, and these boys had clearly been in a few. They were on me in a second, the lad on my left grabbing me around the throat and the one on my right landing a hard punch on my chin before Johnno had even finished falling to the ground. I got in a couple more punches myself, but it was anybody's guess where they landed. Then the sheer press of bodies made it impossible for me to do anything at all. My arms were caught and pinned: two fists gripped my hair and forced my head back.

Out of the corner of my eye I saw Johnno climb to his feet, the lower half of his face masked in blood, like a red bandanna. He stared at me with impossibly wide eyes. At the same time, not breaking that gaze for a moment, he held out his hands, palms up. Someone put a knife into each of them. Oh great. I was about to be carved up by the two-blade kid.

But as he stepped in towards me the eager crowd moved, reluctantly, to let someone else squirm through. It was the kid, Bic. He stepped hastily in front of me, blocking his brother's path.

'I'll tell Mum,' he said.

'Fuck off, Bic,' Johnno yelled, brandishing the two knives over his head like a picador.

'I'll tell Mum,' Bic repeated, and collapsed at my feet. His head made a hollow sound as it hit the concrete.

8

As though a voice had yelled 'Cut!' from the darkness beyond the street light, everyone instantly lost volition and direction. The hands holding me fell away. Johnno blinked three times, each slower than the last, as he stared down at his brother's sprawled body. His bloodthirsty cohorts looked at a loss, almost embarrassed, unable even to hold each other's gaze. I knew how they felt: some tremor had passed over and through us, and this was the pained lull between the quake and the aftershock.

I knelt down and lifted Bic up, gently, in my arms.

'Open the door,' I said to the nearest bravo, hooking my head to point. He moved to obey, and as I stepped forward the ranks of Johnno's gang parted. One burly acned teen put his knife-hand behind his back with incongruous shyness, as though he'd been caught flicking ink pellets at school.

I walked into Weston Block, past Kenny's door – it was still standing open, as I feared – and on to the door at the end where Jean Daniels and her family lived. I didn't look behind me, but I knew I had an entourage. I decided not to chance my luck with another direct order, though. The spell could break at any moment. Or had it already broken? Was it the earlier drug-hazed bloodlust that was the enchantment? In any event, I kicked the door three times with my foot.

After a few moments there was the sound of someone fumbling with lock. The gang scattered like cockroaches when you turn the light on, so when the door opened I was alone.

A stocky middle-aged man with an inelegant comb-over stared out at me, backlit by the hall light so that I couldn't see his face.

'What the fucking hell do you call this?' he asked, sounding despite the words more mystified than heated. Then his gaze fell to what I carried. 'Oh God! Oh bloody hell!'

He scooped Bic out of my arms and turned on his heel, stumble-running back into the flat. 'Jeanie!' he bellowed as he went, heedless of the late hour and the neighbours' slumbers. 'Jean!'

I followed more slowly, into an infinitesimal hallway the exact same size and shape as Kenny's, – it smelled faintly of fried fish – and through into a living room that was completely dark apart from the light spilling in from the hall. The man – Tom Daniels, I had to assume – laid his son down very carefully on the sofa of a three-piece suite that was too big for the room. Then the light clicked on behind us and we both turned to look at Mrs Daniels, who ignored us completely as she saw Bic laid out on the sofa.

In that first moment, maybe inevitably, the worst possible conclusion was the one that jumped out and ambushed her. She gave a wail like the first note of an ambulance siren, when it's still climbing towards its ear-hurting peak, and I stepped aside hastily as she strode past us to the sofa. She went down on her knees and put her hands to Bic's face, huge sobs shaking her thin frame the way a hurricane shakes scaffolding.

'Billy—' she moaned. 'Oh my baby!'

Tom Daniels turned to me, his eyes wide with surmise and his fists clenched.

I stood my ground. My blood was still up from the fight outside and I had to struggle against an urge to raise my own fists in response. What was it with this place? 'He's not dead,' I said, from between gritted teeth. But Jean had discovered this for herself by this time.

'He's all right,' she wailed, still on the same painful, rising note: her relief sounded very much like her grief. 'Oh thank God, he's all right.'

Speaking personally, I wouldn't have gone that far. Bic had just tried to throw himself off the walkway in what seemed to be a full-blown trance state. He was back in that state now, with the possibility of a concussion to add spice to the mix.

'Mrs Daniels,' I said, still watching her husband for sudden moves. 'Jean. I don't think he's all right at all. I think he's very, very unwell. Even in danger.'

She raised her head to look at me, her face tear-stained and hectic. 'What do you mean?' she demanded. 'Tom, ask him what he means.'

'Answer her,' Tom Daniels ordered me belligerently. 'What happened to our Billy? Where did you find him?'

I followed my instincts and went for the truth again. Lies hadn't worked all that well on Jean the first time I'd met her. 'Right outside,' I said, nodding towards the window. 'On the walkway. I'm thinking he must have walked in his sleep. At any rate, he was up on the parapet and about to jump off. I got to him just in time.'

I was expecting another wail from Jean, but instead she gave a strangled sob and buried her face in Bic's narrow chest, where there was scarcely room for it. Tom Daniels swore and shook his head, but then came back onto the attack.

'Did anyone see all this?' he demanded, glaring at me again.

'Your other son and his friends came along right afterwards,' I said. 'They didn't exactly see it, but Bic told John—'

I stopped because John himself had come into the room – or at least, into the doorway. He stood there uncertainly, like a vampire who hasn't been invited in yet and so can't cross the threshold. I stared at him, slightly baffled. He was the same kid I'd met outside on the walkway, very obviously, but he was also different in some not-so-subtle ways. Calmer, for one thing, and with less of an edge to him: less of a narcotic turbo-tilt to the movements of his eyes.

'Stevie Rawlings saw,' he mumbled. 'He was over by Sandford, on three, and he said . . . what this bloke said. Bic climbed up on the ledge, and he just stood there. Stevie shouted to him, but Bic didn't answer or anything. Then he leaned forward, like he was gonna jump off, and this bloke caught him in the air, kind of thing. Pulled him back, before he could go over. That's what Bic said, too, before he fainted.'

The mood in the room changed, as I went from potential enemy to something less easily definable.

'I'm calling 999,' Tom Daniels muttered, crossing to the phone.

Jean stroked her son's cheek again, and then stood up on legs that seemed understandably shaken. She wiped her bleary eyes with the heel of her hand.

'You were here before,' she said, giving me a wary, searching look. 'Yesterday.'

'To see Kenny Seddon,' I confirmed.

'He's in the hospital. He was mugged.'

I let that word slide, although it seemed pathetically inadequate to describe the frenzied industry of Kenny's attacker; the threshing of his flesh with a straight razor until the floor of his car filled up like a well with his blood. 'I know,' I admitted.

'And you're . . . nothing to do with the church, are you?'

'No. I'm an exorcist.'

She nodded as though that answer confirmed something she'd already guessed. She started to say something, but that was when her husband got through to the emergency services, and his clipped answers to the standard questions cut her off short. 'This place is sick,' was all she said, and then she returned her attention to her unconscious son.

There wasn't much she could do for him, but such as it was, she did it. She got John to go and get a cold flannel to drape over Bic's forehead, although the heat of the day had faded by this time and the room actually felt a little chilly. Hedging her bets, she brought a blanket in from one of the bedrooms and covered him with it. She fetched some pillows, too, but then seemed to have second thoughts about whether or not his head should be raised, so she made John take them back again and bring a glass of water so she could wet Bic's lips.

By this time Tom Daniels was finished on the phone. 'They said there'll be an ambulance along inside of half an hour,' he said to his wife.

'He could be bloody well dead by then,' she said bitterly. 'God forbid.'

'He's breathing steadily,' I pointed out. 'And you can see his eyes moving under the lids. I don't think he's in any immediate danger.'

Jean picked up on the apparent contradiction, staring up at me hard from where she knelt at Bic's head.

'Then what did you mean before?' she said. 'When you said he was.'

I hesitated. On the one hand, I didn't want to worry these people and add to the problems they already had on their plate – particularly given how little I really knew about what was going on here. On the other, I didn't want to fob them off with some bullshit when their kid was lying comatose on the sofa – and had been an inch away from killing himself a moment before for reasons that seemed more geographical than psychological.

'You said this place is sick,' I said. 'I think I know what you mean. And I think that Bic – Billy – has caught the same sickness. He didn't seem to know what he was doing. He was in a trance state of some kind.' I looked from her to Tom, and then to the older boy, John, who was back loitering in the doorway again. I could have added that John had seemed pretty out of it too, in a different but equally scary way, but I suspected that it would derail the discussion into a pointless argument. I appealed to him as a witness instead. 'Bic told us that, didn't he? That he wasn't sure what he was doing there, or how he got there.'

John nodded but didn't speak.

'Well, we'll take care of it now,' Tom said, turning his gaze from his older son to me and keeping it there until he was sure I'd got the message. I nodded, accepting the brush-off without argument. He was right. I had no business being here.

But as I headed for the door, Jean spoke a single word. 'No.'

I stopped and turned. Jean released her hold on her son and stood again. Husband and wife exchanged an asymmetrical stare: surprised and affronted on his side, cold and calm on hers.

'You heard him,' Jean said. 'He's an exorcist.'

Tom huffed out breath in an exasperated grunt. 'Oh not that bloody rubbish again! Didn't we have enough of this with that frigging nutcase in the white coat?' I pricked my ears up at that. Gwillam? Gwillam had been here? Why? But Tom Daniels was still talking and there was no opening to slip the question into. 'It's just his mind, woman. It's bloody sick ideas he's got in his head from the other little psycho, isn't it? Poems and bloody pornography! I've sat by and watched and I've said nothing, but enough is enough. That filth poisoned his mind, and any other man would have smacked it out of him long before now. He doesn't need an exorcist, he needs to – he needs a—!'

Words failing him, Tom brandished his clenched fist to illustrate what Bic needed. Jean stared at it as if it was a slug she'd found in a lettuce. After a moment he lowered it again, some of his belligerence fading as he realised how little impression it had made.

'The day you touch him,' Jean said, her quiet voice sounding very distinct after Tom's little tirade, 'will be the last day on this earth that you have a family. I'll go out that door and they'll go with me.'

Tom blinked. I saw a guy once get hit in the eye with a piece of a car tyre, when the tyre exploded after he over-filled it. That was how Tom Daniels looked, more or less: as though some mechanism whose workings he was sure he knew had just blown up in his face and left him bloody.

'John,' Jean Daniels said after a strained pause. 'Go and wait on the street for that ambulance. Tell them where to come. They could waste ten minutes traipsing around this place.'

John protested half-heartedly, but gave it up on the second repetition and did as he was told. Jean crossed the room to close the door behind him. Tom stared at her with troubled eyes, clearly aware that there'd just been a *coup d'état* and – it seemed to me – not wanting to put a foot wrong before he'd had the new constitution explained to him.

'There's things that have been going on,' Jean told me, with a catch in her voice.

'You never saw very much of her,' Mrs Daniels said. 'Mrs Seddon. Did you, Tom?'

We were talking in the kitchen so as not to disturb Bic – or perhaps because we were talking about things that Jean didn't want her son to hear. It was a cramped, func-tional little galley: there was room for the three of us in there, but not a lot left over. The kitchen knife that Jean had been wielding when I first saw her lay in the sink, protruding from a plastic bowl full of unwashed dishes. My eyes kept straying to it as I listened.

'Hardly ever saw her at all,' Tom agreed. 'Only she did the shopping, some days. You'd see her coming up the stairs with her bags. Never had a word to say to anyone.' He was pathetically eager to please: a willing collaborator with the new regime of Jean the First.

'And once . . .' his wife prompted.

'Once she had a black eye, and a sort of a cut on her lip. It looked like someone had given her a bit of a hiding. If it had been anyone else, I'd have asked them if they were all right, but I didn't feel like I could. Not to someone I'd never even spoken to. It would have felt like nosing.'

I thought of Jean's monologue at the door the other day. *Nobody said a thing, did they? Nobody ever does.* 'Did you tell anyone else?' I asked. 'The police?'

Tom rolled his eyes and Jean scowled bleakly. 'I called *them* a few times,' she said, with a contemptuous emphasis on the pronoun. 'Not just then, but later on when they had the fights. Smashing things and screaming at each other at two in the morning. I knew he was hitting her. I didn't need to see it. I could hear it.'

'Hear what, Jean?' I asked, wanting to be sure I was getting the right end of the stick.

'Hear him hitting, and her – making the noises you make when you're hit.'

'Crying out?'

She shook her head. 'No. Not exactly. Grunting. Gasping. She didn't ever scream or cry: she was as tough as nails, that one. I don't think she wanted to give him the satisfaction.'

'You're talking about her in the past tense,' I said. 'Did something happen to her?'

'She left him,' Tom Daniels said, with flat and absolute conviction. 'For a younger bloke. A real flash Harry, he was. Used to work for some builder's merchant's down Blue Anchor Lane, but he looked like an Italian waiter with his long black hair and his motorbike. And he had this palaver all over his face.' He gestured vaguely towards his own forehead. 'Earrings on his eyes, sort of thing. I don't know why anyone would do that to themselves, and on a man . . .' He tutted, leaving the obvious verdict unspoken. 'He used to come and see her on a Saturday afternoon when Seddon was on his allotment down Surrey Square. Ten in the morning till one in the afternoon, every Saturday. As long as the weather held, he never missed it. And from what I heard, neither did she.'

Jean winced at this crude single entendre, but she confirmed Tom's version of events with a curt nod, only qualifying it with a 'Well, there's always talk.' As a defence of Mrs Seddon's virtue, it was less than spirited. 'He went mental when he found out she'd gone,' she went on. 'Seddon did, I mean. Running up and down the stairways shouting after her, asking everyone if they'd seen her. He had the police in and everything, only they said it was a missing-persons and they don't investigate a missing-persons unless there's . . . you know. Unless they think there was funny business.'

'How long ago was this?' I asked. 'That she left Kenny, I mean?'

'Nineteen months, now,' said Tom promptly. 'Just before Christmas, it was. Has to have been, because he pulled down all their decorations after she went. I reckon Christmas was like bloody Lent for that poor lad that year.'

'For her son?' I clarified, and Jean nodded.

'That was what I was coming to, really,' she said. 'The young lad. Mark. After she left, he used to hang around here like a lost soul. He'd left school by then, but he was too young to be on supplementary, so he didn't have any money to spend. He didn't run with any of the gangs.'

'Didn't seem to have any mates at all, to be honest,' Tom chipped in.

'He just sat, out there on the walkway, the livelong day. Bouncing a ball off a wall, or reading a comic sometimes. And sometimes some of the younger kids would sit with him, on a weekend or after school, because he had the comics – the American ones, you know, with Spiderman and whatnot – and he'd let the little ones take them away when he'd finished reading them.'

'So that was how Billy got to know him.' Jean's tone became more sombre and her eyes defocused. This part she was remembering more vividly. 'He'd sit with Mark for an hour or more, just talking about superheroes and super-powers. And he'd come in with an armload of Superman and Spiderman and X-Man and Daredevil-Man, and sit on that sofa –' she nodded towards the living room, one skin of brickwork away on the other side of the wall that faced her '– for hours. In his own little world.

'Then I found the poem.'

Tom's face darkened at the word. 'Show him,' he suggested. 'Show it to him.'

'I don't know if I kept it,' Jean said. And then, abandoning the subterfuge immediately, 'All right.'

She got up and turned her chair round. Using it as an ad hoc stepladder, she climbed up onto the seat and reached into the space on top of one of the kitchen cabinets. A moment later she got down again and handed me a sheet of paper: lined, folded into four, ragged along the left-hand edge where it had been torn from a pad or an exercise book.

I opened it up and read in silence. Twelve lines in small, neat handwriting with only one crossing-out.

If I could talk, I'd talk. It's the easy choice.
But I can't, so my knife has to be my voice.
I sing. Do you hear me sing? But what you don't know
Is what that sounds like inside me, in the depths below.

I'm full of pain. Like a bottle full of coke.
I take the blade and it just needs one stroke.
It comes out, but it changes as it flows.
Water becomes wine. My wound becomes a rose.

The pressure is balanced, outside and in.
The torment is over, the future can begin.
In that moment I know where I belong.
So you see why I need the blade to make my song.

The crossing out was in the fifth line. *I'm full of pain* had originally been *I'm full of darkness.*

'Mark wrote this?' I asked.

Jean nodded. 'Or copied it from somewhere. And he gave it to Billy as a present. Because he thought Billy

would get what he was going on about, Billy being such
a bright little lad. So after that—'

'I put my foot down,' Tom said. 'I told him to have
nothing to do with Mark. Not even to talk to him. I said
if he did, I'd stop his pocket money and pull him out of
the school football team.'

Jean took the sheet of paper out of my hands and folded
it up again, as though its dangerous doggerel had to be
silenced. 'He's a good boy,' she assured me. 'So that was
that, we thought. And then in the summer – I suppose
that would be a year ago, wouldn't it, so you're right, Tom,
it must be longer since she went – in the summer Mark
jumped off the walkway out there and killed himself. And
it came out at the inquest that he'd been cutting himself.
For years. Which was what he was telling us, if we'd only
cared enough to listen.' She waved the sheet of paper like
a tiny white flag of surrender. 'What can you say, Mister
Castor?' she demanded bitterly. 'What kind of love did he
get at home, if his mother ups and leaves him for a brickie
with a fancy hairdo, and his father is an animal who just
hits out all the time at everyone around him? It was for
me to say something, and I only thought about Billy.
About my own.'

She relapsed into dismal silence. Tom seemed thrown
by the sudden detour into moral philosophy, but he struggled on manfully.

'We didn't discuss it with Billy,' he said. 'John knew
all about it, of course, because they were talking about it
up and down the estate, but Billy mostly stays at home
and does his own thing, like. He's got his Playstation and
his books. Or he goes off wandering, sometimes, with his

mates. There's half a dozen of them – no harm in any of them, not like the bloody teenagers we've got round here.

'But as Jeanie says, Billy's not stupid. He knew Mark had gone, and I imagine there was talk at school about what had happened. Must have been, mustn't there? Anyway, he started brooding about it. Next thing we knew, he's cutting stuff out of the newspapers and taping bits off the TV news. I suppose it hit him hard, this lad living right next door to him and being sort of his friend and everything.'

'His best friend,' Jean said softly.

Tom looked at her and shook his head. 'No, no,' he said. 'There was five years between them.'

'He gave Billy the poem,' Jean said, talking to me more than to her husband. 'That had to have meant something. I told you he had no friends his own age, Mister Castor. I think he thought Billy understood him. I think it must have hit him very hard when Billy stopped talking to him.'

She trailed off into silence.

There was an elephant in the living room with us, and I felt that it was time to try wrangling it a little. 'When did Billy's hands start to bleed?' I asked.

Tom blanched at this blunt wording, but Jean took it squarely on the chin. 'That was later,' she said, her voice almost level. 'The dreams came first.'

'He dreamed about Mark?'

She shook her head. 'Not really. At least, he didn't see Mark in his dreams. He dreamed about a place. It was really dark there – so dark you couldn't see anything, not even yourself. And he'd stumble around for a while, trying to find a way out. But he never could, so in the end he'd just sit down on the ground and wait.

'The ground . . .' She hesitated, as if she really didn't know how to say this. 'He said it was warm. Like skin. But not soft like skin: it was all ridged and rough and shiny. He said it was like lava after a volcano. When it's cooled, he said, you get miles and miles of this stuff like the surface of the moon.' She smiled faintly. 'He'd just done volcanoes at school.

'And then he'd start to hear this voice, in the darkness. And he was sure it was Mark's voice, even though he said it didn't sound anything like. But there it was, this voice droning on and on. Not really talking to Billy, so he said. Just talking.'

'About what?'

She gave me a slightly haunted look. 'What do you think? About hurting yourself. Cutting yourself open. About the way it feels when you cut into yourself and let the pain out. About how wounds are roses and blood is wine.'

One of those leaden silences fell between us: the kind where everyone is expecting someone else to be the next to speak, and it gets more awkward the longer you leave it.

'Did the news articles mention that Mark was a self-harmer?' I asked.

'Some of them,' said Tom. 'But he could have got most of it from the poem, couldn't he? It's all there. We just tried talking him out of it at first, because he's bright and he's a good lad, like Jeanie said. We thought it would be a nine days' wonder, like most things are when you're that age. We took the tapes and all the bits of paper away and locked them in a cupboard. And we kicked him out when he got back after school to play in the adventure playground or over in the park. We thought he just needed his mind taking off it.'

'And that,' said Jean, with heavy finality, 'was when the bleeding started. Just a drop, at first, but how can you have blood, Mister Castor, if you haven't cut yourself? And the more we wiped it away, the more it came. We took him in to see the GP, and then a dermatologist, but they don't have a clue. They were talking about our Billy being a haemophiliac, as though that explains it. But his blood clots normally if you test it, so it isn't that.'

'And that bloody priest . . .' Tom interposed, but then he seemed to think better of that line of discussion and left the words hanging.

'The priest?' I echoed. 'Is that the man you mentioned before? The man in the white raincoat?' Tom didn't answer, but the look he threw at Jean was of the he-already-knows variety. 'Was his name Gwillam?' I asked.

After a strained pause, Jean nodded. 'That's him.'

'What did he want? Was it something to do with Billy?' Another look passed between them.

'It was my fault,' Tom muttered, 'for mentioning it to Father Merrick at Bethesda's. I should have kept my mouth—'

'I don't think it's something I feel comfortable talking about, Mister Castor,' Jean broke in, her tone as tense and taut as if Gwillam had put an indecent proposal to her. 'I'm sorry.'

That left me somewhat high and dry. 'Okay,' I said. 'Look, it's not my place to ask. And I'm grateful for what you've told me already.' I stood up. 'See what the hospital says about Billy,' I said. 'Hopefully he'll just wake up tomorrow not remembering any of this. But I'd get him out of this place, if you've got anywhere else to send him. He needs to be in a different atmosphere for a while.'

'There's my sister's,' Tom said doubtfully. 'In Croydon.'

The thought of sending anyone to Croydon for their health was as surreal as anything else in this conversation. 'Yeah,' I said. 'That sort of thing. Just for a couple of weeks. You've got the school holidays coming up. Pack him off out of this.'

But Jean was shaking her head. 'He stays here,' she said, 'with me. Or we all go together. If my boy is going through something bad, then I'm the one who looks after him. Thank you for your time, Mister Castor.'

There was no misinterpreting her tone. The consultation was over.

'I think it's this place more than anything else that's making him sick,' I said, persisting with my diagnosis in the teeth of her new-found determination. 'It's your choice, obviously. And I know it's complicated. It always is. But look, if anything should come up that you want to talk to me about . . .' I gave them my card, with the solemnity of someone who hasn't been doing that kind of thing for very long. The card is a recent innovation, obtained from a printer who offered to do me a job lot of a hundred for free by way of an introductory offer. If he'd known the size of my client base he would have cut that back to ten.

Jean turned the card in her hand, and Tom looked over her shoulder at it, his expression changing to a slightly pained frown.

'Spiritual services,' Jean read aloud. 'That's what you get from an exorcist, is it? What does it mean, exactly?'

'It means a lot of different things,' I said. 'I set up wards against the dead, advise people how to make their houses safe, that sort of thing. I persuade ghosts to go away if they're making a nuisance of themselves, or else I find out what it is they want. I can tell you if someone you haven't seen for a while is alive or dead, and if they're dead I can invite them over to talk to you. I do kids' parties too, sometimes. Don't ask for references on that, though, because I haven't had any satisfied customers yet. The number on the back is my landlady's: if I don't pick up on the office number, you can leave a message for me there.'

Jean gave the card to Tom to look after, and he slipped it into a back pocket. I stood up, feeling like I'd over-stayed my welcome.

'Thank you, Mister Castor,' Jean said, giving me a slightly awkward handshake. Tom didn't put out his hand, and I didn't feel inclined to offer mine.

'Seriously,' I said to Jean. 'If you need me, call. I'm only an hour away.'

She nodded.

'He'll be fine when he wakes up,' Tom said, with brusque conviction.

But Bic was still sleeping – or unconscious – when I left, and the ambulance still hadn't arrived.

I noticed as I walked past that Kenny's door was now closed. That was good, as far as it went, but I wondered who was going around behind me, covering my tracks. I also wondered what business Gwillam could have with the Daniels family – and why it didn't bear repeating.

I was lost in thought as I walked down the stairs. But as I came level with the third-floor walkway, a movement at the corner of my eye made me turn my head. It had come from outside, from the walkway itself, which meant I was seeing it through the grimed glass of the swing-doors. What had made it noticeable was that there was a light out there – one of the few functioning street lamps – and whoever had moved had momentarily occulted it from my perspective: light-darkness-light, a Morse-code flash.

I stopped and stared. There was a figure standing on the walkway, her back against the street light. Not a bad position to take up if you were watching Weston Block, because to anyone looking back you'd just be a backlit silhouette. But I *knew* the silhouette: I'd seen it only a day before, and the ponytail was a dead give-away. It was the woman I'd seen with Gwillam.

I took an involuntary step forward. Despite the stern tone I'd taken with Nicky, I was itching to find out what Gwillam was up to down here. Maybe the ponytailed woman would be willing to give me a few hints if I did my Rudy-Basquiat-consulting-detective routine again. You never know until you try.

But as I headed for the doors she saw me too. Her gaze had been fixed on the higher levels of the building: now it flicked down and caught the movement nearer to hand, and she was gone out of the circle of light before I even had the door open.

I went after her at a flat run, along the full length of the walkway and into the gaping doors that led into the next tower block in the daisy chain.

The doors facing me – doors that led out onto another stretch of walkway – were still swinging. I headed in that direction, but something – some mistrustful gene that's probably a precious part of my Liverpudlian heritage – made me slow and listen for half a second even as I took the bait. It was half a second well invested: the woman's rapid foot-steps were clearly audible from the echoing stairwell off to my right, and from below me. I slewed round and followed, taking each flight of stairs in two giant strides.

I guess Juliet is right about my aversion to planning: this kind of whimsical improvisation has got me into trouble more times than I care to count. But I only wanted to talk to the woman, in a spirit of bluff and intimidation, and maybe get a hint about how the Salisbury fitted into the Anathemata's world-view. Plus my blood was up now: I was filled with the thrill of the chase.

That was probably why I walked right into what was waiting for me at the bottom of the stairs. As I rounded the final bend, still a dozen or so steps above ground level, a big hand thrust itself out of the shadows in the dank lobby, grabbed a generous swathe of my lapels and hooked me through the air to slam me hard against the wall.

It was Gwillam's other friend: the tall, lean man with the planed and spirit-levelled face. He held me pinned against the wall with surprising strength, his hand pressing against my chest so hard that he squeezed the breath out of me like the air out of a bellows, making it impossible for me to inflate my lungs. He looked round inquiringly at the ponytailed woman, who was standing up against the street doors, which she'd pushed half open. She looked breathless and angry.

'Scrape him off,' she snapped. 'Then fold and follow me.'

The flat-faced man brought his face up close to mine, staring at me slightly quizzically with his head tilted first to one side, then to the other. His movements were staccato, punctuated by perfect stillness.

'Bad boy,' he said, in a voice that was both deep and hollow, like an oracle speaking from a cave or from the bottom of a well. His tone was detached, though, despite the disapproving words — and his mouth, as I'd noticed the day before when he was talking to Gwillam, moved all of a piece, as though his lower jaw, like a puppet's, was a piece of wood hinged at the ends.

I locked both of my hands on his one, and tried to lever it away or at least relieve some of the pressure so that I could draw a breath. Nothing doing: this guy wasn't particularly thickset, but he was terrifyingly strong.

'You — ' he said, and he let the word linger while black dots clustered and spread behind my eyes. ' — really need to take a rest.'

He pulled me back and slammed me forward again so that I crashed against the wall once, twice, three times. I tried to let my head sag forward, but on the third beat he got the angle just so and the back of my skull smacked off the wall, turning the black dots into impressive techni-colour Catherine wheels.

There was one further impact, but it came from a different angle. I was dimly aware that the big man must have thrown me, or maybe just let me fall. Through the spiked fug of near-unconsciousness, I deduced that I was horizontal and used that as a clue to what it might take to get upright again. But my limbs had forgotten the effortless cooperation they'd developed over thirty-some years: I must have looked like Bambi on ice.

Unfortunately, Flat-face had lingered to make sure I stayed down, and he seemed to take my trying to get up as a deliberate provocation. I saw his foot draw back for a kick, aimed squarely at my head. I raised a feeble, futile arm to fend it off.

'That's enough,' said a voice from over by the street doors. 'Leave him alone.'

Flat-face lowered his foot and turned. Blinking my eyes semi-clear, I looked off in that direction too. The newcomer stood framed in the doorway, holding the double doors open with fully extended arms, but there was a querulous note in his voice that clashed badly with the dramatic pose. It wasn't the voice of a man who knows he's going to be obeyed.

'Who says it's enough?' demanded Flat-face in a dangerous basso rumble.

'I do, obviously.' The newcomer took a step towards us. 'I mean it, Feld. Look at me if you don't believe me.'

Flat-face stared down at the newcomer. I stared at him too and I probably would have gasped if I'd had any breath left to do it. The big man didn't gasp: in fact he didn't respond in any way that I could see. But after a moment or two he flexed his arms and adjusted his cuffs, first left and then right.

'I'll take advice,' he said in the same deep voice.

'You do that,' the other man agreed.

I watched Flat-face groggily from my floor-level ring-side seat as he stepped carefully around the newcomer, staring at him the while as if to show that his readiness for mayhem hadn't abated by a single degree. Then he walked out into the night, opening the doors by the novel expedient of slamming his head into them so hard that they flew back to their full extent. They hit the wall on either side like a pistol shot in badly synched stereo.

My rescuer helped me to my feet, which took a couple of attempts because I was embarrassingly weak and groggy after my recent anoxic experiences.

'Out for a late-night walk?' I asked sardonically.

He shrugged. 'Just be thankful I was here. You make friends everywhere you go, don't you, Felix? You really should think twice before coming into a place like this at night.'

There were lights going on up above us now, and faces peering over the banisters on the upper levels. Only a natural impulse towards self-preservation had prevented anyone from coming down and seeing what all the noise was about, but it could only be a matter of moments. Better to have this conversation somewhere else, far from the madding crowd: especially considering how spectacularly madding they could get around here. We left Weston Block, our shoes crunching on broken glass.

'Well, it's good of you to take an interest,' I said as I led the way between the towers, heading north across the estate. 'But any place that's good enough for you and your friend Gwillam is good enough for me.' Considering he'd probably just saved my life, the satisfaction I took in his startled expression was a little ungenerous. But I was starting to see a pattern, and it was one I liked even less than red and green Paisley.

There was one final broad flight of steps that led down from the concrete plain towards the New Kent Road. I took it, limping slightly, and my rescuer followed me.

'I thought you gave up the pastoral stuff,' I muttered over my shoulder.

'Where you're concerned, Felix?' Matt answered with a sorrowful inflection. 'I think I'll always be my brother's keeper.'

9

'You've got a visitor' were the first words that Pen said when she opened the door to me. Then she noticed Matt, standing in the puddle of moonlight behind me. 'Oh,' she appended, without enthusiasm. She walked away, leaving the door open behind her.

We came out of the warm sticky night into the warm sticky hallway, and followed Pen downstairs into her chthonic domain. *Tales From Topographic Oceans* was playing softly from below us, the occasional crack and hiss making it clear that we were listening to vinyl being played on Pen's old Dual 2.2 turntable. Gary Coldwood was sitting on the shapeless leather sofa with a glass of brandy in his hand. Edgar and Arthur perched on the sofa's back on either side of him, clearly acting as chaperones. They needn't have worried: Gary is in love with his job.

He set the glass down as we came into the room so that he could look more like a copper when he stood up and scowled at me.

'Two reports came in at Uxbridge Road within ten minutes of each other, Fix,' he said, as I crossed the room and uncorked the brandy bottle. 'Both from the Salisbury Estate. A breaking and entering and an affray. Would you know anything about either of those?'

The brandy burned as it trickled down my throat — and since Pen hadn't seen fit to put out the good stuff I let it trickle fairly liberally. Then I set the bottle down and belched, more for effect than anything. I noticed a smear of blood on the neck of the bottle where my hand had held it: I'd scraped my palms when I went down the second time, and they were raw and stinging. 'Gary Coldwood,' I said, hooking a thumb over my shoulder, 'Matthew Castor. *Father* Matthew Castor. My big brother. I don't think you've ever met. Gary's a cop, Matty: you'd better get an alibi ready.'

Gary refused to be deflected, but he looked at Matt with unmistakable interest. 'Two men fled the scene,' he pursued grimly. 'One was described as wearing a long coat of some kind – maybe a mac or a heavy overcoat. So, second time of asking: were you there? If you were, I need to know about it. I may be able to come between you and the shit-storm if I know what it is you've done.'

'I may occasionally enter, but I never break,' I said, slumping down on the sofa because standing up was feeling like a real effort. 'And I've been with my brother all evening. He's a man of the cloth, did I say? Sit down, Matt, you're making the place look untidy. Pen, have you got any anti-septic salve or anything?'

'I've got cider vinegar,' Pen said, heading for the kitchen. 'That'll do just as well.'

'And make me smell like a bag of chips,' I said, glumly.

'Fix—' Coldwood was glaring down at me.

'Gary.' I stared back, deadpan. 'I've been down in that neck of the woods tonight, I won't deny it. I was there for quite a while, so you'll find no shortage of people who can give you my description. But you know how peaceable a soul I am. I wouldn't dream of getting involved in an affray, even if I was invited. I'm just sniffing around, trying to figure out what it was that Kenny was trying to tell me. How's he doing, by the way? Dead or alive?'

Gary swore, coarsely and caustically. 'Sniffing around,' he repeated, with biting emphasis. 'It *was* you, wasn't it? You broke into the house of a man you might end up charged with murdering.'

'I just told you I didn't, and I'm sticking to that. So Kenny is—?'

'No change. But the longer he stays in the coma, the less likely he is to recover. Did you at least wear gloves?'

'For a quiet evening walk with my brother, the priest? Of course not. We've had our differences in the past, but it's never come to blows. And if it ever does, I think it's likely to be a bare-knuckle fight.'

Gary shook his head in grim wonderment. 'Are you insane?' he asked me.

'Are you?' I countered equably. 'Two calls come in from right next door to your crime scene and you come here? Why aren't you getting a head start on Basquiat the big blonde battering ram, Gary? You're not letting her steal the case out from under your nose, are you?'

'I'm fucking homicide, Fix,' Gary almost yelled. 'Burglary and random bottlings are as relevant to my working day as minding your own business is to yours. I only came here because I can read the bloody signs by now. I had this vivid sense of you drawing yourself a tall pint of razor blades and getting ready to take the first swig. Tell me I'm wrong and I'll walk right out of here. Go ahead.'

I considered him in silence. Pen came back into the room carrying a bottle of vinegar and some torn-off lengths of kitchen towel: also a couple more glasses for the booze.

'Right,' Coldwood said, tersely. 'Thought so.'

I wadded up the kitchen towel and applied vinegar to my abraded hands – noticing in the process that the palms were still itching insanely. Edgar and Arthur bated at the intense, pungent smell, but they were usually present when Pen did her witchy conjurations, so they were used to worse. Coldwood, meanwhile, had finally turned to Matt who was still hovering uneasily by the doorway. He gave him a perfunctory handshake.

'Pleased to meet you, father,' he said. 'You're the oldest, right?'

'Just Matt,' said Matt. 'I'm three years older than Felix, yes.'

'And where did this evening walk of yours take you, besides the Salisbury Estate?'

Matt thought about this for a long moment. 'Nowhere else,' he said at last. 'I met Felix there. I was already passing – walking – I was in the area. I heard the sound of a fight and intervened.'

'A fight?' Coldwood's expression of exaggerated surprise was straight out of the silent movies. 'You found Fix involved in a fight? And him so peaceable? No wonder he looks like an elephant wiped its arse with him.'

I dropped the vinegar-soaked kitchen towel onto the table and went for the brandy bottle again, but Pen intercepted me, grabbing hold of my wrists and turning them over so she could view the damage. 'How do they feel?' she asked.

'Painful,' I said. 'And mildly pickled.'

'I'll make you a sulphur poultice later,' she promised.

'Maybe I'll get lucky and die from gangrene.'

Pretending to be offended, Pen released my wrists and

made a gesture that told me I was divorced from her mercy
and goodwill. I took the opportunity to pour myself some
more liquor. 'Tell me about the lab data, Gary,' I said. 'Have
you got any better idea of what happened in that car?'

Coldwood grimaced and didn't answer. I refreshed his
glass and pushed it across the table towards him.

'Two men,' I prompted. 'One of them was Kenny. The
other one wasn't me.'

'Two men,' Coldwood agreed, picking up the glass and
taking a solid swig. 'Two men *besides* Seddon. All three of
them touch the razor at different times – lots of different
times, shifting their grip. It looks as though the razor was
a major fucking talking point.'

'Do we know whether it belonged to Kenny or one of
these other guys?'

He shook his head. 'No idea. But if it belonged to one
of the killers – I mean, the assailants – then he definitely
used it mainly for shaving.'

'What do you mean?'

'I mean that anyone who knew how to handle a malky
wouldn't have made such a frigging dog's breakfast of it.
To look at the wounds, you'd think Seddon had been done
over with a potato peeler. And then switched to a tin-opener
for the actual kill. Sorry, father.'

Matt did look a little pale and introspective. He'd sat
down at last, on the huge wooden chest in the corner, as
far removed from these discussions as he could get. He swallowed audibly. I was going to tell him where the bathroom
was, forestalling any further degradation of Pen's already
grimy carpet, but Gary was still talking and I didn't want
to interrupt in case it was hard to get him started again.

'We've got some fibres,' he said, 'from the other guys' clothes. No footprints, though. The car was parked on a slope, with the bias towards the driver's side. Easy enough to bypass the blood if you go in and out by the passenger door. But with the fingerprints and the other bits and pieces, there's no margin for error.'

'So we'll know these guys when we find them,' I summarised.

'Which *we* is this?' Gary went and leaned against the fireplace as though putting some distance between himself and me. 'You don't work for me any more, Fix. Ruth Basquiat doesn't see you as part of any we. And she's I/C on the case now, so you'd better not expect any favours.'

'Basquiat is—?' I echoed. This wasn't good news. 'When did that happen?'

He shrugged. 'As soon as we hauled you in for questioning. You heard me backing off on that. Basquiat thinks the conflict of interest is deep enough to be fundamental, and she was prepared to bring the DCI in. She's not seeing you as the chief suspect, but she wants to be free to go wherever this takes her. She told me not to get in her way.'

'And you took that?' I was incredulous.

'Yeah. I did.' Coldwood's tone was harsh. 'Because she's right. Look at it from her point of view – which the DCI is bound to share if he's got half a brain. If you are involved somehow, then she knows you'll try to play me. And if it's anyone else then the big question at trial will be why we didn't go after you properly out of the gate. We'll look about as bent as a nine-bob note, and razor-boy will walk on a technicality. Either way I'm a defence lawyer's wet dream. So there you go. I'm still dancing but Ruth is leading.

And that – before you ask – is the other reason I came here tonight: because I thought you ought to know. The weather's going to get colder.'

I mulled that unpalatable fact over for a moment or two: brandy didn't sweeten it.

'Okay,' I said. 'Thanks for the warning. Listen, Gary, you're already digging into Kenny's past, presumably. Any leads there? You know what happened to his wife and kid, right?'

'Common-law wife,' Coldwood corrected me. 'She's MIA. Walked out on him a year or so back, according to the neighbours. The son belonged to her, not to him, and he's dead. We're still getting the details.'

'Would that include calling up the autopsy report?' I asked.

Coldwood shrugged and raised his eyes to Heaven.

'Could I get a copy of that?'

'For Christ's sake, Fix!'

'All right, all right. No harm in asking. What do you make of the other wounds on Kenny's arms? The older ones?'

'Botched suicide attempt? Wouldn't be too surprising, would it? When you think about what he's been through . . .'

'I think he might have been self-harming,' I said.

Coldwood stared at me.

'Why do you think that?' he asked.

'Because I – sorry, because whoever broke into the flat found a hurt-kit in the bedroom. Not the boy's bedroom. Kenny's.'

'We already went over that room.'

I blew out my cheeks. 'Yeah, but I bet you did it politely. It isn't a crime scene, and Kenny isn't a suspect. I almost missed it myself.'

'You keep defaulting back to that first-person stuff, Fix,' Gary pointed out testily. 'Work on it. So are you saying that Seddon—?'

Matt stood up abruptly. 'I am finding all this talk . . . unnerving,' he confessed. 'I think I might leave now. I'm teaching at a seminary in Cheam and I have a very full day tomorrow. If you don't mind—'

'I do mind,' I said firmly. 'Come on, Matt, we haven't seen each other in, what, must be a year and a half. And I bet you hear a lot worse in the confessional.'

'Well, I was leaving anyway,' Gary said, putting his empty glass down. 'I've got to be on my feet again in four hours. Mind how you go, Fix. And keep your fingers crossed that the floating-pronoun burglar didn't leave too many prints behind him in Seddon's gaff. Even my C2s can't be relied on to miss everything that's under their noses. I'll tell them to take another stroll around that bedroom.'

He thanked Pen for the booze and hospitality and let himself out. And then there were three.

'So how are you doing, Matt?' Pen asked my brother. 'I didn't know you were teaching now.'

'For six years,' Matt said, killing that line of conversation stone-dead. Pen was only trying to be nice because the last time Matt had come visiting she'd hit him in the nose with a tea-tray. It hadn't been in the course of a theological debate, either, although that wouldn't have been much of a surprise: Pen takes her spirituality pretty seriously.

But I hadn't insisted on Matty staying behind so that we could discuss the good of his soul. It was something else that was bugging me, and I needed an answer now.

'We'll see you in the morning, Pen,' I said, getting to

my feet. 'We've got some things we need to go over in private.'

'Take the bottle,' Pen suggested. I lifted it, started to say thanks and noticed it was empty. She was just making a point, in her own inimitable way. 'I'll get another in the morning,' I promised.

'Just pay me some rent,' she riposted, stroking Arthur the raven's glossy back.

I led the way up the stairs. Matt lingered by the front door for a moment, as if contemplating making a break for it. 'I'm serious, Matt,' I said. 'We're having this conversation sooner or later, and I did you the courtesy of not having it in front of a copper. So let's make it sooner, eh?'

Without protest – in fact, without reacting at all – Matt followed me up to my attic room. That put two clear storeys between us and Pen: enough so that she wouldn't be disturbed by raised voices or colourful language.

There's only one chair in the room. I waved Matt to sit down, but he crossed to the window instead and examined the badly repaired plasterwork around the sill. 'This is where your sex-demon friend jumped through after she almost devoured you,' he reminisced. It was such a transparent attempt to put me off balance that I felt a sudden wave of affection for him. It took me by surprise, reminding me of brotherly feuds long past, and the kind of dirty pool we always played against each other before he found God and lost the rest of us. Maybe for that reason, I came straight to the point instead of dancing around it looking for an unfair advantage.

'What were you doing at the Salisbury, Matt?' I demanded.

He turned to look at me. His blue-grey eyes, otherwise unknown in the Castor family, held my gaze unblinkingly. 'I was just walking,' he said, with immaculate calm. But I knew from way back how good he was at the straight-faced kidding.

I nodded. 'Nice,' I said. 'Hell of a walk, from Cheam, but they're your shoes. I saw someone else just walking there recently – Gwillam. That shitehawk from the Anathemata Curialis. You remember him?'

'Of course I remember him,' Matt said, with guarded emphasis.

'When from?'

'I'm sorry, Felix?'

'When do you remember him from, exactly? When did you last see him, and what's he got you doing on the Salisbury?'

'Felix—'

'Don't get coy, Matty.' I pushed the chair around so that it faced him. 'That was Gwillam's man you hauled off me right now, and you called him by name. And it makes sense, doesn't it? He's a self-righteous lunatic fighting a one-man crusade against the undead. You're just a priest who can't say no. Somewhere you were bound to meet.'

Matt still refused to sit. 'You're wrong, Felix,' he said.

'Am I?'

'Yes. It's not a one-man crusade. The Anathemata probably has upwards of a thousand members – a couple of hundred in the UK alone. It's not an official arm of the Church any more, but it's still highly respected in many circles. And Thomas Gwillam is a hugely influential voice when it comes to . . .' he faltered for the first time, but it was a short hesitation and a good recovery '. . . the more controversial aspects of the afterlife.'

'Thomas,' I mused. 'Probably named after the popular saint.'

'Probably.'

'Whose unique selling point was that he had those doubts, yeah? Amazingly, he wasn't always a hundred per cent sure he was doing the right thing. I could really get behind a saint like that.'

Matt sighed – a long-drawn-out sound that was more indicative of exhaustion than of resignation. He did look tired, now that I looked at him properly: tired and a bit beaten down, as though something serious and distracting was weighing on him. 'Aquinas, Felix,' he said. 'Saint Thomas Aquinas, not the apostle Thomas. You know this. You went to church too, and to Sunday school. You only pretend to be ignorant.'

'But we are what we pretend to be, Matty,' I countered. 'Kurt Vonnegut, chapter 1, verse 1. So if you pretend to be a carpet-chewing religious bigot, that's how you end up. What the fuck are you doing mixing with the likes of Gwillam?'

There was a long, strained silence.

'You take a lot of things for granted,' Matt said. His voice trembled slightly.

I shrugged. 'Well, that's me,' I said. 'Always jumping to conclusions. I see the head of a secret Church organisation hanging around on a street corner. Then I see my brother, who's a priest, hanging around on the same corner less than twelve hours later. And I think to myself, something's going down. Something's got the 'if-it's-dead-bust-its-head' brigade well and truly steamed up. And I start wondering what that something might be.'

Matt clenched his fist in a very uncharacteristic gesture, but then only massaged it absently with the other palm. 'That's absurd,' he said. 'I'm not even a member of the Anathemata.'

I shrugged. 'If you say so. Lying's a sin, so I'm sure you'd never do that. But you are from the arse-end of Walton. And you did take your holy orders at Upholland, just a few miles down the road from where we grew up. So if anyone was looking for a priest with a Liverpool 9 background, yours would be the first CV to pop up, wouldn't it?'

'Who would look?' Matt asked, still meeting my gaze and still looking both weary and unmoved. 'Why would they look?'

'Because of Kenny Seddon,' I said, and I saw the name hit home. Matt shook his head wordlessly, but his expression was almost a wince. 'There's something really strange going on over at the Salisbury,' I went on, not giving him a chance to interrupt. 'Something in the air that's driving people crazy. I don't know what it is, even though I've felt it. It's not an emotion I can give a name to. It's more like an impulse, moving people in different ways. Tonight I saw a kid try to kill himself, and I think it was because he was possessed by this – whatever it is. This spirit. This peripatetic emotion.

'And two nights ago, Kenny Seddon met a couple of guys a mile down the road for a quiet chat. Relaxed. Informal. Bring your own razor. And whatever it was they talked about, the conversation – as you just heard with no trace of surprise – ended with Kenny carved up like a Christmas turkey. And I mean the way Homer Simpson carves up a Christmas turkey.'

Matt held up a hand as if to correct me on a point of fact. I rode right over him. 'Now maybe those things aren't connected, but I'm working on the assumption that they are. Because the last thing Kenny did, as his nifty little urban runabout filled up with his own blood, was to write my name on the windshield. He called in an exorcist, Matty. The only exorcist whose name he knew. Leaving me with a lot to explain to the boys in blue, but making bloody sure I got to hear about what had happened to him. Why do you think that was?'

Matt's brow constricted into a frown. 'It wasn't . . .' he began, but then he shook his head as if despairing of shifting me from my point of view. 'I have no idea,' he said. 'I have no idea at all.'

'Me neither. But if I'm right – if the Anathemata is sniffing after something at the Salisbury, and if Kenny is a part of that something, then is it too much of a stretch to imagine good Father Thomas Aquinas Gwillam sifting through all the tools in the box until he finds the one Catholic priest who happened to know Kenny when we were all kids? Like I said, he's got that kind of mindset. So I could see him asking you, Matty. I think that's well within the bounds of possibility. Don't you? The only thing left to wonder about is what answer you gave him.'

Instead of answering, Matt made to walk past me, heading for the door. I stepped into his way, forcing him to stop. Although I didn't touch him, he backed away as if he was rebounding from a physical barrier. There was genuine pain on his face now.

'Please, Felix,' he said. 'You really don't understand. And I'm—' He drew a slightly ragged breath. 'I'm desperately sorry that you got involved in this. It's unfortunate, and unforeseen. You should walk away, as quickly as you can. It's not something that needs to concern you. It doesn't bear on anything that you know about, or need to know about.'

He was grinding his clenched fist into his open palm again.

'Are your palms itchy?' I asked. He looked down at his hands as if only just realising they were there. The skin of my own hands felt like it was crawling with bugs, although the sensation seemed to have peaked and was now starting to fade. I'd forgotten it until Matt's nervous gesture brought it back into mental focus.

'I'm fine,' Matt said, with slightly too much emphasis to be convincing.

I hesitated. We really don't know each other all that well, Matt and me: that lost ground in our childhoods is somehow still there in between us, keeping us at a distance from each other no matter what else happens and what life turns us into. So now, for instance, I didn't know if he wanted me to push it further or not, or even whether he saw me as a friend or an enemy.

From one point of view, Gwillam and I ought to be natural allies. I used to be an exorcist, at least after a fashion, and that put me on one side of a line that more and more people seemed to be keen to draw: between us and them; between the people who still lived and breathed and the people who'd passed through the veil only to bounce right back again. The Anathemata were on the same side, building bulwarks of faith against the rising tide of the dead.

But I didn't like that company much. And I didn't see the dead – or the undead, for that matter – as the enemy.

'Matty,' I tried again. 'Toss me a bone, will you? I'm not walking away from this because I can't afford to. You heard what Coldwood said: I'm in the frame here, and the woman in charge of the investigation hates my guts. So I really need to know what the hell it was that Kenny was trying to tell me. If I'm wrong – if what's going on down on that estate has got nothing to do with him and nothing to do with me – then tell me what it's all about and I'll leave it at that. Swear to God, I'll mind my own business. If you don't trust my honest face, trust me to be a selfish bastard.'

Matt was silent for long enough that I believed he was really giving that proposition some serious thought. But when he spoke it was only to repeat himself.

'I'm sorry you've become involved in this. You need to get out of it again and stay out. Whatever happens – I don't believe you'll be incriminated.'

'I've already been incriminated,' I yelled, grabbing his lapels and giving them an exasperated shake. 'Haven't you been listening?' It was the first time I'd touched him, and he brought up his arms to break the contact, smacking me away forcefully. In Matt that looked like a scary lack of control: he's so used to turning the other cheek he can do the whole Linda Blair thing and rotate his neck three-sixty. It startled me, and made me take a step back, not sure for a moment if he was going to follow it up and turn this into a real fight.

He didn't. He just stood there with his hands raised in a guard stance, like an ecclesiastical Bruce Lee. The effect was a little spoiled, though, by how badly he was shaking.

'You saw what happened tonight,' he blurted out. 'And what almost happened. I mean it, Felix. Keep your distance from it. Don't even ask any more questions. Whatever it looks like — it's not yours. Not your kind of thing. Nothing — nothing at all to do with you.'

He was having to force the words out by this time. His face was pale and there was an audible catch to his breathing.

'So you won't trust me?' I said, more quietly.

'Oh, I trust you, Fix,' Matt said tremulously. 'I know exactly what I can expect from you. I've known ever since the first time I took your confession.'

I didn't see that one coming, and it silenced me as effectively as a punch in the gut. Before I could answer, Matt pushed violently past me, barging me out of his way, and ran from the room. By the time I got out onto the landing he was onto the second flight of stairs, taking them at a run.

I followed more slowly, not trying to catch him. It seemed like we'd reached a conversational impasse.

The door slammed below me, and as I came down into the hall Pen came up from the Stygian depths and met me at ground level. She looked at the door, then back at me.

'Well, that was loud,' she said.

I shook my head, too uneasy about what had just happened to bother to hide it. 'Sorry,' I said. 'I took it as far away from you as I could. I'm sorry you got landed with Coldwood too. Did he ask you about Rafi?'

Pen nodded. 'I just said what you told me to say. I haven't visited Rafi in more than a month, and I don't know where he is.'

'Good. There's nothing to prove you had any part in it. He can't get from me to you.'

She didn't seem to want to pursue that topic any further. 'So did you sort it all out with Matt?'

'No.'

'Didn't think so. Come on down and talk me through it.'

I normally keep Pen at arm's length from my professional life, but on the few occasions when we've got down to cases, as it were, she's turned out to have some pretty shrewd insights. I looked at my watch. Too little left of the night now to make an issue of it anyway, and I was at that stage where you're too close to what you're looking at to see it at all. Not to mention the fact that Pen had probably weaselled a lot of the story out of Coldwood already. Brandy is a potent lever in her hands, and with the home-team advantage she's pretty hard to beat.

'Yeah,' I said. 'Okay.'

Over lethally potent coffee from her stove-top Moka pot, Pen listened to the whole story in inscrutable silence.

'What did he mean?' she asked, when I got to the confession part. 'You don't go for all that stuff, do you, Fix?'

I gave a scoffing laugh. 'Too many sins,' I said. 'Can you imagine the queue that would build up behind me?'

'Then why did Matt say that to you?'

I didn't answer for a moment. The memory came over me so strongly, I felt like I was there again. That last spring before I left home. The party we threw for Matt at the Railway Club on Breeze Lane, the day after his ordination.

Pen waited, knowing me too well to push: and after a while, speaking softly because this too felt like a confession, I told her the story.

The party was Dad's idea: to celebrate Matt's achievement and to rub everyone's nose in the fact that he had a priest for a son. The Castors would be first in the queue for Heaven from now on: we had our very own inside man.

I wasn't exactly in the party spirit: I prowled around the edges of the good time that was being had, feeling the same old resentments coming to a boil in my mind. Matt had walked out on us back when 'us' was still the barely viable huddle of him, me and Dad: now Matt had come back the hero. I didn't see anything much to celebrate here.

So I swiped a bottle of whisky – a potent liquor I'd only just discovered – and a glass, found a tiny room at the back of the club where they stacked empty beer barrels, and commenced an experiment that Albert Hofmann would have approved of.

Matt appeared in the doorway maybe an hour later. He'd noticed my absence from the party and had come looking for me.

'You okay, Felix?' he asked.

'I'm fine,' I answered, raising the whisky bottle to support the contention. 'Doing good here, Matt.'

'Then do you want to come and join the rest of us? Auntie Lily wants to talk to you about the ghost in her outside loo.'

'Auntie Lily can whistle for it.'

Matt came forward into the room. He was wearing the scrimshaw cross that Mum had just given him: carved with bas-relief thorns to the point where it looked like a bramble thicket, and with the legend INRI inscribed on a scroll at its centre, it was an object both beautiful and grotesque. He took the whisky bottle from my hand. 'I think you've probably had enough,' he said gently.

I took it back and poured myself another large one. 'Probably right there,' I allowed.

'Fix—' Matt hardly ever used my nickname, so this was a sign of some preternatural unbending. 'I know you could have done with having me around, the past few years. I just – felt that this was something I really needed to do. Something I was *meant* to do. They say if God wants you to be a priest he speaks inside you so you can't mistake it. And it was like that, it really was. Like something pulling me, that I couldn't refuse. But it was terrible having to leave you and Dad. I'm going to try to think of ways to make it up to you.'

'You are?' I asked. 'That's cool, Matt. You're a prince.' He looked pained at the sarcasm, which encouraged me to go on. But I was drunk as a bastard by this time, and it took me a while to think of anything good. I was about to ask him what sort of penance he thought was suitable for sodding off for five years and leaving us all up the Swanee, but the word itself – penance – set off a chain of associations that led to a better idea.

'Take my confession, Father Castor,' I said.

Surprise and consternation crossed Matt's face, but only for a moment. He shook his head. 'If you're serious about that, Fix, go to St Mary's and talk to Father Stone. You don't want absolution from me. I want it from you, but that's beside the point.'

'I *am* serious,' I persisted. 'There's something that's weighing on my mind. It's been troubling me for twelve years, and I can't share it with anyone. Except you, Matt. Because you're family and this is family business.'

I held him with my stare, like the Ancient Mariner. He

wanted to leave – wanted not to have come in here in the first place – but I had him by the balls, from a clerical-pastoral-tragical-historical point of view. He couldn't say no in case I meant it: and what with the booze and the baggage, that was a question that I couldn't have answered myself.

Matt sat down on a barrel.

'Go on,' he said.

'Do it properly,' I slurred.

He took the hit with an impatient gesture. 'Then stick to the script,' he countered.

I spoke the familiar, disused words with a prickling sense of unreality. 'Bless me, father, for I have sinned. It's been eight years and some odd months since my last confession. I have one sin on my conscience.'

'Just the one?'

'Just the one, Matt. I don't want to keep you from your adoring fans.'

He didn't answer, so I went on.

'After Katie died . . .'

The words just hung there. Whatever I'd been about to say drained out of my head like oil from a cracked sump. Nothing came to replace them.

'After Katie died?' Matt repeated, prompting me. 'Go on, Felix. What happened after Katie died?'

Why had I started this? What had been the point of the joke? I filled my glass from the whisky bottle, discovering in the process that it was still full from the last time. The pungent liquid ran down my fingers and spattered on the ground.

'After Katie died . . . ?'

I couldn't look at him, so I stared at the brimming glass:

at the shivers and ripples chasing themselves across the meniscus. 'I killed her again.'

'What does that even mean, Felix?' Matt's voice was still mild, but I felt the tension underneath the words.

'Her ghost. Her . . . spirit came back. She came into my room.'

'You imagined she did. Your grief—'

'No, Matt. Katie. Katie herself. You know I can see things that you can't.'

'I know you've convinced yourself that you can.' The tightness was right there on the surface now. Matt had known about my death-sense ever since we were kids, but we'd never discussed it since he took holy orders. It was the elephant we danced arabesques around every time we talked.

'And I made her go away by . . . singing,' I went on. 'By chanting. I think she just wanted to talk. I think she was scared, and she wanted to be where she belonged, with the family. But I sent her away. And she never came back.'

The silence stretched.

'Go to her grave,' Matt suggested at last. 'Pray for her. Pray that she found her way to Heaven, and pray for her forgiveness.'

I turned the over-full glass in my hands and more whisky oozed over the rim of it to trickle down the sides of the glass like sweat or tears.

'Do you hear me, Felix?'

'Yeah,' I said. 'I hear you.'

He smacked glass and bottle out of my hands. The glass shattered, the bottle didn't: it just skittered away across the floor, coughing up booze like a docker at chucking-out time.

'Then say the Act of Contrition,' he suggested.

I started in. 'Deus meus, ex toto corde paenitet—' But it had been too long and I didn't remember the words. Matt recited them for me and I parroted along, finding my feet again at 'adiuvante gratia tua.' It was just words, and I didn't believe there was anybody listening.

But there was, of course. There was Matt.

He put his hand on my shoulder, gripping hard enough to hurt.

'Your sins are forgiven, you drunken, selfish bastard,' he said. 'Go in peace.'

When I looked up, he was gone. Or maybe it's fairer to say that I didn't look up until I was sure: until his footsteps had faded into silence. The music and shouting rose to a peak and then fell to a rumble again, announcing the opening and closing of a distant door.

I sat breathing whisky fumes like profane incense, still feeling the weight of his hand on my shoulder. I didn't feel like I'd been absolved: it was more like I'd had my collar felt by some holy constable of the spirit. I knew two things, and two things only: that Matt's vocation was real, and that as far as absolution went, a few soggy prayers weren't going to cut it.

Pen heard me out in silence. When she spoke – pagan gods bless her infallible instincts – it was to change the subject.

'So this thing that you're feeling when you're over there at the Salisbury. Do you think it's a geist of some kind?'

Pen speaks the argot, and she was using the word in its technical sense. To an exorcist, a geist is a human spirit that takes no visible form but can still have powerful – almost always destructive – effects.

'I don't know,' I said, stating the obvious. 'But I don't think so. Most geists move things – physical things. They break bottles, throw furniture around, blow candles out, fling people through windows. This is . . . intangible. It's just a feeling. And it seems to be really pervasive – I mean, it spreads across the whole estate, where a geist would tend to stick to one small locus.'

Pen inhaled the steam from her coffee cup, eyes closed, like Nicky drinking the wine breath. Then she downed it in one swallow. I waited patiently, knowing she was thinking it through.

'The people on the estate,' she said, when she finally opened her eyes again. 'Do they know this thing is there? I mean, obviously it's changing the way they feel and the way they behave, but are they aware that it's happening or are they just submerged in it?'

'The second, I think. I'm aware of it because—'

'—Because of your built-in radar.'

'Exactly. But to anyone else I think it would be like a sound that's been in your ears for so long you can't hear it any more – you just hear the silence when it stops. It's subtle. Powerful, but really subtle. To tell you the truth, I'm starting to wonder if there's a demon mixed up in this somewhere.'

Pen nodded as though she was coming to the same conclusion at the same moment.

'Then you should talk to an expert,' she said.

10

As it happens there are two demons within my immediate circle of acquaintances. Pen had Rafi in mind, for many reasons besides the strictly pragmatic, but of the two of them Juliet is the easier to deal with by a factor of a million: and Juliet was already on the case, in a way, so I dropped in on her first.

I tracked her down at the library in Willesden where her partner, Sue Book, now works. Juliet was waiting for Sue to finish her shift, after which they were going to some kind of a book launch and public reading together. The two of us sat in the children's section, because children at least were immune to Juliet's lethally intense sexual aura. But there were a few mothers and fathers dotted around the room, too: Juliet ignored their uneasy, covetous stares and heard me out while I described my latest adventures at the Salisbury.

But she didn't offer any insights of her own, and in the end I had to put the question directly.

'So did you make it down there? If you didn't, no pressure – I know you didn't make me any promises and you don't owe me anything. But this has got me scratching my head, Juliet. Anything you could throw me would be good.'

'I was there,' Juliet said.

I waited for more, but more didn't come. Juliet looked

down at the book she was reading: *The Very Hungry Caterpillar*. It was a subversive enough juxtaposition to throw me a little off my stride.

'So what did you find?' I asked, when it was clear that she wasn't going to volunteer anything further.

She looked up at me again. A human woman – or man, for that matter – would have looked at the book in order to avoid eye contact, but Juliet was incapable of feeling embarrassment or social awkwardness. She was a stone-cold fact, exquisite and unapologetic, in a world of nuances. So she was looking at the book because something I'd said or something she was thinking had made a connection. To hunger? To caterpillars? To metamorphosis?

'I can't discuss this,' she said.

I took a look at the other people in the room. It was true that there were a lot of eyes on us – or rather, on her. 'Okay,' I said, reluctantly. 'But if I hang around until after the reading, could we—'

'I don't mean here and now, Castor. I mean ever. This isn't a subject that can be raised between us.' Her stare was cold and stern: she knew me, and she knew how hard it was for me to take no for an answer. She was warning me with her eyes that any subsequent answers would be smackdowns.

But fools rush in, as they say. 'It kind of already has been,' I pointed out. 'Raised, I mean. Can you at least tell me whether you felt this thing?'

'No.'

'Or whether you recognised it? Whether it's something you've met before?'

'No.'

'But you're a ghost-breaker,' I pointed out. 'This is your living, right? What if I hired you to—'

'I said no, Castor. I'm not for hire. If you can handle this yourself, do so. If you can't, don't come to me for help or try to pick my brains with one of your stacked games of twenty questions. It will cause friction between us. It could even compromise our friendship.'

Before I could think of a question that wouldn't sound like it was a question, Susan Book crossed the room and joined us. She put a hand on Juliet's shoulder: Juliet took it in her own, touched it to her lips and then replaced it.

Susan beamed at me. Being with Juliet had made her blossom: turned her from a shy, conflicted little mouse with a self-effacing stammer and a tendency to blame herself for other people's failings into a woman with confidence and quiet charisma. Sex is magic, and she was tapped into the wellspring. I'd be lying if I said I didn't envy her that.

But in case the point needed to be made, that unobtrusive little kiss on the back of the hand reminded me that there was a lot more to this relationship now than sex. Susan loved Juliet, wholly and desperately and unquestioningly. And Juliet – felt something too. Something that made her protective and a little possessive and occasionally exasperated when Susan wouldn't do as she was told or see things as they obviously were. Might as well call that love, too: it had a lot of the hallmarks.

'Hi, Felix,' Susan said. 'Are you going to come along with us to the Martin Amis thing?'

'And be lectured about how Muslims ought to smack their kids more? Nah,' I said. 'No, thanks. You crazy kids go and enjoy yourselves.'

I stood up, trying not to let my consternation and annoyance show on my face. Juliet had warned me once before this – about a year before, if memory served – that certain subjects would always be taboo between us. Heaven and Hell were on the list, and so was God, and so were her own nature and origins. It would be useful to know which of these, if any, were operating here: but Susan's arrival had made it impossible for me to fish any further.

'We will,' Susan said, presumably referring back to my begrudged 'Have a good time', or whatever it was I'd said.

Juliet made a sour face. 'Ideas,' she said.

'Nothing wrong with ideas, Jules,' Susan chided gently.

'No. But my comfort zone is flesh.'

On which note I said my goodbyes, feeling none too happy.

If Juliet wasn't going to play ball, I was left with Asmodeus. And Asmodeus was a different proposition altogether.

Bigger, for one thing. Meaner. And living inside my best friend.

Rafi only started playing with black magic after he met me and saw the things I could do. This was during my brief, abortive stint at university, when he was an elegant wastrel and I was a working-class Communist with a chip on my shoulder the size of the Sherman Oak. We vied briefly for Pen's affections, although Rafi never had any doubt that he'd win in the end. He always did: he was one of the people who life went out of its way to accommodate.

Rafi was never part of the exorcist fraternity: he was

just an enthusiastic amateur with a sharper mind than most who mixed and matched necromantic rituals until he put one together that actually worked. But he was never a completer-finisher, either, which was the first part of his downfall. He left out one of the necessary wards, and the magic circle that should have kept Asmodeus safely contained was fatally flawed. The demon – one of the most hard-core bastards in Hell – battered his way out and into Rafi's soul.

A lot of things could have happened at that point: demonic possession is a fairly new phenomenon, and not all that well documented. What actually happened was that Rafi became delirious and got so hot he actually seemed in danger of catching fire. His girlfriend called me, and I tried to carry out an exorcism.

That was the *coup de grâce*. I'd never encountered a demon before, let alone one as powerful as this. I screwed up badly, welding the two of them together in a way that I couldn't undo. Asmodeus has lived inside Rafi ever since, the senior partner in a very unequal alliance.

For Rafi it was effectively the end of any kind of normal life. A human soul is pretty lightweight when weighed against one of Gehenna's finest, so Asmodeus would surge up and take the driving seat whenever he felt like it. After a couple of ugly incidents, Rafi was sectioned under the Mental Health Act: there are aspects of the way we live now that the law hasn't caught up with yet, and this was one of them. Being realists, though, the senior management at the Stanger wrote 'Schizophrenic' on the paperwork, while at the same time they lined Rafi's cell with silver to curb the demon's worst excesses.

For three years we bumped along and made the best of a bad job: I went along to the Stanger every so often and used my tin whistle to play the demon down so that Rafi got some peace, and Doctor Webb, who ran the place, was happy so long as we kept the money coming.

Happy, that is, until he got a better offer from a former colleague of mine: Jenna-Jane Mulbridge, the director of the Metamorphic Ontology Unit at Queen Mary's hospital in Paddington. Jenna-Jane was just a ruthless monster back when I worked for her, but for the past couple of years she's been reinventing herself as a crazed zealot, convinced – just as Father Gwillam is – that humanity is now engaged in a last-ditch, apocalyptic struggle against the forces of darkness. As far as I can tell, she sees her role as broadly similar to Q's in the James Bond films: humanity's armourer and engineer, forging the weapons that we're bound to need when the dead and the undead back us up against the wall and finally come squeaking and gibbering for our throats.

But before she can be Q, she has to be Mengele. She's turned the Helen Trabitch Wing at Queen Mary's into a little concentration camp over which she rules with loving, obsessive sadism, and she's managed to persuade the CEOs of the hospital trust that this still counts as medicine. She's got an amazing variety of inmates there: werewolves, zombies, the oldest ghost ever raised and some tragic nutcase who thinks he's a vampire. About the only thing she hasn't got is a demon, and she's got her heart set on acquiring Rafi.

About a month back, the cold war between me and J-J got a little hotter, as it periodically does: it looked like she was going to be able to persuade the High Court to overturn a decision made by a local magistrate, which had given Pen power of attorney over Rafi. She was looking to have Rafi transferred from the Stanger to the MOU, with the connivance of Doctor Webb, whose balls she seems to have in her pocket.

But I've started a ball collection too, and the afore-mentioned magistrate is part of it. I got my own court order, immaculately forged, and went in first. Webb and J-J woke up the next morning to a fait accompli. Rafi was gone, having traded the dubious hospitality of the Stanger for the ministering hands of my good friend Imelda Probert – known to most of London's dead and undead as the Ice-Maker.

It was a spoiler run, and it was desperate improvisation. At the Stanger, Rafi was penned in a silver cell and Webb and his team had a dozen or more ways, ranging from subtle to brutal, of keeping Asmodeus in check when he rose into the ascendant. Now all we had was my whistle, and Imelda – who had never thought that this was a good idea in the first place.

As I trudged back to the Tube, I imagined the ructions I was going to have with her, and the sheer gruelling agony of whistling the hell-spawn up and then back down again in a single session. It was going to be bad. Bad for me, anyway: Pen would see it differently, because she'd be able to visit with Rafi while I – assuming things went to plan – consulted his bad-ass alter ego.

But when I went back to Pen's to give her the equivo-cal tidings, she was waiting with the phone receiver still in her hand and some news of her own to pass on.

'Someone called Daniels,' she told me. 'They said it was about Billy. Billy's awake.'

'That's great,' I said, but Pen was looking solemn and troubled.

'Apparently not,' she said.

It was practically on our way: a crow flying across London from Turnpike Lane to Peckham and sticking to the rules would pass within a spitball's distance of the New Kent Road. Pen wasn't eager to break the journey, but I had two trump cards. One was that Tom and Jean Daniels were potential clients: Pen likes me to earn money, because I owe her a vast amount of the stuff and every little helps.

The other was what Coldwood had said about someone watching Pen's house. I'd had my radar out since then, looking for tails, but there hadn't really been anything at stake until now. If it was Jenna-Jane, hoping I'd lead her to Rafi, then the more twists and turns we added to our itinerary tonight, the better. We had to be damn sure that when we got to the Ice-Maker's we'd be alone.

So we went to the Salisbury, and as we passed into the shadow of the first two concrete monoliths Pen gave an involuntary shudder.

I stared at her curiously. 'You feel it?' I demanded.

'I'm just cold,' Pen muttered.

'Billy's awake,' Jean Daniels said, almost before we'd got inside the door, 'but he's not himself, Mister Castor. He's wandering in his mind. Tom was sitting with him up until an hour ago, but he had to go and sign on down at the job centre.'

She pointed me through to the living room. Bic still

lay on the sofa where I'd deposited him the night before, but in his pyjamas now rather than his street clothes, and with an old overcoat, by way of a blanket, covering him up to the waist. The pyjamas were red and blue: Spiderman fought Doctor Octopus across the front of them.

Bic's eyes were open, but he didn't seem to see me. He was restless, his fingers moving with small fluttering motions as though he was a guitarist trying to remember a chord sequence with no instrument ready to hand. His lips were moving too, although no sound was coming out.

'What did they say at the hospital?' I asked.

Jean flicked a doubtful glance at Pen, seeming reluctant to drag out family business under the eyes of a stranger.

'It's okay,' I said. 'This is Pen Bruckner. She's my landlady. She's also sort of a shareholder in the business, on account of I owe her more than I'm worth.'

Jean accepted the explanation with a hapless shrug: needs must when the devil drives, she seemed to say. 'They told me he might have a concussion. Then he woke up and they said he didn't. Then he started to talk all funny, and he didn't seem to know who I was, so they decided they weren't sure. They gave him some tests but they wouldn't tell us what any of the results were. It was obvious they didn't have the faintest idea what was wrong with him. We were there for five hours, waiting on some consultant or other, and when he came he only said again that it wasn't a concussion and Billy would probably be all right inside of a few hours.'

She rubbed furiously at her eye, more as though she wanted to force a tear back inside than to wipe it away. 'They were going to keep him in,' she said, her mouth setting tight at the memory, 'but when I asked them what they were going to do they couldn't give me a straight answer. Keep him under observation, they said. As if that's going to make him better all by itself. So we brought him home. But he's getting worse, Mister Castor. It's like he's got a fever, only he isn't hot. So I told Tom we should call you, and we had a big row about it and he said I could only do it when he wasn't in the house because he doesn't believe in any of the things you were talking about. I suppose I didn't either, until all this happened. But there's no point sticking your head in the sand. This isn't a medical thing, is it? It's not a medical thing at all. Not with the bleeding and the dreams and all that. It's . . .' She shrugged helplessly. 'Well, I think it has to be something more in your line, doesn't it?'

I nodded, but for a moment I didn't speak. The miasma – the migraine buzz in the air, the prickling sense at the back of my skull – confused my death-senses to the point where they were almost useless. I honestly couldn't tell right then if Bic was one of the loci it was coming from or not. On the other hand, I'd seen him the night before about to sleepwalk off the edge of a balcony sixty feet above the ground. And I'd seen his hands running with blood despite the absence of a wound. If it wasn't possession, then what was it?

'Yeah,' I said at last. 'In my line, certainly. But I'd be lying if I said I knew exactly what it was, Jean.'

'I don't need to know,' Jean said, her voice thickening. 'Just bring him back. That's all I want. If you can do that, I'll pay you anything you want.'

It was an empty boast. How much could she afford,

if Tom was on job-seeker's allowance? Even a tenner would probably stretch the budget. But why had I come here if it wasn't to do the job? And how could I smack this woman in the face with charity after everything else she'd been hit with? It was a knotty problem whichever way you looked at it.

And then there was the matter of my own professional competence, which I reckoned we'd better get sorted right now before we went any further.

'I don't know if I can do it or not,' I told her. 'Because like I said, I don't know what I'm dealing with. If I *do* bring him back, it's not likely to be on the first pass. It could take a few days, and a few visits, with nothing promised at the end of it. I'm prepared to try. That's the best I can offer.

'As far as money goes – I'm sort of already working this case for another client,' I said, shading the truth without blushing. 'So I can offer you a discount. In fact, under these circumstances I'll work COD. I won't charge you anything up front, but I'll send in a bill if Billy gets better and doesn't get sick again.'

'A bill for how much?' Jean persisted, no doubt being far too used to the foibles of debt collectors and money-lenders to fall for vague expressions of goodwill.

'A hundred,' I said, plucking a figure out of the air. 'A hundred quid.'

Jean did some quick mental arithmetic, her eyes moving from side to side as she shunted invisible beads on an invisible abacus.

'All right, Mister Castor,' she said at last. 'A hundred it is.'

I took out my whistle. Jean stared at it a little blankly.

'I'm on my way to another appointment,' I said, which was also true. 'But I'm going to do a preliminary examination now and see what I can find out. Then I'll come back later – or more likely tomorrow – and spend some more time with him.'

Jean looked at me forlornly. 'Tomorrow?' she repeated.

'I don't know what I'm dealing with,' I reminded her. 'So it's the best I can do. If it's a ghost, or –' I skirted around the word *demon* '– something like a ghost, then I need to get a fix on it. Kind of a psychic mugshot. I can't do anything else until I've got that. I still think getting Billy out of here would be the best medicine for him, but if he has to stay on the estate then I'm going to have to do what I always do, which is to work the thing out in stages. Or you can tell me to bugger off, if you want. But either way, I don't want to give you any false hopes.'

Jean looked at the whistle again, and shook her head. She wasn't turning down the offer: I think she was just struck with wonder at how slim a reed she was clinging to.

'All right,' she said. 'No false hopes.' She tried to laugh, but it just loosed the tears at last and she broke down in front of us, which was what she'd been struggling so hard not to do all this time.

Pen scooped her into an embrace, saying the usual consoling nothings. We exchanged a glance over Jean's bowed head, and I pointed towards the kitchen.

'Let's get ourselves a cup of tea,' Pen suggested, taking Jean in hand and steering her in that direction with the magic of artificial good cheer. 'I can talk you through what

Castor does while he's doing it, and then we won't be getting in his way.'

They went through into the hall and I pushed the door to. Pen hadn't needed to ask why I wanted to be alone for this. She knows from past experience that when I'm putting a tune together for the first time – using the music as sonar to zero in on a dead or undead presence that I haven't got a proper fix on yet – the two things that are most likely to screw me up are strong emotions and external sounds.

I turned to look at Bic. He had carried on twitching and muttering all through our conversation, his eyes wide and unseeing. *Lost in his own little world*, Jean had said, describing what her son was like when he was reading superhero comics. Well, he was now, that was for damned sure. And wherever that world was, it was a long way from South London.

Sitting on the arm of the sofa, I closed my eyes and fitted the whistle to my lips. I blew a few exploratory notes, drawing them out long and slow, not even trying to fit them together into a phrase. They faded from the air but remained in my mind and on my inner ear: something to build on. The next notes had a suggestion of melody to them, although it was a melody that kept changing its mind, rising and then falling, approaching a resolution and then shying away from it, breaking into discord and then finding the key again when you thought it was out of reach. Gently and painstakingly, I assembled braided ropes of sound and sent them out into the room. And as they grew in complexity, my sense of the room itself faded. I drifted in an undefined un-place, drawn along in the wake of my expelled breath like a sailboat making its own headwind.

Two presences hung off to the right of me, one small and bright, the other huge and sprawling and dark: the boy's soul and its passenger. But bright and dark were metaphors in this case, because I wasn't seeing them with my eyes: it was more like how a bat sees a moth, through the shapes made by the distorted echoes of its own shrill cries.

I tried to stifle the surge of triumph that I'd found the thing so soon, because finding it wasn't the same as driving it out. But it seemed like a good omen, all the same, and I couldn't resist the urge to push it a little further. I played an atonal sequence that approximated to a stay-not: a crude command to the dark thing to piss off out of here before things got rough. The notes rolled straight forward from my mind like the bow wave of my will and consciousness. They touched the edges of the dark thing.

It backed away from me, in some direction that wasn't up or down or left or right or anything else I could find a name for. It receded or shrank, and I pressed it hard with more and louder trills and elisions, the tune becoming a hurried, spiky thing with no grace to it but lots of momentum.

Bourbon Bill Bryant, the former ghostbreaker who used to run the Oriflamme, the exorcists' pub on Castlebar Hill, told me once that one of the biggest mistakes you can make in our profession is to go hunting bear with a pea-shooter. Pretty self-evident, you'd think: but that was the trap I'd fallen into. I was chasing this thing just because it was running away, forgetting that until I had a clear enough mental impression of it to feed into the music I was not only wielding a pea-shooter – I hadn't even brought along any peas.

Suddenly, the darkness was no longer receding. It was standing still, and I was rushing towards it. It seemed to grow, not continuously but in a series of flickering freeze-frames, becoming denser and deeper and bigger by the moment. I was sailing into a storm, and there was nothing ahead but blackness.

I modulated the tune, letting it dip almost into silence, letting the wind drop. But the darkness was moving toward me now of its own volition, and it was so huge that I had no sense any more of where it began and ended. It was the world around me. It was the hungry void in which I floated, and although it already filled the sky it was still getting closer.

When it was right on top of me, my skin prickling with the ghost-sense of imminent contact, I forced myself to open my eyes. It felt like I was hefting two bowling balls, one on each eyelid. My sight was swimming, both eyes watering and stinging as though I'd jammed slivers of raw onion into my tear ducts. There was a ringing in my ears. But I was back in the real world, so abruptly that it felt like that moment just before sleep when you jolt back into wakefulness with a feeling like you've fallen out of thin air onto the bed.

Bic wasn't moving any more. He was preternaturally still. Very distinctly, he said, 'I got the sword.'

'What sword is that, Bic?' I asked, my voice scraping against the sides of my dry throat.

'Wilkinson's. Wilkinson's Sword.'

*   *   *

'Just those three words?' Pen demanded.

'Yeah. Just those three words.'

'But what did he mean?'

I shook my head, walking faster so that she had to trot a little to keep up. We could have grabbed a cab down to Peckham, but I was restless and walking felt like a good way to burn it off. A little unfair to Pen, though, whose legs, although in perfect proportion to the rest of her, are a good bit shorter than mine.

'You don't know either?' Pen asked.

'I know what the *words* mean,' I muttered. 'I'm just not sure who was saying them.'

'Fix, am I going to have to drag this out of you one syllable at a time? Either tell me or—'

'Wilkinson's Sword,' I said, 'is a well-known and popular brand of razor blade, second only to Gillette in UK market share.'

Pen digested this in silence for a moment or two. 'The boy who died,' she mused.

'Mark. He was a self-harmer. So is Kenny.'

'The bully who beat you up when you were a kid? Are you sure?'

'Reasonably sure, yeah. He's kept his dead kid's hurt-kit and there's so much scar tissue on his wrists he'd have a hard time putting his hands in his pockets.'

'Is there a connection?'

I shrugged irritably. Having to tell Jean Daniels that I'd blown the gig had left me in a sour mood. I'd promised to come back and try again, but for the time being all I'd managed to do was calm Bic down a little and leave him in a light, seemingly normal sleep. It was some considerable way short of a command performance. Whatever this thing was, it had stopped me cold. But then again, I'd gone in half-cocked, so I had nobody but myself to blame.

Which was about as much of a consolation as it ever is.

We were on the outskirts of Peckham by this time, and Pen's excitement was becoming a palpable thing. Short legs and all, she was outstripping me now: but then, I was only going to have a chat with a demon – a process that always carries the risk of agonising death – while she was going to meet her lover. On balance, her jubilant horniness took some of the edge off my unease.

And there's a darker side to Peckham, too, once you get in deep: a side I like a lot more, because I identify with the past and prefer even worm-eaten wood to wipe-clean plastic. If you set your back against the kitsch-Bauhaus folly that is Peckham library and walk half a mile south towards the common, you'll eventually find yourself walking through streets that the property developers haven't found their way to yet: streets where endless curved terraces of turn-of-the-century three-storey town houses, like the tiers of some city-sized amphitheatre, have been left to fall in on themselves at their leisure. There's a hectic tubercular beauty to them.

The two of us threaded this maze, thinking our own separate thoughts. I knew what Pen's were, more or less, because her walk was halfway to being a run by this time, and her hands kept clenching and unclenching from sheer nervous energy. Mine were focused on the question of whether we were being followed. By this time I was almost a hundred per cent certain that the answer was no: not because I hadn't seen anyone – that didn't mean a thing – but because I'd added enough loops and squiggles as we went from Pen's place to the Salisbury to force any tail either to drop us or to show himself. I was satisfied that we were safe, but I remained in paranoid mode because it has its uses.

Imelda Probert's place stands on a cul-de-sac that reminds you of the literal meaning of that term – the arse end of a bag. There was precious little beauty to be found here: just the ugly functionality of boarded-up windows, basement-level front lightwells turned into skips and ship-wrecked cars lying dormant under birdshit-spattered tarpaulins.

We ignored the front door, which had been screwed immovably into its frame in aeons past, and went in via the side alley. That meant braving the yard, where weeds grew to the height of men and every clump of grass hid a broken bottle. Pen led the way with reckless speed: I followed more cautiously, knowing from previous visits how treacherous this terrain could be.

We walked up the stairs in the sullen twilight of a forty-watt bulb. On the second floor Pen's eyes strayed to a door that was scrawled over and over with makeshift wards and sigils and had been closed with a heavy padlock. She slowed for a moment. This was the lodestone that had been drawing her, and it was hard for her to walk on past it. But she knew there was no way into that room except with me and Imelda to act as Virgils to her Dante.

Imelda is a faith healer for the dead. Most of her work comes from zombies, who find that a laying-on of hands from the Ice-Maker slows down the processes of organic decay for a month or so at a time. That's a precious boon to zombies, whose biggest problems are the ones that arise from a limited shelf life. But Imelda's motto is 'come one, come all': she'll help *loup-garous* keep their animal side in check at the dark of the moon, arrange for bereaved spouses and parents to meet their lost loved ones, and probably do a lot of other things besides that she wouldn't advertise to a practising exorcist like me.

We continued our ascent to the third floor, where we knocked politely and waited. No wards on this door: no sprigs of hazel or hawthorn or stay-nots in crude, dyspeptic Latin telling ghosts and the undead to shove off without passing GO. Imelda likes the undead and makes them welcome. She's a lot less certain about me, though.

From inside the flat there came the sound of a great many bolts being drawn back, and then the heavy door creaked open to reveal the wary but curious face of Lisa, Imelda's sixteen-year-old daughter. She grinned when she saw me.

'Oh, look what the cat sicked up!' she said, in gleeful imitation of her mother. She stood aside and we walked through into Imelda's hallway, which was no better lit than the landing but a lot more spacious: her flat may be falling apart but it's built on a grand scale. The floor under our feet was actually slightly concave, a sign of some deep malaise of the floorboards hidden from sight by the bilious green carpet.

'You're looking well,' I said to Lisa. 'Does that mean you're pregnant again?'

She punched me in the arm, which I took as a fair riposte. In fact Lisa had never been pregnant in the usually accepted sense of the word, but the ghost of a dead baby had taken up lodgings in her once – a regrettable side effect of having no wards on your door – and Imelda had called me in to persuade it to go elsewhere: that had healed a rift between me and the Ice-Maker, and it had made it possible for me to approach her when I had a problem of my own that seemed to need the touch of her skilled hands.

'Your mother in?' I asked, rubbing my arm because Lisa packs a powerful punch for such a skinny little kid.

'I dunno. I'll go see,' Lisa said, and then without moving from the spot she bawled 'Mummmmmmm!' at the top of her voice.

A door slammed open in the recesses of the flat and heavy footsteps sounded, heading towards us. The rest of the building is empty, so any time you move you raise echoes as hollow and resonant as if you're walking on a drumhead. Imelda likes it that way, though: she never has to keep the noise down for fear of what the neighbours will say, and there's nobody to object to the odd hours she keeps or to the inevitable stream of mostly posthumous late-night callers.

Pen and I both looked off left as the footsteps approached the other side of a door whose paint looked not so much chipped as partially boiled. It swung open and Imelda loomed into view, stepping out of a room that was completely unlit. She was a formidable black woman, in her late fifties now but as imposing as she'd been at thirty, with a hard, beautiful face like sculpted ebony and arms like a pair of late-autumn hams. She was dressed in a midnight blue Ashoke-style dress that flowed like churning water when she walked. The Met office would issue a storm warning as soon as they caught sight of her.

'Hello, Felix,' she said, civilly enough. Then she turned to Pen and beamed all over her face. 'Pamela! He's been asking after you, honey. Doing nothing but. And when he's not asking after you he's thinking after you. I can tell every time, because he gets a Pamela look on his face that I can't mistake for anything else.'

Pen smiled weakly but gratefully. 'Can I see him, Imelda?' she asked, putting her hand on the older woman's arm.

Imelda patted it reassuringly. 'You mean private?' she said. 'Of course you can. Just as soon as me and Felix have gone in there and done the necessary.' And then to me. 'Felix, shall we make a start?'

'Absolutely,' I said. 'But then I'm on again after Pen. I need to talk to Asmodeus.'

There was a moment when a pin dropping would have sounded like a steel band.

'Now that wasn't in the deal,' Imelda said with dangerous mildness. 'Not the way I remember it.'

'I know,' I said. 'We won't be talking about the weather, Imelda. I wouldn't be here if it wasn't important.'

The Ice-Maker wasn't impressed. 'I got a kid here,' she said, waving a hand towards exhibit one. 'You think I want to be summoning up demons in my own house?'

'I'm not a kid, Mum,' Lisa protested, scenting excitement. 'I'm sixteen, for Christ's sake.'

'Don't use that kind of language!' Imelda snapped.

'I think the pair of us can handle him,' I said. 'And you know you can lock him away again when we're done. He'd be within the wards and he'd be on the leash. The whole time.'

'There isn't a leash short enough for that kind.'

'There are two of us and one of him.'

Imelda shook her head, not only unconvinced but angry. 'We had an agreement,' she said. 'I said I'd let that sick man stay here, and I said I'd keep his fever down – but that's all I swore to do. He stays in that room. I go in to him whenever he needs me. End of story. Now you're asking me to raise the fever up instead, and that goes against the grain of me. The stink of a demon in my place – it will make everything I do harder. I'll live with it for weeks, and I'll feel like I've got the damn flu the whole time. And that's the least of it. Calling him makes him stronger, you damn well know that. So why should I do it, Castor? What have you got to tell me that will make me think it's worth it?'

That was a good question. I decided to duck it until I could think of a good answer. 'Let's go ahead and get Rafi ready to receive visitors first,' I said. 'Then we'll see if we can cut a deal.'

With an expressive look at me, Imelda swept away. I followed, and Pen remained behind. At this stage of the game, her presence was a wild card that we surely didn't need.

Down on the first floor, Imelda traced a line around the padlock with a stick of charcoal that she took from the blue-black folds of her gown. Then she spoke to it before she unlocked it and left it hanging on the hasp. There were two further locks on the door itself and they both got the same treatment. Then she stood back and I led the way into the room – the moment of greatest risk, reserved for me because this whole thing had been my stupid idea in the first place.

I'd taken a lot of pains setting the room up in the week or so before we made the raid on the Stanger, so it was a big improvement over Rafi's cell back there. It had furniture in it, for one thing, and a bookshelf with books on it – including his precious Kerouacs, Corsos and Ginsbergs – and an icebox with a few cans of Fosters floating in cold water that had been ice the evening before. All the comforts of home, give or take: nothing electrical, no TV or fridge, because things of that nature interfere with Imelda's wards. But back at the care home, Rafi lived in a bare silver box and was given nothing that Asmodeus might use to raise mischief. Even his clothes had to be free of buttons and zips. By contrast, this was one of the corner suites at Claridges.

Rafi was lying on the bed reading the previous day's *Guardian* when we entered. He sat up and nodded to us both.

'Hey, Wonder Woman. Hey, Fix. What's new? Are we still good?'

'Still fine, Rafi,' I assured him. 'No news is good news. Webb doesn't seem to be missing you very much.' I was watching Rafi as I spoke, alert for any trace of the demon Asmodeus in the way he moved or spoke. There was nothing. The Ice-Maker had touched him and he was still chilled.

All the same I played him a binding tune, and Imelda touched him some more on the head and face and shoulders, murmuring to herself in throaty Gabon French as she did so. It was the first time we'd worked in tag-team format like this, but we fell in with each other's moves without needing to discuss it.

Rafi didn't talk either, until we'd finished. Then he voiced the question that had been on his mind ever since we'd walked into the room. 'Is Pen with you?'

'Nah, she had to do her hair,' I said, and then, before his face could register either dismay or disbelief, 'She's upstairs. She clocks on as soon as we clock off.'

'Then don't let me keep you,' he said, waving us towards the door. 'Oh, did you bring the whisky, Fix?'

'I'll drop it in later,' I promised. 'Before I leave, there's something I want to talk to you about.'

While Pen got her conjugals, securely locked in with Rafi behind the barricade of wards, I explained to Imelda what I'd seen and felt on the Salisbury estate. She was about as impressed as I thought she'd be. 'You need to drink a little less coffee, Castor,' she told me stonily. 'Your nerves are getting jumpy.'

'I'm serious, Imelda,' I said, not rising to the bait. 'This is real, and it's nasty.'

'Then go do that thing you do.' She said this with a contemptuous edge in her voice: like I said, to the Ice-Maker the dead are friends and clients. Consequently she doesn't have a whole lot of time for exorcists.

'I intend to,' I said, flatly. 'But I'd like to know how the land lies. You don't defuse a bomb by picking it up and shaking it to see what rattles. You check what kind of trigger it's got.'

'What in God's name do you know about defusing bombs?'

'About as much as I know about freestyle tap-dance,' I admitted. 'But I do know about frying the undead – saving your presence – and I know I've got a better chance of coming out of this on my own two feet if I get some decent intel.'

We argued it backwards and forwards a little without getting anywhere. And when it was clear that Imelda wasn't going to concede the point, I shifted my ground.

'What if Asmodeus gets out anyway?' I asked her. 'We've got him under control at the moment, but that might not last. Wouldn't you like to test the strength of those wards on the door while you've got me around as back-up?'

By way of answer, Imelda stood up and beckoned me to follow her. We went across the barren space, smelling slightly of decay, that she calls her waiting room to a doorway, on the far side of which Lisa was reading *Hello!* magazine by the light of a stub of candle.

'So say we test the wards, and they fail,' Imelda said. 'That's my sweet girl there, Castor. The only thing I'll leave behind me when I'm gone to show I was ever here. I stretched a point already, letting you bring an *âme raché* into my house. I stretched it as far as it's going to go. Do I want to test the wards? Hell, if that thing gets out of him, all the wards in the goddamn world aren't going to slow it down for the time it takes you to fart, Castor. I'm relying on the strength of my hands. They've never failed me yet.'

I threw up my hands in a gesture of surrender. I could see I wasn't going to carry the point. By this time Pen's hour was up and we were getting into overtime. We went downstairs, letting our feet fall heavily to announce us. When Imelda was finally done with the locks and bolts, Pen and Rafi were sitting demurely on the bed together, just holding hands.

I held out the whisky and Rafi let go of Pen's hand to take it.

'Jameson's,' he said without much enthusiasm. 'I asked for single malt.'

'You get single malt when I get a paying gig,' I told him, and he grunted in disapproval. 'Okay,' I said. 'I guess we'd better hit the road.'

'I thought you had something you wanted to say to me.'

I shrugged. There was nothing else I could do. 'It'll keep,' I said. 'Pen, whenever you're ready.'

They embraced, long and lingering: in the end I made a throat-clearing noise and they peeled apart reluctantly. Don't think I was just being an arsehole here, by the way: we'd learned by trial and error that the heightened arousal Rafi gets from being around Pen tends to undo the effect of Imelda's benediction and my playing. An hour is safe. An hour and a half is usually okay. Two hours or more is asking for trouble.

'You're working on the Tune, right?' Rafi asked me. When he says it that way, with the capital letter, it only ever means one thing: the music of unbinding, the tune that will sunder him from Asmodeus and leave him once again as sole tenant in his own skin.

'Always,' I told him, which was as good as saying 'No news since the last time you asked.'

He nodded slowly, staring me in the eyes the whole time. He knows the only leverage he has on me is my guilt and so he plays it up, afraid that I might one day forget who carries the lion's share of the blame for what he is. He doesn't have to worry on that score, but you can understand why he doesn't take it for granted. I broke that ancient-mariner stare and turned to leave, my hand already on the handle of the door.

The whisky bottle hit the wall right next to my head and shattered spectacularly.

I turned with my mouth open on an oath, but the look on Rafi's face silenced me. He was staring in shock and horror at his own left hand, which was rotating on his wrist as though he was flexing before some strenuous exercise. I saw the truth in his eyes. Then the hand and arm lifted, against Rafi's straining efforts, and beckoned me to return.

I didn't: not straight away. First I went upstairs to get pen and paper.

'So let's be absolutely clear,' I said, looking not into Rafi's eyes but at his twitching left hand. A black biro was loosely propped between his thumb and forefinger, and a page from the newspaper was spread across the table between us. 'Asmodeus?'

The moving biro wrote, and having writ moved on. A single word. *Yes.*

'Son of a bitch,' Imelda murmured in her throat. Pen just gave a forlorn moan.

'How?' I demanded.

Rafi wrote: *The usual way.*

'So you're building up an immunity to Imelda's treatment. Very kind of you to let us know. We'll try harder next time.'

The hand twitched and scribbled, the pen held at a crazy angle, the letters produced gradually by what seemed at first to be random strokes and slashes. *You'll be civil. If you want answers.*

I tried to keep a poker face: Asmodeus had the left hand, and clearly he could hear me, too. Safest to assume he was also looking out through Rafi's eyes. 'You've got some answers for me?'

Ask me a question.

Might as well go for broke. 'What's happening on the Salisbury estate?'

A door opening, Rafi wrote. *An eggshell breaking across. Call it metamorphosis. Call it transformation.*

Great. Who's up for a game of twenty questions? 'So what's changing into·what?' I demanded. 'Or are you getting writer's cramp?'

Rafi's hand laid down the pen, flexed and unflexed, then picked it up again. *You'll laugh when I tell you. It's a huge joke, mostly on you. But there are two sides to every deal, Castor. You haven't asked me what my consultation fee is.*

And here we were, at the top of the slippery slope. 'Okay,' I said. 'How about this? You tell me what I need to know, and I'll keep doing whatever's necessary to make sure Jenna-Jane doesn't get to add you to her zoo.'

But you do that for your friend, not for me. I need

The sheet of paper was now completely filled with angular scrawl. I flipped it over – Rafi's hand twitching all the while as though the flow of nerve impulses couldn't be stopped or slowed – and Asmodeus went on as though there'd been no interruption.

something else.

'Like what?'

Entertainment. Delectation. Tasty morsels to gladden my jaded heart.

Despite the situation, I almost laughed. The images

conjured up by the words were too grotesque to take seriously. 'How about an Indian takeaway and a belly dance?'
I suggested.

My tastes run otherwise.

'Be specific. I'm no way signing you a blank cheque.'

You feed me. And I'll feed you.

'Meaning?'

*Bring me to it. This thing you want to kill. Set me free, so
I can carve off a little piece of it for myself, and enjoy it at my
leisure. When I've eaten my fill, I'll tell you how to deal with
whatever's left.*

I sat irresolute. I looked into Rafi's eyes but Rafi only
shrugged brusquely, his shoulders hunched and his mouth
set in a grimace. This was nothing to do with him, and
he obviously wasn't enjoying the experience.

Imelda saw my hesitation. 'No deal,' she said, a warning
note in her voice. And I knew damn well she was right.

'Tell me a way to do this that doesn't leave you loose
in the world when it's over,' I said to the invisible presence. 'Meet me halfway, Asmodeus. If this is something
you really want, make it possible for me to say yes.'

The hand stopped its restless movement and lay still
for a few moments on the paper. Then Rafi, with a wince,
lifted it to head height and massaged the wrist with his
other hand.

'That fucking hurt,' he said.

Pen was at his side in a moment, embracing him fiercely.
Imelda turned to me, her face hard. 'What did we miss?'
she demanded. 'What trick did we miss?'

I shrugged. 'We didn't miss a thing. I think he's been
building up to that. Keeping a piece of Rafi under his

control so he could pull a little coup when the right time came.' And why would that be now? I wondered but didn't say. Why had he shown his hand?

Because he felt pretty damn sure that I'd be taking him up on his offer, either now or later.

Rafi disentangled himself from Pen's consoling arms and stood.

'You've got some more work to do,' he said to me and Imelda, a tremor in his voice.

'Yeah,' I admitted. 'You're right.' I took out my whistle and blew a low, sustained note while Imelda clamped her strong hands to either side of Rafi's skull. We got busy.

Again.

II

I made the tail after I'd seen Pen onto the train at Peckham, and my feelings passed quickly from terrified alarm through consternation to a sort of dogged puzzlement. This guy was at best an enthusiastic amateur, making himself obvious by keeping his movements broadly in synch with mine, keeping his shoulders hunched and his head lowered as if he was afraid of looking anyone in the face, and once stopping dead when I turned and looked back the way I'd come.

That first clear glimpse gave me a prickly feeling of recognition, although I couldn't remember where I might have seen the guy before. He had the etiolated skin and painfully slender build of a smack addict, and black hair that hung to his shoulder: a look distinctive enough that I ought not to have had to grope too long for the newsflash from my long-term memory, but nothing was forthcoming. His dark eyes flicked to left and right as though they were following a metronome, effectively solving the problem of not looking fixedly at me by not looking for more than a fraction of a second at anything. He wore a dark grey flak jacket and a silver-grey scarf only marginally thicker than a necktie – maybe trying to signal that he was tough but in touch with his feminine side.

The memory nagged at me but at first it wouldn't come clear. Then I got another blink-and-you-miss-it glimpse of him reflected in the glass of a swinging shop door as it closed. The tiny dark dot over his right eye was the trigger that loosened my mental logjam. The guy on the stairs at the Salisbury, with the BO that was probably grave stench. The dead man walking, who'd said he thought he knew me.

In a way, it was good news: if he was a zombie – and particularly, if he was following me *away* from Imelda's place – then he wasn't one of Jenna-Jane's people. He must have hooked onto my coat-tails at the Salisbury, which was why all my ducking and diving on the way there from Pen's house hadn't shaken him off: whoever he was, he didn't seem to be part of the professional two-man tag-team Gary Coldwood had spotted. So maybe – just maybe – I hadn't just blown the secret of Rafi's current location to the last person in the world I wanted to have it.

I needed answers, though, and in the aftermath of that nasty shock I yielded to an evil temptation. Why not turn the tables on this born-again little scuzzball and see if he had anything to say for himself?

I picked up speed walking across McNeil Road, hurrying between cars and buses as though I was late for an appointment. I didn't look back any more: I didn't want to scare the guy off. I just had to trust that he'd stay on-task until I'd scouted out a good place for an ambush.

Peckham has some of my favourite place names in the whole of London, although mostly the places themselves don't live up to their billing. Love Walk falls squarely into this category. There's nothing about it you could love unless you were a dog looking for somewhere new to piss. But it has a feature I remembered from previous visits — somewhere just off it there's an even narrower street that straddles the railway line before Denmark Hill station, and at that point there's a flight of steps leading to an elevated pedestrian footbridge, narrow enough so that two people have trouble passing each other on it. Actually, maybe that's where the place gets its name from: anyone you pass on the footbridge you're going to get to know quite well, so maybe love has been known to blossom there.

I didn't have love in mind: I just wanted me and my shadow to meet up in a place where there was nowhere to hide and where even turning around was going to be problematic. Then we'd see what we'd see.

Still walking briskly, I got to the wooden steps and went on up them at a jog. It was important that he shouldn't get too much time to think about this: I wanted him to commit himself right at the outset and then repent at leisure.

I walked out across the wooden footbridge, my footsteps echoing loudly. Overhead was an arched tunnel made out of steel loops and torn wire mesh. Once upon a time it had been there to stop suicidal passers-by from ending it all, or at least to move them along a little way and make them someone else's problem: now there were so many gaps and rents in it that it couldn't even do that. I made as much noise as I could, bringing my feet down heavily on the wooden planks. All part of the show: I wanted my tail to feel safe closing the gap, under cover of the racket.

Casting a furtive glance back and down through the gaps between the heat-warped planks, I caught a glimpse of his grey jacket and the top of his head as he climbed the steps in a hurry, trying to match my pace because he'd lost the line of sight. Great stuff.

At the far end of the walkway I scooted down a second, identical set of steps. Then I just ducked to the side, behind a narrow parapet wall maybe three inches taller than my head, and waited. Now I could hear him coming, because he was out on the bridge and there was no way to cross those echoing boards both quickly and quietly: and by the same token I was hoping that, because the noise he was making drowned out the noise I wasn't, he didn't know that I'd stopped.

I tensed, getting ready to jump him. He hadn't looked too hefty, but it was probably still better to hit hard and ask questions afterwards. I had plenty of questions I wanted to ask.

But the sound of footsteps died away above me, just as they reached the top of the stairs. Had I blown my cover somehow? I glanced up, saw nothing between the slats.

The moment stretched, way past the point where it could have been explained by the guy tying a shoelace or pausing to catch his breath. From where he was, he presumably had a good view both up and down the street: maybe he'd waited up there to see which way I went: in which case he had to have twigged by now that I hadn't come back into view, so unless he was a peerless moron my pathetic ambush stood revealed. I was just about ready to jump out of hiding, sprint back up the steps and see if I could catch the guy before he bolted. But before I could, the sound of footsteps resumed. Someone was coming down the steps towards me: coming down slowly, with long pauses for thought or reconnaissance.

Reverting to Plan A, I got myself into a tackling crouch. The steps at my head height creaked one by one, in descending sequence – an arpeggio of protesting wood.

But maybe on some level I'd already registered that there was something wrong with the footsteps. At any rate, when the old man came out at the foot of the steps, sighing audibly as he paused to get his breath back, I was able to check my forward lunge in time and I didn't actually punch him in the head. He walked on down the road, weighed down by two bulging bags in Sainsbury's livery: he hadn't seen me at all, which might have seemed odd if he hadn't been wearing glasses as thick as the portholes on a bathysphere.

Stifling an obscene oath, I went back up the steps at a run, but I was locking the stable door when the horse was already at the airport with a false passport. The walkway was empty: my tail must have waited for the next pedestrian to come along, lingered just long enough to watch me from above as I stepped out of cover, and then – having verified beyond any doubt that I'd made him – done a quick fade back the other way. The old gent's footsteps coming down the stairs would have covered his heading back the way he'd come.

I was chagrined – and frustrated. I'm too constitutionally lazy for real detective work, and I'd found the prospect of leaning on someone else for information very attractive.

But there was nothing doing, clearly. Next time, I promised myself, I'd move a little faster and give the slick bastard the benefit of one less doubt.

I was still thinking that when I caught a sudden movement off to my left. Honed reflexes made me turn right into it, and something hard and heavy smacked against the side of my head. The zombie had been clinging to the outside of the suicide netting, having crawled through one of the many gaps in its mesh. He knew damn well that his biggest handicap in a fair fight was speed – dead nerves and dead muscles taking their own sweet time to answer the call to arms – so he'd made damn sure the fight wasn't fair, turning my own ambush back on me.

The first blow made me see stars and tweeting birds. I staggered and fell against one of the steel beams supporting the suicide nets. That put me beyond the reach of my assailant's hands, but he got around that by kicking me in the face. The back of my head slammed into the beam: I caught hold of his foot at the same time, hauling him down on top of me. We sprawled and wrestled in an un-dignified heap, until he got his hand free and it came up again. I saw what was in it this time: a builder's hammer, with one flat and one clawed end. Like I said, an enthu-siastic amateur.

The hammer came down, clawed end first, and buried itself in the wood of the planking as I twisted my head aside. I would have been doing okay except that the first whack to the head had left me dazed, my movements logey and slow. Since the hammer didn't serve his turn, the zombie butted me hard in the bridge of the nose, then locked both hands around my throat. I brought my knee up into his groin, but with no noticeable effect: a half-rotted nervous system has its upside.

With a frown of effort, the dead man leaned hard into the business of throttling me. His grip tightened, and all strength went out of me in a black, liquid tide. I shouldn't have bothered with the knee to the groin, I should have been trying to break his grip. I scrambled for his hands now, but I couldn't make my own hands move in synch or take a tight hold of anything. I was sinking into a swamp sown with broken glass. I was broken myself, and every ragged edge of me was shrilling in atonal discord like the factory sirens of Hell. My eyes were still open, but the seat of my consciousness seemed to drop from its usual position right behind them, plummeting into stippled darkness.

Time to fight dirty – assuming you count a knee to the balls as fighting clean. I went for the dead man's eyes, hooking my thumbs into the sockets and squeezing with as much force as I could bring to bear.

The zombie rolled off me with a spluttered curse, one hand raised to his face, the other groping blindly at the planking. I rolled away in the opposite direction, struggling to get my knees back under me. That was the wrong move, because the dead man wasn't groping blindly at all, he was reaching for the hammer. It swung around in a tight arc and staved in my third rib.

I screamed in agony, further tearing my already badly mangled throat. The dead man went two for one, smashing me in the chin with the blunt end of the hammer as he brought it up for another blow. I jackknifed, kicking out with both feet because it was the only thing I could do. Luck was with me, and my right foot met the guy's arm as he brought the hammer down again. It went spinning out of his hand end over end, ricocheting off the suicide nets and fetching up ten yards from us.

But that was all I had in me. I slumped back onto the boards, my vision filling with black, granular static.

I think I actually blacked out for a moment or two. The next thing I was aware of was movement: the movement of my own body. Someone was lifting me, strong arms hooked around my lower chest. The pain was indescribable, because the pressure was right against the rib that had been damaged by the hammer.

'It's all right,' said a voice. It was a woman's voice, soft and low and very gentle – a stark contrast to the strong grip around my middle. 'It's all right, Fix.'

It wasn't all right. My head was still swimming and the gorge was rising in my stomach. I was terrified of what would happen if I threw up: involuntary muscular spasms would tear through my tortured throat and bounce me off the diving board of agony in a spastic triple salto. I tried to pull away from my rescuer's grip, but she wasn't having any. As I sank she raised me up again, whether I liked it or not.

I was too close to the rail and my balance was off. I was still rising, and my Good Samaritan was leaning against me from behind now, pressing me hard against the rail.

'Hey—' I choked out.

She shifted her grip, clamping one hand on the back of my neck to push me forwards through a gap in the suicide nets. Then she got hold of my leg with the other hand and lifted my feet off the ground.

'I can't let you do it,' she said, her voice strained and breaking. 'God forgive me, but I can't. I'm sorry. I'm so sorry.'

There was the distant honk of a train's klaxon, and the rails below me gave a tinny death rattle.

My eyesight cleared for a moment, at the worst possible point in the proceedings. I was staring down at the tracks far below, and even though there was a slight red shift to the scene I knew exactly what it meant.

I was about to impact on those rails at a modest but effective nine point eight metres per second – head first. And then the train was going to roll over me.

I got a good grip on one of the steel uprights and squirmed in the woman's arms, leaning my weight backwards to mess up her leverage. That brought my head around to the point where I was staring straight into her face.

His face. Paler than pale, and with a steel ring punctuating his right eyebrow.

Despite the unmistakably feminine voice, this *was* the dead man. My two attackers were one and the same.

Shock took the strength out of my arms. He gave one last heaving push and I fell towards the tracks below.

The freight train shot past at the same second, more or less. I caromed off the roof of the first carriage, bounced through the air like a matador who'd picked on the wrong bull, and went arse over tip into the neck-high gorse and brambles beside the track. The impact knocked the breath out of me, and the last vestiges of consciousness.

I came back to the world again slowly, and piecemeal. From where I was lying, the walkway above cut across my field of vision like a bend sinister. There was no sign of anyone up there, which was kind of a relief.

Taking it very slowly, I made a tentative pass at the whole complicated business of sitting up and then standing. It hurt a lot, but in some ways it had the abstract fascination of a crossword puzzle: finding joints that still pivoted and muscles capable of doing some actual work, and putting them together so that I moved in the directions I wanted to go.

Moving forward was even more of a challenge, because my head was full of fizzing static and my eyes were still refusing to focus or even to combine their efforts and look in the same direction. A concussion? That would be bad.

Inching my way along the rail, I made it to a fence and – after a few false starts – scrambled-slid-slipped over it into a narrow alley that led out onto the street. I had some vague idea in my head about knocking on the first door and asking them to call an ambulance, but a woman with a yappy little dog screamed when she saw me and in no time I'd drawn a small crowd. Someone helped me to sit down again, at the side of the kerb, and I hovered at the ragged edge of consciousness while another someone called for an ambulance. 'Love Walk. Love Walk in Peckham. Yeah, I think he's been mugged. His face is covered in blood and he's—'

What? Luckier than he had any right to expect? Probably, because when I surfaced again for real underneath a sardonically winking strip light in the corridor of some cavernous casualty unit (back at the Royal London, by a grim irony) floating on the wave of amiable invulnerability that comes with tramodol, it was to the good news that most of my internal organs seemed to be intact and functioning: two cracked ribs were a minor nuisance, or would have been if one of them hadn't punctured the lining of my left lung. The broken finger on my right hand was scarcely worth mentioning, and my nose hadn't broken after all, although it had swollen up spectacularly and the orbits of my eyes were deep purple.

The young Australian doctor decided to keep me overnight for a brain scan and a bit more prodding about in my chest cavity to see if the lung itself had been damaged in any way. But he was cheerfully optimistic about the whole concussion thing because I could count to five without clues and I knew who the prime minister was.

So all things considered, I'd come out ahead of the game. My attacker had come from the Salisbury: he was nothing to do with Rafi, so our cover was still safe. I hadn't been killed or even crippled. And I knew something about that dead man that might come in handy somewhere down the line.

All the same, I decided, enough was enough. It was time to take a leaf out of Juliet's book, and start going for some throats.

12

'They feeding you okay?' Nicky asked, taking a tentative sniff of the plastic pitcher of orange cordial – I'm using the word 'orange' to refer to the colour, not to the taste – that stood on my bedside table. Evidently it was less enticing than wine breath. He put it down and shoved it away firmly to arm's length.

'You any good at syllogisms?' I countered.

'Socrates is my bitch.'

'Then work it out. Everyone in a hospital eats hospital food. Everyone in a hospital is sick. Conclusion?'

'Right. I heard it was even worse than the shit they give you in prison.'

'Makes sense. In prison, most people are strong enough to fight back.'

It was around lunchtime of the next day, and a lot of my aches and pains were maturing rather than fading. I had a huge dressing on my cheek that made me look a little bit like Claude Rains as the Invisible Man, and I was doped up to my eyeballs on drugs that had lightened my discomfort by shutting down large and important parts of my brain.

Things being how they were and the day being overcast, Nicky had volunteered to come around in person and fill me in on the progress he'd made with my data. He normally prefers to avoid away games and make me come to him, but I think he was curious to see how badly I was damaged. Of course a hospital is a safe, antiseptic environment, cooled by air-conditioning and wiped clean regularly with powerful disinfectants: that hits Nicky where he used to live. And on top of all that he was enjoying the attention, aware that the orderly who'd come through briefly with the medicine trolley had run off to tell all the junior doctors that they had a zombie in the place, and that a small horde of them were now watching him from the nurses' station while pretending to sign prescriptions. They were all aching to dissect him and to debrief him about life after death at the same time. The ones with the strongest curiosity and the weakest morals would probably end up on Jenna-Jane's staff at the Queen Mary MOU.

By contrast, my fellow patients were mostly ignoring him: but then, we were all of us fire-damaged, chipped at the edges or generally shopworn. This was a recovery ward, but the term was being applied fairly loosely. There was a guy with hair so lank and plastered to his head that he looked like he'd been given the first part of a tarring and feathering, who twitched and chewed his knuckles a lot and seemed to be in some kind of withdrawal; another, much older man who drifted in and out of sleep with a look of faint surprise perpetually dissolving back into torpor; a kid probably still in his teens, his pyjamas drenched with sweat, who wore cordless headphones and rocked gently to his own inner beat. And there was me. Mostly we respected each other's space – or in some cases were maybe unaware of each other's existence.

That suited me fine. I was looking at this brief stay in the way that old lags look on short stretches of imprisonment:

you do your time, interacting with your environment as little as you can, and then you walk. I've already told you why I hate hospitals: the teeming multitudes of ghosts are as distracting as mosquitoes, as spirit-sapping as a constant hangover. That aside, though, this was a new-ish ward with reasonable decor. Reproductions of Van Gogh's sunflowers, Picasso's *Man With the Blue Guitar* and one of Andy Warhol's soup cans looked down on us from the walls, and the fluorescent strips were the kind that are meant to simulate outdoor light. Despite my bitching, it could have been a lot worse.

'Okay, you're kind of spoiled for choice,' Nicky said, dropping a thick wodge of computer printouts on the table in front of me. Actually, 'thick' doesn't cover it: it looked like a Central London phone book. Propped up in bed in tee-shirt and pyjama trousers with every muscle in my body aching, feeling like I'd been rolled up wet and put away dry, I could only stare.

'This is—?'

Nicky gave the massive accumulation of data an affectionate pat. 'Incidents on the Salisbury estate involving a police report or a newsfeed write-up. I went back two years – and I widened the net to include an area of a few blocks on all sides of the Salisbury itself. I didn't know how tight your brief was.'

'So tight I'm having trouble breathing,' I said, fingering the bandage across my chest. 'Jesus, Nicky, how many incidents are we talking about?'

'I didn't tally up. And bear in mind, there's a lot of redundancy in there – some things popped up in a lot of different places, and I didn't bother to filter out because, hey, you don't pay me enough for the deluxe service. Also, I set the bar real low. If someone's bike got stolen, it's in there. Or say little Timmy went missing for an hour or two and turned out to be round at his gran's . . . So long as someone called the cops and the call was logged, I threw it all in the pot. I didn't discriminate.'

He paused. I could tell it was a pause rather than a dead halt because there was something in his voice – the eagerness to spill that Nicky feels when he's unearthed something good.

'But?' I prompted.

'But there's a lot of good stuff, too. I mean, if you were looking for evidence that the Salisbury is a snake-pit, then you've got it. Standouts from this year included a guy cutting up his teenaged daughter with a carving knife because she stayed out too late, and a bunch of kids who caught a cat, dismembered it and posted the pieces through all the letter boxes in Boateng Block. Last year someone celebrated Christmas by hanging a tramp with a noose of barbed wire in the doorway of an empty flat where he was squatting. A while before that, a kid took a swan-dive off the eighth-floor walkway head first onto the concrete.'

I pondered this. 'Is all of this inside the bell-shaped curve, or out of it?' I asked him.

Nicky's face lit up as he answered, with the fervour of the data-rat. He's never happier than when he's slinging some choice statistics.

'How many people live in that towering shithole, would you say? With full occupancy, I'd say it would be pushing three thousand. But some flats are in between tenants and some have been certified unfit for human habitation. Call it two thousand, for the sake of argument.

'Average percentage for public-disorder offences involving violence is 2.2 per thousand head of population. That's across the whole of the UK mainland. For London it's 2.9, and on the worst sink estates you can expect to be up past five. The magic number for the Salisbury holds steady at six all the way from 2000 up until late last year. Then it jumps to more than three times that. Okay, across small populations you can expect crazy year-on-year variations, but I'd say this is something special – especially given how wild and wacky some of these incidents are. It reminds me of that time last year, you know? When your friend Asmodeus got loose inside a church and made the whole congregation turn rabid.'

Nicky dropped his voice for this last part, because the guy with the greasy hair had turned to look in our direction a moment ago, when Nicky's tone became more animated. I nodded. I'd made the same connection myself.

'I tried to get Juliet on the case, too,' I murmured. 'She went down there to take a look at it for me. But she's being real cagey about what she found.'

'Cagey?'

'She won't discuss it at all. She more or less said she knows what it is but she's out of it. On the sidelines.'

Nicky thought this through, obviously fascinated. 'Did she seem scared?' he asked. 'Was it, like, this is too big for her? She doesn't want to get in deeper than she can deal with?'

I shook my head. 'No, not that. Or at least, it didn't feel like that. I just don't know, Nicky. She's never bailed on me before. Well,' I amended, 'for a while on the Myriam Kale case, when she was seeing it as a sisterhood thing, but even there she came around. I don't get this at all, but I've seen Juliet face off against everything from were-kin to God Almighty. I don't think there's anything out there that she's afraid of.'

Nicky acknowledged the point with a nod. 'Well, anything else she tells you, I want to know about it,' he said.

'Why?'

He looked at me as if that was the stupidest question he'd ever heard. 'Because knowing things is my shtick,' he said. 'Remember?'

'Okay, Nicky.' I made my tone emollient because I was too tired and sore right then to want an argument. 'What about Kenny Seddon? You turn anything up there?'

He shrugged with his eyebrows.

'A little. I mean, I got what was there to be got, but there wasn't much. And none of it is what you'd call illuminating.'

'Go on.'

He pointed at the thick stack of pages. 'It's in your reading material,' he said.

'Give me the highlights.'

'What highlights? He's born, he lives, he maybe dies. Bit of a cliffhanger ending there, but that's as good as it gets.'

I held his gaze, and after a few moments he took an in-breath so he could sigh theatrically. 'Okay, whatever. Full name, Kenneth Christopher Seddon. Born, Walton, Liverpool, late 1960s. The exact date is in there some-where. He gets to age fourteen without incident, then has his first run-in with the police – possession of stolen goods. Court appearance, rap on the knuckles, off he goes. That's the beginning of a beautiful friendship – he turns up on the magistrates' court dockets six more times before he hits eighteen. Couple of affrays, couple of B-and-Es, drunk driving, and one moderately juicy wounding with intent.

'Then he cleans up his act. Puts away childish things and doesn't put a foot wrong for about five years or so. Or so we assume. Certainly doesn't leave any footprint on the world. I've got a few possible pings on the name from Glasgow and Oldham – credit checks of one sort or another, mostly – so maybe he was on his travels.'

'Maybe,' I allowed. I'd already left Liverpool myself by that time, and truth to tell I hadn't gone back much since. I'd never seen Kenny on any of my brief trips home, but then, I hadn't been looking for him. I had no idea whether he'd stuck around. A lot of my generation were shaken loose when the slums around the hospital were knocked down and new estates were built there. A lot more had already gone, deserting the sinking ship that Liverpool had looked like back in the Thatcher/Hatton era.

'But then we get a solid sighting in January 2001,' Nicky went on. 'In the exuberant spirit of the new millennium, your man Kenny head-butted a cop after being pulled over on the M25, which places him in London and tells us something about the deficiencies in his survival instincts.'

He made a gesture towards the sheaf of paper. 'I decided to narrow the search then, and hit a rich seam. There's a K. Seddon working casual shifts at a haulage firm in

Newport Pagnell in August 2001. He doesn't stick around long, but then he pops up again at a Lada garage in Welham Green, where he works for a year on and off. Pays his taxes, keeps his nose clean.

'He's down on the council register in Brent in 2002, on the waiting list but not yet in residence. He gets sick of that, presumably, and heads south. Bribes, blags or begs his way onto the list in Southwark and in due course gets his offer. Not the Salisbury, at first. Somewhere a bit classier than that. He lands in a two-bedroom conversion in Curtin's Grove – the only council estate in South London where most of your neighbours live in fucking Grade Two listed buildings. And two bedrooms makes you think, doesn't it? There's no mention of dependants on the application form, but obviously there had to be some. Presumably it came up at the screening interview, and the records were filed with the housing department's formal assessment. Which was erased, as per the stipulations of the Data Protection Act, when he left that address.'

I was momentarily distracted by the memory of that stark, unlived-in second bedroom at Kenny's flat. *The son was hers, not his,* Gary had said. *And he's dead.* Details to follow.

'So then he moved to Weston Block?' I asked.

Nicky nodded. 'July 2003 to present day,' he said. 'But you're missing out the best part, which is the reason why he moves. Those mysterious dependants? He keeps beating on them. Three domestic call-outs in five months, one of which involves an actual court appearance and a charge of assault, for which he does a month because he's got some previous. That means we get a name at last.

Kenny's live-in is a Ms Blainey. Tania, Tina, something like that. You've got all the details there, but it's a name that leads nowhere. I know, because I chased it.

'Anyway, all of this bullshit is too rich for the neighbours' blood. Complaints and formal warnings follow, and the housing department, as soon they've made their nod to the house rules, pick Kenny up by the scruff of the neck and drop him into the oubliette. I mean the Salisbury. There are no employment records from around then, by the way, but we've got him signing on at the social and showing up in the DSS database. He's got a dodgy back and he's on some kind of invalidity benefit. But he's still got the two bedrooms, so I guess we can assume that his lady friend sticks around despite the abuse. Maybe the bad back makes him less free and easy with the backhanders. She goes AWOL soon after, though. Kenny reports her missing on 16 December 2005. Police file the report, then do nothing, which is fairly typical copping for a missing-persons notice. File hasn't been added to since and, like I said, the name goes nowhere.'

He started in on a fairly arid list of other official agencies whose records proved Kenny's continued existence. 'What about the kid?' I said, cutting him off before he could get a head of steam going: I needed to see the wood right now. Individual trees could be examined later.

Nicky looked aggrieved. 'I was coming to the kid.'

'I know, Nicky. But visiting hours are almost over. Let's not piss off matron any more than we can help, eh? This is Mark, right? The boy who died?'

'Right. Birth certificate has Mark Blainey. Local school records had him down as Mark Seddon.'

'But he's not Kenny's son?'

'No reason to think so, since he's living with his mother at seven different addresses that don't have Kenny in them before they all wind up together in Walworth. But she tends to give him the surname of whoever she's shacking up with at the time. Maybe she's an old-fashioned girl at heart – or maybe she thinks it helps the family to bond. But it's kind of a moot point now, since, as you already pointed out, the kid is dead.'

I felt a twinge of formless regret, thinking of that bare bedroom like an inadequate mausoleum: a memorial to a life, but from which all the visible signs of that life had been scrupulously erased. Didn't grieving parents keep their kids' rooms the way they were when the kids died? Wasn't that how it was meant to work?

In my mind's eye I'd given this lost boy the face of Bic, the prescient kid with the bandaged hands. And I suddenly realised that the hands were the link I'd unconsciously followed. Bic's hands were wrapped up in grubby dressings: Kenny's were criss-crossed with the scars of old wounds. Even the ponytailed woman who was hanging out with Gwillam had her hands wrapped up. And my hands, when I'd visited the Salisbury for the second time, had itched so badly that I'd wanted to tear the skin off them.

You need hands to hold a little baby, Max Bygraves crooned lugubriously in some imperfectly locked room in my memory. When I was about eight, there was a certain level of drunkenness that would cause my mum to break out her LPs late at night and play them loud enough so that the sound came up through the floorboards to the bedroom I shared with Matt. *SingalongaMax* was one that we came to dread.

'Tell me about that,' I said. 'I mean, how he died.'

'He was the jumper. I told you there was a jumper, right? Maybe eighteen months ago. Jumped off the walkway between Weston and Beckett Block. Lot of alcohol in the blood, and a lot of speed, too, which is never a good combination. Couple of people saw him climb up on the concrete parapet, yell something and then jump. Verdict was accidental death, mainly because of the bloodwork. He probably wasn't sober enough to make up his mind to kill himself and then stick to it.'

'How old?' I asked. Jean Daniels had already told me, but there's never any harm in checking against the records.

'Eighteen. Just.'

Okay. So here it all was in black and white, just as Jean had laid it out for me. This was the tragedy that she didn't think Kenny had ever got over: a tragedy maybe slightly qualified by the fact that this wasn't his own flesh and blood. But that wasn't the main issue here, was it? That wasn't what was niggling me. It was just that I found it hard to imagine Kenny Seddon loving anyone. Beating up his girlfriend in a drunken rage, that I could see: and then turning his hatred on his own body when he ran out of other targets. Kenny sitting in his bedroom, on the double bed he now slept in alone, and carving out his indignation on his wrists and forearms . . . that was no stretch at all. But Kenny mourning a dead child? That wasn't such an easy fit. And the bare room belied it, too, unless he cleared out all the kid's stuff because it aroused memories that were too painful to bear.

I suddenly saw another anomaly, though, and the vivid picture faded.

'Wait,' I said. 'If Kenny's girlfriend had left, why was the son still living with him? Didn't he move on with the mother every other time she switched boyfriends?'

Nicky shrugged. 'Yeah,' he said. 'That seems to have been the pattern. But not this time. This time she hit the road and he hit the concrete. Everyone leaves the nest sooner or later.'

I found I wasn't in the mood, somehow, for Nicky's flippant little homilies, but as I opened my mouth to launch a put-down a nurse stuck her head in through the door and called out 'Five minutes!' in a ringing tone to the room at large.

'Man, you should ask for a cavity search,' Nicky scoffed. 'That's all you're missing for the full institutional experience.'

'That and some decent food,' I reminded him. 'Nicky, did you get anywhere with that drawing? The teardrop thing?'

'The shiny vagina? Not so far,' Nicky confessed grudgingly. 'Still working on it.'

'Okay. I want you to do me another favour.'

'Well, Jesus, what a surprise.'

'Gwillam. Find out where he lives.'

Nicky's eyes lit up, but he couldn't resist the cheap shot when it was sitting there right in front of him. 'I thought that was Humpty-Dumpty territory,' he reminded me.

'It is. But hey, they cracked me once and I didn't break. Not all the way. So now it's my turn.'

'Then I've got some good news for you.' Nicky reached inside his pocket, fished out a folded sheet of paper and waved it in front of my face before dropping it onto the sheets. 'I took the liberty. He hides himself pretty fucking well, and it took a while. But it was a labour of love.'

I unfolded the sheet. It was an address in St Albans: The Rosewell Ecumenical Trust, Church Street.

'That one you get for free, by the way,' Nicky added. 'Truly, this is the ending of days.'

'Get well. And get bent.'

He walked away with a laconic wave, and I immediately turned my attention to the papers he'd left me. Not Gwillam's address – that would keep – but the incident reports and statistics.

They would have made dry and difficult reading even if I'd been in better shape than I was. Nicky's hacks get him into all kinds of interesting places, but he usually loses a certain amount of formatting along the way, so I was facing vast blocks of prose with pretty much no punctuation apart from line breaks.

And in that typographic ocean, dark shapes moved of their own volition, against the sluggish tide. People hurt and killed each other, or themselves: broke against pavements, were impaled on railings, swallowed razor blades, carved gnomic messages on their own flesh or the flesh of their loved ones. There was blood, and there was pain. It drew me in, until I couldn't see the land any more.

Was self-harm just another current within that sea, or was it something else? Mark, the dead boy, had cut himself and written poems about it: the wounds were clearly part of his inner life; the most intense and precious part. And Kenny had got the habit, too: as though it was something you could catch. As though . . .

'Felix Castor!'

The voice was acerbic, angry, the emphasis very pronounced. I came out of my grim reverie and found myself looking up at the nurse, who was standing at the foot of my bed with my chart in her hand. And I understood her tone immediately, because she already knew me. But not by that name.

'Nurse Ryall,' I said, weakly. 'Petra.'

The redhead quirked her head and flashed her eyes meaningfully. 'Detective . . . Basketcase, was it?'

'Basquiat,' I said. 'Would you believe I'm here undercover?'

She thrust the chart back into its holder with more vigour than was necessary. 'It doesn't matter what I believe,' she said. 'That bloke upstairs was under police guard because someone had tried to murder him. I don't know how you got in there, but I'm going to report it to the shift registrar and let her decide what to do with you.'

I tried to jump up out of the bed to head her off, but the pain relief I'd been given was working too well for that. I slumped back down onto the banked pillows and she turned on her heel.

'They'll want to know why you didn't ask to see any ID,' I called hastily.

Nurse Ryall hesitated, and then turned back to me with a flush of anger on her face.

'You told me—' she began.

'No, you just made an assumption,' I countered. 'And I played up to it. Look, give me a minute to explain. I can't stop you from reporting me, but if you do we're both going to be in the shit for nothing.'

She stared at me wordlessly for a long time. I held on for the answer, keeping my stare locked with hers.

'Go on,' she said at last, her tone verging on grim.

I pointed to the chair that Nicky had left vacant. 'Why don't you sit down?'

'Because you said you'd only need a minute.'

'That was poetic licence. I'll need ten.'

She consulted the watch she wore pinned to her chest. 'I don't have ten minutes,' she said. 'I'm on ward rounds.'

'Then come back later. Seriously, there's an innocent explanation for all this.' If you stretch the word 'innocent' out to its functional limits, I thought to myself, and then knot it into a balloon sculpture. Nurse Ryall looked unconvinced, but after another painfully overextended pause she finally nodded.

'All right,' she said. 'In two hours, when I'm on my break. But it had better be good.'

'I'll see you then,' I confirmed, feeling weak with relief. Well, feeling weak generally, if the truth be known, but relief was in the mix.

Nurse Ryall stalked away, accompanied by the concatenation of her heels like the hoofbeats of apocalyptic horsemen.

I tried to wade into the haunted depths of Nicky's paper trail again, but my attention was shot to hell. Giving up, I thought about the few things I thought I knew and the many, many more about which I was totally in the dark.

Something – quite possibly something demonic – was haunting the Salisbury estate. And the ripples seemed to be spreading in the form of an increase in violent acts of every kind. Even in that cautious formulation, I was naggingly aware that there was something I was missing.

But my mind was too distracted by drugs and discomfort to pin it down.

Kenny, who had a ringside seat from the eighth floor of Weston Block, and whose own stepson was one of the victims, had tried to warn me about something. Or at least, while dying in his car of an overdose of slash wounds he had written my name on his windscreen in his own generously flowing blood. He'd got my attention, at somewhere considerably over the market price.

And the Anathemata Curialis, an ultramontane Catholic sect dedicated to the overthrow of the risen dead and undead, was now doorstepping the flats on the Salisbury – raising subjects that Jean Daniels hadn't wanted to discuss with me. I'd tried to step in on that dance and had got myself well and truly bounced by the big man, Feld. Clearly this gig was invitation only – and the invitation seemed to have extended to my brother Matt, even if it hadn't quite reached all the way to me.

A consultant on his late-evening sweep was working his way down the ward, looking at charts without enthusiasm and making a few observations now and again to his retinue of admiring interns. The procession stopped at my bed briefly, but seeing that I presented nothing more interesting than a punctured pleura and a few bumps and bruises, there was nothing to keep them.

Bored and restless, I tried again to make sense of the paperwork. It wasn't just the unappetising format that was making it hard for me, it was the content, too. It was like looking through a tiny, smeary window into one of the circles of Hell. A drunken fight where one of the combatants had pulled a can opener instead of a knife, and had put it to a use not too far removed from the one it was designed for; a late-night duel with sharpened pool cues; home-made shurikens and caltrops, piano wire and cheese graters . . . Okay, we were talking about a span of well over a year, but were the residents of the Salisbury so much in love with blood that they spent their time devising new implements for tapping it? The sheer invention on display was disturbing in itself, although it paled next to the terse, unreflective case histories. This wasn't right. Nothing here was right.

A clitter-clatter of heels jolted me out of my reverie, and I looked up to see Petra Ryall approaching, grim-faced. She looked around, her expression defensive and resentful, but the consultant and his teenage sidekicks had moved on to pastures new, the fat man and the twitching guy were asleep and the kid was lost in his own world of high-fidelity audio input. She pulled up the chair, sat down, glanced at her watch once to note the start time.

'Ten minutes,' she reminded me.

'Okay,' I agreed. 'Well, for starters, I'm not a detective. I'm an exorcist.'

That got a sceptical eyebrow-flash, but no other response. Nurse Ryall stared at me, waiting for more.

'I bind and banish the dead,' I translated.

'How?'

'With a tin whistle.' I spoke over her next question, because I've had this conversation a lot of times with a lot of people. 'No two exorcists do it the same way. It's music for me. For someone else it could be pentagrams or incantations or automatic writing or interpretative dance. It doesn't matter. You make patterns, and things happen.'

'What sort of things?'

'I can make a ghost come to me by calling it. Sometimes I'll use an object – some personal effect or keepsake – as a focus; other times I just get the sense of the ghost by being close to it, and I can play the tune that makes it come. Then if I want to I can bind it and send it away.'

'With music?'

'Exactly. And I can do that with other things, too. Not just ghosts but . . .' I hesitated. It was a big enough morsel to swallow already, without going into the full catalogue. 'Let me tell you about Kenny,' I suggested. 'Maybe that's the best way of explaining this.'

I started with the story of how me and Kenny had fought our one-sided duel on the roof of the tinworks, jumped forward to Kenny bleeding out in a car with my name on the windscreen, then went back and filled in as many of the gaps as Nicky's brief orientation lecture and my own ferreting around the Salisbury would allow. I played down the demon-weavings, played up the wanting to find out what it was that Kenny had to tell me that was worth wasting a pint of his own blood to do it. From about two minutes in, I could tell from her expression that Nurse Ryall wasn't buying it. Her frankly lovely face looked like a hod full of hard-core. And as soon as I'd finished, she shook her head.

'If what you're telling me is true,' she said, 'then why were you interested in the other man on the ward, too? The one with the puncture wounds.'

She had me there. By putting the emphasis so much on me and Kenny, I'd left out too much of the bigger picture – which maybe she needed to make sense of the other stuff.

I tried again, this time telling her about some of the stuff that was happening at the Salisbury — the epidemic of violence, the weird graffiti, the tranced kid trying to jump off the walkway. But it made things worse, not better. There wasn't any thread of logic connecting these things, and that became more and more obvious the more I talked about it. I was just whistling in the dark, trying to make a whole out of a bunch of parts that I didn't even understand separately. I decided to finish what I'd started, but more from mule-headedness than from any feeling that it would do any good. By the time I got to Nicky's stats, I could hear the hollow echo of my own words in the silent ward, and when I finally wound down Nurse Ryall didn't make any answer at all.

But her expression was unhappy, and it was noticeable that she wasn't telling me that I was a rabid dog who ought to be put down for the good of humanity. I waited her out, and at last she spoke.

'Can you walk?' she asked, very quietly.

'Normally, I'm proficient,' I said. 'Tonight, I don't know, but I'm prepared to give it a shot. What do you fancy? A movie? A Brick Lane curry?'

She didn't seem to hear the lame joke. 'Get your dressing gown on, then,' she instructed me. 'I've got something to show you.'

I threw the covers aside and swung my legs off the bed. Taking my weight on my hands, I touched down on the frigid tiles like Neil Armstrong making his one small step. But then Neil Armstrong was certified drug-free by NASA, and he was only contending with low gravity, whereas gravity seemed to be pulling me in a whole lot of random directions.

'We haven't got all night,' Nurse Ryall said testily.

I stood up with barely a stagger, which I thought deserved at least a short round of applause. My paletot was in the bedside locker. I shrugged it on, to Nurse Ryall's pained surprise.

'You're wearing that?'

'It's in right now,' I muttered, concentrating on my vertical hold. 'Rat-shit brown is the new black.'

She shook her head in disapproval, turned and strode off without a word towards the door. I followed her, assuming that she was leading the way rather than just giving up on me.

We went along a short corridor lit by fluorescent tubes that seemed agonisingly bright after the subdued lighting in the ward. There were backless benches along one wall where patients sat in some forlorn limbo, either waiting to be seen or just taking a breather somewhere on their personal roads to Calvary. Some of them looked hopefully at Nurse Ryall, as though they thought she might be their guide for the next stage of that journey: but not tonight.

We went out into the open air, across a courtyard where a few vans and a single ambulance were parked, and then back into a different part of the main building. It was darker and older here, and I started to recognise this or that turn in the corridor, this or that loitering spirit. We came to the main staircase: Nurse Ryall looked back once to see if I was following her, then went up. We were going to Kenny's ward.

The cop on the landing – fortunately not the one I'd met two days ago – gave us a questioning glance as we approached the forbidden door. Nurse Ryall nodded to him, showed her ID and said nothing about me. She entered the code and pulled, but the door stuck for a moment as the lock's old and cranky wards failed to pull back all the way. The cop took the edge of the jamb and added his own heft to hers: she thanked him politely.

I knew where we were going, but I didn't know why, so I let Nurse Ryall keep the lead as we crossed the narrow space to the door of Kenny's ward. There were still just the two beds occupied, Kenny and his roomie both asleep and breathing heavily. Nurse Ryall turned to me with an expectant look on her face.

I hesitated for a moment, glancing around the room. She said she'd show me something, but there was nothing to be seen.

'What?' I said.

She made an impatient gesture. 'Listen.'

I did. Nothing but the rough-edged breathing of the two men that would have been snores if there'd been more strength in their chests to push them out. I was about to say 'What?' again, for lack of any better ideas, but then the two men stirred in their sleep and spoke.

It was just the usual half-formed mumble of a dreamer almost but not quite breaching the surface of consciousness. The kind of sound in which you can perceive the melted outlines of words without being able to separate them out or decode them. They ended in a subdued, lip-smacking swallow, a slightly tremulous sigh.

Both men. Together. The same sounds, in perfect synchrony.

13

I swore, very softly, and Nurse Ryall nodded.

But she'd asked me to listen before the men spoke, and now I realised why. I could see it as well as hear it: Kenny's chest and the other man's rising and falling in unison, their in-breaths and out-breaths coming at exactly the same time.

With a slight sense of unreality, I looked at the nurse and she looked back at me. There was a strained inquiry in her expression: *What does this mean?*

'When did you notice?' I asked her, ducking the issue just for the moment.

'Two nights ago.' Nurse Ryall's voice was tight, unhappy. 'You can listen to it for ages and not hear it. Then it just . . . hits you.'

'Do you have any other patients in here from the Salisbury?'

'From the what?'

'From the same postcode. The Salisbury Estate in Walworth.'

She consulted her memory, shook her head doubtfully. 'I don't think so. I'd have to look in the admissions book.'

'Is that up here or somewhere else?'

'In the shift room. Listen, Mister – sorry, what was your *real* name again?'

'Castor. Felix.'

'What could make them do that? It's not even possible!'

I crossed the room and picked up the black man's chart. 'Women living in the same house will synchronise their periods,' I said. 'Not right away, but after a while. Their bodies respond to each other's hormones. Maybe this is like that – something autonomic that only kicks in after a while.'

'That explains the breathing. It doesn't explain the talking in their sleep.'

I looked up at her. 'Do they do that a lot?' I asked.

'What's a lot? They've done it before. Just like that, in chorus. But none of the other duty nurses has heard them do it. I know because I asked every last one of them.'

'Anything you could make out?'

'One word, sometimes. It sounds like "more" or "ma". The rest is just gibberish.'

More? Ma?

'Mark,' I suggested.

Nurse Ryall nodded. 'It could be that. Why?'

'Because Kenny here –' I pointed to the other bed '– had a stepson named Mark who died last year. Fell or jumped off a high building. And it hit Kenny hard – at least, according to some.'

Which explained nothing. I needed more than I had: needed a thread to follow through the maze, but Nurse Ryall had given me all she had. And she was well aware that I hadn't returned the favour.

'What is it?' she demanded. 'What is it really?'

'Demonic possession,' I said, deciding not to beat about the bush.

She gave a pained, incredulous laugh. 'What, and you'd know?'

'I'd know. I've seen it before.'

'With two people? Two people at the same time —' she groped for a phrase '— hooked up to each other like this?'

'No,' I admitted.

'Well, then—'

'Last time it was two hundred. The entire congregation of a church in West London. They all caught a dose of the same demon, and they all went out into the night to do unspeakable things to each other and to anyone else they met. I know about this shit, Charge Nurse Petra Ryall, because this shit is what I do for what I satirically call a living. They're both possessed, and it's one entity that's possessing them. I don't know what, and I don't know why, but I might have a way of finding out. Is anyone else likely to come in here?'

She stared at me, her face a menagerie of misgivings. 'At twelve. When the shift changes.'

'Okay.' I slid my hand into one of the paletot's many inside pockets and took out my tin whistle. 'Watch the door. If that cop makes a move, even if it's just to scratch his arse, or if anyone else comes along, let me know. You'll probably need to shake me or punch me in the shoulder or something. I may not hear you if you just whisper. Or even if you shout out.'

Nurse Ryall looked unconvinced, but she nodded.

I turned the chair beside Kenny's bed to face me and sat down on it the wrong way round: there was no telling how long this would take, and if it dragged on it would be useful to have something to rest my elbows on.

Nurse Ryall watched me with uneasy fascination. 'You're going to do an exorcism?' she asked.

'I'm going to try,' I said. Then I shut her out of my mind.

I started to play, random notes shaping themselves quickly into a sort of loose, aimless proto-tune. It was hard at first. It was only the lining of my lung that had been damaged, not the lung itself, but still the sharp pain whenever my chest muscles worked meant that everything cost me more effort than usual.

This part of the gig is like what bats and dolphins do: you throw out a sound and you wait for it to come back to you, subtly changed as it bounces off the world's various bumps and hollows. And from those changes you work out what the place you're in looks like: whether it's high up or low down; what natural hazards there might be; what sort of company you're keeping.

My death-sense rides the music as a wolf spider rides the wind, trailing a single thread of silk across a thousand miles of ocean. It doesn't have any volition or direction – not at first – but the music takes it where it needs to go, and in return it shapes the music until the feedback loop that runs through my ears to my brain and on down to my fingers and my pumping lungs narrows and refines the formless feeling into something patterned, perfect, vivid – like hearing your own name softly spoken in a roomful of bellowed arguments.

This is the first stage of the exorcism ritual, known variously as the finding or the summoning. Sometimes it comes quickly, sometimes it's agonisingly drawn-out, and sometimes it doesn't come at all. Tonight it was slow but inexorable like the building of a huge wave that towered over me like a wall – a wall I was mirroring in sound, climbing the scale and letting the volume build at the same time.

'Someone's going to hear you,' Nurse Ryall warned, but right then her voice was just another feature of the room that the music bounced off, briefly: a bubble in the flow.

There was something there: behind the room, behind the merely physical space in which I sat and the two wounded men lay. Something was looking in at us from a direction so strange and so nebulous that I couldn't turn around to meet its gaze. All I could do was keep playing, feeling its contours in the steady rise and rise and rise of the tune. It was coming towards me, and it was coming into focus: a tenuous presence that brought its own echo with it, a shadow with a darker shadow attached.

Then the wave broke over me and the darkness was absolute. I was almost thrown by that – by the suddenness and the force of it, the black slamming down from above and wrapping itself round me with disturbing intimacy. I could still feel the chair underneath me, the cool metal of the whistle between my fingers, but I couldn't hear anything now except the music I was playing – and rising behind the music the broken rhythm of the two men's laboured breathing. The world had gone away. I was alone in the dark, the tune my only lifeline.

So I carried on playing, my chest on fire now: there was no other choice.

And as I played, the darkness revealed itself to me: it had within it variations of tone, anfractuosities of depth and texture. It wasn't a curtain, it was a three-dimensional landscape executed in monotone: vertical and horizontal expanses that I could imagine as cliffs and fields, mountains and plains. I was looking at a black world on which a black sun shone, casting shadows of black on black.

Something within that landscape was staring back at me.

It had some kind of camouflage that didn't depend on colour, so I couldn't detect its outlines: only the pressure of its gaze, because an exorcist can always tell when one of the dead or the undead fixes its attention on him. It sat perfectly concealed, watching me without a sound.

And all sound had died now: my fingers were still moving on the stops of the whistle, but the tune I was playing had fallen away on the far side of some shearing blade, leaving me here in this silent immensity.

The hidden thing shifted, very slightly, and the sense of being watched and weighed shifted with it. Time passed, but there was no way for me to measure how much or how little.

Mark? the thing said. Or rather didn't say, because there was no sound here.

I couldn't answer. To answer I would have had to stop playing, and some instinct told me that if I did that I wouldn't be able to find my way back out of this place.

The thing that lived in the darkness growled soft and deep. It didn't like being ignored. *Mark*, it said again, and this time it wasn't a question.

I don't have him, I thought. He's dead. He's already dead.

I was starting to lose the feeling in the tips of my fingers. I had no idea what stops I was pressing, what notes I was sounding. My chest felt impossibly constricted, as though it might shut down at any moment and stop the flow of air across the whistle's mouthpiece.

The thing moved towards me, leisurely but with a heavy weight of purpose.

Not, it said.

I tried to back away, but my body didn't really exist here and it didn't even try to respond to the nerveless impulse. I was just a double handful of stiff, arthritic fingers groping along the cold metal of an object whose purpose I was starting to forget: a halting bellows blowing air over a spark I couldn't see.

leave

I took the tune out into a wild cadenza – or at least I tried to, but I'd lost the feeling for it now. Playing on autopilot is a lost cause, ultimately. And it looked like I was one, too.

The unseen thing crouched to spring. How did I know, when I couldn't fucking see it? Because I was tracking its voice through the muffled air – a diachronic line graph expressing an equation whose solution was my spilt intestines.

this

I blew a fingernails-on-blackboard discord – the last shot in my armoury. Sometimes it stops zombies and *loup-garous* undead in their tracks. Sometimes.

place!

Its hot, fetid breath was in my face, and there was a hideously suggestive sound — a sound like knives being stropped on a thick leather belt. I tried to flinch back, and couldn't even do that.

So I did something else. Since my hands were the only part of me that could still move, I punched straight forward with both of them, the whistle still gripped between them, and they made contact with something that was moving fast towards me. In fact, they did more than make contact: they sank, forearm-deep, into a rushing, blood-warm mass. A jolt of pure agony shot through me: a pain that was to the twinges of last night's beating what crack cocaine is to Coca-Cola.

The thing's own speed and strength carried me backwards. The darkness broke into bright staccato fragments of light and sound. There was a moment when I was weightless in a booming void, my thoughts spilling out of my head like blood as I turned towards a distant pinprick of light — attuned to its feeble radiance like a sunflower on Pluto.

Then I was falling out of the chair onto the ward's tiled floor, with as much momentum as if I'd been pitched out of a moving car.

'Castor!'

It was Nurse Ryall's voice, and Nurse Ryall's hands on my forehead, stopping me from smashing my brains out as I spasmed. Every muscle in my body was convulsing at once, and I could taste my own blood in my mouth. I was fighting for breath but the band of pain across my chest made breathing almost impossible. I was lapping air with my tongue, drinking it in agonising sips.

'Castor, it's all right! It's all right!'

It was, eventually, although the violent tremors running through me felt like small electric shocks. As they subsided, they left behind an enormous lethargy and lack of volition: a feeling that the only way I was ever going to move again was if someone rolled me down a grassy bank into a ditch. Nurse Ryall took my pulse and said soothing things: I could tell that from the tone of her voice, although the words themselves were just sounds. She wiped the bloody froth off my face where I'd bitten deep into my tongue. She helped me into a sitting position when I seemed to be capable of dealing with it. And the first question she asked, although I could see she was brimming with a million others, was 'How many fingers am I holding up?' She was waving just the one in front of my eyes to see how they tracked it.

'One,' I said thickly. 'Index. Right. Dark pink nail varnish.'

'Fuchsia. What day is it?'

'Tuesday.'

'What's your name?'

'Currently? Felix Castor.'

Nurse Ryall smiled in spite of herself – but sadly she also disentangled her body from mine, correctly judging that mine was sufficiently recovered now to go solo. She stood up and brushed off her uniform. What is it about nurses' uniforms that makes men fantasise about them? Mostly when you meet a nurse both your charisma and your libido are at their lowest ebb.

'So did you get anywhere?' she demanded, as I got up

slowly and carefully on Slinky-spring legs. The footboard of Kenny's bed was called into service.

'Oh yeah,' I said. 'I got somewhere.' But I didn't make any attempt to say where. That night-black *terra incognita* was beyond my power to describe.

'And what is it? Is it . . . what you said? Some kind of shared possession?' She had trouble getting the word out, but she did it anyway. I like a woman who doesn't flinch from absolute madness.

I nodded slowly. I would have nodded vigorously but I was afraid my head would fall off. 'I'm nearly certain,' I said.

'Then you can deal with it?'

And that brought us to the crunch. I made a non-committal gesture.

'I mean . . . that's what you do, isn't it? You said you were an exorcist.'

She had me there: I did say that. It's even still true, up to a point. But there were a number of reasons why that didn't immediately translate into ultra-macho demonslaying.

The first is that demons are mostly pretty damn hard to slay. Human ghosts are easy, most of the time. You get the sense of them, the measure of them, by staying in their proximity for a few minutes, hours or days – the precise time varied from job to job, and from one ghostbuster to another – and then you did whatever it was that you did: the peculiar schtick that channelled your power. With me it was music, but everyone's got their thing. If you do it right, then when you've finished the ghost is gone: permanently, irrevocably gone, and nobody (despite what they may tell you) has any idea where to.

Loup-garous are a bit more complicated. When you've

got a human spirit anchored in animal flesh – which is all a werewolf is at the end of the day – you can drive it out easily enough. You just set up an interference between the spirit and its host, so that the body expels the invading ghost and becomes its normal, animal self again. This isn't the same as a straight exorcism, although we still call it that: the ghost isn't permanently banished, it's just temporarily evicted. If that sounds like a pussyfooting distinction, look at it this way: it's the difference between what an assassin does and what a bailiff does. Who would you prefer to get a visit from?

And demons – demons are different again, mostly because they know how to fight back. Demons are sensitised to exorcisms, to the point where even the preliminary rituals shrill out to them across enormous distances like a police siren. Probably there's a Darwinian explanation for that: the demons that lacked this sensitivity were the ones that went under. The ones that are left, by contrast, have both a certain level of resistance to an exorcist's patternings and a tendency to counter-attack: they've been known to back-navigate the psychic trail like a shark following a blood-spoor, until they find the exorcist and stop the spell in progress by, say, eating his brain.

But the other element in the mix here is the exorcist himself, and my feelings on the subject underwent a bit of a revision a while back. I started to wonder where it was the ghosts went to when we dispatched them so casually – a question I should maybe have been asking way back when I performed my first exorcism on my own sister. Belatedly, my itchy trigger finger got a little bit arthritic, and I made a decision not to perform exorcisms on demand. I take each case on its own merits these days, as you've maybe seen. If a ghost is genuinely dangerous, I'll bind it or even banish it and pocket the cheque. For demons, excluding personal friends and acquaintances, my standards are even lower. But – call it a weakness, or an eccentricity – I like to know both who and what I'm dealing with these days before I get out the bell, book and candle. I don't empty the whole clip into every room as I kick the door down: that's for amateurs and idiots.

'I don't know,' I said, by way of abridging all this angst and introspection into soluble form. 'I need to find out more about what this thing is – and how it's tied up with Kenny.'

Petra seemed to find this answer unsatisfactory. 'Through the boy,' she said, bluntly. 'Mark. If that's what they're both saying in their sleep—'

'If,' I repeated, cutting across her. 'And even granting that that's true, we still don't know why, or how. Mark is dead. Did someone raise the demon to get vengeance for him? Is it looking for Mark's spirit for some reason? Did Mark himself bring it to the Salisbury – whether he meant to or not – by something he did? There are just too many ways it could all fit together, and if I go in without knowing the answers, I'm probably going to last as long as a marsh-mallow in a microwave.'

Petra stared at me.

'You're afraid of this thing,' she said. It wasn't a taunt – just an observation.

'Oh yeah.'

She looked at the two fitfully sleeping men, then back at me. 'But you're – awake. Healthy. It can't hurt you, can it?'

'When I fell over just now, it was about a heartbeat

away from doing something to me that the English language doesn't even have a verb for.'

Nurse Ryall nodded uncertainly, visibly rearranging the furniture in her conceptual space. 'Okay. So what should we do?'

I noted the 'we', and I was impressed. Scared as she was, she wasn't just writing this off as somebody else's problem. 'Right now,' I said, 'we should get out of here. There's nothing more I can do until I get some of my facts straight.'

We left the same way we came in, under the bored eyes of the duty cop who didn't even ask us what the music was all about. Maybe he thought a late-night serenade was something that NICE had approved for general therapeutic use.

Back on my own ward, I stowed my paletot thoughtfully while Nurse Ryall picked up Nicky's printouts and flicked through them with unashamed curiosity.

'Are these the facts you were talking about?' she asked.

'Some of them,' I allowed. 'The rest I'm going to have to pick up on the ground.'

I thought she'd just make a desultory pass through the frankly soul-deadening bulk of Nicky's transcripts and then put them down again. But half an hour later she was still reading, while the kid with the headphones communed with his inner ears and the fat man woke, looked around in surprise and suspicion, dozed off again. I let her read, covertly admiring the furrow of her brow, her lower lip unselfconsciously thrust out in deep concentration. I like intelligent women. It's a pity they're mostly too smart to get involved with me.

After a while she looked up at me, turning the sheaf of documents so that the top sheet faced me.

'Incised wounds,' she said.

'What?'

'Is that what this is about? Incised wounds?'

I was momentarily at a loss. 'There are a lot of wound-ings in there, Nurse Ryall,' I acknowledged. 'But as you can see, there's no pattern. We've got every weapon under the sun, including some that came as news to me, and every variation on murder, suicide, self-harm and lethal ambush. It's hard to think of a kind of wound that isn't in there.'

She stared at me wide-eyed. 'Are you serious?' she demanded at last.

'I thought I was.'

'Then you really needed to ask an expert.' She counted them off on her fingers. 'The ones that aren't in there? Blunt-instrument trauma. Crush and impact trauma. Abraded wounds. Gunshot wounds. Not to mention, if you widen the field a bit, burns, fractures, dislocations, concussions and sprains, strangulation, suffocation—'

I held up my hands, partly in surrender and partly to rein her in a little. 'Okay, fine. What does that leave?'

'I told you,' Nurse Ryall said, with slightly exaggerated patience. 'Incised and puncture wounds – and you've got one of each of them up in that ward. Almost all these cases fall into one of those two basic types: the damage was done either with a point or with an edge – or sometimes both. Stabbing and hacking, basically. Hurting people with things that are sharp.'

'You must be a lot of fun at playtime,' I said sardonic-ally. It was either that or break into full applause, and I didn't want her to get too cocky at this early stage in our relationship.

'Nursing diploma – BSc equivalent. I'm studying four nights a week.' She said, stiffly on her dignity. 'So I don't get much playtime, Felix Castor. But I do get to know everything there is to know about wounds. Or did you think that was just prurient curiosity?'

'Fix,' I said.

She bridled. 'What is?'

'My name. It's Fix. Short for Felix.'

'Oh.' She looked only slightly mollified. She stood up, briskly, as if she was suddenly conscious of other things she ought to be doing. Her break must have ended long ago. 'Well, you can carry on calling me Nurse Ryall. It shows respect.'

'Good enough,' I agreed. 'And since you're the expert, can you do me one other favour?'

'Possibly.' Her tone was cold. The playtime remark had gone badly awry. 'Depends what it is.'

I gave Nurse Ryall another one of my rare and precious business cards, having palmed one from the pocket of the paletot earlier. 'Keep an eye on Kenny for me,' I said. 'And an ear. If he says anything else that you can make out, or if anything else happens that strikes you as weird, or even if he just gets better or worse, will you keep me clued in?'

She took the card, but she looked disapproving. 'Why?' she demanded.

'Because it'll be another fact,' I said. 'And I'm collecting them.'

'Wide range of wounds,' she scoffed. I took that as a positive sign: she wasn't saying no.

'So sue me,' I said, with a comic shrug. 'I bet you don't know anything about medieval grimoires.'

'I can see what's in front of my face, though.'

Her breasts were on a level with my eyes. 'Me too,' I said.

'Don't push it, Castor.' She dropped Nicky's printouts onto my tray table with an audible thud. The top sheets sloughed off in a loose concertina.

'Thanks,' I said, sincerely.

'You're welcome. And thank you too, I suppose. At least now I know that I'm not going mad. You should get some sleep.'

'Yes, nurse.'

'And I should get over to casualty, or I'm going to be on report.' She started to walk away, got halfway to the door and then turned back.

'You didn't pick me up on the almost,' she said.

'Almost what?' I asked.

'I said *almost* all the cases on your printout were incised or puncture wounds,' she said. 'But the odd one out is a big one.' She clearly wanted me to ask, so I obliged — mainly to make up for the earlier off-colour innuendo.

'Big in what way?'

'It's Mark,' Nurse Ryall said. 'Mark thingumajig. Mister Seddon's stepson. You said he fell, didn't you? From high up. So that's a crush injury.'

As exit lines go, it wasn't all that punchy, but it left me staring at the door long after it swung to behind her.

Wounds. Points and edges. And one long, lonely fall to the ground. Or two. There would have been two if I hadn't stopped Bic from stepping off the ledge the other night.

What the fuck did it all mean? And where did I go to fill in the gaps?

14

The next day dragged on like a wounded snake across a barbed wire entanglement. It still hurt me to breathe, and I still couldn't walk very far without resting up every few steps to let my lungs reinflate. I could have checked myself out of the hospital, but I was stiff and sore enough to find the prospect daunting, and I wasn't sure yet where I was going to go. Something was crystallising in my mind, but it was taking its own time coming.

A junior intern changed the dressing on my ribs, giving my fingers a cursory examination along the way. I asked her how soon I could expect to play the tin whistle again: she looked at me like that was meant to be a joke, and then suggested that I take up comb and paper. Later on, a nurse came round to inspect my stitches and declared that they were doing nicely.

'Then I can expect to leave soon?' I asked.

'Oh yes, I should think so. We'll be needing the bed for someone else.'

'Tomorrow?'

'When the doctor says.'

On and off through the day, I read through Nicky's downloads and transcripts, looking for insights that didn't seem to be there. Nurse Ryall's hunch about the wounds played out strongly across the board. The dense, dry prose was full of people puncturing each other and themselves, carving and slicing and severing human flesh in every way imaginable. And in the middle of all this, one boy jumped off an eighth-storey walkway and kissed the concrete.

Or rather, not in the middle: Mark Seddon's death predated everything else on Nicky's list. It was as though he'd opened the door to something that had come spilling out like toxic waste across the entire estate.

Feeling restless, and enervated from doing nothing else but lie or stand or sit up on the ward, I went for a walk around the rest of the wing. Inspiration didn't come, and if anything the ghosts with their alarming array of stigmata and their disregard for walls and floors were even more of a distraction than the kid with the headphones. But it felt good, in some obscure way, to be moving – even if I was going round in circles.

In the evening, when I was sitting up in bed again with the notes spread out in front of me, chewing over random horrors until they were bland and flavourless, I had a visit from Detectives Basquiat and Coldwood. Basquiat said she wanted to ask me a few more questions. She was carrying a black leather document wallet which looked disturbingly full of something or other: also a micro-tape recorder which she switched on and put down on my bedside table. Gary seemed to be there purely to act as chaperone, which probably didn't bode well for me at all.

'What happened to your face?' Basquiat demanded, after she'd cued in the tape with date, time, people and place. There was a glint in her eye that was far from solicitous: she was interested because she didn't believe there was an honest way to come by bumps and bruises on such a heroic scale unless you were in police custody at the time.

'Cut myself shaving,' I said.

Gary opened his mouth, probably to tell me to do myself a favour and stop pissing about, but Basquiat signalled for him to let it pass. 'I'd like to come back to the question of your movements on the night when Kenneth Seddon was attacked,' she said.

'What I told you last time still stands,' I said.

'Meaning that you were at home with your landlady, enjoying a takeaway curry and a few cans of Special Brew.' She was only so-so as a poker player: she kept the edge out of her voice and her face as expressionless as the keyboard player in Sparks, but there was a set to her shoulders that betrayed an underlying tension.

'I don't drink Special Brew,' I temporised. 'It was probably Theakston's Old Peculier. Or maybe some kind of Belgian blond—'

'You were at home,' Basquiat repeated, cutting across me. 'You didn't go out the whole night until Detective Sergeant Coldwood came to collect you at four a.m.'

Backed into a corner, I gave a straight answer. Too bad it had to be a straight lie. 'Yeah,' I said. 'To the best of my recollection, I didn't go out.'

'Not even to pick up a pack of cigarettes?'

'I don't smoke.'

'Nicotine patches, then.'

'I don't smoke because I never got started.'

'Dry-roasted peanuts. Salt-and-vinegar crisps. A DVD rental.'

'No, no, and no.'

She nodded, satisfied. 'And your landlady will corroborate this?'

I looked over Basquiat's head at Coldwood, who was studying Van Gogh's ever-cheerful sunflowers and didn't meet my eye.

'Ask her yourself,' I suggested.

'In good time. I'm just asking you if you're happy with your alibi, from a structural point of view. Is it fit for purpose, Castor? Will it take the strain?'

I looked her in the eye. 'Alibi?' I repeated, as if it was a word I'd never heard before.

'If you were down in South London that night, you might not want to tell us about it.'

'I can't even remember the last time I was south of the river,' I said. 'Well, I mean before this thing broke.'

'Days? Weeks? Months?'

'Months. Must have been.'

'How many months?'

'At least six.'

Basquiat didn't answer, but she did finally unzip the document wallet. On top of the papers inside was a small stack of A4-sized photographs, one of which she held up for me to see. It was a grainy enlargement from a badly framed original, taken at night without a flash but with some kind of light-enhancement technique that made everything into an over-contrasted soot-and-chalk cartoon. It showed a white Bedford van, stationary at a traffic light. Someone had drawn a ring around the registration plate in thick black marker.

Basquiat flicked that photo down onto my bedsheets like a blackjack dealer, revealing the second one behind it. This was a zoom in from the previous image, focusing on the driver. He was hunched over the wheel, squinting sideways at the red light that had stopped him in his tracks as though he could make it turn green just by facing it down. The resolution was surprisingly good: it was me at the wheel, beyond any reasonable shadow of a doubt. Basquiat dealt me that one too and showed me the third: a close-up on my face, the image looking a little washed out and raggedy-edged this time. So did I, for that matter. My mother would have said 'Poor Felix!' by automatic reflex.

'Speed camera?' I asked, conversationally.

'Do you see any motion blur? Bus-lane camera, Castor. St George's Road, Elephant and Castle. You tried to over-take a truck in the left-hand lane and got caught by the red at just the wrong moment. This was three weeks ago. The night of the third. '

I handed her the first two photos back. Might as well keep the whole set together.

'Okay,' I said. 'You got me. Being vague on dates isn't evidence of murder, though.'

'No, just of having something you needed to lie about. We traced the reg back to a dodgy little runt in Cheshunt. Name of Packer. The worst kind of dodgy little runt, in a lot of ways – the kind that's on parole, and caves in at the first whiff of a search warrant. He was telling us first of all that he'd hired the van out to a Greek gentleman named Economides. But I reminded him that every time a lag on probation actively colludes in a criminal enter-prise, a fairy dies. After that he was only too happy to put your name in the frame.'

Thanks, Packer, I thought sourly. I owe you one, mate. But hard on the heels of that thought came the twin realisations that he didn't have any choice and it didn't make any difference. Once they had the van they had as much supporting evidence as they liked. My fingerprints would be all over it in any case. Basquiat had found a smoking pistol — but it was the wrong pistol, and the wrong crime. Looking for evidence that I'd tried to murder Kenny, she'd found the trail that linked me to Rafi's escape.

I waited for her to tell me I had the right to remain silent, but she didn't seem in any hurry to wrap this up.

'So what were you doing in Elephant and Castle at half past midnight?' she asked sarcastically. 'Getting into line early for the tropical house? Or crossing over into South London by a route that wasn't the shortest line between your gaff and Seddon's?'

This was bad. Worse than bad, probably. At the Stanger we'd been careful not to park anywhere within range of the one visible security camera, but the nurse on reception had seen the van and presumably the description was right there in the police report. I was caught between a rock and a hard place. The only way I could get myself off the hook for attempted murder was to put myself on a different hook labelled *grand theft Ditko*. Either that or pray that Kenny would come out of his coma and agree to be a character witness. Under the circumstances, dumb insolence was the closest thing to a strategy I could scrape up.

Basquiat didn't mind. She was keeping her end of the conversation up very well without me.

'So we've got you in the vicinity of the Salisbury Estate,' she summarised. 'Admittedly, some weeks before the attack on Kenny Seddon, but — to make things more interesting —

in a van you took the trouble to hire under an assumed name. And we've got you lying about it in evidence freely given to an investigating officer – both now and when I asked you the first time down at the Cromwell Road nick. Are we having fun yet, Castor? Because it gets better.'

I looked at Coldwood again. This time he met my gaze. He touched his lips, which were closed, presumably to indicate that I had nothing to gain by running my mouth off here. It was a fair point, but not one that I needed coaching in.

'You were seen on the Salisbury Estate,' Basquiat went on. 'Two nights ago. Barely twenty-four hours after you were released from police custody. I've got positive ID from two separate sources. I ought to be embarrassed about how easy you're making this, but hell, these days it takes a lot to make me blush. Now tell me what you were up to, and maybe when you come out on the far side of this you won't be quite old enough to claim your pension.'

Her tone had become even colder and more clipped in the course of this speech, and she was leaning forward, her face just a little too close to mine. Two separate sources? I thought irrelevantly. Was one of them Catholic? Was the other Gary? Where did the Pope shit these days, anyway?

'I was looking into the attack on Kenny myself,' I began, 'because it seemed pretty likely that I was going to end up in the frame for it—'

'You built the bloody frame,' Coldwood growled – his first contribution to the proceedings. I knew what he meant. I couldn't have put myself in a shittier position if I'd been trying. But hope springs eternal, especially when you've got nothing else to fall back on.

'Kenny was sending me a message,' I said. 'The words on the car windscreen were like – the last throw of the dice. He wanted me to look at what was happening down on the Salisbury, so he did the only thing he could think to do as he was bleeding out.'

'And you felt like you had to honour his last request?' Gary concluded. Basquiat clenched her fists and swung round to give him a look, but she was too late to stop him from spoiling her game plan. I took the sucker punch to the chest, not to the chin.

'Kenny's dead,' I said, feeling a momentary sense of vertigo.

'About three hours ago,' Basquiat confirmed. 'So it's not wounding with intent any more, Castor. It's murder. And this is your last chance to level with me about your part in it.'

'My part?' I couldn't make my brain work, and I couldn't figure out what her game was – the way she was playing this. But my hopes of Kenny coming round and explaining how all this was just some amusing mistake had just gone up the Swanee. 'Basquiat, for the love of Christ!' I said, almost pleading because I really felt like I needed not to be arrested right now. 'I didn't kill Kenny. You know I didn't. You've got two other men's prints on the fucking razor.'

'But the razor wasn't the murder weapon,' she reminded me grimly, her face still almost shoved into mine. 'The last blow – the one that counted – was struck with a short knife, none too sharp, that we haven't been able to retrieve yet. What's the fascination with the Salisbury Estate, Castor? Why do you keep going back there, if it's not to get paid or cover your tracks or coach someone down there through their story?'

'I was checking the place out,' I persisted doggedly, 'because Kenny's message—'

'And you called in some back-up of your own, didn't you? I almost forgot that part. But you were smart there, at least. Kept it in the family.'

'In the family?' I echoed, missing her point for a moment. Then I realised what she was talking about and felt sour anger flare in my stomach like a progress report from a perforated ulcer. 'Yeah, right. Of course. I teamed up with my brother, who's a fucking priest, and we carved Kenny up because he stole our football back when I was ten. Basquiat, Matt wasn't even with me when I went to the Salisbury. He was there by himself, under orders from another priest named Thomas Gwillam. If you want to know more, look him up in the Yellow Pages under rabid religious conspiracies.'

'The two of you were seen at the Salisbury together.'

'Because we were both there for the same reason, I suppose. I mean, because of what happened to Kenny. But we didn't arrive together and we didn't . . .' I faltered for a second, lost my thread, because I was listening to my own words and I could see, very abruptly, how little sense they made. Everything was tied together. It had to be. But maybe I was wrong in putting Kenny at the centre of it. When I first saw Gwillam on the walkway at the Salisbury, it was before any word of Kenny's death could possibly have got out to him. And the first thing he'd done, as far as I could make out, was to knock on the Danielses' door.

Incised wounds. Puncture wounds. Bic didn't have either kind. And I suddenly realised that that might be the point.

Basquiat was still looking at me expectantly. 'Didn't what?' she prompted.

'Didn't anything,' I muttered. 'We ran into each other, we talked, and then we went our separate ways.'

'You ran into each other.' Basquiat didn't even need to inject any sarcasm this time: the words just hung there, limp and ailing in the unsympathetic air.

'I didn't call Matt to the Salisbury,' I said.

'So he was there for reasons of his own.'

'Obviously.'

'Before Kenny Seddon was attacked, or after?'

'Like I said, ask Gwillam. There's a church-based group called the Anathemata Curialis—'

At this point the main door of the ward swung open and Charge Nurse Petra Ryall walked in, wheeling the meds trolley. She immediately looked across at the little group by my bed, and her gaze lingered. Basquiat's power dressing is multifunctional, but you couldn't mistake Gary for anything but a cop.

'Find Gwillam,' I suggested again. 'Ask him about all this. Matt is part of whatever he's doing. You ought to be able to get chapter and verse on that from your two fucking sources—'

Basquiat stood up, so abruptly that I was taken by surprise and stopped in mid-curse. 'I'll do that,' she said. 'And in the meantime, I suggest you don't leave town. Can you promise me that, Castor? Because if I have to come chasing after you, when I find you I'll nail your balls to the table to make sure you stay where you're put.'

I stared at her, mystified. The absence of handcuffs, verbal cautions and statutory phone calls caught me so far off balance that all I could think of to say was 'What?'

'Stay at your regular address,' Coldwood interpreted. 'Or check with us before you go anywhere. We'll be in touch again soon.'

'Ending interview at ten-sixteen a.m.,' Basquiat said. She picked up the tape recorder, turned it off, and slipped it back into her pocket. 'Very soon,' she confirmed, and stalked away without even blowing me a kiss. She stopped and looked back, though, when she realised that Gary wasn't following her. He was still loitering by the sunflowers.

'I need a minute,' he said.

'Off the record?' Basquiat's tone was dangerous.

'Off the record.'

'No.'

'How exactly are you going to stop me, Ruth?'

Her eyes narrowed. 'By telling you no,' she said. 'I'm senior officer on the case and I conduct the interviews.'

'This isn't an interview.'

'Then send him a bloody postcard.'

Gary waited her out. In the end she made a gesture of disgust and walked on through the door, pushing the meds trolley out of her way. Petra Ryall muttered something that could have been either an apology or an imprecation, but Basquiat wasn't listening in any case.

I looked up at Gary, and he looked down at me. He reached into his pocket and pulled out a few folded sheets of paper, which he handed to me wordlessly. I looked a question at him.

'Mark Seddon's autopsy report,' he said. 'Only he's down as Mark Blainey. They went by the birth certificate.'

'Bloody hell.' I picked up the sheets and stared at them with a certain wonder. 'Thanks, Gary. I wasn't expecting this.'

He didn't answer, but it was clear from his face that there was something else on his mind, so I waited for him to spit it out. 'Fix, I took a hard fall for you last year when you had me looking into that crematorium thing. And you never really told me what it was all about.' It wasn't an accusation. His expression was sombrely reflective.

'A lot of people ended up dead,' I reminded him. 'I didn't want to put you in an awkward situation.'

'You never apologised to me for getting my legs broken, either.'

'I said sorry in my own way, Gary.'

'By never referring to it again and dodging the subject whenever I brought it up.'

'Exactly.'

He shook his head. 'You can be a right bastard when you want to, Fix,' he said.

'All right,' I agreed. 'I'm a bastard. It's a gift. But I failed the police entrance exam so I never turned it into a career.'

Gary didn't seem to be listening, so my attempt to drag the conversation back onto the well-worn tracks of our usual repartee fell flat.

'But bastard or not,' he said, 'you usually look as though you know what you're up to. As though you've got some kind of a game plan. This time – it's like you're flailing around waiting for someone to tell you what to do. Or waiting for Ruth to put the collar on you.'

It was close enough to the truth to sting a little, but I shrugged it off because I got the distinct impression that Gary was trying to tell me something.

'It's more complicated than it looks,' was all I said.

'Oh, I'm sure.' Gary nodded sourly. 'And if I came out and asked you, as a friend, if you knew who'd killed Kenny Seddon, what would you say?'

'I'd say, Gary – as a professional exorcist and former police informer – that I don't have a fucking clue.'

He searched my face. 'Honestly?'

I nodded. 'Honestly. Why, you think Basquiat's right? You think I'm in some kind of conspiracy?'

'If she thought you were in a conspiracy,' he pointed out dourly, 'you'd be nicked already and sitting in a remand cell in Jackson Road.'

'In hospital pyjamas.'

'Until they could fit you for prison ones. She didn't arrest you because she's got a warrant out on someone else. We matched one of those sets of fingerprints.'

Relief left me momentarily speechless, the conclusions I'd been building to falling down like a card house inside my head. 'Who?' I demanded, after a long pause for thought.

Gary shook his head. 'I wouldn't want to put you in an awkward situation,' he said. The echo of my own earlier words was deliberate, and done with ruthless finesse. I acknowledged it with a nod.

'If you change your mind, I'm still here,' he said. 'I don't know how much I can do to help. Depends on what you've got to tell me.' He reached into another pocket, brought out a brown paper bag whose contents had leaked and stained its corners dark red. He set it down on the tray table.

'Grapes,' he explained, and left.

Once I was alone, the sense of relief turned out to be short-lived. It drained away, to be replaced by a greater puzzlement and unease than before. If Basquiat had someone else in her gunsights, then her not arresting me made a little more sense. But then why come in and brace me in the first place? And what kind of help was Coldwood offering if I wasn't even in the frame any more?

Maybe I was unconsciously hiding from the answers – not wanting to go in the only direction that made any sense. In any case, before I could put my thoughts in any kind of marching order, Nurse Ryall came over with the meds trolley. I ordered tramadol with an amphetamine chaser, but the à la carte menu was off.

'That looked heavy,' she observed.

By way of answer, I held up my hands for her to inspect. 'Look, ma. No cuffs.'

'But that was the police, right? The *real* police, I mean?'

I nodded ruefully. 'Not just the real police, but the real Sergeant Basquiat.'

Her eyebrows went up. 'Rudy actually exists?'

'Yeah. But he's a Ruth.'

'You should have introduced us. Listen, I'm on duty in the new wing today. I only came in here to tell you that your man had died. But she told you that already, didn't she?'

'Yeah. But thanks, anyway. I appreciate the thought. Did he—?'

'Say anything before he popped off? Not while I was

around, no.' She stared at me in silence for a moment or two while I tried to digest all this and found parts of it sticking in my throat at odd and uncomfortable angles.

'How do you feel?' Nurse Ryall asked.

I looked up, startled.

'About Kenny being dead? I'd be lying if I said I felt anything at all. It's been too long. It's like being told they knocked down a pub you used to drink in a long time ago. Actually that would probably affect me more, because I really like booze, and when you come right down to it Kenny was a bit of a turd.'

'Then why are you looking so mardy?'

Why indeed? Because he'd died at a sodding awkward time: invited me into his seething nightmare of a life and then pissed off to join the choir invisible, leaving me facing a murder charge and an invisible monster with a sweet tooth for what Petra Ryall so charmingly called incised wounds.

It was a neat trick. Not quite the same kind of bullshit he used to pull on me when we were kids, but definitely not a major change of direction.

'Because I'm still a suspect,' I said, abridging the more complicated truth. Coldwood had told me that I wasn't, but that was less comforting than I would have expected. Even if they did get the guy with the straight-edged razor and his mate with the blunt knife bang to rights, Basquiat's investigations were still likely to nail me to the board for the crime I really had committed that night – taking Rafi Ditko out of the Stanger care home with forged papers. And then there was the demon at the Salisbury, which I was reasonably sure I'd met the night before, up on Kenny's ward. Something had to be done about that. In a way, it wasn't my problem: but I thought about Mark Blainey's bare room and about Bic's attempt to re-enact his death, and I knew I couldn't just walk away from this.

Something hit the sheets next to me with a soft thump. I stared at it for a few moments before realising what it was. It was the plastic canula from a surgical drip, still slightly stained with the rusty brown of blood. I looked from it to Nurse Ryall, who shrugged almost apologetically.

'Just a thought,' she said. 'When you told me how you people work, you said you could use personal effects to raise a ghost. Maybe you could have another go at Mister Seddon. I mean, correct me if I'm wrong, but by dying he's put himself right in your comfort zone, hasn't he?'

Kenny. The man, not the demon. It might work, at that. I nodded slowly, giving Nurse Ryall a look of frank appreciation that she took without a flinch or a blush. 'I like the way your mind works,' I said.

'You don't know the half of it,' she assured me, deadpan. 'By the way, you asked me to check the admissions records. We've had dozens from the Salisbury over the last year and a bit. Two a week, sometimes. Over the past couple of months, more than that, even. And they've almost all been incisions and puncture wounds.'

By this time I would have been surprised to hear anything else. But those figures confirmed the sense that I'd been getting from Nicky's printouts: the sense of a slow-building epidemic, cresting like a wave; of the Salisbury as a raft of lost souls in the path of some sundering flood that was going to get much, much worse before it got better. Assuming it ever did.

Once again, Bic's was the face that came into my mind: the tiny human figure by which you measure the scale of something enormous.

'What does it mean.' I asked Petra, 'when you put your head in the lion's mouth and it doesn't bite down?'

She shoved her lower lip out while she thought. 'Is this a metaphor?' she asked.

'Yeah. For the lion, imagine that scary blonde who was in here just now. The one with the badge.'

'Oh. Got you. You mean—'

'She hates my guts, and she could have arrested me for – I don't know. Something. Conspiracy, at least. Wasting police time. Consorting with known felons. Something would have stuck, and she knew it. So I'm wondering why she didn't at least make the effort. It's enough to make a man feel unloved.'

'I'm sure you've got used to that by this stage in your life,' said Nurse Ryall sweetly. And she was gone before I could think of a comeback.

The open ward didn't seem like the right place to summon Kenny's ghost, and the middle of the afternoon didn't seem like the right time. But it would be a long time before the sun went down, and contrary to what you may have heard, ghosts aren't any more active by night than they are by day: they're just easier to see.

In the end I locked myself into the disabled toilet on the corridor outside the ward, put the canula down on the floor in front of me and played while sitting on the toilet. I took it slowly, because the pain from the previous night's musical exertions was still very fresh and very vivid.

It felt strange in a way, summoning a spirit that was already so familiar to me. Okay, it had been a long time since Kenny and I had met – at least, with both of us actually conscious – but most of the ghosts I raise are strangers and even after seventeen years Kenny was a long way from being that. Also, most ghosts don't scare me: Kenny had been a monster to me back when I still believed in monsters, and locking myself in with his spirit was something that I did with a slight prickling of unease, even though I hated myself for that atavistic weakness.

The tune was slow in coming, and it was only partly because of my aching chest and shortness of breath. I had to overcome a powerful reluctance to open myself up to the music – to start the process that would bring Kenny's wandering essence into focus in this place, at this time. It was as though a part of me was trying to back away and another part was holding me in place by the scruff of the neck. And the part that wanted to retreat was about twelve years old, which paradoxically gave it an edge against the adult, rational Castor that wanted to play the summoning: on the lost highways of the id, reason is a bike with no wheels.

But it happened in any case, the tune pulling me onwards in spite of myself: a fractally branching tail winding out through the disinfectant-soured air and wagging me like a dog. I closed my eyes, tried to keep my embouchure reasonably tight and let it happen.

Consequently I felt Kenny before I saw him. That's how it works for me most of the time, of course: the death-sense drives the music and the music turns into a negative image, a sound-painting that describes the thing it wants and brings it by describing it.

He was close. Of course he was close: he'd died in this very building only a few hours before. The sense of him went from tenuous to vivid to claustrophobic within the space of maybe a dozen heartbeats.

I opened my eyes again. The air darkened in front of me and he began to appear, in separate splotches of deepening tone that spread and merged like blood from a shaving cut soaking through tissue paper. As soon as I thought that, I tried to banish the image from my mind, but that was what Kenny was like: a wound in the air that my skirling music had incised.

Some ghosts don't know where or even who they are: they get lost in a memory or an emotion, replay a past moment like a ragged piece of vinyl being ceaselessly sampled by a demonic DJ. Kenny stared at me in silence, and I saw the recognition in his eyes. Unlike the living Kenny, he wore no bandages, which meant that his body was criss-crossed with wounds so dense and interconnected in places that they looked like words in some hieroglyphic script.

I lowered the whistle to my lap, and he didn't fade.

'All right,' I said. 'You called me. What did you want?'

The ghost looked down, turned its hands over to examine its ravaged wrists. Its lips moved, and although I didn't hear the word it spoke I could read the shape of it.

'Mark,' I agreed. 'What about him, Kenny? Is that what you wanted to tell me about? How he died? What's been happening since?'

The ghost shook its head slowly from side to side, but I wasn't sure whether it was in disagreement or just in bewilderment. This time when he spoke I heard the word as a tinny, baseless whisper in the air: the hum of a breath-less mosquito.

'Mark . . .'

'Did he bring it? The thing that's living in the Salisbury now, and making people cut themselves? Did he summon it, in some way? With his hurt-kit instead of a magic circle? Is that what happened?'

Kenny blinked, but he had no tear ducts now to wash the surface of those fleshless eyes. A grimace spread across his face in slow motion.

'Angry,' he whispered. 'Because . . . an . . . an . . . an . . . an . . .'

After each repetition of that syllable, the pauses length-ened. Whatever he was trying to say, it was a gradient which his cooling consciousness refused to climb.

'Who was angry?' I asked. 'Mark? Mark was angry?'

The ghost whimpered, bringing its hands up to chest height with the fingers curled like hooks. It looked as though it wanted to rend its own breast, but of course that wasn't an option.

'Cut,' it said, very distinctly. 'Again. And again. An . . . an . . . an . . .'

A ripple passed through it, so that for a moment it looked like a piece of washing hung out on a line. I was reminded, grotesquely, of how kids pretend to be ghosts by draping sheets over themselves.

'Who killed you?' I demanded, cutting to the chase. 'Who was with you in the car?'

The ghost's desolate gaze travelled along the length of its right arm, starting at the wrist and finishing at the shoulder; then on down its hacked and sliced torso.

'Oh,' it murmured brokenly. 'I didn't – I couldn't – He's too big now and he made me—'

'Kenny—' I said, but its head snapped up suddenly to fix me with a pleading, agonised stare.

'Castorrrrrrrrr!' it shrilled.

'Shrilled' is the wrong word: there was nothing behind that voice to push it up the register either in pitch or in volume. It was a broken fingernail making a forlorn pilgrimage across a blackboard without end.

Kenny broke into pieces, shattered by the note of his own grief and pain. Abruptly I was alone again, apart from the hideous echoes of that sound, clawing their blind, blunted way around my brain.

I lurched to my feet, groped for the bolt on the door and found it, stumbled out into the corridor as though I was a ghost myself, breaking free from my own tomb. My heart was hammering arrhythmically and my body was drenched in sweat. I leaned against the wall as the sweat cooled and the hammering slowed.

I went back to the ward, my feet shaky enough to require two further stops. Once there, I fell with relief back into my own bed.

Death had brought no relief to Kenny, that was clear. He didn't seem to be enjoying himself much at all. And for all I'd learned from raising him, I might as well have stayed in bed and messed around with a ouija board.

The dark mood engendered by the summoning refused to lift from my mind. Giving in to it, I picked up Nicky's sheaf of notes again and made to pick up where I'd left off the night before. I wasn't expecting the endless catalogue of perforated bodies to yield anything new in the way of insight, but I knew with a gloomy certainty that my mind wouldn't settle to anything else.

Then I belatedly remembered Gary Coldwood's little gift. Mark Seddon's autopsy report. It was still lying where I'd left it on the bedside cabinet. I picked it up and unfolded it.

I scanned the name and address details with a cursory eye and went straight to the physical indexes. They were as grimly, relentlessly thorough as you'd expect, compiling to a full but oppressively abstract description of the kind of damage cold poured concrete will do to a body that hits it at a velocity of forty-some metres per second. There were even photographs, but fortunately they were so dark and lacking in contrast that you couldn't really see what they were of. Except for one of them, and I stared at that one with slowing gathering shock and unease.

A terse note underneath the photo identified it as a tattoo on Mark Seddon's left shoulder. It was a stylised teardrop shape surrounded by radiating lines.

I sat propped up on my pillows staring at that inscrutable, unrevealing image for the best part of a minute. Then, since I couldn't look away from it, I tried to hide it by putting the cover sheet back over it. Doing that gave my system its last and maybe biggest shock of the evening: or maybe the nasty stutter of my pulse was an after-effect of the summoning, with its combination of physical and psychological exertion.

The cover sheet was where all the name and address details were set down. Mark Seddon, place of residence 137 Weston Block, Salisbury Estate, Walworth. Father's name left blank. Mother's name given in full. Not a Tina, or a Tania.

Anita.

Married name, Anita Mary Corkendale.

Birth name, Anita Mary Yeats.

My stomach did something complicated and self-destructive, and suddenly I was fighting to keep my hospital dinner – which was already inclined to defy gravity – down in the hold.

Anita.

That downtrodden chattel, who went from Brent to Walworth as part of the property and appurtenances of a boyfriend who beat her up every night as regularly as another guy might put the cat out.

Anita.

Why? What fucking sense did that make? She'd seen through Kenny when we were kids. She'd cut a slice out of him to save me, but then did a quick-fade before my balls dropped and I could ask her out on a date.

How could she end up with Kenny, even briefly? How could she give his name to her kid?

My phone rang, making me start so violently that my chest muscles spasmed and my fists clenched from the sudden pain as my damaged lung reported in still not fit for duty.

I hauled the greatcoat off the back of the chair and rifled the pockets with trembling hands. They didn't seem to be in the right places, and the phone had stopped ringing by the time I found it. I checked last-number redial, but the number wasn't one I recognised and it refused to take a call. So I waited.

After maybe a minute it rang again. I flicked it open. 'Hello?'

'Felix.' It was Matt's voice, and hearing it I remembered

how our last meeting had ended: probably that was why his tone sounded so guarded. But maybe he'd had second thoughts about letting me in on what he and his dubious friends were up to at the Salisbury.

'Hi, Matt,' I said. 'How's your soul?'

There was a long silence. Maybe it wasn't the most tactful way of starting the conversation, but then I was feeling too bruised and battered to be interested in my brother's tender feelings. 'Something you want to share?' I prompted him. 'Or are you calling me out of the blue because you decided that "brother's keeper" line was too cheap a shot to let stand?'

Another silence.

'This is my statutory phone call, Fix,' Matt said at last, his voice unnaturally calm. 'I'm at Cromwell Road police station. I'm under arrest for murder.'

15

The interview suite at Cromwell Road reminded me of
the classrooms at the Alsop Comprehensive School for Boys,
where I spent the years between changing up from short
trousers and leaving home. The resemblance wasn't immediately obvious, because the classrooms at Alsop mostly had
windows whereas the Cromwell Road interview rooms are
below ground and therefore don't. And you never had to
be swiped in through the doors at Alsop by a burly
constable wearing a hundredweight of ironmongery at his
belt. Moreover, the teachers at Alsop were for the most
part saintly men and women who got little reward for
plucking the flowers of higher learning and strewing them
at our ungrateful feet: you'd be hard put to it to find a
saint in a London cop shop, unless he'd just been done for
resisting arrest.

So I suppose it was just the institutional thing: not
quite 'Abandon hope, all ye who enter here', but the feeling
that you're handing over some portion of your life into
someone else's hands, to be tagged and bagged and given
back to you later, maybe, if they can find it again and if
it's still identifiable as yours. Fatalism descends on you
like a stifling woolly blanket as the door closes behind
you.

Gary Coldwood was sitting in a tubular steel chair with
a red plastic seat – some kind of Platonic archetype of

cheap, nasty, totally disposable furniture. But he stood up as I came into the room.

The surroundings were sparse. Just a table and two chairs, a green plastic wastebasket and, for some reason that escaped me, a poster on the far wall advertising all the many benefits of using a condom. When having sex, I assumed, rather than, say, for piping crème de chantilly or impromptu party decorations.

'Go and get Matthew Castor from the remand cells,' Gary said to the cop with the keys. 'Sign him in here for thirty minutes on my bounce code. Seven-thirteen.'

The uniform hesitated. 'Can't use these rooms for visits, sarge,' he said, in a timid tone that sounded like it didn't know what it was doing in his square-jawed, bushy-bearded mouth.

'It's not a visit,' Gary said. 'It's an interview.'

The uniform still didn't seem entirely happy. He shot a look at me that spoke twenty-seven volumes plus an appendix. 'But, you know, for an interview,' he said. 'If there's a civilian observer, you've got to fill in a—'

'What civilian do you mean?' Gary asked mildly.

The constable thought this through, and eventually got there. 'Right you are, sarge,' he said, in a nudge-nudge-wink-wink kind of voice, and he went on his way.

'Thanks,' I said to Coldwood.

'You're welcome.'

'And thanks for the heads-up, too, you duplicitous bastard.'

Coldwood nodded. 'Which is why we're in here,' he said, 'and all on our lonesomes. Get it out of your system, Fix.'

'You fucking knew she was going after Matt.' I thrust a finger at his face. 'You knew it, and you didn't tell me.'

Gary nodded. 'Right. I knew it. Did you?'

'No!' I exploded. 'If I'd had the slightest fucking inkling, I'd have warned him. And I'd have kept my mouth shut in front of you and your better half, you back-stabbing little pig-farmer.'

'I'm going to have to smack you,' Gary admonished me.

'On an interview?'

'You had the marks when you came in. You've seen how reliable a witness PC Dennison is.'

'Gary, why the fuck didn't you at least give me a—'

'Because it's an open and shut case,' Gary said. 'And your best bet, if you really had nothing to do with it, was to stay well clear. Whereas if I'd told you we were about to arrest your brother, you'd have gone barging in like a fuckwit, probably got yourself seen tampering with the evidence and ended up on a bloody conspiracy charge. Because what you're short on, Fix – what you do not have even a bastard trace of – is peripheral vision. You only see what you're going for, and you walk right into every bleeding thing else.'

Gary had been talking in his usual voice when he started that little speech, but he was shouting when he got to the end of it. I opened my mouth to shout back, and – to my complete and absolute amazement – he was as good as his word. He clocked me a solid one on the mouth.

It wasn't hard enough to knock me down, but it made me stagger. I blinked twice and shook my head. Licking my lips, I tasted blood. 'Son of a bitch,' I growled, and I started forward with my fists up. But Gary just stood there, staring me down, and after a moment I let my hands fall again.

'Are you ready to listen to reason now?' he asked.

I spat on the floor – a thick red gobbet – then met his gaze. 'Have you got any?'

Gary breathed out heavily. 'What I've got, Fix, is evidence. Which I'm about to share with you out of the goodness of my heart – unless you piss me off so much that I sign off early and forget you're stuck in here until the morning. If you're interested, sit down and shut up. Otherwise, say something really clever and sarcastic and I'll be happy to leave you to it.'

After a moment's painfully weighted silence, I sat down in the other chair, giving him a shrug and a wave.

'The writing on the windscreen,' Gary said.

'Points to me,' I observed.

'No. It doesn't.'

'What, you know another F. Castor, Gary?'

'We put the lab boys on it, Fix. The letters had been washed or smeared away, but the oil traces from Seddon's fingertip were still there on the glass. He didn't write "Felix Castor". He wrote "*Father* Castor".'

I opened my mouth to speak, but the words fled away into my hind-brain and my mouth just hung open, waiting for them to come back.

'So then we looked at your brother's movements,' Gary said. 'He was seen leaving that Saint Bon Appetit place around midnight, although he'd previously told a colleague that he was turning in for the night. We've got his car on CCTV twice, once in Streatham and once at Herne Hill. And – get this, Fix – the priest in the room next to his is woken up at four the next morning by the sound of someone crying. Loud, uncontrollable sobbing, in his own words, coming from Matthew's room. And he's prepared to go on record that it was Father Castor he was hearing.'

I found a word floating somewhere in the void that seemed as though it might be relevant and serviceable. 'Circumstantial,' I said. 'It's all circumstantial.'

'Maybe it is,' Gary allowed. 'But it was enough to get us a warrant. And the Basilisk was careful to shake you first, before she went in, just in case the forensics didn't play. She got your statement, which placed Matthew Castor at the Salisbury both before and after the fact.'

I shook my head in protest. 'Not before. I couldn't eyewitness him before. I just said he was with Gwillam, and Gwillam—'

'None of it matters, Fix.' Gary cut across me impatiently. 'Because the forensics did play out. Matthew's fingerprints and boot print match, a hundred per cent. And this just in – we shagged the phone records for the place where Matthew teaches. Him and Seddon were gabbing away every day for a week before the killing. They met up in that car, and your brother brought a straight razor with him. He brought an accomplice, too, and we're still working on that. But we've got him, Fix. If he's innocent, then this is a fit-up so immaculate that only God could have pulled it off.'

And that was out of the question, of course, because God loves Matt. He loves all His little children, of course, but Matt is actually on His team. I just sat there, not saying a word, and Gary sat there watching me, until PC

Dennison swiped the door lock again and then leaned inside
to hold the door open for Matt.

Matt was a mess: unshaven, red-eyed, his hair up in a
tousled Stan Laurel peak. They'd left him his own clothes
but had taken his shoelaces and his belt. Being put on
suicide watch must be particularly hard for a practising
Catholic.

'Felix,' he mumbled. 'Thank you. Thank you for coming.
I'm – it's all been a little crazy, since—'

He faltered into silence, blinking fast as he stared at
me with pleading, bewildered eyes. I got up and crossed
the room to him. Neither of us was ever very big on
physical shows of affection – something we got from Dad
– and Matt would have cringed if I'd tried to hug him,
but I put my hands on his shoulders and squeezed: a
clumsy, truncated gesture of solidarity that he didn't even
seem to notice.

'It's okay, Matt,' I said, going against both the evidence
and common sense. 'It's going to be okay.'

Coldwood made for the door. 'Knock on the glass when
you're done,' he said, brusquely. PC Dennison was still
holding the door open: Gary swept through and he let it
fall to again with the decisive clunk of a solid mortice lock
that I could probably have identified just from the sound
if my mind hadn't been otherwise occupied.

'I need to sit,' Matt said, and I stood aside so he could
get to the chair. He lowered himself into it a little too
carefully for my liking.

'Are you all right?' I demanded.

'I'm fine,' Matt said. 'But my side is a little sore, where
one of the police constables kicked me.'

Indignation flared inside me like heartburn. 'They worked you over?'

Matt shook his head emphatically. 'No. I fought them. I panicked, I suppose. I punched one of them in the face. It was a disgusting thing to do. They had to . . . subdue me. I wasn't really in control of my own actions.'

I closed my eyes and massaged them with the heel of my hand. It was too much to take in. 'How long ago was this?' I asked. 'Have they let you see a lawyer?'

'I haven't asked for one, Felix. I don't . . . I have no experience in these matters.'

'Well, I do,' I said. 'Say nothing, Matt. Not until you're behind a protective wall of sharks. I'll call Nicky Heath and get him to recommend someone. In the meantime you just . . .' I ran out of steam mid-sentence again. 'How the fuck did this happen?' I asked, lamely.

Matt looked at me briefly, then back down at his own lap. 'They came to Saint Bonaventure's,' he said. 'I was teaching, but they waited until the end of the session, for which I'm very grateful. Then they asked if they could speak to me, in private, and I took them into the clerestory, which is only used on Sundays. And then they – told me they were arresting me. For Kenny's murder. It was about seven o'clock, I think. I don't really remember. No, it must have been earlier if I was still in a lesson.'

'Fuck!' The invective was for Basquiat and Coldwood. They must have gone straight from me to Matt. Basquiat probably had the warrant in her pocket the whole time she was talking to me.

'Okay,' I said. 'Tell me about it. You and Kenny hooked up. How? They've got you in the car, and that's their strongest piece of evidence right there. Tell me what happened, and we'll see what we can do to beat this — thing.'

This time Matt looked at me for a lot longer. 'You haven't asked me the obvious question, Felix,' he pointed out.

I laughed without a trace of humour. 'You mean whether or not you did it? I grew up with you, Matt. Remember? If I had to ask, I wouldn't be here. Tell me what you were doing in the car.'

Matt finally lowered his eyes again. 'I can't,' he said, simply. He folded his hands in his lap, like a saint accepting martyrdom. It was only a gesture, but it set alarm bells off in various parts of my skull: this really wasn't the time to turn the other cheek. In my experience, that time doesn't come very often.

'What do you mean?' I asked, angrily. 'Why not?'

'I just can't.'

'Then tell me how you and Kenny hooked up. What you talked about.'

'Kenny . . . called me. Suggested that we should meet.' Matt spoke slowly, as though choosing his words with care. A jury wouldn't have been impressed.

'Out of the blue?' I said, falling automatically into the role of prosecutor.

'Yes. No. Not entirely,' Matt said, floundering slightly. 'We'd met a year before, by chance, so he knew I was in London. I don't know how he got the phone number of Saint Bonaventure's, but I suppose it's not that hard to find. The faculty lists must be online somewhere.'

'So Kenny called you. Why did you say yes, Matt? You

couldn't have wanted to see him again. I thought we all got more than enough of him when we were kids.'

Matt drew in a long breath and then let it out again, shuddering audibly. 'He said he could help me,' he said. 'With something—' Abruptly he jumped to his feet and walked away from me. A few steps brought him to the far wall, where he had to stop. He put up his hands as though to support himself. His right hand happened to fall on the let's-all-wear-condoms poster, and I thought incongruously of the oath they make you take when you give evidence, with your hand on the holy text of your choice. *I solemnly swear . . .*

'Matt,' I said urgently. 'I'm on your side. What are you afraid of?'

He bowed his head, shoulders hunched. His voice was thick and barely audible, as though his mouth was full of something choking and hot and he had to try to speak through it. 'I didn't kill him,' he said again.

'I know that!'

'But I think I did something – worse.'

The words made a space for themselves as they fell: made the dead silence that followed them seem like a police-incident barrier around their sprawled, unlovely outline. Nothing to see here. Keep moving. It's all over.

'Worse than murder?' I said, as soon as felt like I could muster a detached, sardonic tone again.

Matt turned to look at me, a strained and terrible grin on his face as tears welled up in his eyes. 'Worse than murdering Kenny? Yes. Oh yes. A lot worse than that. God help me, Fix. Oh God help me.' He raised his hands to his face as though he was going to bury them in it, but instead he just clamped them on either side of his forehead and held them there, rocking slightly backwards and forwards in an autistic pantomime of grief and pain.

This time I did throw my arms around him, if only to stop that scary display. Violent shudders were running through him like peristaltic waves.

'It will be all right,' I said again, between my teeth. 'But you've got to trust me, Matt. You think the room is bugged? They don't do that, because it would shoot the case down as soon as they tried to use it in evidence. And Coldwood wouldn't pull that shit on me in any case. What is it you think you've done?'

'I can't—' Matt moaned. He lowered his head onto my shoulder, not for comfort but as though he was about to faint and couldn't hold it upright any more. 'I just – what I've done is—'

He didn't seem able to make it any further. The next word couldn't be 'unforgivable' of course: all sins can be forgiven if they're truly repented of, and it's never too late. *For Christ did call the thief upon the cross, and offered him comfort.*

Matt was far from comfort right then: he was host to some terrible secret that was ricocheting around inside him like a bullet, breaking everything it touched.

'Tell me,' I said again. But if there'd ever been a moment when he was going to do that, it seemed to have passed. He pulled himself away from me, raised up his hands to ward me off.

'Don't let Mum know,' he choked out. 'Don't let anyone know.'

I threw out my hands in a gesture of helplessness. 'That

a Roman Catholic priest has been arrested for killing someone with a straight-edged razor? Matt, it's going to come out. It can't be hidden. Gary may be able to run a bit of interference for us, but as soon as you show up on a court docket you're front-page news. The only way you can help yourself is to tell me the truth.'

He was still crying, but the shuddering had stopped now: he was visibly getting himself under control, one piece at a time.

'No,' he said at last.

'Why?' I yelled, beyond all patience. 'Even if you're right – even if what you've done *is* worse than murder – you ought to confess it. That's how the drill works, right? You confess, you do your penance, the world goes on. Whereas if you keep your mouth shut, you're probably looking at twenty to life.'

Matt didn't seem to have heard me. He went back to his chair and sat down, wiping his eyes with the back of his hand. His expression had come back to something like calm, although it was a calm of balanced forces: the stillness of a man whose limbs are tied to horses pulling in opposite directions.

'Don't let her come here,' he said, and I guessed he was talking about Mum.

'I'm not making you any promises,' I said grimly. 'Not unless you let me in on this. What did Kenny want with you, Matt? And what did you want with him? What's this really about? Gwillam? Did Gwillam set this up?'

'I'm not with Gwillam,' Matt muttered, and I could see from his face that he was telling the truth. 'They approached me once. That's how I knew Feld, and how I was able to call him off when he attacked you. But the Anathemata only wanted me because of my name. Your name. They thought I might have the same – skills – that you have. When they found out that wasn't the case, they lost interest. This was years ago. I haven't seen any of those people since.'

'Then why—?' I began, but Matt made a brusque gesture and cut across me.

'No more questions, Felix. I appreciate you coming here. I – was glad to see your face, and you've given me strength to bear this. But you can't help me now.'

He put the matter beyond debate by banging on the glass and summoning PC Dennison to take him back to his cell. Matt went without looking at me again, or saying goodbye. I don't think he trusted himself to do either of those things with dignity.

Coldwood waited until Dennison was clear and then let himself back into the room.

'How did that go?' he asked.

'Like a bastard picnic, Gary. Why wouldn't it?'

He blew out his cheeks, shrugged. 'His faith will be a comfort to him. And believe it or not, he does have a guardian angel.'

'Meaning you?'

'He lamped a copper. Priest or no priest, he would have had it a lot harder if I hadn't put the *tupp nicht* out on him.'

He was right. I knew that. But I still couldn't bring myself to thank him right then. 'Drop you anywhere?' he asked as we walked together up the badly lit stairs to the ground floor and the reception area.

'I'll walk,' I said. Just bravado, of course, but I didn't feel like taking Gary's charity right then.

'I'm not your enemy, Fix,' he told me.

'You said.'

'And I'm still here if you need anything I'm in a position to give.'

I walked out into the night without bothering to answer.

There was no point going back to the hospital. I'd left a few bits and pieces there, but nothing I couldn't pick up again on the move. My coat was on my back and my whistle was in my coat. The rest was just details, really. I knew where I had to go, and more or less what I'd do when I got there.

I took a cab back to Pen's, found her still out on the town, so I borrowed an overnight bag from her wardrobe and left her a note. But while I was writing it, I thought of another piece of unfinished business that was hanging over me. And since I didn't know how long I'd be away for, now seemed like the best – if not the only – time to do it.

I went down to the kitchen and found Pen's car keys where she always left them, in the bowl of dusty imitation fruit on top of the Welsh dresser. Ten minutes later I was driving around the North Circular towards Wembley.

I called Juliet while I was en route to tell her where we were going, and who we'd see when we got there. She didn't ask for any further details. 'I'll be ready,' was all she said.

Juliet and Susan live in a minuscule terraced house in Royal Oak that had formerly belonged to Susan's mother. It had been a tip in old Mrs Book's day, but they've done it up really nicely now – although I suspect, without any evidence beyond the obvious, that all the nesting instincts are on Susan's side. It's hard to imagine Juliet with a paint roller in her hand. Someone's still-beating heart is more her speed.

When I knocked on the door, Susan Book answered. Her face was a little troubled.

'Jules is just coming, Felix,' she said. 'But are you sure you need her for this? It's very late.'

I reflected for a moment on the implications of this: that succubi tend to prefer early bedtimes, possibly with a mug of cocoa, and might get peaky and over-tired if they stayed up past midnight. Of course, being the person who shared Juliet's bed was bound to give you very strong opinions about how much time she spent in it.

'It was kind of her call, Sue,' I said. 'I'm visiting an old acquaintance, and Juliet told me a while back that she wanted in.'

Susan still didn't look altogether chipper about the whole deal, which made me wonder if she'd already quizzed Juliet about it and failed to get a straight answer.

'It shouldn't take us long,' I promised. 'I just want to deliver a message.'

Susan looked at me doubtfully. 'But who to?' she demanded.

'Someone who isn't going to want to sit still and listen. But there shouldn't be any trouble. The someone in question won't make too many waves because this will be at his own place, where he's got to worry about keeping up appearances.'

'I'm here,' Juliet said, walking down the stairs at that

exact moment. I was relieved, because any further questions were neatly forestalled.

Susan stood aside to let Juliet walk on by. A glance passed between them.

'I'll just be an hour,' Juliet said. 'Perhaps an hour and a half. If you're still awake when I get back, I'll massage your back.'

A series of mostly pornographic images flashed on my inner eye, but I strove manfully to censor them for decency and good taste.

Susan nodded and the two women kissed. It went on for long enough that I had to take an interest in the wallpaper so as not to feel like a voyeur.

'Let's go,' Juliet said, when she had sole possession of her own lips again.

Susan squeezed her hand, gave her a slightly brittle smile. 'See you later,' she said.

On the A1081, as we breached the M25 ring and headed north towards St Albans, Juliet broke the silence that had fallen between us.

'You're making no progress,' she said.

'At the Salisbury? No, you're right. I'm getting nowhere fast.'

'And you blame me.'

I thought about that one. 'I wish you'd picked another time to get strong and silent on me,' I admitted. 'This has turned into a fucking nightmare.'

'But still you invited me to come with you tonight.'

'Well, you asked. And to be honest, I might need the back-up. He's a whimsical little sod, and he's got it into his head that we're playing on different teams.'

'Is he wrong?'

'Usually, no. But this time, I think I might be able to bring him round to my way of thinking.'

Juliet digested that statement for a moment or two, various emotions passing over her expressive face. The last time Juliet and Gwillam had crossed swords, he'd managed to get the drop on her with a Bible reading – the Good Book being to him what a tin whistle is to me. It had rankled with her for a long time afterwards, because it meant that she'd been in his power, however briefly. He might even have been able to banish her to wherever demons go after they're exorcised, which is nowhere good: or possibly just nowhere, full stop.

'I'm looking forward to seeing him again,' she said at last. 'It will be . . . interesting.'

'But I don't want any trouble unless he starts it,' I clarified. 'This is a public-information campaign, not a vendetta.'

Juliet looked at me with detached curiosity. 'And why is that, Castor?'

'Because he's more use to me as an ally right now than as a corpse,' I said bluntly.

'And if he refuses to be an ally?'

'Then we'll have to see.'

Church Street turned out to be a very narrow road in the middle of a bewildering one-way system at the further end of St Albans High Street. I left Pen's car illegally parked in front of some gates that led God knew where, and we looked for the Rosewell Ecumenical Trust. It was a modest-looking building that seemed to have been made by knocking two old workmen's cottages into one structure. The sober, black-painted door looked fairly solid, but came equipped with both a bell and a knocker. I applied myself to both.

While we waited for an answer, Juliet examined the wards that were nailed to the doorposts and the stay-not painted on the wall. They were intended to deter the dead, and the undead, from entering this place.

'Anything likely to slow you down?' I asked.

She shook her head brusquely. 'Not for a moment. They make my skin itch a little, but they won't keep me out.'

There was a sound from inside of bolts being drawn. A very unecumenical face stared out at us: pug-ugly and brimming with surly suspicion, topped with black hair in a military-length razor cut.

'Yes?' it said.

'We're here to see Father Gwillam,' I said, giving him a beaming smile.

He tried to shut the door in our faces, so Juliet slammed it back into his. Then she pushed him up against the wall of the narrow vestibule and I walked on in past him. He rallied, driving a punch into Juliet's kidneys that actually made her frown slightly. She gripped his throat, slapped him across the face hard enough to make his head snap round a full ninety degrees, and then pitched him out into the street where he fetched up in a heap against a parked car. Its sidelights started to flash and it wailed on a rising pitch as its alarm went off.

Juliet closed the door on the intrusive sound. I looked around me. The ground-floor layout of the place was what an estate agent would have described as deceptively spacious: we were in a hall with a tiled floor, from which three doors opened off. The decor was High Victorian, which in the Catholic Church almost passes for contemporary. The inadequate light came from uplighters high up on the walls and from a heavy and unlovely wrought-iron chandelier suspended from three evenly spaced chains.

I kicked open the first door, seeing a roomful of books beyond and smelling the contemplation-and-dust smell of a library or study. The second was a broom cupboard. I was going for the third when running footsteps sounded from our right: we turned to see two men coming down the stairs towards us. One of them was Gwillam, a book in his hand and a pair of reading glasses on his nose. The other was a slight, bald man in a plain black suit, whose teeth were bared in a subtle but permanent snarl.

Gwillam opened his mouth to speak, but he was too late because Baldy was already in the air, launching a flying kick towards Juliet's face. Not a bad opening gambit, all things considered, but when his leading foot reached its intended destination, Juliet wasn't there any more. She leaned sideways, her movements seeming almost lazy because they were so perfectly timed that there was no need for haste. Her right arm flicked out and flexed at the elbow, intersecting the bald man's trajectory and punctuating his leap with a queasily suggestive impact sound. He jackknifed in mid-air, his forward momentum catastrophically sabotaged, and hit the floor in a rolling heap of limbs. He didn't get up again.

Gwillam's gaze was locked on Juliet's face. He recognised her at once, on a level deeper than sight: he knew her for what she was. He began to intone as he descended the stairs towards us, his voice an octave lower than its normal register. 'Would you tarry for them till they were full grown? They found a plain, in the land of Shinar, and they dwelt there. The right hand of the Lord hath done—'

'One more word,' Juliet said, unconcerned but a little stern, 'and you'll die where you stand.'

Gwillam fell silent. He was good, and he was quick, but he knew he couldn't complete an exorcism before Juliet reached him. He'd only managed to bind her last time because neither of us had seen his particular MO before.

But he lowered the book, allowing us to see that he was holding something else in his other hand. It was a handgun.

'No,' he said. 'You won't touch me.'

Juliet stared at the gun for a moment in silence. Then she laughed softly, richly. 'Is that for me or for yourself, servant of Heaven?' she murmured deep in her throat. 'Either way, the distance between us is too small for it to matter. Perhaps if it were already pointed at your head, and your finger on the trigger, you could pulverise your own brain while your purpose still held. But see, you stand there listening to me, and seeing me, and smelling me, and it's already too late. So now –' her voice had sunk to an insinuating whisper, and her eyes narrowed as she spoke '– what will you do?'

Gwillam was staring at Juliet in fixed astonishment. His mouth had fallen open a little way, as though he'd been about to speak and then been struck by some insight that took his breath away. He made a strangled sound that had no consonants in it.

'Come to me,' Juliet said, raising her hand.

Gwillam came, stumbling down the stairs with a rocking gait. His movements were as stiff and uncoordinated as a zombie's: so much of his mind was taken up with Juliet that there was barely enough left to handle basic motor functions. He walked right up to her, and then stopped when she raised a hand to signal that he'd come close enough.

She stood facing him, her breasts thrust forward, her head on one side in a parody of coquetry. They stared into each other's eyes, and for a long time neither of them moved. A lazy, terrible smile spread slowly over Juliet's face: Gwillam's breathing became louder and more laboured with each gulp of air he took.

'You may love God, Thomas,' Juliet growled, 'but now you've learned a different love. I hope you think of me often. And I know that whenever you think of me, God will be far from you.'

The joke was getting a little thin. I'd needed Juliet to get me in here, and I guess I'd known all along that she wasn't going to let Gwillam go with a warning. Maybe I was looking for a little payback myself, for the hurt the good father had put on me already, but I wasn't comfortable watching this sado-psycho-surgery.

'Break it up,' I told Juliet.

'When I'm finished. Kneel, Thomas. Kneel and pray to me.'

Gwillam was about to comply when I punched him in the mouth and sent him sprawling. The gun flew out of his hand and clunked away end over end into a corner.

Juliet shot me a look of pure rage, which was actually something of a relief. I didn't want to feel what she'd just made Gwillam feel: I'd been there, and seeing it happen to him had brought the whole thing back: the seismic, heart-stopping lust, the almost unbearable pleasure, and the black abyss of cold turkey afterwards.

'Your point's made,' I said. 'My turn. My show.'

Did you ever play cards for money? And if you did, can you remember a time at the end of a desperate night when you bet everything you had on a lousy hand, knowing the only way you could win was if everyone else bought the bluff?

That was me right then. Except that I knew Juliet wouldn't buy it for a moment, because she could smell my fear the way dogs are supposed to be able to. So actually I was betting on something else, and the odds were pretty easy to calculate: two years on Earth, against fifteen millennia in Hell.

My number came up.

After maybe five or six seconds – long enough for most of the late 1980s to flash before my eyes – Juliet relaxed and shrugged. She shot Gwillam one last glance, where he lay at the foot of the stairs, and he gave a ragged moan as her gaze swept over him, as though he'd just been lashed raw and her stare was a splash of vinegar on his open wounds. 'I'll wait in the car,' she said, and walked away, stepping over Baldy's sprawled unconscious body.

I got Gwillam into a sitting position. His breathing was still uneven and his eyes wouldn't focus at first. I half-led and half-carried him through into the study, dumped him into a chair that looked like an eighteenth-century antique, and while I was doing that I noticed a decanter of brandy standing on a dresser. I poured a shot, which I managed to get down Gwillam's throat after three tries: I took one myself, too, purely for medicinal purposes.

Slowly the good father came back to himself, anger and hatred filling the void left by his recently discovered passion.

'You consort with demons, Castor,' he sobbed, his voice breaking. 'This one, this succubus, and even worse. You think we don't know that you took Asmodeus from his cell? You profane this place and imperil your soul.'

'My soul?' I touched the dressing on my cheek, made a half-shrug with just the one hand. 'Well, I'm gambling on a deathbed conversion, so I'm hoping I've got a bit of leeway yet.'

Gwillam had been staring at the empty brandy glass. Now he looked up at me, his pale face streaked with sweat. 'Without sincere repentance,' he said, 'I can promise you, God won't listen to your apologies. Some sins are mortal.'

I leaned down to bring my face in close to his.

'Yeah,' I agreed. 'They are. And being as stupid as a hatful of arseholes is one of them. You screwed up, you sanctimonious fuckwit. I thought I'd stop by and tell you that before things at the Salisbury get even worse than they are. Because I've got other places to be and this was your mess before it was mine.'

From somewhere, Gwillam found the strength to stand. He thrust his face into mine, his eyes wide and his face white with rage. 'You persist in thinking that, don't you, Castor? That the whole world is full of the waste products of other people's mistakes? That your role in life is to clean them up, and take the thanks for it? But Asmodeus alone is proof enough to refute that.'

'I'm all that's keeping Asmodeus locked down,' I pointed out, wiping a little spittle from my face.

Gwillam's eyes narrowed. 'You took that monster from a place where he was safely contained,' he said. 'Under control. Who knows what you've started? Or what we'll have to do to stop it if it gets away from you. Because it will be us, Castor. It will be the soldiers of God – the ones with an actual vocation – who clear up after *your* mistakes. Just as it has been through the world, down through the ages. We watch, we weigh, we decide, and then we act. You simply cut out the first three stages of that process!'

As he spoke, something clicked into place. Watch? Weigh?

'You had a tail on me,' I said.

Gwillam gave a choking laugh. 'Is that meant to be an accusation? Yes, we followed you – as soon as the Mulbridge woman deigned to alert us to what you'd done. If she'd called us at once – but there's no point in repining after the fact. God works in his own way – and although you didn't lead us to Rafael Ditko, you did lead us to the Salisbury, and to William Daniels. We don't trawl the sink estates of the world looking for miracles. God made you an instrument of his light and truth. He does that, whether you like it or not.'

Gwillam smiled coldly. His composure was coming back to him at a steady trickle, bringing with it the unshake-able sense of his own rectitude.

'The situation at the Salisbury,' he said, 'is one that a faithless man like you can't understand. So there's nothing to be gained by discussing it.'

By way of answer, I held up my right hand, fingers spread.

The red, inflamed flesh in the centre of my palm was clearly visible. Gwillam's eyes widened as he stared at it.

'And that's after only a few hours on the estate,' I said. 'How holy do you think I'll be if I rent a flat there?'

Gwillam started to speak, but I rode right over him. 'You should have been like your namesake, Father Thomas, and looked for a little more proof before you threw up your hands and started singing hosannas. You find a boy with wounds in his hands and you think he's a saint in waiting, right?'

'I won't discuss—'

'Don't waste my fucking time. You already said the boy's name, and his mother told me you were there. She just couldn't bring herself to tell me why, but then she was seeing Bic's wounds as part and parcel of the other sick shit that was going on in his life. It must have stuck in her throat a bit when you told her it was good news from Heaven.'

Gwillam was silent for a moment, but he found his voice again soon enough. 'The appearance of the stigmata *is* a miracle,' he said. 'One that recurs down the centuries, as a sign of Christ's manifested blessing.'

'Either that or hysteria,' I said. 'Only this time – this time, Gwillam, it isn't either of those things. It's a demon.'

He stared at me in amazement, and then in undisguised scorn.

'A demon?' he echoed.

'Yeah.' I nodded. 'A demon that loves wounds. That seems to *live* in wounds, somehow. Some poor kid who was into self-harm summoned it. I think he did it without even meaning to, just by being on its wavelength. It makes people cut themselves, or other people. It fills their dreams and their waking minds with the eagerness to see blood spilled. And it makes blood well up from healthy flesh, as though there were wounds there. That's what Bic has got. A curse, not a blessing. Unless Jesus has got a really fucked-up way of showing that he loves us.'

I took the thick wodge of Nicky's printouts from my inside pocket and let them fall on the carpet in front of Gwillam. 'Read it,' I suggested, 'and weep. And after that, go and fucking do something.'

I left him sitting there, visibly reassembling the armour of his righteousness. No way of telling whether he'd believe me or not, but if he did there were things he could do while I was away to stop the situation at the Salisbury from reaching a crisis point. It was better than nothing, anyway.

As we drove back into London, Juliet maintained a thoughtful silence. I did the same thing, for a while, but then I thought what the hell: we were already on rockier ground than we'd been at any time since she decided to live on Earth instead of killing me. What did I have to lose by pushing the boat out a little further?

'Is this thing a friend of yours?' I asked.

I didn't look around, but I felt the pressure of her gaze on me.

'I mean,' I said, 'don't get me wrong here, okay? If this is another of those off-limits topics, just tell me. But if it's not, I wouldn't mind knowing. Does this thing that makes people cut themselves into ribbons so it can nest in the torn flesh go way back with you? Is it a friend of the family? Did it bounce you on its knee when you were a little girl?'

We'd gone another couple of miles before she spoke, and I'd stopped waiting for an answer.

'They're called the *Oleuthroi*. And I've never met this one before. In fact, I haven't seen any of his breed for twelve centuries. And the last one I saw was an adult, very old, enormous, that I and my sisters rousted up in the fields of Varhedre and killed for sport.' Juliet's voice was eerily distant, as if thinking about the past had carried her back there in some way.

'They're very rare,' she said, and then paused. 'Now. Now they're rare. It wasn't always so.'

'And what, you're into conservation? They're an endangered species?'

Juliet was silent for a while.

'I tried my hand at exorcising this thing before I came away from the estate,' she said at last, returning her gaze to the road ahead. 'Without result. I've told you what I can, Castor. More than I should. Be grateful. Or at the very least, be quiet.'

We said no more to each other. When I pulled up in front of Susan's house, Juliet got out without saying a word: I thought, but couldn't be sure, that I saw her turning away from Susan's door and heading off into the night, which embraced her as eagerly as ever.

By the time I got back to Pen's, it was after midnight. I called Jean Daniels, which I should have done from the hospital: to explain why I hadn't been in touch and to ask her how Bic was.

More or less the same, was the answer. He slept a lot, and when he was awake he drifted in and out of his right mind — talking in his own voice one moment and in a strange polyglot growl the next. He hadn't tried to hurt anyone, but he was unmistakably still possessed.

'And now you're going away?' Jean asked, dismayed.

'For a day,' I said. 'Two days, tops. I'm looking for Anita Yeats. I think she might know something that could help both your son and my brother.'

'Know something about what, Mister Castor?' Jean demanded. She sounded plaintive, and it made my stomach churn to be letting her down like this.

'Two separate somethings,' I admitted. 'About Kenny's death, and about Mark's hobby. She's the only person I haven't managed to talk to, and there's one obvious place where she might have gone.'

'Which is?'

'Home. Liverpool. But I'll come and see Bic as soon as I'm back. Unless you want to get someone else in, which I'll understand. I swear to God, Jean, I'll see this through if you still want me to. I just – have to do this other thing first.'

'We can't afford to get anyone else,' Jean said, her tone bleak. 'Come as soon as you can, Mister Castor.'

She hung up, and I finished packing, wondering how late the last train would go. They'd probably run through the night, I thought. But then I was overcome with weariness: my brain felt like it had been scraped clean with wire wool, and my chest was throbbing again. I had to sit down until the pain and weakness passed.

I woke late in the morning to find Pen putting a cup of coffee on the bedside table – next to a double chocolate muffin with a lit sparkler embedded in it.

'Welcome home,' she said.

'Thanks,' I muttered, sitting up slowly. Christ on a crutch, I thought. Losing half a day wasn't an auspicious start to the quest.

'You slept in your clothes,' Pen observed.

'Didn't mean to sleep at all,' I muttered, taking a scalding sip of coffee.

I told her about Matt, and she filled the pauses with expletives. 'Murder my arse!' she said when I'd finished. 'Your brother would do ten Hail Marys if he farted in a lift!'

'True,' I admitted.

'So what are you going to do about it?'

'I'm going to find Anita Yeats,' I said. 'All I've got is random facts that don't connect. I think she might be the one person who can join the dots for me. Can you lend me some cash, Pen?'

There was a square tin box in the kitchen that had once contained tea, or at least said it had. Now it contained ten-pound notes, stored up by Pen against a rainy day. She assessed the current storm at a hundred quid, counting the notes into my hand one at a time. Then, after a short tussle with her conscience, she forked over the rest. 'Just bring me back what you don't spend,' she said.

She dropped me off at Turnpike Lane station, and from there it was a short hop down the Piccadilly Line to Kings Cross. Trains for Liverpool were three or four to the hour, according to the Virgin Trains website, so there was no need to book.

Can't help? I thought.

Fucking try me, Matty.

16

In England it's not biology that's destiny, it's geography. London rules the roost and runs the show not because there's something aristocratic and splendid in the Cockney gene pool but because the Thames flood plain provided the geographical trifecta of rich, fertile soil, a navigable river and a billion acres of forest to make ships out of. Spread your sails and sell your surplus to the world, then come home and throw together the mother of parliaments on your days off. Before long you're not only ahead of the game, you're making the bloody rules.

Taking the Richard Branson Express from Kings Cross up to Liverpool, you go out through a whole string of towns that were never in with a chance of becoming the capital of England because they could never get over the accidents of birth: inland, becalmed, bucolic, they surrendered their produce and then their souls to the great maw of London: went straight from farming communities to dormitory suburbs without a protest or a qualm. Now they're trying to bottle nostalgia and sell it to the tourist trade, but it seems like fewer and fewer people are buying. Stands the church clock at ten to three? Well, that's bloody British workmanship for you.

Then again, maybe I was just feeling jaundiced because the pain in my ribs wouldn't go away even though I was popping ibuprofen like Smarties.

And because the guy sitting just down the carriage from me was a werewolf.

Don't get me wrong, I don't mean he was making a big thing about it. He wasn't hairy and slavering and going for my throat. In fact, he was just a young guy in an FCUK tee-shirt with a spiked haircut that was black at the roots and blond at the tips. He didn't look like anything out of the ordinary, apart from the impressive upper-body musculature rising out of a dancer's waist. But my death-sense spiked into jangling chords whenever he looked at me, which was often, and having to run for the train had left a faint film of sweat on his forehead, so he wasn't a zombie. That meant he was either carrying a passenger of his own, like Rafi, or else he was a *loup-garou*. Odds favoured the latter.

He'd boarded the train at Bedford, along with a very striking young woman in salwar kameez who got out her laptop straight away and never once looked up from it, two gloomy, overweight guys in painters' overalls, a half-dozen suit-and-tie grunts and a couple of amorous teenagers. He'd brought a four-pack of Tennent's Extra by way of a picnic lunch, but once he realised he was sharing his space with an exorcist he forgot about the beer and fixed his state on me with feral fascination. I've never even got close to working out why this is, but the death-sense thing cuts both ways: we know when we're in the presence of the risen, and they know when they're looking at someone who can send them down again. Once Mister FCUK had reached that conclusion his gaze never left my face.

I'd have been very happy to pretend I'd seen nothing.

He wasn't hunting and neither was I. But something told me it wasn't going to be that easy. The *loup-garou* held up one hand to me in what looked like a wave, all four fingers raised and spread. Then he popped a can of beer and drained it in a couple of swigs.

When it was empty he held up three fingers. Then he opened and polished off a second can, at a somewhat more relaxed pace. A countdown. *First I'll take my refreshment: then I'll take you.*

I pretended to take an interest in the scenery while the *loup-garou* worked on beer number three and I tried to make up my mind how to handle this unfortunate situation. I felt like shit: if anything, even stiffer and wearier than I had the night before. My dreams had been full of Kenny's feeble, shrieking plea, and I'd drifted between sleep and waking with no clear sense of the boundaries.

Finally I got tired of calculating the odds.

I stood up, exaggerating my movements slightly like a mime artist doing 'I'm going to take a little stroll now.' I took my tin whistle out of the inside pocket of my coat, laid it down on the seat and walked away with my hands in my pockets.

I made a sortie to the dining car to buy a styrofoam container full of coffee-coloured beverage. Then instead of going back to my seat I loitered by the door in the little non-space between the carriages, leaning against the wall and looking out through the open window at the fields and trees strobing by. I had one hand on the window frame, the other holding my coffee cup.

After a few moments the door at my back hissed open. The ontologically challenged youth stepped through, the door sliding closed again behind him, and stood watching me, at the edge of my field of vision.

'The whistle is your *thing*?' the *loup-garou* snarled. His voice had a dry rasp to it, so loud that it sounded as though he had a skiffle board in his throat.

'Yeah,' I said, not looking round. 'Music, generally, but the whistle's the best medium I've found to work in. Key of D. I'm sure you understand.'

A half-second of silence, heavy with incomprehension.

'Then why'd you leave it behind? You think I care two fucks about killing an unarmed man? Or was that your way of waving a little white flag?'

I gave him a look, keeping my expression more or less neutral. 'Look,' I said, mildly, 'I'm off duty. Good news for both of us. Why don't you buy yourself a few more beers, work on doing your liver a bit more damage, and at Lime Street we'll wave each other goodbye? No harm, no foul. Sound good?'

The *loup-garou* stared at me. His lips peeled back from his teeth, which is never a good sign in a werewolf. I noticed that they consisted entirely of incisors.

'You're a toaster,' he said, spitting out the word as if it was something unpleasant that he'd swallowed. I could have called that hate-speech, but exorcists coined the term themselves to describe their core business: ghost-toasting. Banishing the dead, with malice aforethought, whether they were threat or nuisance or just a drag on property values.

'And you're a fuckwit,' I said, without heat. 'Go and get drunk.'

'I think I'd rather kill you,' the *loup-garou* observed,

leering. His face was flushed and his eyes, like animal eyes, had no whites. Part of that was just the animal and the human trying to reach a tense accommodation about what their shared body should look like, but I think he was substance-abusing too. I mean, besides the alcohol.

'Have you done it before?' I asked.

He laughed shortly – a single exhalation pushed out through his still-bared teeth. 'Killed? Oh yeah.'

'Taken on an exorcist,' I said, with heavy emphasis. His face registered the word in a micro-momentary flicker of some emotion that I couldn't quite pin down.

But he ignored the question, or at least fended it off by throwing one of his own. 'You got any money?' he asked.

'Why?' I pretended to take a sip of the coffee.

'You pay me – a hundred, or a couple of hundred – maybe I'll let you live.'

I sighed and shook my head. 'You died young,' I said, trying one last time. 'The first time around, I mean. Probably because you got yourself into some stupid pissing contest like this one. Learn from your mistakes, eh? Let it lie in the long grass for once, and see if there's another way besides the hard way.'

The *loup-garou's* fingers were curved like claws now – and actual claws had slid into view at the tips of them. He took a step back, presumably because whatever animal his flesh had originally belonged to liked to go for the run-and-jump approach, and a train carriage barely gave him room for it.

I dumped the coffee in his face. I'd asked to have it scalding hot, and I'd made the girl at the counter in the dining car put it back in the microwave twice, until it was almost too hot to hold even through the styrofoam and the cardboard sleeve. This was why I'd only pantomimed drinking it earlier on: it was for offensive use only.

The *loup-garou* gave a gargling scream, ducking and covering reflexively even though it was too late. He must have been in agony, the near-boiling liquid blinding him and filling his exquisite senses with the roaring static of pain. I knew exactly how he felt, but it didn't affect my game plan.

I let go of the door, which I'd already unlocked and was only holding closed with my free hand. As it swung open in the train's slipstream, slamming against the flank-wall of the carriage, I kicked the *loup-garou* in the place where nothing male, whether living or undead or anywhere in between, likes to be kicked. Then I grabbed him by the shoulders, two-handed, and pitched him forward. A hooked foot in front of his made sure that he kept right on going, falling head over heels out into the rushing noise and the world we were leaving endlessly behind us.

It was over inside of five seconds. It had to be, because if I'd let him get those claws into play even once, this would have been my arterial swansong. Leaning out precariously I caught the window frame again and pulled the door closed, just as the connecting door to the carriage swung open and the Asian woman with the laptop poked her head out.

She stared at me in some surprise. 'I heard a noise,' she said, without much conviction.

I pointed to the door. 'It wasn't locked properly,' I said. 'It swung open, but I managed to get it closed again.'

She hesitated for a barely perceptible moment, perhaps noting my flushed face and trembling hands — or perhaps just seeing the spilled coffee on the floor. But she nodded and withdrew at last, if not satisfied then at least not wanting to make an issue of it. I waited a few moments, until my hammering heartbeat had returned almost to normal, and then went back to my seat.

The rest of the journey was without incident. I couldn't shake off a sombre mood, though. I was thinking about kids: about Mark Seddon, and about Bic. Even about the cocky little bastard I'd just tangled with. I hadn't picked the fight; and once I was in it, I'd won it in the only way I could think of. And he might even have survived, because *loup-garous* are as tough as weeds. If not, his spirit could find another animal host and start the make-over process all over again in its own sweet time.

I still felt like I'd just pulled a switchblade on a puppy dog. But then again, I hadn't had the option of a rolled-up newspaper.

Pulling into Lime Street for the first time in so long gave me a peculiar kind of double vision.

Three years. Not so very long, really, if you count it in calendar terms: but in terms of what I'd lived through since, it was about two ice ages ago. The last time I'd walked out through those oversized doors and got the Mersey's gusty, vinegary breath full in my face, it had been before Juliet. Before Rafi, even. Back when banishing the dead for fun and profit had seemed like a reasonable way of making a living.

Coming north had taken me a piddling two hundred

miles closer to the Arctic circle, but the afternoon air had a slight chill in it all the same. A green double-decker in the livery of the MPTE rolled past me, and as I crossed the road I glimpsed first the tower of the Playhouse rising above Forster Square and then, off to the right, the heroic frontage of St George's Hall. Amidst the welter of new roads and shitty poured-concrete frontages, they were like old friends standing on the fringes of a party where they didn't know anybody.

I waited at the bus stop, out of sheer force of habit, for the number 93. I could have grabbed a cab, but I'd always gone in and out of town by bus. Neither of my parents had ever driven, and I hadn't even taken lessons myself until I'd moved down to the Smoke.

I checked my itinerary off in my mind. I was looking for Anita, first and foremost: notwithstanding my own bad example, those born and bred in Liverpool 9 have a strong homing instinct, and this was my best guess as to where she would have come after life with Kenny lost its lustre. I was thinking that I'd shake down her brother Richard – Dick-Breath – and see if he knew where I could find her. If not, I'd get what I could by putting my questions to him instead.

I was also thinking of talking to some of the other Seddons if any of them had hung around in Walton. Kenny's brothers Ronnie and Steven might know something about Kenny's state of mind in recent weeks, and it was always possible he could have let something slip in a phone call or an e-mail.

Two women talking behind me in the queue disrupted my thoughts. After so long an absence, it was impossible not to tune in to the nasal poetry of Scouse.

'He loves the bones of her, he does.'

'Oh, aye. You've only got to look, haven't you?'

'But if he thinks she's getting that money down the bingo, he's living in a fool's paradise.'

'She's a dirty mare.'

'She's a hoo-er, is what she is.'

That was how my mother always pronounced the word. Not whore: hoo-er. Two syllables, drawn out with censorious relish.

Concentrate on business.

Anita.

Kenny.

And one other outstanding item, which had to come first.

The bus took me out of town along St Anne's Street, and then up through the asphalt and concrete runway which is all that remains of Scotland Road. As you drive out from the centre, Liverpool opens itelf up to you in concentric bands of squalor and almost-affluence – although for real affluence you had to swing all the way east to Woolton, and that was nowhere near my destination.

I got off two stops past where I should have done, at the Queen's Drive flyover. Queen's Drive is the Liverpool ring road, although Liverpool being a crescent-shaped city jammed in against the banks of the Mersey it's really only half a ring. When John Brodie started building it in 1903, Walton was a village. By the time he downed tools and signed off on the job two and a half decades later, it had become a borough of the city, but there were streets behind St Mary's Church that still kept that parochial charm. Other parts, particularly the streets around Walton

Hospital, underwent a further metamorphosis into a slum, but as kids we had no standard of comparison. For all we knew, the queen had bedbugs too.

The hospital stands just outside of Queen's Drive's tight embrace, at the northern end of Breeze Hill. But when I got off the bus I turned the other way, past the church and on down County Road. In the mid-1980s the city council had finally decided to pull the beam out of its eye and had torn down the shithole where I'd been born, relocating most of the inhabitants either to a new development on the Walton Triangle or to council houses a couple of miles further in towards the centre.

A couple of miles. Tops. But geography is destiny in Liverpool, too, and for some reason the distances are strangely compressed. A hundred yards can be decisive in determining who you are, and what you are.

For my dad, who'd already lost his daughter and his marriage, moving out of Walton into Everton Valley was the third strike: the one that finally took him out of the game. It meant leaving behind an ecosystem as complex and fragile and non-portable as a coral reef: an ecosystem where kids tended to end up living in houses on the same street as their parents, or the next street over, where you could call on twenty or thirty cousins within a half-mile radius, and where every family had inherited alliances and feuds stretching back at least as far as the First World War.

Cut loose from that support mechanism, John Castor succumbed to colonic cancer and died within the space of a year. It was as though he'd made his mind up to it and saw no point in hanging about.

I was travelling backwards in time as I walked: County

Road was my bathysphere. From my father's death, I descended a decade or so to my parents' break-up. Probably that would have happened a lot sooner, too, if they'd been living in Everton back then. Probably conservatism is a kind of social cement. The kind of conservatism that comes without a capital letter, I mean: we all know what the other kind is. At any rate, my mother's infidelities and my dad's heroic binge drinking might have made their marriage shake like a Tokyo skyscraper, but it took actually walking in on Mum *in flagrante* to make Dad finally call time, and even then it was all nuance. You find your wife naked with another man, you beat him senseless and throw him through the bedroom window onto the shed, that's understood. But the 'don't darken my door' routine was probably for form's sake. Mum just chose to take it literally this time.

My life, and Matt's life, became a strange and fractured thing after that. Mum went away, we lived with Dad. Matt went away, and I still lived with Dad but it was more like two guys just sharing rooms, seeing each other occasionally and finding they had less and less to say to each other when they did. Then Mum came back, which raised the possibility of us all being a proper family again, but she moved in with her lover, Terry Lackland, instead and it just meant that Dad's bad temper got an additional scary edge to it, and that there was one more place where I didn't really feel at home.

Now Dad was dead, and Terry was dead, and none of it meant anything any more. Except that the impassable terrain was still there between us shell-shocked survivors. The débris. I was walking on it now.

Mum's house was ex-council, now owned by a private landlord called the Inner City Partnership. Mentioning their name was a quick way to elicit a spectacular torrent of abuse from her, but there was no denying that this was a step – if not a whole damn staircase – up from Arthur Street. The door wasn't covered by a slab of particle board, for one thing. And it had a bell.

I rang, and silence answered. After a while, I rang again.

Mum answered on the fourth ring, just as I was giving up. She opened the door and stared at me for a moment or two, blank-faced and bleary-eyed, before recognition kicked in.

It was hard for me, too. In my mind, Barbie Castor always has a heroic, larger-than-life stature, as one of those Walton women of whom it was said, with approval and respect, 'she fights like a man'. As a kid I used to look up to her in a literal and physical sense too, but her generous build and rugged independence made her the sort of person who it was easy to hide behind, easy to shelter in and rely on. Even her walking out on us hadn't tarnished that image of her: if anything it had helped, because just when I was hitting my iconoclastic teens she wasn't around any more to be measured against reality and found wanting. Consequently, when I thought of her at all, I saw her from the ten-year-old Felix's perspective, which meant looking up from close to ground level.

Mum was still big, but – like one of those packages sold by weight, not volume – her contents had shifted in transit between the past and the present. Her bulk had a softer edge to it now, and her short-sleeved top showed me that some of the definition had gone from her finely muscled upper arms. It had gone from her face, too, her eyes passing over me once and then twice rather than pinning me to the wall until she was good and done with me.

'Felix,' she said, with a rising inflection, and then again, with slightly more conviction, 'Felix!' She took me in her arms, briefly but with feeling.

'Hello, Mum,' I said. Anything was going to sound banal under the circumstances, so I settled for, 'How's it going?'

'All right,' she said. 'I'm all right. Come on in.'

She led the way into the living room, which in true Walton style opened directly off the street with nothing in the way of a porch or hall. It was a room that exemplified my mother's virtues: four-square, clean, and without a book or an ornament to be seen, apart from her much-loved print of Edward John Poynter's *Faithful Unto Death* – which shows a Roman soldier remaining at his post, nervous but steadfast, as the ashes of Vesuvius rain down around him. The picture has taken on a darker and darker yellow-brown cast over the years, caused by nicotine deposits staining the glass despite regular and vigorous polishing.

There was a single armchair and a narrow two-seater sofa, both in gaudily patterned fabrics, a portable TV about the size of a matchbox with an indoor aerial sitting on top of it, and a coffee table much marked with the whitened rings left by a thousand cups of hot tea – which brought to mind, rather too vividly, the young *loup-garou* on the train. There were no teacups on it now, though: just two bottles of Worthington's pale ale, one empty and one half-full, and a glass with beer froth around the rim.

'Bit early in the day, Mum,' I said, trying to make it sound like a joke.

'Away, away with rum,' my mother said, quoting Mike Harding's mock-temperance song: that was always her answer, whenever anyone commented on her drinking. She's not an alcoholic, not by her own definition: she never lets herself get drunker than the business of the day requires. 'You'll be sticking to tea, then, will you, love?' she added, with a meaningful roll of her eyes.

'I will for now,' I said, hedging my bets.

She went through into the kitchen, and I stayed behind in the living room. Channelling Sherlock Holmes, I looked around for fag ends. But if Mum had started smoking again, she wouldn't need anything as formal as an actual ashtray, and in any case I would have noticed as soon as I walked into the room: because it would have had that smell – somewhere between despair and dysentery – that smoking rooms in old hotels have.

Lots of empty beer bottles on the mantelpiece, though. Putting them there was an atavistic impulse: when I was growing up they'd served the same function as clothes pegs, holding Matt's and my smalls in place while they dried in the warm air coming up from the fire. Now the fire was a log-effect gas burner, and the bottles just looked like old soldiers who know that the ceasefire has sounded and are waiting for the order to stand down.

Mum came back into the room, carrying a mug of milky tea in which a teabag still floated. She'd never really been into the idea that we eat first with our eyes. She handed it to me, then kissed me on the cheek, putting her hands on my shoulders and squeezing tight.

I cast around for something to say, but found nothing. I wasn't even sure if she knew, until she buried her face in my shoulder and let out a single, throat-tearing sob. Mum never cried: not actual tears. Maybe when Matt got his ordination, but tears of pride are different. The world had never wrung one millilitre of tribute out of her in any other way; and even now, her eyes were dry as she raised them to stare into mine. Hollow, troubled, red-rimmed, but dry.

'If it had been you, Felix, I would have understood.'

'Cheers, Mum,' I said.

'I don't mean that I wouldn't have cared, love. But Matty's world is different from yours. It always was.' She shook her head, giving it up. 'I just don't see how this could have happened,' she said mournfully.

'He didn't do it,' I said. 'I can tell you that much.'

Mum flared up, but not against me: against the world that was misjudging her son. 'I bloody well know that!' she said. 'Didn't I raise him? Isn't he mine? Of course he didn't bloody do it!'

'Well, okay then,' I said. 'Just making the point, that's all.'

Mum sat down heavily in the armchair, picked up her glass and took a deep swig of beer, then refilled the glass with what was left in the bottle. I took the sofa, which meant I had to sit on the edge of a cushion, balanced on a single buttock, in order to face her. I put the mug of tea down on the table's bare wood, adding another ring to the many already there. Maybe you could use them to tell its age.

Mum was looking at me with a solemn, musing expression, the heat of her anger gone as quickly as it had come. 'Three years,' she said, softly. 'Three years, Fix.'

'I did call,' I countered, but it was a feeble defence. The last time had been more than a year before, to ask her how she was doing when Matt had told me she was recovering from a chest infection. It had turned out to be low-grade pneumonia, and I'd still found reasons not to come up and visit. Given the distances involved, there *was* no defence. From London to Liverpool is three hours or so with good traffic: in America people drive further than that to pick up a carton of milk.

So I brought her up to speed on my life, going light on the succubi, zombies and were-beasts and heavy on my recent wanderings after Pen kicked me out of her house. I know my audience, you see: Mum favours Matt because he went to God and I went to the devil. So when she asked me if I was seeing anyone, I ducked the whole story of my infatuation with Juliet, and how a demon from Hell had ditched me for a Sapphic fling with a church warden. 'I've been seeing a nurse,' I told her, which was unassailable truth and could be said without blushing.

All of this was really just a way of not talking about Matt, and when I ran out of anecdotes that were fit to print, I found I still wasn't ready to go there.

'You getting out much?' I asked, throwing the ball of procrastination into her court.

Mum shook her head emphatically. 'What for, Fix? I've got everything I need here in this room. I watch the telly, listen to the radio. Put a bet on, when it's the flat season.

You know me and my accumulators. Three cross doubles . . .'

'. . . And a treble,' I finished. 'The mini-Yankee. Yeah, I remember. Still listening to Sing Something Simple?'

'It's not on any more,' she said. 'But there's still Billy Butler on a Saturday.'

Billy Butler, and his Sony bronze award-winning show, *Hold Your Plums*. It used to have Matt and me giggling our heads off when we were kids. Only Scousers could come up with a radio quiz based on a fruit machine, with a robotic voice telling you what was showing on each reel.

'Billy Butler,' I said. 'Christ.' It was the only comment that seemed to fit.

'Oh aye,' Mum agreed. 'I never change, me. I've had enough changes in my life, Fix. I'm happy with what I've got, these days.'

What you've got is nothing, Mum, I thought but didn't say. Everyone you used to know is dead or somewhere else. And you're stuck here in Walton like a fly caught in amber. Although pale ale doesn't quite have that golden-brown lustre to it. It's more the colour of piss.

'Ever see anyone from Arthur Street?' I asked.

This time Mum didn't answer. She looked at me thoughtfully, waiting for more. 'Anyone from the old days, I mean,' I clarified.

Still nothing. She took another long swig from her glass.

'I know a lot of people moved to the Triangle,' I went on. 'After they knocked down—'

'What are you here for, Fix?' Mum asked, putting down her empty glass. 'Really?'

'You mean besides seeing you?'

'That's what I mean, yes.'

'It's about Matt,' I said, bluntly. 'You know who it is he's meant to have attacked?'

'Kenny Seddon.'

'So I was thinking I'd shake the tree a bit. Talk to some people who might know more than I do about what Kenny was up to before—'

'Before someone sliced him up like a bacon joint.'

'Well, essentially. Yeah.'

Mum nodded, straight-faced. 'Go on, then. Who's on your list?'

'Anita and Richie Yeats,' I said. 'And Kenny's brothers, Ronnie and Steve. Do you have any idea where they ended up?'

'The Yeatses are over in Bootle now,' Mum said, counting them off on her fingers. 'That's Eddie and Rita Yeats, I mean – Rita Brydon as was. I haven't seen Anita in donkey's years. Richie was living with them, or so Ernie Hampson said, but I heard they gave him down the banks and showed him the door.'

Her expression told me that something momentous was being left unsaid. 'Why was that, then?' I asked. 'Gave him down the banks for what?'

Mum pursed her lips. 'Well,' she said, 'you know. A grown man, and he's never done a day's bloody work in his life. He's a waster, Fix, and there's nothing down for him. Some people are never going to do any good for themselves if you give them a hundred years. And he's – you know . . .' Mum made the limp-wrist gesture.

'He's gay?' I said blankly.

Mum pursed her lips and nodded.

'You're saying they kicked him out because he's *gay*?'

Mum stood her ground. 'Well, you don't want your son bringing strange men into the house, do you?' she demanded. 'Some of these people—'

'Thanks for the tip, Mum,' I said, cutting her off. And thinking of Juliet I added, 'At least he didn't go outside his own species.'

I think the homophobia must be a generational thing: it's certainly not class or geography, because you can meet the same bullshit in Hampstead just as easily. I remembered now that Richie had made some non-standard life choices even as a kid – he was the only boy in my circle of acquaintances with a skipping rope – but I'd never read anything into that. Maybe someone else had, though: maybe the nickname Dick-Breath was more than just a whimsical *jeu de mots*.

'Now Ronnie Seddon –' another finger went down '– he was selling drugs at the Palm Tree, until he tried to sell them to a couple of plain-clothes coppers, so that was the end of him. He got three years in Walton. Mind you, there's more drugs in there than there is anywhere else, from what I hear, so he's probably happy. Teresa Size's lad, Philip, was saying they smuggle them in over the wall from the cemetery on Hornby Road. They use catapults, he said. Just tie Jiffy bags full of heroin to old batteries and shoot them in with catapults.'

Mum recounted this with relish. Her favourite reading matter had always been true crime, although she preferred a good murder to any amount of aggravated robbery.

'Then there's Steven Seddon,' she said. 'He was at the docks for a while, back when they still had a few ships coming in every now and then. But he gave that up in the end and went to some night-school thing. He's at a law office in the Cunard, now, and he wears a suit. I've seen him waiting for the bus up at the broo, looking like Lord Muck. I wouldn't trust him with a bloody paper clip.'

'Would any of them still drink at the Breeze?' I asked.

Mum made a sour face. 'Richie might, though it's a bloody mystery to me why anyone would go back to that place. Harold Keighley is the most miserable bastard of a landlord I've ever met, God forgive my language. He opens the doors when he puts the towel up, so the place gets as cold as a fridge.'

The description made me grin: I remembered those winter nights when the determination to finish your last drink clashed with the onset of hypothermia. 'Does he still do that, then?' I asked.

'It's hard for a leopard to change its spots, Fix,' she said sententiously. 'And Keighley doesn't even change his bloody underwear more than twice a year.'

Mum got up and went into the kitchen again, coming back with two bottles of pale this time. She opened both with a kitchen tin opener – one of the old kind that have two hooked blades, one large and one small, and look like exotic torture implements. She handed a bottle to me, and I took it because I knew if I refused she'd drink them both herself.

We drank, and reminisced, as evening fell outside. At half past seven there was a pause while Mum watched *Coronation Street* and I made a foray to the off-licence at the top of the street. Then we drank and reminisced some more.

'Mum,' I said, when I judged that she was mellow enough to roll with the impact, 'Matt left home around the same time I did, didn't he?'

Mum nodded. 'Same year,' she confirmed. 'His first parish was in Birmingham. Our Lady of Zion. You went to Oxford in September, and Matty left in December. He gave his first sermon two weeks before Christmas. You remember? We all came up for it.'

'Yeah,' I said. 'I remember. But he was ordained in April. So what was he doing in between times?'

Mum gave me a look that was a couple of centuries too ripe to be merely old-fashioned. 'He was learning to be a priest,' she said. 'He'd been ordained, aye, so he wasn't a deacon any more, but it isn't like an assembly line, Fix. They had all sorts of things he had to do first. Seminars, he called them. A seminar here and a seminar there. All up and down the country, he was, and living out of a suitcase. Except it wasn't a suitcase, it was just a big shapeless bag with two handles that he got from the Army and Navy. Six feet long.' She illustrated with her hands. 'He looked like he was carrying a bloody bazooka, honest to God. If it was nowadays, someone would think he was a terrorist and shoot him.'

That brought her too close to the painful subject of Matt's current situation, so she shied away from it again. 'He was everywhere,' she concluded. 'Running around like a blue-arsed fly.'

'But he was still living at the seminary? Over in Skem?'

'In Upholland? No, after that big – you know, passing-out parade thing, where the bishop put the oil on him, and gave him his Jezebel – they needed his room for someone else. He stayed there until the autumn, when they had the new lads in, then he came back here.'

'Jezebel' was Mum's mispronunciation of chasuble, the sleeveless robe that a priest wears on top of all his other vestments when he does the business at Mass. I was never sure whether it was a joke or an actual mistake: after all, her mangled renderings of song lyrics, including turning Fun Boy Three's 'Our Lips are Sealed' into 'Olives to See You', were legendary.

But what made my ears prick up was the revelation that Matt had come back home in between the seminary and his first ministry. I was already off out in the world by that time, screwing up my degree course, and I don't think I came home once in the first two terms.

'Back to Walton?' I asked, making sure I was getting this straight.

'Back to this house, Fix. Where else was he going to go?'

I nodded, conceding the point. 'So he was around for three months,' I said. 'Back in circulation. Looking up old friends.'

Mum sniffed. 'I don't know about that. He saw some of them, aye, but he wasn't going to walk in the Breeze and stand at the bar with them, was he? It's not that kind of life, when you're a man of the cloth. You've got to stand aloof.'

The conversation veered off in other directions, by virtue of some unspoken agreement that passed between us. Nostalgia and beer are a potent combination in themselves; and when Mum got the photo album out and cracked it open in the middle we had the emotional perfect storm. There we all were: Matt and me in short trousers, Dad all tanned and handsome – 'a dark horse', my grandma used to call him, with mingled disapproval and admiration – and Mum looking like a million dollars.

'Where did it go?' I asked, wonderingly. 'We just—' I couldn't find a word for it, so I pantomimed it instead – holding my hand in front of my face with the fingers pursed together, then opening it wide. 'Where did that come from? One minute we're a family, the next we're . . . in the wind.'

Mum didn't answer. She just turned a few pages in the book back and folded it open at a page we hadn't seen yet. There were three photos on the page: the first, Mum holding a baby, the baby all swathed in pink blankets and pink bonnet and pink everything; the second, the three Castor siblings in school uniforms, wearing the pained grimaces children always put on when they're told to smile; and the third, Katie by herself, aged four, smiling a smile that was altogether more believable – a smile with secret, solemn little-kid thoughts behind it.

I stared at the photos, suddenly sober despite the seven or eight beers I'd downed.

'It took a while,' Mum said, her tone soft. 'It didn't happen all at once.'

17

I didn't leave Nimrod Street until almost ten p.m., by which time I'd drowned that little nugget of cold, hard sobriety in a few more beers and a lot more talk. But the talk was getting harder and harder to sustain, and the question of where I was going to spend the night was getting more and more pressing.

Mum had offered me a bed, which I'd declined with thanks. The impassable ground again: the conversation leading us into the middle of a minefield and leaving us there without a map or a metal detector. She'd asked me about Matt. When had I last seen him and how was he doing? I'd passed the question off with some made-up bit of news about his teaching work, because the truth was that I never asked Matt about his life. I never had asked him, I realised now, since the day when he'd walked out of mine.

I walked back up to County Road and grabbed a cab up to Breeze Lane. I could have walked it, but I wanted to get to the Breeze – my Mum and Dad's old local, ruled over with a rod of rusty iron by the aforementioned Harold Keighley – before the towel went up.

The pub hadn't changed. They'd rebuilt the entire neighbourhood around it, but the Breeze remained its own sad-ass self, like the filament of platinum in that bullshit metaphor of T. S. Eliot's. You dip it into a mixture of oxygen and sulphur dioxide and blam, you've got sulphuric acid – but the platinum stays the same, unaffected by the reactions it catalyses. The metaphor sort of falls apart at that point, though, because the Breeze was never the catalyst for anything apart from a thousand drunken fights about who was looking cross-eyed at our Karen and whose grandad had stolen whose great-uncle's ration book back in the austerity years.

It's a Tetley pub, probably built around 1920, and since the size of the plot gave the architect no room in which to exercise his imagination it's just a big blockhouse coated in rough-cast and painted white. The sign is a little classier, because it's topped with an iron silhouette, painted in bright red, of the liver bird – the mythical short-necked cormorant invented for the purpose by the desperate gofers of the school of heraldry back in the eighteenth century. That was when the city – flush with its winnings from the slave trade – slipped the heralds a backhander and asked them to run up a quick coat of arms.

Call me a sentimentalist, but I've always felt a sort of kinship with that bird. It belongs to no genus, but everyone confidently declares it to be a stork, a pelican, or whatever else they need it to be to fit the theory in hand. Whereas actually it's a sleight of hand, a brazen forgery passed off on man and nature. As a symbol for my home town, it's not bad: everybody thinks they know what Scousers are like, but the closer you look at us, the less neatly the individual details seem to add up.

Inside, the Breeze continued to give that same impression of inelegant confinement. The main room is long and narrow, with the bar running the whole length of it: there's just enough room between the bar and the wall for one row of people standing up and one row sitting down.

When my parents were regulars here, social propriety dictated that the standing drinkers were men: tonight there was a fair mix, but I noticed that there was a heavy age bias, with most of the faces — both at the bar and along the wall — belonging to my mum and dad's generation. The Breeze clearly wasn't managing to sell itself as a happening place for the younger social drinker: no widescreen TV, no games machines, no jukebox even. There was a one-armed bandit sitting in an unfrequented corner, which probably made less income in a month than the bar staff earned from tips, but that was the only concession to the modern era.

I didn't recognise more than half a dozen people, and none of them seemed to recognise me. Life is the best disguise of all, and I'd been through a lot of it since the last time I'd bought a round in this place.

But Harold Keighley hadn't changed a bit. Standing dead centre at the bar, he was pulling a pint of Stingo from a chipped black hand pump with a golden liver bird perched on its apex, expertly tipping the glass to a shallower angle as it filled so that the head would be an even half-inch or so. He'd always been a big man — Hungry Harold, Harold the Barrel — and now he'd filled out to even more heroic proportions: his size, and his fearsome flatulence, were legendary, as was his refusal to treat drinking yourself into oblivion as anything other than a strict business proposition. His face, which I couldn't remember in any other condition than flushed hectic red, was heavy-jowled and pugnacious, topped with a full head of hair the colour of the snow you're not supposed to eat. Mind you, it would probably have been pure white if Harold hadn't been a forty-a-day man: even now, in defiance of the recent ban, he had a fag hanging from the corner of his mouth – inspiring other, similar beacon fires around the room.

He finished pulling the pint, set it down, took the money, gave change. I waited patiently while he dealt with two other customers who were at the bar before me. A younger guy with a nose-stud who was also serving asked me if he could get me anything, but I sent him on his way with a curt shake of the head. Harold had seen me by this time and I waited patiently while he worked his way around to me.

'Matty Castor,' he said, wagging his pudgy finger at me. 'I thought you were a priest now.'

'He is,' I confirmed. 'I'm not. I'm the other one. Felix.'

'The little bugger who used to steal the beer mats.'

'The same. I'm done with them now if you want them back.'

He pursed his lips as though he was actually considering the offer, then made an obscene gesture. 'What can I get you?' he asked.

'Pint of Guinness,' I said, not being a big fan of Tetley beers. While he poured it I took another look around the room. Still just that thin leavening of people I vaguely knew, none of them likely to lead me onwards in the direction I needed to go in, even if they decided to talk to me.

So I went for the big man instead.

'Richie Yeats still drink in here, Harold?' I asked.

The Guinness was on an electric pump, so Harold didn't need to give it much attention as it sluggishly climbed the glass. He looked at me shrewdly. 'Well, now,' he said, with a humourless smile. 'If I had a fiver for every time I got that question . . .'

'Yeah?' I was interested. 'Who else is looking for him, then?'

'Who isn't, these days?' Harold countered. 'That'll be two sixty.'

'And whatever you're having.'

'I'm having rectal surgery. Stick it in the lifeboat.'

He took my money and gave me my change: true to his word, he'd just taken the cost of my pint, refusing the offered drink. Since I mentioned Richie, the temperature had cooled. I fed my change into the RNLI money box, a coin at a time. Harold waited, staring me out.

'What about Anita?' I asked, changing tack. 'Ever see her around?'

To my surprise, Harold's dour face suddenly cracked open in an involuntary smile that had real warmth in it. 'Not in too many years,' he said. 'Light of my life, she was. Even as a kid. She should have gone on the telly or something. A girl like that, her face is her fortune, innit? Her fortune or her falling down, as our Nan used to say.'

That reflection seemed to sour his mood again. He shook his head, his lower lip jutting out like a shelf weighed down with all the world's woes. Down at the other end of the bar some other guy's hand was waving with an empty glass in it. Harold noticed it and turned, starting to head in that direction: I put my own hand out to detain him.

'Could I leave a message for Richie?' I asked.

He stared at me hard, frowning so that his eyes almost disappeared as the topography of his corpulent face shifted seismically. 'Could you what?' he echoed.

'I just want to talk to him,' I said. 'About Anita. She's missing and I'm trying to find her. He knows we used to be friends. If he wants to meet up he can leave a message here. Or he can just call me.' I fished a pen out of some recess of my greatcoat and wrote my mobile number on a beer mat, then held it up for Harold to take. He hesitated for a moment, then nodded brusquely at the counter .top, indicating that I should put the beer mat back where I'd found it.

'If I see him,' he said, 'I'll tell him. If I remember. I'm not saying I'll remember.'

'Thanks.' Harold walked away and I drank the Guinness, which in Liverpool is almost as good as it is in Dublin. Then for the hell of it I went over and fed a few coins into the one-armed bandit. There's something about watching your hard-earned cash disappear very quickly into a machine's impassive maw that encourages philosophical detachment. It's a very pure transaction: almost spiritual. All you're buying is a few seconds' worth of flashing lights, and a near-subliminal flicker of hope.

The towel was up by the time I'd finished that pint, and true to form the doors at either end of the bar were standing open. It doesn't have quite the same impact in summer, but I was done anyway. I left the pub, walked down to Rice Lane and caught yet another cab: this time out to Aintree, where there was a small B&B I remembered. It was called the Orrell Park. It took in a lot of travelling sales reps, and consequently stayed open all hours. They had a room for me at a knock-down price, and it was – just about – worth every penny. It even had a kettle and some sachets of Douwe Egbert's, so I made myself a treacly black coffee and ate a complementary pack of digestive biscuits: not much by way of supper, but I'd make it up with an artery-hardening English breakfast in the morning.

In the meantime I lay on the bed with my shoes off and worked out a plan of campaign for the next day. There were a few other people I could shake down for a possible sighting of Anita or Richie, but they could wait until the afternoon. My morning was going to be devoted to Steven Seddon.

I wondered about Harold Keighley's sudden changes of mood. He definitely hadn't been happy to hear Richie's name, or else to hear that I was looking for him; and he'd said in so many words that I wasn't the only one. Maybe Dick-Breath had landed himself in some kind of trouble and was lying low for reasons of his own, using the Breeze as a *poste restante*. But in any case he was only relevant to me as a possible bridge to Anita, and if Harold was right and she hadn't been seen around in a long while, then I was probably just chasing my own tail to start with.

How in the name of all that's fucked up and untenable had she ended up with Kenny? What tortuous byways of destiny and dumb lucklessness had led her to live with a guy she already knew was a coward, a bully and an emotionally unavailable gobshite?

Nicky had filled in some of the gaps, of course, but it hurt a little to think about that: about the long succession of other men she'd lived with, only to move on once the magic wore off or the hard-core abuse set in. Why had she made so little of her life? Become a casual adjunct to a bunch of losers, one of whom had even given her a kid without that making the slightest difference to his level of commitment? She'd seemed like the best of us, in a lot of ways. The most alive, anyway.

But where was she now?

And assuming I even found her, could she give me any

clue as to why Kenny hated Matt enough to put him in the frame for murder?

I fell asleep still chewing on these unpalatable little nuggets, and as a result I slept very shallowly, coming awake from disconnected dreams and then dozing off again in a cycle that made me feel more tired when I woke the next morning than I had been when I went to bed.

But as sometimes happens when you've been through a night like that, your mind like a computer that's hung in the act of shutting down, you wake up with fragments of the recent past stuck in the forefront of your consciousness. For me, the fragments included Matt's first sermon at Our Lady of Zion. The text was from Numbers 23: 'Let me die the death of the righteous, and let my end be like his.' A pretty downbeat choice for your first Mass at your first ministry, I thought at the time. But I never asked him why, and I realised now what a shitty thing it was I'd done to him. Yeah, I came along to wave the flag and mark the occasion. But Matty was hurting: he'd told me so as clearly as he knew how. And I'd walked away without saying a word.

Later for that. Business is business.

The Liver Building is the iconic face of Liverpool: pure white stone, golden at sunset like an emperor's palace floating on the muddy Mersey, and guarded by those two mythical cormorants with their well-chronicled fondness for honest men and virtuous women. The Cunard is the big ugly bread box right alongside: as squat as a stool and as elegant as the stump of a limb. I worked there myself in the summer before I went off to college, as an office assistant for the Regis Shipping and Forwarding Company. I'd almost died, but that was mainly the systemic shock of having to get up at half past six in the morning and put in a full day's work. I was pretty sure that my destiny lay elsewhere: God couldn't be that cruel.

That was eighteen years ago, but the place hasn't changed much. The war memorial with its winged Victory is still standing in the forecourt. The foyer is as imposing and unwelcoming as ever, with its massive Doric columns designed to put generations of junior clerks firmly in their place. And the elevators still play Dvorak's *Slavonic Dances* with enough crackle and hiss to drown out the music, which makes you wonder if in some secret chamber in the heart of the building they've got an endless supply of identical pre-Dolby eight-track tapes that Mr Cunard boosted from some fire sale in a spirit of waste not, want not.

A single phone call to Nicky from the Orrell Park had established the fact that Steven Seddon, MSSP, worked as a law clerk for Sedgewick & Stacey, a firm of solicitors specialising in contract law, with three partners on permanent retainer to half a dozen Liverpool-based shipping lines. 'Clean, as far as that goes,' Nicky had said. 'No obvious bad smells, anyway. Seddon. Any relation to the late Kenneth Seddon?'

'Brother,' I confirmed.

'He's been there three years and a month. Should have been promoted last year when he got his paralegal diploma, but he squeaked in with the lowest pass grade you can get. It was a skin-of-the-teeth kind of thing, and they decided to bump him a year.'

'You got all that from their website, Nicky?'

'Nope. I'm in their personnel files. It's all up on the office intranet. Restricted log-in, but what's a password between friends? I'm currently one of the senior partners, a Mister John Loose. As in "fast and . . ." Oh, and by the way, guess which demon-haunted estate in South London made the news last night?'

I felt a prickling on my scalp and the back of my neck. 'What happened?' I demanded.

'There was a fight. Couple of gangs met up by prior arrangement and had a bit of an altercation. Nobody dead, but lots of blood spilled. Cops came in to break it up, and here's the bizarre part. The good citizens sided with the gang-bangers. Cops were pelted with all kinds of shit from up on the walkways. Bricks. Bottles. A widescreen TV. It got kind of intense. And while I'm watching this on the nine o'clock news, what do I see but the other bastard walking right past the camera.'

'What other bastard?'

'Good old Tom Gwillam. The Pope's plausibly deniable leg-breaker.'

'So he's still there,' I mused. 'Well, he can't have too many illusions about what's happening now. And maybe he can do some good.'

'What, with the power of prayer?'

'Something like that.' Actually, Gwillam was an exorcist, and a pretty damn powerful one. He got the drop on Juliet once, which was more than I'd ever managed. 'Thanks, Nicky. I owe you, man.'

'Oh, indubitably.'

So here I now was, sitting in Sedgewick & Stacey's reception area, which was about the size of Lime Street station but had considerably more potted palms, waiting for Steve to put in an appearance. He seemed to be in no hurry at all to do that, but I was prepared to be patient. That was my main bargaining chip. I was comfortably dressed in my jeans and greatcoat, and I had a good greasy breakfast under my belt, so I just sat reading the magazines while other clients came and went, and while the receptionist, shooting the occasional frosty glare in my direction, called Steve on the intercom at ten-minute intervals – which I timed by the clock above her desk.

Steve broke before I did, which is where my money would have been if I'd been making book on this. He came out of the inner office after barely an hour, looking harassed and hunted. I knew him at once, even though his complexion had cleared and he didn't have the words LOVE and HATE written on his knuckles in red biro, as he had when I'd seen him last. He'd grown up without filling out, so he was basically just an attenuated version of his childhood self with a line of bum-fluff on his upper lip. He was wearing a suit, and it looked like a pretty good one except that it was brown. I couldn't remember the last time I'd seen a brown suit, but I was nearly certain that Norman Wisdom had been wearing it.

Steve nodded a begrudging acknowledgement to the receptionist to show that he was taking care of this, then crossed to me as I folded my magazine and stood up.

'Hey, Steve,' I said.

'Hey, yourself,' he growled back at me, if you can growl while you're keeping your voice half a hair above a whisper. He gave me a look of the up-and-then-back-down-again variety, his lip curling. 'Christ, it really *is* you, isn't it? Felix bloody Castor! Well, take the bloody hint, okay? I don't want to talk to you, and you shouldn't want to talk to me. You're probably prejudicing that fucker's case just being here.'

'Fucker?' I queried.

'Don't play thick. Your frigging loser of a brother.'

'Wow,' I reflected. 'Free legal advice! Do the partners know you give it out for nothing, Stevie? Or are you planning to hit me with a bill on my way out?'

'I'll hit you with the toe of my frigging boot,' Steve hissed, with another panicky glance towards the receptionist, who was still watching us with undisguised interest. 'Piss off, Castor. I mean it. Do you want me to tell the prosecutors you came here to offer me a bribe?'

'I don't want you to do anything that would niggle at your conscience, Steve,' I said. 'Children and lawyers should get a completely free ride, in my opinion. Karmically, I mean. But then you're not actually a lawyer yet, are you? You're still slogging your way up the ziggurat, and it's got slippery sides. All the more so when you barely scrape a pass in your tests and your kid brother is up Beddie Road doing time for drugs. So I'm hoping we can have a civilised conversation here and not make a scene. Because a scene would be ugly and demeaning and it might mean you miss out on your promotion for the second year running. In fact,' I added, poking him lightly in the stomach, 'if we make it just ugly and demeaning enough, you could be out of a job altogether. What do you think?'

Steve stared at me, nonplussed. 'Fuck you,' he said at last, shaking his head in wonder at my impudence.

'Fuck me,' I agreed. 'But quietly and discreetly, yeah? So as not to wake the neighbours. Sit down and let's talk. Or I will, I promise you, blot your copybook here beyond any chance of unblotting.'

Steve laughed indignantly. 'I'll just have you thrown out.'

'Then I'll go out screaming that you raped my teenaged sister after I refused to sell you any more drugs.' I shot him an affable smile. 'Sit down,' I said again. 'Last time of asking.'

A heroic psychomachia played itself out in his face. To my chagrin, it looked as though he'd decided on the 'publish and be damned' option, but the receptionist, who had left her desk and crossed the room to join us, intervened at the tipping point by pure chance.

'Is everything all right, Mister Seddon?' she asked, with heavy emphasis.

'It's fine, Karen,' Steve said, instinctively shrinking back from the edge of the abyss. 'I might have double-booked an appointment time, but I'm sorting it out. Thanks.'

He stared at her, a stiff smile on his face, until she retreated again, with a begrudging nod. She knew something wasn't kosher, but she couldn't push it any further in the face of Steve's stonewalling. And Steve, as soon as she was out of earshot again, gave up the unequal struggle. He sat down opposite me, giving me a venomous look.

'How long ago did you talk to Kenny?' I asked him, feeling in no mood for small talk.

'You mean before your brother killed him?' Steve shot back, his voice sinking to the lower limit of audibility.

'I just mean how long ago, Steve. Give me straight answers and you'll get me out of your life a lot faster.'

'Months ago. A year, almost. We don't talk.'

'Why is that?'

'Why do you think?' Steve's tone was sharp.

'Because you're trying to become a lawyer, and everyone else in your family is a petty crook with a rap sheet as long as a nun's nightie?'

'There you go.'

'But you knew who Kenny was shacking up with, right? Up until a couple of years back? The big love of his life, until she left him for a builder's merchant with a moped?'

'Anita Yeats.' Steve spat out the name as though it was something poisonous that he'd almost swallowed.

'Exactly. How did that happen, Steve? How did the star-crossed lovers meet up again so far from home?'

'How the fuck should I know, Castor? And why the fuck should I care? Kenny always had a thing about her. I wouldn't have put it past him to go looking for her. Or pay someone else to. He couldn't be made to see sense on that subject. Anita Yeats was a frigging bike, and he talked about her like she was the Blessed Virgin.'

'Couldn't be made to see sense?' I echoed. 'Did you try? Was that something you talked about a lot?'

Steve rolled his eyes, shrugged in exasperation. 'We didn't talk about *anything* a lot!' he said. 'He was two hundred miles away, Castor, and we didn't have a blind bastard thing in common to start with. If we talked once a year, it was all we did.'

'But you had strong opinions about Anita, obviously,' I observed. 'You didn't think your brother should be taking up with her.'

Steve shook his head. 'Not just Kenny,' he said. 'Anyone. Fucking psycho-bitch from Hell! You know what she did to him with that bit of steel. And anyway she wasn't worth picking up off the street. She was a scissor-reflex slut, like all the women in her family. Getting herself knocked up before she was twenty, then carting the kid around with her from pillar to post while she was looking for another shag!'

Steve's face twisted with distaste. I raised my voice as I answered, loud enough for the earwigging receptionist to hear me very clearly from across the room. 'Let him who is without sin cast the first stone, Steve. Sexual morality's a funny thing, when you think about it. One man's meat, kind of thing.'

Steve cringed, hunching his shoulders. 'Keep your frigging voice down,' he whispered hoarsely.

'Then keep it respectful,' I counter-suggested, 'In case you've forgotten, the psycho-bitch from Hell episode was when Anita saved my life from your much more scarily psycho brother. So remove the beam from your own eye first, eh, Steve?' Another thought struck me, so I pushed on, dropping my voice again. The receptionist wasn't even trying to pretend not to eavesdrop now, so I threw her a friendly wave over Steve's head. He started and turned, the hunted expression coming back onto his face. 'Who was Blainey?' I asked. 'The guy she named her kid after, I mean. Did you ever meet him?'

Steve opened his mouth to speak, and judging from his expression it was going to be another mouthful of bile. But our eyes met and he hesitated, then changed gear. 'I saw him a couple of times,' he said. 'He was . . . nobody. Really, nobody. A gobshite from Childwall Valley who was stupid enough to let her bring another man's kid into his house.'

'Nobody?'

'Nobody.'

'Then why do you remember him after sixteen years?'

Steve was silent for a moment. In case he was trying to come up with a lie, I pressed him again. 'Why do you remember him?'

Steve exhaled: a world-weary sigh of resignation.

'Kenny sent me and Ronnie over there to have a look at him,' he said.

'What? Why did he do that?'

'I have no fucking idea. Because he never saw sense where Anita was concerned.'

I turned this fact over in my mind. 'Just to look, or—'

'No. We warned him off. Told him that if he didn't drop Anita, someone with a flick knife and no sense of humour was going to drop him.'

'And did that work?'

'Yeah. She was on her travels again in short order. We did it a couple of times after that, too. In the end she packed her bags and fucked off south. Which was always what she was going to do, but you couldn't tell Kenny that. He thought that if he terrorised enough of her boyfriends, in the end she'd come running back to him because he'd be the only viable option. Dozy fuck.'

Steve looked away towards the windows, where the Mersey flowed by in its sluggish brown majesty. 'Well, it took him sixteen years,' he said bleakly. 'But he got there in the end, didn't he? Got the both of them. Anita and her fucked-up kid, too. Fantastic, eh? A real Hollywood happy ending. Except that Anita still couldn't stand him, really. And her brat thought cutting pieces out of himself was the best game in the fucking world.'

'Pot, meet kettle,' I said.

Steve stared at me, half mystified and half annoyed. 'What?'

'Kenny was a self-harmer, too.'

The annoyance won out. 'No, he bloody wasn't. Kenny cut lots of people in his time, but he never cut himself.'

'I saw his body, Steve,' I pointed out.

'So what?' Steve demanded, unimpressed. 'I'm telling you, Kenny never cut himself. It used to drive him apeshit when the kid did it. He gave him a proper fucking hiding whenever he caught him at it. The last thing he'd do was . . . you're full of shit, Castor!'

His indignation at this slur on Kenny's memory was overriding even his sense of self-preservation. The receptionist was now talking on the phone to someone, casting urgent glances in our direction. I could see that this conversation was going to have to be curtailed.

'Forget it,' I said. 'It doesn't matter. If Kenny found Mark so creepy, why did he let him stay on after Anita bailed?'

'No idea,' Steve said. 'But I can tell you it wasn't for love. What he had going with Anita was fucked up seven ways from Sunday, and we've all suffered for it. But the kid he just despised.'

That blew one theory that had been growing slowly at the back of my mind: that Mark had been Kenny's kid, belatedly acknowledged. It would have made sense in that case for Anita to have come back to Kenny, even if she'd taken her time doing it. But it seemed like that kite wouldn't fly.

I was about to ask Steve to explain the little crack about suffering, but at that moment two building security guards in ever-serviceable black uniforms lumbered into view behind him, separating to approach me from opposite directions. It seemed like I'd worn out my welcome.

I stood, raising my hands in a shrug of acquiescence. Far be it from me to make any trouble. 'Well, it's been a pleasure, Steve,' I said. 'Using the word in the sense of "worth the bus fare into town". Good luck with the law.'

'You can drop dead. You and your bastard brother,' Steve riposted. The word 'brother' almost stuck in his throat, it came out with such a freight of bristling hatred.

'I'll tell him you said hi,' I promised.

The men in black saw me to the door, but with no laying-on of hands, and I walked out into bright sunshine. But after their ninety-three million mile sprint, the dazzling rays faltered in the final straight and didn't seem to reach me. I was like some guy in a bloody Leonard Cohen song.

My mobile buzzed as I walked down towards the Pier Head. I took it out and put it to my ear.

'Hello?'

'Castor.' The voice was instantly recognisable: Dick-Breath sounded like his balls still hadn't dropped.

'Yeah,' I said. 'It's me. Hello, Richie. Thanks for getting in touch.'

'You're welcome. Keighley said you wanted to talk. I want that, too.'

'Great,' I said. 'Do you know where my mum is living now? It's just on the—'

'I can't come to Walton,' Richie said, categorically.

'Why's that, then, Richie?'

'I just can't. I'll tell you when I see you. But choose somewhere off the street, Castor. Somewhere where nobody will see us. And it needs to be out in the open.'

'Why?' I asked again.

'So I can see you coming,' Richie said.

18

The Linacre Lane cemetery in Bootle was looking a lot less overgrown and graffitied than when I'd seen it last. There were fewer used condoms on the ground, too, so someone was clearly making a real effort; but I wasn't here to admire the view.

The 61 bus put me off within sight of the gates, but I walked on by and did a circuit of the place first – both to see if I'd been followed and to think about what I'd already picked up while I'd been here.

Not the jackpot, obviously – that I could only get from Anita herself – but a few little nuggets of possibility. Kenny's obsession with Anita meant that the two of them playing house together two hundred miles from home was a smaller camel to swallow: particularly since Kenny had done his level best to drive Anita away from the 'Pool in the first place. Mind you, I reflected, there wouldn't have been a lot keeping her here: as a single mum in Walton with no man in tow, she would have taken a lot of cheap shots, a lot of innuendo and collateral contempt from the matriarchs of my mum's generation. There would have been no shortage of places where she'd have set tongues wagging and heads shaking: and, little by little, that kind of shit wears you down.

And then there was Steve's obvious hatred of Matt. It had shown in his face, both times he'd been mentioned.

Steve disliked me cordially, that was obvious, and I didn't blame him; but there was some additional weight of animus when he talked or thought about Matt: something that gave his aggression a whole lot more forward momentum. Maybe his mother had been frightened by a rabid priest while he was still in the womb: they say that leaves an impression.

Lastly, there was Richie's paranoia about being seen in public, which I was evidently starting to share. What had he done that had caused him to drop off the map so precipitously? And did it have anything to do with either his missing sister or Kenny Seddon?

Finally, satisfied that nobody was dogging my shadow or shadowing my dog, I turned in at the gates. I'd told Richie exactly where to meet me, and I'd described the spot with enough circumstantial detail so that not even a blind man could have missed it. There was a chestnut tree, for one thing: one of the dozen or so mature trees that were still permitted to stand within the cemetery grounds, even though their roots spread out a long way and put some of the ground off-limits for burials. And there was a headstone a couple of aisles away where a stone angel had been painted by some street artist who for once had some ideas in his head besides writing his own name: painted in gilt and silver and metallic blue, so that she now looked like some cybernetic robot seraph come down from Silicon Heaven, which of course – as even Kryten finally had to acknowledge – doesn't really exist.

Richie was pacing backwards and forwards under the tree, sucking on a fag: it wasn't the first, either, as the dog-ends at his feet testified. He looked up as he saw me coming, took the nearly dead dimp out of his mouth and flicked it into the long grass with evident ill humour.

I watched it smoulder. 'You remember seeing the Smokey the Bear cartoon at school that time?' I reminisced.

'You're late,' Richie said with asperity.

I nodded. 'Which gave you plenty of time to get into position so you could see me coming. Your ground rules, Richie. Now what the fuck is going on?'

He tapped me on the chest with a finger. 'You tell me,' he suggested. 'I'm only here because you asked me to come.'

Unlike Steve, Richie had grown outwards as well as upwards. His voice might still be a choirboy's, but his frame was a full-back's, and he seemed to be on something of a short fuse. He jerked his head to the side suddenly, a nervous gesture that flicked his long blond hair out of his eyes, and an avenue of memories opened up in my mind, so that I could see him doing the same thing a hundred times, in a hundred different places.

'Where's Anita?' I asked him.

'Why?' Richie snapped back.

'Because Matt's in jail.'

This seemed to be news to Richie, and it gave him a moment's pause. He blinked twice, staring at me. 'What for?' he demanded at last.

'Murder. Kenny Seddon's murder. Someone sliced him to ribbons in a parked car, and the police think it was Matt.'

Richie laughed, but it was from incredulity rather than amusement. 'Kenny's dead?'

'Yes.'

'Kenny Seddon is dead?'

'Still yes.'

'And your brother did it?'

'Well, that's where me and the official version part company,' I said. 'I don't think he did. He was in the car with Kenny – they've got his prints on everything up to and including the murder weapon. But he says he didn't kill him, and I believe him.'

Richie shook his head in wonder. I waited for him to say something, but he took out his fags again and lit up first. 'I don't care who did it,' he said, blowing smoke out of his nose. 'I'm just glad the cunt is under the soil. That's the best news I've had all year, Castor. Thanks. Thanks so much.' His voice shook a little.

'You're welcome,' I assured him. 'But at the risk of repeating myself, where's Anita? She was living with Kenny until a couple of years back. She might know who the real killer is.'

Richie held my gaze for a moment, his expression turning into a grimace of remembered pain. Then he looked away, up into the branches above.

'Richie . . .' I said.

'I get it.' He waved me silent. 'You want Nita to get your brother out of the shit by fingering someone else.'

'Well, ideally, yeah. And if she can't do that, then maybe she could give me some leads. Something to go on.'

'I could ask what he's ever done for her,' Richie said, still staring at the sky through the interlacings of the chestnut branches. 'For any of us. But I won't bother, because you already know the answer. Give it up, Castor.'

'Why?'

'Because Anita's dead.'

The words hit my stomach like slingshot stones: or rather, not so much the words as the absolute conviction with which he said them. Here we were, then: at ground zero.

And it looked like I'd come all this way on a fool's errand.

We sat with our backs against the stone, facing towards the cemetery gates because Richie still wasn't sure that some unspecified enemy wasn't going to try to sneak up on him while we talked. Consequently his gaze wasn't on mine and I could watch him while he talked; look for any chink in that heavy armour of certainty.

'She was living in Derby when he found her,' he said, his beautiful voice elegaically lowered. From his tone, you knew that as far as he was concerned, that was where Anita's death had begun. 'He paid some private-detective bloke to chase her down, with some bullshit cover story about how they were separated but he wanted to give it another chance, and then he turned up on her doorstep one morning.'

He stared into the past, saw nothing there to give him any comfort. 'She was in a bad way,' he said, flatly. 'She had a bit of a habit. Heroin, I mean. And sometimes . . . You know how it is. Some times are worse than other times. When Kenny showed up, she'd just been thrown out of a job and she didn't have any money coming in. He practically said he'd keep her fucking supplied. Anything to get her to go back and live with him.

'I told her. I frigging told her. You know yourself what he's like. You know he can't control himself. Even as a kid he was fucking dangerous, so what do you expect him to be like as a man? People like Kenny Seddon don't change. He'll hurt you, Nita. He'll hurt you worse than . . . worse than you've ever been hurt in your life.'

It was as though he were having the argument with her now. As though she was standing there on the grass in front of us, visible only to him, talking only to him. The cigarette between his fingers burned down unnoticed, growing a longer and longer beard of ash.

'She didn't care,' he said, shaking his head. 'She knew I was right, but it didn't make any difference. "I don't deserve any better," she said. "Look at me, Richie. Look at how I'm living. He'll put a roof over our heads. He'll be a father to Mark. Fuck knows, somebody's got to be. I can't go on like this." And all the rest of it. Like it was a rational decision. Like what she was doing made sense. But it didn't, Castor. And I'll tell you why.

'She knew. She went back knowing what he was going to do to her. In fact, that was *why* she went back. Because Kenny could be relied on to treat her the way she thought she deserved.'

The cigarette burned his fingers. He gave a convulsive start, let it drop and put the tip of his finger in his mouth, tears gathering in his eyes. I didn't think it was because of the blister.

'How can you be so sure, Richie?' I asked gently. 'What makes you think she's dead?'

He shot me an impatient look, as if it was a stupid question that didn't deserve an answer. 'Because she moved a hundred times in ten years,' he said, examining the damaged finger irritably, 'and we never once lost touch.

Now she disappears without a trace. No, Castor. It doesn't work like that, not between us. If she was still alive, she'd have called me. She always called me. And she would have taken Mark with her when she left, like she did every other time.'

'Unless she thought Kenny was doing a good job of being a dad,' I suggested.

Richie swore caustically. 'If that was meant to be funny,' he said, 'I'm not laughing. He was as good a dad as he was a human being, Castor. You can't bring out what isn't there in the first place. I saw him with Mark, and he never even tried to pretend he gave a fuck.'

'There was another man,' I said, changing tack. 'A builder's merchant or something, from what I heard. Did Kenny find out that she was seeing him? Do you think he was jealous?'

'Roman,' Richie said.

'Roman what?'

'That was his name. And yeah, maybe . . . that could have been what happened. I don't know.' He gave a weary, barely perceptible shrug. 'It was a game they played,' he said glumly. 'Nita found guys to sleep with, and Kenny beat her up. They both knew the rules. But . . .'

'But?'

'But Roman wanted her to leave with him. Set up somewhere else. See, normally she picked guys who were cynical enough to just use her and then get out when things got complicated. But this time she made a mistake. Roman seemed to really care about her.'

'What was he like?' I asked. 'Did you ever meet him?'

'Only the once.' Richie considered. 'I was up there for

the weekend and we slipped out for a curry behind Kenny's back. He was . . . good-looking, I have to admit. Sort of Mediterranean looks. Open shirt, lots of bling, leather jacket with the sleeves rolled up. You know the sort of thing. He didn't really push my buttons, but I could see where he'd push Nita's.'

'Did he have a piercing?' I asked. 'Over his right eye?'

Richie looked at me in mild surprise. 'Yeah,' he said after a moment or two. 'He did. Why? Do you know him?'

'No,' I said. 'Not to talk to, anyway. But I'm starting to feel like I didn't know Anita very well, either. Richie, is there some connection between this and you living like a submarine? Who are you hiding from?'

I wasn't expecting the reaction I got from that question. The corners of Richie's mouth quirked up and he smiled: a smile that most reasonable people would have wanted to back away from.

'From the Seddons,' he said. 'Because I hit the bastards back, where it hurt them. And I'm going to keep on hitting them back until there's nothing left of them but fucking greasy stains. If your brother took Kenny out, then it was the best day's work he ever did in his God-bothering life — and if it was someone else, then whoever he is, he's got my blessing. I love him. I take him to my bosom. I would have done it myself if I had the bottle, but I don't. I couldn't kill someone. So I got Ronnie the best way I could.'

Somewhere in my overstretched cerebellum, the other shoe dropped.

'You grassed Ronnie up?'

'Oh yeah.' Richie nodded emphatically. 'Just had to get the timing right. He always did the Red Pepper on a

Friday night, so I placed a call to the Greater Merseyside drug squad and told them exactly where and when to flash the bacon.' He smiled even wider: he was evidently enjoying the memory. 'And I'm going to get Steve, too,' he said in a more meditative tone. 'I've been following him for months and I finally struck gold. The stupid bastard is seeing prozzies down the Dock Road and I'm getting pictures of him doing it. When I've got a nice thick photo album's worth, I'm going to send it in to his boss. Should fuck him over nicely, don't you think?'

I nodded, because there was no way of disagreeing. 'You blame them all, then?' I said. 'For – whatever happened to Anita?'

'They hounded her from pillar to post,' he said, grinding out the discarded dog-end with his heel as though it were a Seddon he'd inadvertently missed. 'They wouldn't let her rest. And then when they'd hounded her all the way back to that bastard down in Walworth, they walked away and let him kill her. Yes, Castor. I blame them all. I blame a lot of people. Don't get me started.'

I was prepared to take that advice, but there was one more thing I needed to know. Well, two things, now that I thought about it.

'Richie,' I said. 'Don't take this the wrong way or anything, but . . . it wasn't you, was it? With the razor? You didn't go down to the Smoke on a day return and – you know – do a bit more pruning?'

Richie gave a sardonic snort. 'I wish,' he said. 'But I already told you, I'm no good at that stuff. I must be a throwback or something, mustn't I? A Walton kid with no taste for aggro.'

He sounded like he meant it; and the accusation hadn't got the smallest response beyond that weary, self-hating derision. 'Okay,' I said, feeling obscurely relieved. 'Then answer me this and I'm out of your hair. Can you think of any reason why Kenny would have had a grudge against Matt? A big enough grudge that he'd frame him for murder? Because that was the last thing he did, as he was drowning in his own blood. And it seems like a strange . . .'

I tailed off into silence, because Richie was looking at me with enormous, astonished eyes.

'Why Kenny would hate your brother?' he echoed.

'Yeah.'

'Castor, who do you think you're talking to? And what fucking tree did you just fall out of?' Richie's tone was pained and angry.

'Okay,' I said, cautiously. 'I'm assuming those were rhetorical questions. You think there's something obvious I'm missing, then? Something you know, and you think I should know, too?'

He stood up. 'Here's the thing,' he said. 'It wasn't me in that car. I already told you that. But if it had been, and if I was someone else instead of me – a macho psycho killer kind of someone, in the real Walton style – then I wouldn't have stopped at Kenny.'

He brushed the grass off his jacket, wincing as the movement chafed his blistered finger.

'I'd have killed your brother, too,' he said.

Then he seemed to recollect where he was; or perhaps he read the expression on my face. Either way, his gaze fell from my face to the name on the headstone we'd been leaning against, and he had the decency to look abashed.

'Okay,' he muttered. 'Shitty thing to say. I'm sorry. It's just – fucking priests, you know? Is there one of them out there who can—? Never mind. Forget it. There are degrees, aren't there? Maybe he said a few Hail Marys and squared himself with God. But he'll never square himself with me.'

He walked away before I could ask him what he meant by that. I was left staring at the gravestone, still feeling the ghost-echo of it against my back. Feeling as though her name had been burned on my skin, through the cool stone and through the fabric of my coat.

CATHERINE PAULINE CASTOR
BELOVED DAUGHTER AND SISTER

Just those words, and the two dates: the two dates so very close together.

My phone, which I'd set to vibrate, squirmed like a rat in my pocket, startling me out of a grim reverie. I put it to my ear.

'Hello?'

'Castor.' I couldn't place the voice at first, but the slight muffling effect caused by a fat lip gave me the clue I needed. 'Gwillam. How's life?'

He didn't bother to answer. 'You were right,' was all he said. 'Get back here as soon as you can, because we need to talk.'

The mix of old tragedies and current irritations made me curt. 'Do we? About what?'

'About the Salisbury. Come and save these people, Castor, because they're in Hell. And I'm not strong enough to get them out.'

19

The towers were silent, and most of the lights were out. Here and there a single window blazed yellow-white, the random elevations and distances making the Salisbury seem like a constellation that nobody had got around to naming yet. I watched some of those windows for a fair old while, but nothing moved behind them.

Nothing was moving where I was, either. I'd taken a taxi from Kings Cross, but told the driver to stop on the overpass where Kenny had been attacked, now open to traffic again but not so busy at this time of night that we'd be in anyone's way. I'd thought about calling in on Matt on the way, but I didn't know how to frame the question I wanted to ask him. If I was wrong, it was the sort of thing that could wreck a sturdier relationship than ours.

So here I was: the Lone Ranger riding to the rescue with no six-guns. All I had was another piece of the puzzle, and the sour knowledge growing inside me that the price for anything better was going to be higher than the one that Faust paid.

With the taxi driver's suspicious gaze on me every step of the way, I got out of the cab and walked over to the edge of the parapet, staring out towards the Salisbury. I didn't bother with the whistle because I really didn't need it: I just focused my concentration on my death-sense, closing down my eyes and ears the better to see and hear what was in front of me.

It was seething. The miasma hadn't widened, but it had deepened: it was an indelible skein of screaming wrongness impaled and spread out across that sector of the skyline. It hung in front of me like mouldering curtains, so vividly present that I felt I could reach out and touch it: part the veil and look into some other place entirely.

A penny for the peep-show.

'Are we going anywhere, mate?' the cabbie asked from behind me. Even on the meter, he clearly didn't like his time being wasted. Which was a pity, because I would have been happy to draw this out a lot longer.

But there was nothing else I could do from a mile away, and it was more than time that was being wasted. I got back into the cab.

'New Kent Road,' I said. 'The Salisbury Estate.'

We pulled back into the traffic, and I thought about what I had to do. Promises to break. Innocent people to lie to. Stupid, blind risks to take while I pretended that I knew what I was doing. Just another day at the office, really. Maybe I should have worked harder at giving the children's-party entertaining a fair trial.

It took five or six minutes to get to the Salisbury, the air seeming to thicken and congeal around me with every yard we travelled. I paid off the cabbie and walked up the steps to the concrete apron, where I saw with little surprise a small posse of Gwillam's merry men and un-men waiting to meet me. The flat-faced man – Feld – was there, but I didn't know the others. There was a short swag-bellied man in a shabby suit who looked like he might be someone's fat, jolly uncle, although the Father Christmas effect was slightly spoiled by a horrendous scar that ran diagonally down his face in a bend sinister of rucked and hardened flesh, and a hard case who was dressed entirely in black: ready for night ops, and maybe trying just a bit too hard. He had impressive muscles, though: but then, being around born-again Gwillam's menagerie would obviously leave an ordinary baseline human feeling like he had something to live up to. Poor sod was probably at the gym all the hours God sent.

'Mister Castor,' said the man in black. 'I'm Eddings, and this –' pointing to the fat man '– is Speight. He'll brief you as we walk.' He didn't bother to introduce Feld: perhaps he knew that we'd already met.

He turned and led the way across the concrete. Speight fell in beside me as I followed, and Feld brought up the rear. Nobody else was in sight, and the silence was more profound than ever. It wasn't just that there was no noise from the towers nearby: the voices of the city itself, the noise of the traffic on the road only a few yards behind us, the rumble of trains and shouts of convivial drunks, were stilled as we walked forward. The curtains: we'd passed through them, and they'd fallen closed behind us.

'Last night was very bad,' the little man, Speight, was saying in a cultured voice with a slight Welsh lilt to it. 'There were fights, last night.' He pointed. 'The police were called, but the fight spread to the walkways. A lot of people got hurt, some of them very badly. Even the ambulance crews, when they tried to treat the injured, were attacked.'

'Tonight's an improvement, then,' I said, looking up at the hulking, menacing shapes of the towers: dark giants with asymmetrical eyes.

Speight looked at me, as if he suspected me of trying to make a joke. 'No,' he said, lingering on the syllable. 'Tonight is worse.'

Gwillam was waiting for us at the foot of Weston Block, with a Bible in his hands and another small gaggle of multi-purpose zealots clustered around him. He watched us come, and Speight said nothing more: obviously it was the boss's prerogative to fill me in on the rest of the big picture.

Gwillam nodded to me, and I nodded back. There didn't seem to be much point in small talk, given that I'd laid his face open the last time we'd met. He seemed to have recovered from that, although I couldn't help wondering if he'd bounced back so easily from the more spiritual pummelling that Juliet had laid on him.

'It's a demon,' he said flatly.

I shrugged. Presumably he hadn't dragged me all this way to tell me what I already knew.

'It seems to have an affinity for wounds, as you said,' Gwillam went on. 'And its presence twists people's perceptions – subtly, at first, but with more and more pervasive effect. I've got my people on two-hour shifts, rotating. But we're barely containing it.'

'You seem to be doing a good job,' I said. I gestured at the stillness all around us. 'No riots. No things going bump in the night.'

'That doesn't mean it isn't trying,' said a woman standing to Gwillam's right. She was tall and well built, attractive in a Junoesque way. I registered that first: then the ponytail, and then the cat's cradle of string that was wound around her hands. It was only then that I realised I already knew her. When I'd seen her standing out on the walkway it had been dark, and before that, when she'd been with Gwillam, I'd mistaken the tightly looped string on her hands for bandages. In fact it must be the way she focused her power. She was an exorcist, like me, and like Gwillam. So I turned to her, if only for a fresh perspective and an excuse not to look at Gwillam's sour face any more.

'Go on,' I said.

She looked to Gwillam for permission and he gave it with a resigned wave of the hand.

'We tried a straight exorcism,' she said. 'But it fights back. It tries to take you onto its own ground.' Thinking about my own ham-fisted efforts at the hospital, and the black pit where I'd briefly faced this thing, I knew exactly what she meant. I nodded and she went on, her clipped, emotionless tones making a strange contrast with the horrors she was describing. 'Peyer went in first, and then – he tried to put his own eyes out. He succeeded with one, but Feld managed to stop him before he got to the other. After that we used strength of numbers: one exorcist doing the binding, two or three others watching over him, weaving stay-nots around him so the thing can't get close.'

She held up her hands as if I could read their failure in the complexity of the woven threads that covered them.

'It doesn't work,' she said flatly. 'Because its focus isn't really this place. It's more – like it—'

'Like it lives in the wounds,' I finished.

She nodded. 'And most of the people on the estate have got broken flesh of some kind by now. So it's all around us. In a hundred or a thousand different places. You drive it out of one vessel and it goes. It retreats. Then it flows back as soon as you look away. We've been here all night, and the best we can say is that the thing is focused on us, so it's not making any mischief anywhere else. But we can't keep this up for ever. And if anything it seems to be getting stronger.'

That wasn't surprising at all. If wounds were its joy and its sustenance, and if there were a thousand wounded people crammed into these few hundred square metres of space, then the demon's cup must surely be running over. And if every man, woman or child who got hurt, who got cut, gave it a new anchor and a new home, then its growth could become something truly exponential and unstoppable.

'So we feel we need a fresh approach,' Gwillam summed up tersely, giving me a cold, expectant look. 'And since you knew most of this before we did, we hoped you might be able to advise us on where we go from here.'

'Sorry to disappoint you, father,' I said, 'but you've got further than I have. When I met it, I was lucky to get out with both balls and a soul.'

Out of the corner of the eye I saw the woman's shoulders sag. Gwillam shook his head. 'Then you've had a wasted journey,' he said. 'And I'm sorry to have taken up your time. If you'll excuse us, we'll return to our labours, however futile they may ultimately turn out to be.'

'There is one other thing we could try, though,' I said. He was already turning his back on me, but he stopped and waited.

'The boy,' I said. 'Bic.'

'William Daniels,' Gwillam translated.

'Exactly. You thought he had Jesus as his co-pilot.'

'Castor, I've already admitted that I was mistaken about what was happening here.'

'But you thought that for a reason, right?' Gwillam stared at me, waiting for me to go on. Everyone else had their gaze on me, too, and I could feel the quickening of interest behind every pair of weary eyes: they made such a lovely audience I would have loved to take them home with me. If home was Guantánamo Bay. 'He was the first,' I said, impatiently. 'The first by a long way, I'm guessing. This thing found him long before it did anything to anyone else. He's a sensitive: he's got some sort of gift that lets him pick up what you're thinking and feeling. Most exorcists have got a touch of it, too, but he's got more than most. He's like a radio satellite pointing into inner space. And he picked up the wound demon.'

'Is that why it came?' the little man, Speight, demanded in his lisping voice.

'No,' I said, shaking my head. 'It came because of another boy. Mark Blainey, who died here a year ago. He was a self-harmer. He found wounds, or the inflicting of wounds – I don't know, exciting, I guess. Appealing. He thought about them a lot. He obsessed on them. He cut himself in a lot of different ways, with different kinds of objects. And somehow, somewhere along the way, this thing noticed him. It came looking for him. I heard it speak his name, when I met it in that place where it lives. It came looking for Mark, but it stayed because it found Bic. And now it's expanded its friendship group. That's what I think happened, anyway.'

Gwillam considered, and all eyes now shifted to him because he was the authority, the giver of truth. That's the trouble with the Church: it's a top-down hierarchy where everyone does what they're told by the guy on the next rung up. Which would be fine, I suppose, if it was me on the top rung instead of God.

'We learned about Mark Blainey in our researches here,' Gwillam conceded. 'We thought him an early symptom.'

'So did I, at first,' I agreed. 'But a nurse at the Royal London put me straight on that one. He's not a symptom, Gwillam. His death sticks out like a bishop in a brothel, saving your presence. No puncture wounds involved: no blades, no points or edges. He just jumped right off the walkway. So it's a fair bet that this demon wasn't what drove him to his death. He didn't die from it: he brought it, and then died of something else.'

And I probably know what the something else was, I added inside my own head. *He may square himself with God, but he'll never square himself with me*, Richie had said. No, I reckoned Matt was going to be in trouble on the God front, too: there was no getting away from sin on this scale.

'So you think if we attempt an exorcism on William Daniels—' Gwillam began.

'No,' I cut in impatiently. 'I already tried that. That might have worked back when he was the only one affected, but it's not going to work any more. Like you said, the thing has got its hooks into too many people now. It can just shift its ground and come back at you from a different angle.'

'Then what?' Gwillam asked impatiently.

So I told him what I had in mind.

I hadn't expected the next part to be easy, but even so I'd underestimated Gwillam's sheer, unremitting stubbornness in the face of something he didn't trust and couldn't control.

He was appalled at what I was planning to do, and he dug his heels in fast and hard. He wanted names and addresses, just for starters. He also wanted to take charge of the operation and leave me here as a hostage with his people to ensure the cooperation of the other parties I wanted to involve. And he wanted to keep his options wide open with regard to other sanctions – up to and including exorcising or otherwise destroying any non-humans who ended up playing a part in the operation.

I told him, in a certain amount of detail, exactly what positions he might use when he fucked himself.

We argued it backwards and forwards for half an hour before finally reaching an impasse. Gwillam had the entire place sewn up, with at least one of his people on every walkway, and he flat-out refused to let me take Bic off the estate even if his parents consented – unless he got to come along in force and run the show. I told him that couldn't work, and that he was condemning the residents of the Salisbury to the death of a thousand cuts, and he said – in effect – that their suffering was part of God's great plan.

I gave up in the end and left them to it. At least they didn't stop me from going up to the eighth floor of Weston Block to look in on Bic and his family, which might have been interesting because he had serious muscle and I was in a black enough mood to have pushed it. But as it was I walked on across the forecourt and in through the double doors while Gwillam was still deep in murmured confab with his minions.

But the lifts were out, so I went around to the external staircase and started my trek into the sky, not looking round in case I locked eyes with Gwillam and he called me back. But while I was trudging up the stairs I heard hurried footsteps clattering behind me. I turned and waited, so that at least I'd be meeting whoever it was head-on: in this place, it was best to take nothing for granted.

It was the tall woman with the cat's cradles wound around her hands.

'Father Gwillam changed his mind,' she said, simply, stopping three steps below me. I noticed, impressed, that she wasn't out of breath after her sprint up the stairs. A childhood infatuation with Ellen Ripley stirred in the depths of my hindbrain and reminded me of the space where once it had sat enthroned in my libido.

'About what?' I asked.

'About the boy. He said if you let one of us come with you, to make sure nothing goes wrong, you can do it.'

'I already told you—' I began. But she lifted a school-marmish finger to shut me up.

'Double blind. Whoever goes with you doesn't get to know the address, and you do whatever you need to do to make sure they don't get a clear look at the route.' She looked at me expectantly. 'We're meeting you halfway, Castor. It's up to you to figure it out now. One of us has to come, but it can be on your terms. Okay?'

'I'll think about it,' I said, but it was only for form's sake. I wasn't going to get a better offer, and we didn't have any other choices left. Rather than let her see how emphatically and irrevocably up against the wall I felt, I turned and started walking again.

She fell in behind me, keeping a respectful three paces' distance until we got to the eighth floor.

'I don't need an escort,' I said over my shoulder.

'No? Still get it for free, do you?'

It wasn't the kind of comeback I expected from a woman who was big in the Church – even if we were talking about the Church's black-ops division. Then again, Sue Book had been a verger when I'd first met her and now she was in a more than civil partnership with a demon. You never can tell with these mission dolls.

'I'm celibate,' I said shortly. 'Only the pure in heart can seek the Holy Grail.'

Walking past Kenny's door, which was now nailed shut and sporting police-incident tape, made my skin tingle as though I was showering in battery acid. I was nearly certain it wasn't psychosomatic, although by now I had a vivid enough sense of the horrors that must have been enacted behind that door that I didn't have to go reaching for supernatural explanations. Did the wound demon have a physical locus after all? Would an exorcism undertaken in Mark Blainey's bedroom have a better chance of succeeding?

Another missed opportunity, I was willing to bet; like Bic. Although with Bic we still had one final chance to make good. If 'good' was the right word.

Jean Daniels answered to my knock, looking like a woman who was self-medicating in order to perform open-heart surgery on her own ventricles, and had been called away in the middle of the procedure. She stared at me with hollow eyes, seeming to take several seconds to register who I was.

'Mister Castor,' she mumbled. 'You're back. I called you a few times, and left messages, but you didn't . . .'

'I haven't been home, Jean,' I said, 'so I wouldn't have got them. I'm really sorry. Can we come in?'

She nodded brusquely, stepping aside to let me in: then she realised I wasn't alone.

'This is—' I said, pointing towards the cat's-cradle woman. 'Well, actually, who the hell *are* you?'

'Trudie Pax,' she said, holding out her hand to Jean. 'I'm with Father Gwillam.'

Jean took a step back, as though Trudie's hand was contaminated in some way. 'We've already told Father Gwillam that we've got nothing more to say to him,' she said coldly.

'And we've accepted that,' Trudie said sweetly. 'In any case, Mrs Daniels, we don't believe any more that your son has been touched by God. The way things have gone over the past few days has proved us wrong. But Castor has thought of something that might improve William's condition, and we're here to help in any way we can.'

Tom had come from somewhere to stand behind his wife, so he was hearing this too. He looked almost as wrecked as Jean, and pugnacious with it, but Jean had locked onto the salient point in Trudie's little recitation. Her face as she looked at me lit up with something like hope.

'You can help him?' she said.

'Let me look at him,' I said, by way of a non-answer.

Jean led us through, not to the living room where I'd been before but to a bedroom that led off the hall to the left. Walking through the doorway gave me a premonitory shudder, but it was because of the room itself: because the floor plan was the same as that of Kenny's flat, and Bic's room occupied the identical space in the layout to Mark's.

Lost boys, sharing the same existential billet. But Bic, at least, was loved and looked for: and he wouldn't fall off the edge of the world the way that Mark had done. Not if there was anything I could do to stop it.

He was lying on his bed, on top of the covers, in the Spiderman PJs again. A rumpled blanket lying beside him had presumably been laid over him at some previous point, but I could see why it hadn't stayed there. He was twitching and shaking, his head and limbs moving constantly, and his wide-open eyes darted from side to side, scanning from one corner of the room to another as though he was trying to locate the source of some troubling sound.

He was muttering under his breath, and when I sat down at the foot of the bed I was close enough to hear some of the words.

'Flowering like flowers like it's there because I lost I lost I lost it until I nailed it down. Saves my life every hour, every day. Sewing. Sewing myself with a needle, stitching up the holes but you only see the scars and you don't hear when all these mouths all these red mouths talk talk talk'

I felt his forehead, but as Jean had said the last time I'd been here there was no fever. Bic's skin was cold to the touch.

'Has he been back to the hospital?' I asked.

Tom looked at Jean and Jean, after a moment's pause and a hunted look at Trudie, shook her head. 'What would they do at the hospital?' she demanded. 'Put him on drugs? Cut him open? The only thing that calms him down a bit is me holding his hand and talking to him. It . . . brings him back, for a few minutes at a time. We told the school he had gastric flu, so they wouldn't send anyone round. I'm scared of them taking him. They might think he wasn't right in the head. Might take him somewhere and not let him out again.' She raised a warning finger in Trudie's face. 'You get anyone in here,' she said, 'and I'll split you.'

Trudie ignored the finger, took the threat without flinching. 'We all want what's best for William,' she said.

'Billy,' Jean muttered caustically, turning back to me. 'His name is Billy. So what's the plan, Mister Castor? What have you thought of?'

So it was time to bite the bullet: time to put up or shut up. And like the cowardly bastard that I am, I lied.

'There's another doctor,' I said. 'Only a little way from here. He's kind of an expert in stuff like this, and he owes me a favour.'

Tom and Jean looked doubtful.

'An expert?' Tom repeated. 'In . . . what Billy's got? In this possession stuff?'

I nodded.

'What's his name?' Jean demanded.

'You won't have heard of him,' I assured her, but she continued to stare at me, half-hopeful and half-perturbed but with the balance definitely tilting.

'Ditko,' I said. 'Doctor Rafael Ditko.'

20

When we reported back to Gwillam, he was still pretty sour about the whole deal.

'You realise,' he warned me, 'that in trying to control this menace you run the very real risk of unleashing a greater one?'

'Yeah,' I agreed. 'I know that. And if you can come up with an alternative plan that doesn't involve Asmodeus, then say so. Otherwise, I'm going ahead.'

The priest gave me a hard, pained look. 'This situation . . .' he said, and then seemed to run out of words.

'You were happy with the situation when Rafi was at the Stanger,' I reminded him.

'Yes. Because we were able to monitor him for ourselves. Now you have him somewhere else, and we've only got your word for it that the protections you have in place are adequate to hold Asmodeus in check.'

'Yes.'

Gwillam bridled. 'Yes what?'

'Yes, you've only got my word for it. And that's all you're going to get. Now, are we doing this or not?'

He stared me down for another few seconds, then gave a curt nod and walked away.

But it was a while before we hit the road, even then. Getting myself and Trudie Pax to Imelda's without letting the Anathemata woman see the route we took was fiddly in the extreme, and wasted the best part of an hour. I had to get Gwillam to commandeer a car, then I had to refuse it because while we were waiting for it to arrive I realised that it would be too easy for him to slip some kind of a locator into it. Hell, he didn't even have to: these days a mobile phone would do, assuming Trudie was carrying one.

So I went with Plan B, which involved bringing Nicky into the mix. He's a paranoiac's paranoiac, and I'd already seen how deeply the idea of shafting Gwillam appealed to him. When I called him and asked him how we should handle this, he only pondered for a couple of minutes.

'I'm sending a friend,' he said. 'Be ready. His name's Cheadle, and he does good work. I mean, he's scarily focused. He'll need paying, though.'

'How much?' I asked, briefly thrown as I tried to imagine what 'scarily focused' would mean to a mind like Nicky's. The money didn't matter – Gwillam was going to have to foot the bill because I was a pocketful of small change away from being dead broke – but I wanted to know what to ask for.

'A couple of ton, let's say. And a contribution to the widows and orphans fund.'

'The *what*?'

'It's a gratuity, Castor. You keep the man sweet, he doesn't make any widows or orphans.'

I passed the word along the line, and Gwillam gave his sour, begrudging assent. 'You already have my word,' he told me coldly. 'That ought to be enough for you, Castor. I'm a man of God, and a man of conscience.'

'Sure,' I agreed. 'And this would be what they call a

leap of faith on my part, right? Much valued in religious circles, but elsewhere, poking the bear trap with a stick before you put your foot in it is generally preferred.'

Cheadle drove up ten minutes later in a red Bedford van with DRAINS AND SEWAGE emblazoned on the side in eye-hurting neon yellow. He didn't park out on the street: he drove the van up the shallow steps onto the forecourt and slowed to a halt right in front of us, jumping rather than stepping down from the driver's seat and sizing us up with bullet-grey eyes.

He was a small but very solid man with the kind of natural surliness that dries up small talk over a range of ten metres. He wore shapeless clothes that looked as though they might be made of moleskin, with a few moles still along for the ride. His hair was white, with a nicotine smear of light brown at the front. He carried a small rucksack in his hand by one strap, the other dangling broken.

'Who's Castor?' he said, looking around.

I put up my hand like a schoolboy.

'Right,' he said. 'You ride in the front. I've got the route worked out already, so you don't have to say anything. Where's the other one?'

'That's me,' said Trudie Pax.

'Then get your kit off,' said Cheadle, dumping the rucksack down on the ground, 'and put this lot on.'

Her eyes slightly wider than before, Trudie picked up the bag and examined the contents.

'It's new,' Cheadle assured her. 'I picked it up from the cash-and-carry on the way here. Extra large. If it's too big, it doesn't matter. You can just roll the sleeves and the legs up.'

'I'll need somewhere private to change,' Trudie said.

'No, you won't,' Cheadle demurred. 'You'll do it right here. You can keep your underwear on, and it's nothing I haven't seen before. But no pockets, no hoods, no buttons or zips. That's the deal, love. Take it or leave it.'

Gwillam nodded and Trudie stripped. You can say what you like about religious fanatics, but they show a dedication to the cause that's nothing short of admirable. Some of them have very shapely bottoms, too, I couldn't help but notice.

The contents of the rucksack turned out to be a baggy sky-blue tracksuit with a Nike swoosh on the front that was fooling nobody. Sweatshop chic. Trudie put it on without complaint, and then reached for one of her boots.

'No shoes, neither,' said Cheadle. 'It's a warm night, love. You're not going to catch cold. Now let's have a look at you.'

From a side pocket of the rucksack he took a hand-held electronic reader — to my untrained eye, it looked identical to the ones that the security guys at airports use — and played it over Trudie from head to foot while she stood there with her arms folded, staring at the ground. Her face was carefully blank: if she was feeling humiliated and resentful because of all of this, she wasn't showing it.

'Okay, said Cheadle, 'you're clean. Let's go.'

'I need to bring the boy down,' I told him. 'Bic. Did Nicky explain about that part?'

Cheadle shrugged, already turning his back on me. 'I didn't ask him to. He told me there was three of you, and to bring something for the kid to lie on. All I needed to know. You do what you have to do, I'll get our lady friend set up in the back. Come on, love.'

He led Trudie round to the back of the van and threw the doors open. I went upstairs and collected Bic from his parents.

'You'll keep him safe,' Jean said as I hefted him in my arms – her tone halfway between a plea and a warning.

'Scout's honour,' I said. 'Trust me, Jean. I'm not letting anyone hurt him.' Or at least, it would be over my dead body – and probably a couple of others.

Bic weighed next to nothing: I could probably have carried him one-handed. But my ribs were reminding me of the hard time they'd had of it lately, and I had to pause and get my breath back when I got to the bottom of the eight flights and came out onto the concrete apron. Cheadle was waiting in the van, Gwillam's stooges standing in a cluster looking tough because there was fuck-all else they could do.

Cheadle opened the back door of the van for me. I stopped dead, staring inside. Trudie was cross-legged on the floor, her arms handcuffed behind her back. He'd put something over her head that looked very like a bondage rig: a helmet with a rubber face mask attached, the whole thing secured under her chin and around her neck with two thick straps. There were no eyeholes in the mask.

'Can she breathe?' I asked.

'Course she can breathe,' Cheadle snapped. 'She just can't effing see, is all. The kid goes there.'

He pointed to a bare and maculate mattress thrown down diagonally across the floor of the van. I leaned forward and laid Bic down on it carefully. He was still twitching and muttering, but he never even came close to waking. I wished I'd remembered to bring a blanket.

Cheadle was right, the night was warm enough to make blankets unnecessary: it would just have made this feel less like a kidnapping.

Cheadle slammed the door shut and I went round to the passenger side.

'Trudie is in your safe keeping, Castor,' Gwillam reminded me. 'No less than the boy.'

I nodded, acknowledging the point. 'We should be back inside of an hour,' I said. 'One way or another. Be ready for us. I want to get this over with. And Gwillam – if we're followed, we stop. No second chances.'

I climbed into the passenger seat and there was a solid metallic chunking sound as Cheadle reached down to lock the doors from his side.

'You got a mobile on you?' he asked.

'Yeah,' I admitted.

'Turn it off. They might not know your number, but if they do you might just as well be leaving a trail of breadcrumbs. Better put it in there, for the duration.' He pointed down to a box at my feet. I'd taken it to be a toolbox but when I opened it, it proved to have thicker sides than that, the interior space small and cluttered. Cluttered with telecommunications gear, mainly: esoteric stuff whose purposes I didn't know and didn't care to guess: there were even some naked circuit boards.

'Right,' said Cheadle, 'we're off.'

He backed down the steps again, bumpity bumpity bump, and reversed out onto the road.

'Is Trudie going to be okay back there?' I asked.

He threw the briefest of glances towards the back of the van. 'Should be,' he said. 'So long as she hadn't got any inner-ear problems.' There was an observation window which presumably opened into the van's rear space, but when I went to open it Cheadle put his hand on mine and shook his head.

'No no no. The magical mystery tour is waiting to take her away. This is a full professional service, satisfaction guaranteed, and we put the blanket over the top of the cage so the little birdie can sleep. You got my money?'

I handed over the notes that Gwillam had magicked up from somewhere. Cheadle fanned them out and nodded, apparently satisfied.

We drove around South London for forty minutes, taking every alley and back crack that Cheadle could find. He turned the radio on, but only a dull bass-line thudding came out of it.

'Your speakers are bust,' I said.

'Nope,' Cheadle replied. 'They work all right – but they're mounted in the back of the van. If her indoors is trying to figure out where we're going by the sounds of the city, she'll have her work cut out for her. As for you and me, well, we'll have to make do with witty repartee, won't we?'

That turned out to mean dead silence. I sat back and watched him work.

It wasn't just a case of randomly tacking across the city. He was checking for tails, too, his eyes on the rear-view mirror for so much of the time that I was really afraid we were going to hit something. At one point he stopped, took his own phone out of the reinforced box, turned it on and made a call. He didn't speak but he listened for half a minute, then turned it off and replaced it.

'You do this sort of thing a lot?' I asked, as we drove down Camberwell Church Street.

Cheadle made a tutting sound. 'I do what I'm paid to do.'

'Nicky said you'd worked for him before,' I observed.

'I don't know any Nicky,' Cheadle said shortly, in a tone that made it clear that further questions would not be welcomed.

We rolled up to Imelda's place just as the moon rose, so I guess I'd put the time at about one in the morning. Cheadle waited at the back of the van, leaning against the doors, while I went around the back and up the stairs to talk to Imelda.

She wouldn't have been happy to see me even if my knocking hadn't got her out of bed. She wrapped her tent-like floral-patterned nightgown around her and stared me down with a face like a volley of small-arms fire.

'We had this conversation, Castor,' she growled.

'We did,' I admitted. 'But the situation has changed, Imelda. A kid's life is at stake. You have to let me do this.'

It was – I admit it – a cheap shot. But it was the obvious cheap shot, and I'm way too cheap not to take it when it offers. Imelda is a mother herself, and Lisa is the one thing in her life that she can't be hard-bitten and cynical about.

So I told her about Bic, and I let her make the call. That's how big a bastard I am.

Five minutes later she was unlocking Rafi's door, having previously removed the wards from it. Trudie was with us: Cheadle had freed her hands, but she still wore the helmet and mask. Rafi stared at us in blank amazement as we trooped into the room: me first, with Bic in my arms: then Cheadle, steering Trudie by her shoulders; and Imelda last of all, her expression somewhere close to hangdog.

More explanations, while Trudie sat like a slightly kinky version of Blind Justice on a chair in a corner of the room, and Bic lay moaning and murmuring on the couch. Rafi was unhappy, and scared. Since he'd moved in here, he'd got used to being the only inhabitant of his own brain, and I was proposing to wake up the sleeping sub-letter with a vengeance.

'Is there no other way of doing this?' he asked.

'None that I can think of,' I said. 'But believe me, Rafi, I'm open to suggestions.'

Rafi looked to Imelda in mute appeal, and Imelda shook her head: the rock, crying out *no hiding place*. 'If you're asking me if this is safe,' she said sternly, 'then, honey, I'm going to have to tell you I don't know. Castor and me have been up to the job so far, more or less – kept that nasty little thing under his rock most of the time. But this is different. We're waking him up and we're letting him off the leash. Whether we can put him down again afterwards is a blue-breezing blind guess, and anyone who'd tell you any different would be lying.'

'But it's not just the two of us this time,' I pointed out.

Imelda looked at Trudie, who was missing all the finer points here because of the BDSM harness.

'Can you let her out of that thing now?' Imelda asked Cheadle.

'No,' Cheadle answered shortly. 'But you can. I don't mind what you do here in this room, so long as she's all wrapped up in the ribbons and bows again when we come to leave. I'll be waiting at the bottom of the stairs.

And you can tell madam that if she comes down them with her eyes open, I'll bounce five pounds of loose change off the back of her neck. She might survive the experience, but she won't appreciate it.'

He left without further ceremony. Imelda helped me to undo the straps and we removed the mask from Trudie's flushed, sweating face. 'Thank God!' she said. 'I thought I was going to suffocate in—' She broke off, staring hard at Rafi. After a moment or two, she crossed herself: four short, decisive jabs of her right hand, which she then clenched into a fist.

'The abomination,' she said.

'I go by Rafi,' Rafi answered bleakly.

Trudie nodded. 'I know. You're only the vessel. I've heard of you, of course. We have . . . briefing materials on you. At one time there was talk of killing you, but the prevailing opinion in the society was that Asmodeus would survive, and then he'd be free to choose another vessel. So we left you as you were.'

In the charged silence that followed this pronouncement, she looked from face to face.

'Okay,' she said. 'That was tactless, right? I'm sorry. I'll shut up until I'm spoken to.'

'We're about to wake – the abomination,' I told her. 'And we want to make sure we can keep him contained. Not to mention putting him back to sleep again afterwards. Any ideas?'

'Intravenous silver oxide,' she said, without a moment's hesitation.

I patted my coat pockets theatrically, searched a couple randomly and shrugged, coming up empty.

'Well, you did insist I change out of my regular clothes,' Trudie said, in a slightly truculent tone. 'Wards, then. Lots of them. On the doors and on the walls and probably on his flesh, too.'

'Wards keep him down if he *starts* from down,' Imelda objected. 'They're not going to slow him much once he's up and running. He's too old and he's too sly. Let you nail a thousand signs to him, he's still going to find a way to slip in between them and come for you.'

'A pentagram, then,' Trudie said.

We all stared at her.

'You can draw a pentagram?' I demanded.

She seemed surprised at my surprise. 'Of course.'

'With all the whistles and bells?'

She nodded. 'Yes. Why not?'

'You've had a slightly more catholic education than I would have expected,' I said. 'Small c.'

'We use whatever methods work.' Trudie's tone was cold, as though I'd accused her of sleeping with the enemy. 'We're soldiers, Castor, not pastors or contemplatives. We've got a different brief.'

'Evidently.' I looked at Imelda, who nodded curtly, and Rafi, who gave a resigned and helpless shrug.

'Black magic is how I got into this fucking mess in the first place,' he said, with a touch of bitterness. 'Don't ask me for an opinion.' He paused, swallowed, shrugged again. 'I don't want the kid to die any more than you do. If this is what it takes, then go for it. But if Asmodeus rips your throats out, try not to bleed on my Kerouacs.'

'A magic circle it is, then. Let's go.'

Imelda went and got some chalk while Rafi, Trudie and

I moved the furniture and rolled the carpets back. Bic roused a little when we rolled the couch to the wall, staring at us with slightly more focused eyes.

'The red sea,' he said, more or less distinctly. 'Blood is salt water. That's all.'

'Lisa is asleep upstairs,' Imelda reminded us as she came back in with the chalk. 'Let's do this quietly.'

'We can do the invocation quietly,' Trudie said. 'But we can't be sure that we can control everything the demon does once he rises.'

Imelda closed the door, firmly. 'Thank you for the reminder,' she said, shooting me a look that would have knocked me back ten feet or so if I hadn't already been up against the wall. The room was feeling a little crowded now, since we couldn't walk in the cleared space at the centre where Trudie was about to draw the circle, and the margins of the room were full of displaced furniture.

'I'm going to use the Baphomet sigil, inscribed with the ordinals of Leviathan,' Trudie told us as she started to sketch in the first line. 'Stanislas de Guaita, not LaVey's Hell's Kitchen Baphomet. Mister Ditko, you'd better be inside the circle before I close it.'

'What about Bic?' I asked her. She looked at me, thinking it through.

'Outside,' she said at last. 'If we frame the conjuration right, Asmodeus won't need to cross the circle to touch the boy on the psychic level. And this way there are four of us in total, which is a strong number. Should I perform the conjuration, Mister Castor, or would you prefer to do that yourself? You know this demon better than I do.'

'I'd like to see you work,' I said, which fell squarely

into the 'truth as far as it goes' category. I was curious as to how she'd approach this – and I also wanted to keep my own powder dry in case Asmodeus cut up rough somewhere down the line. My chest was still weak from my injuries, and this was going to be the kind of balancing act I wouldn't normally attempt even when I was at full strength. If I'd had a single other option left in the world, I wouldn't have been trying it.

We placed Bic at the southernmost point of the pentacle – Trudie complaining once again that I'd made her come without her kit so she couldn't check the alignment with a compass – and took our own places more or less at the other three cardinal points, with Trudie as east because this was a Satanic rite and the east is Satan's appointed sphere. Rafi stepped into the circle and sat cross-legged in the middle. 'I'm going to get chalk all over my arse,' he complained. It was probably meant as a joke, but none of us were in the mood for laughing.

Trudie unwound the string from her hands, flexed her fingers, and started to weave a new cat's cradle. She chanted a rhyme at the same time, but it wasn't anything that a practising Satanist – or a practising Christian, for that matter – would have expected. It was a playground rhyme, starting with the familiar sequence 'Apple, peach, pear, plum,' but mostly muttered so fast and so low in her throat that it couldn't be followed.

I caught a whiff of a sour, slightly unnerving smell – like the curdled tang of formic acid when you burn an ant with a magnifying glass. In the centre of the circle, Rafi shuddered suddenly, his shoulders tensed.

'Johnny broke a bottle,' Trudie chanted, 'and blamed

it on me. I told ma, ma told pa—' Her fingers flickered in and out between the strings like the shuttles of a tiny loom. The pattern emerged, one line at a time.

The air in the room seemed to thicken. A cat yowled in the alley behind us and Rafi moaned, both at the same time. It was probably pure coincidence, but it felt as though the power that Trudie was putting out in Rafi's direction was hitting random targets on the same vector.

Her movements quickened, reached a crescendo. She held up her two hands, joined by the cat's cradle, then tugged twice and the string magically fell free, dangling from the index finger of her right hand while her left described an arabesque in the tainted air.

Rafi sagged and then stiffened, his limbs shifting suddenly into a new configuration as his sleeping passenger woke and stretched. I watched the demon surface within the man's flesh. From one point of view, nothing much actually changed: it was more like one of those *trompe l'oeil* drawings where the same sketched outline, seen from two different angles, can be either a woman with a parasol or a charging rhino. The same thing had happened here: Rafi didn't look any different, but he had turned into something else.

I was trying to stay calm and detached, but powerful emotions flooded through me: indignation, that my friend should have to endure this; repugnance at having to wake this thing again against all my instincts and Imelda's arguments; and, bubbling under, the sickening sense of guilt that every contact with Asmodeus brought me – because if I'd been a better exorcist, he wouldn't even have been here.

'Who calls so loud?' the demon asked mildly, raising his head – *Rafi*'s head – and twisting it around to an unnatural angle so that he could stare directly at Trudie. His voice was razor blades shaving your mind too close. 'Come a little closer, girl. Let me look at you.'

'Asmodeus,' I said, from his right-hand side. 'You offered me a deal, the last time we spoke.'

'I'll get to you, Felix,' Asmodeus growled, 'when I'm good and ready. But let me taste the Christian soldiers first, for reasons of decorum. Too much to hope that you've brought either one along as a sacrifice, I suppose?'

'I adjure you to keep in your place,' Trudie said, trying hard not to flinch as Asmodeus leaned forward the better to examine her. 'And – and to make no move without our hest, in plain words stated. *Qui tacet non consentiri videtur.*'

Rafi's handsome face distorted suddenly, the lower jaw sagging like wax to reveal a gaping, shapeless mouth with too many teeth. Trudie's shoulders jerked and her hands came up reflexively for a moment, before she got control of herself and lowered them again.

Asmodeus inhaled deeply. 'Mmmm,' he rumbled appreciatively. 'Scrubbed so clean it doesn't even smell like meat. Pissed yourself just a little, though, didn't you, sweetheart? You were almost sure your little circle would hold, but there's always that little niggling doubt, isn't there? Suppose God is too busy watching the sparrows fall in the market place. Snap. Crunch. Where's little Trudie?'

'You won't be harming anyone in this house,' the Ice-Maker said from directly behind him, her voice cold and hard.

Asmodeus snarled – a long, rumbling sound like distant thunder. He didn't look at Imelda, any more than he'd looked at me; but then, we were known quantities. He'd gravitated towards Trudie because it's in his nature to test out all the variables before he moves. He lowered his head, Rafi's joints making audible clicks and cracks as Asmodeus reshaped his fleshly tabernacle more to his liking.

'No,' he agreed. 'Not yet awhile. You're as safe as if God himself had gathered you into His embrace, my little doves. And Castor – Castor has even less to worry about. Like he said, we've got a deal. Even the meanest little lick-spittle in Hell will tell you that Asmodeus keeps his word.'

Finally his head swivelled round to bring me into his field of vision. 'How did it go again, Felix?'

Meeting that pitch-black gaze was one of the hardest things I've ever done, but there was no way I was going to give him the satisfaction of blinking or looking away. 'You said if I gave you a taste of the thing that's haunting the Salisbury, you'd tell me how to fight it,' I said.

Asmodeus nodded, scratching absently at his chin – at Rafi's chin – and leaving blood-red runnels in his wake – because his fingernails had extended into two-inch talons. 'That's what I said,' he agreed. 'So. Is it Christmas?'

I nodded towards Bic, who was curled up in a foetal position at the pentacle's nadir. Ever since Asmodeus had made his eerie appearance the boy had fallen still, all his mumblings and muscular tics abruptly stopped. He was like a statue now: a study for the starring role in a *pietà*.

'There,' I said.

'That little morsel?' Asmodeus snickered nastily. 'I need enough to get the taste of it on my tongue, Castor.

You want to take advantage of my judgement; my fine discrimination. I can't make up my mind on the first bite, can I?'

'The demon at the Salisbury touched this boy first,' I said, cutting through the bullshit. 'And it put its hand more heavily on him than on anyone else. Trust me, there's enough there for you to work with. What I need from you is a promise – a binding promise – that the boy won't be harmed.'

'Ah.' The demon's gaze flicked back to me, an ironic smile tweaking the corners of his lips. 'We might have a problem there.'

'Oh yes?'

'Oh yes indeed. A *binding* promise? What in all Creation could bind me against my will?'

'Then the deal,' I said, climbing to my feet, 'is off.' I unshipped my whistle and put it to my lips, sounding a chord that Asmodeus would easily recognise: the same tune I always played when my goal was to push him back down into the depths and give Rafi a little respite: a little time alone inside his own head.

'No.' Asmodeus and Trudie Pax said the word at the same time. I watched him and I put out a warning hand to tell Trudie to keep out of this. She was here because Gwillam wouldn't have let me take Bic without her, but that was as far as it went – and it didn't give her a voice in the negotiations.

I lowered the whistle. 'Go on,' I said.

The demon bared his teeth in what could equally well have been a grin or a threat display. 'I have to admit,' he said, 'that my indifference was feigned. I want this.

It's been a while since I tasted another demon's substance. A pleasure too long denied. So I'm inclined to . . . unbend a little to make it happen.'

He paused, staring at me through narrowed eyes. I waited him out.

'Your circle,' he said, 'already binds me in certain ways. If I add the sigils of my own name – my *true* name – to those already present, then your hold on me is that much stronger. You could cripple me if I broke my word to you. If you're strong enough, you'd even have a shot at destroying me.'

'Nice,' I said. 'Except that I've only got your word for it what your true name is, and I can't read your symbols. You could write George W. Bush down there and I wouldn't know any better, would I?'

'The law of analogues—' Trudie Pax began.

'Trudie,' I snapped, 'I swear if you open your mouth again I'll put you outside the door until we're finished.'

She gave me a long, narrow-eyed stare, but she fell silent.

'The lady is, however, entirely right,' Asmodeus said. 'A false name would make your circle convulse and the space within it rupture. We'd all suffer – and I, being inside it, would suffer most of all. You'd know whatever I wrote was truth because I wouldn't be screaming.'

I shook my head. 'I'm not into all this black-magic gubbins,' I said, 'and I'm not taking your word for anything. Try again.'

We locked stares for a moment longer.

'I'll set it to music for you,' Asmodeus snarled.

'Done,' I said at once. Because that was what I'd been hoping for all along.

'Close your eyes,' Asmodeus instructed me. 'And cover your ears. They may bleed slightly, but that can't be helped.'

I put my hands to my ears but kept my eyes open: you can say what you like about my table manners and my love of my fellow man, but Mrs Castor didn't raise any stupid children.

Asmodeus gestured, and a complicated sequence of notes came into my mind from nowhere. I knew, without needing to be told, what it was: it was a portion of his essence – the part of him that could be broken down into sound, and made accessible to my death-sense. He was giving me the wherewithal to destroy him: the magic bullet. A dizzy sense of triumph filled me, and I found it hard to keep my poker face intact. When this was over, I would have most of what I needed to set Rafi free from the burden he'd been carrying for the past three years. I could finally nail Asmodeus to the wall and let my friend walk away clean.

I lowered my hands. My ears were filled with clamour and roaring as though someone had just used my brain as the clapper of a bell. 'Okay,' I said, unable to hear the sound of my own voice, 'this is how it plays. Anything inside that boy that *isn't* boy, you can feed on. Whatever piece of the demon is gripping his soul. Take it out of him, and do whatever the hell you like with it. So long as no harm comes to him in the process, and nothing is left inside of him at the end that isn't human. Nothing of you, and nothing of this other entity. Give me a yes or a no, Asmodeus. Not an inch or an ounce of this is negotiable.'

The demon's lips moved – or rather the man's lips moved

and the demon spoke through them. I couldn't hear the word, but I could read it: and a nod is a nod in any language.

Asmodeus crawled spider-like to the southern tip of the pentagram, where he stared down at Bic with feral delight. Slowly he leaned forward as far as he could, lowering his upper body on jackknifed arms and craning his neck back until the point of his jaw touched the ground a scant inch from Bic's face. The boy seemed asleep, his eyes closed, his body absolutely still and his face perfectly inexpressive.

Asmodeus spoke another syllable – again, I could only see his lips move, not hear the sound – and something rose up from Bic's slumped form like steam from a kettle.

You must have seen a cat with a mouse. Well, if the cat and the mouse were both nine-tenths invisible, and if they didn't move, then that was a little like what we saw: the thing that rose from Bic met another thing that was exhaled in a malevolent hiss from between Asmodeus's clenched teeth, and the air roiled and rocked at their inter-penetration. But it wasn't a battle, because there was no point at which Asmodeus was moved to more than token effort. The thing that was inside Bic, which was a limb of the greater thing that hung over the Salisbury, might be fighting for its life insofar as it had one: Asmodeus was playing, and drawing out the pleasure.

Then finally, after what might have been the better part of a minute, the demon drew in a breath both long and deep, his eyes almost closing, and he tilted his head, first to the left, then to the right, his teeth still bared in a terrible rictus.

He held the pose long enough for the ringing in my ears to die down, and the air in the room, which had seemed to chill precipitately, came slowly back to normal. The goose bumps that had prickled our flesh lay down again, and the cat out in the alley – or perhaps another cat – made a miauling sound that was almost like the cry of a human baby. Bic still hadn't moved in all this time.

'Are you done?' Imelda demanded of Asmodeus, her voice thick with disgust.

'Oh lady,' the demon murmured, 'I am done, and I am satisfied. You cannot know how long it's been since I enjoyed so rich a meal. Small, undeniably, but choice. Very choice.'

'Then give me the goods, you evil bastard, and let's get this over with,' I said.

Asmodeus straightened as slowly as he'd bowed, and then he massaged his right shoulder as though ironing out a cramp. 'The goods,' he repeated softly. 'Oh yes, Castor. I have what you need. I've tasted the part, and so I know the whole. I can give you a nostrum so potent that this new-dropped little runt that dares to call itself a demon will melt away under your ministrations like water drops on a hot iron skillet.'

He held my gaze.

'But you have to say please,' he announced, in a tone that was openly mocking.

'Don't piss me off,' I warned him grimly. 'I've got your number.'

'Because I gave it to you,' Asmodeus agreed. 'But I still feel entitled to a touch of respect, because without me what are you? A dumbstruck cunt-whisker trapped on stage without anything to play for an encore.'

'I can still play *your* exit music,' I reminded him softly, and my whistle was in my hand again.

'No,' Asmodeus said. 'You can't. Not yet. Because if you do that now, you won't have what you came for. Ask me for the ammunition, Castor. You have the tune that means me: ask me for the tune that means this other one.'

'Give me the tune,' I asked him.

'Please.'

'Give it to me, please.'

'Inscribe it in my mind,' Asmodeus coached.

'Inscribe it in my mind.'

'So deeply that it may not be forgotten.'

'What?'

'Say it!'

I swallowed. 'So deeply that it may not be forgotten.'

'It's yours,' Asmodeus whispered, smiling a smile so wide that it almost cracked Rafi's face in half. And just like before, the notes were driven into my brain like tent spikes into frozen ground. Harder this time, and further in, so that the pain made me gasp and stiffen.

And I saw what Asmodeus was doing just a second too late for it to make the slightest bit of difference.

'No!' I screamed.

'Too late,' the demon chided me. 'I have to take your first answer.'

I took a step forward, my arm shooting out by some stupid, gobshite reflex. Trudie Pax tackled me hard from the side and pulled me back before I could step across the circle and into the demon's hands.

'No!' I said again, shaking my head violently as I choked the word out. I was trying to remember: but Asmodeus was writing the new tune – the exorcism that would destroy the Salisbury demon – in the exact same space within my mind where he'd written the one that was his own: over-writing one sequence of notes with another. He'd given me the means to rip him out of Rafi root and branch: and then he'd taken it away again as easily as he'd given it.

'You bastard,' I moaned. 'You cheating, conniving bastard!'

Asmodeus actually laughed. 'I played by your rules, Castor,' he said, shaking his head as he settled back on his haunches again. 'It's not my fault if you don't think things through. Hey, be grateful you get out of this still sane. I could have filled your whole head with that fucking music and left you drooling.'

He licked his lips, savouring the last vestiges of his unholy meal. His gaze clouded.

'But then you wouldn't have got the joke,' he said reflectively. 'And that would have taken away a lot of the point.'

21

It was more than an hour and a half later when we got back to the Salisbury. It had taken a long time to play Asmodeus back down into Rafi's hindbrain: he was disposed to be frisky, and I wasn't exactly on top of the situation. My head was throbbing from having the demon's ectoplasmic fingers poked into it, and I was shaking with anger that I couldn't use and couldn't swallow.

'You should probably take a little holiday when all this is over, Castor,' Asmodeus leered as I played. 'Maybe shoot off to the Caribbean or somewhere. Get yourself drunk, get yourself laid, see if it improves your mood.'

I ignored the cheap jibes and kept banking up the music in front of him in a hot, futile rage, while Imelda sat cross-legged across from me, her head bowed, doing an interpretive dance of a refrigerator. Between the ice and the fire, the demon laughed and took his ease, whistling out of key with my lead-sap lullaby.

This wasn't an exorcism, it was just a soporific: the same tune I'd been playing for Rafi ever since he'd caught his spiritually transmitted disease three years before. It wasn't the tune I wanted to be playing – but then, that tune had been stolen from me.

I'd have to be content with cleaning out the Augean shit-hole over at the Salisbury. That at least I could do now. And Bic was stirring in his sleep towards normal wakefulness, his face calm, his chest rising and falling evenly. Everything had worked out fine, really – except that Asmodeus had found a way to stick a poker up my arse even when I was facing him full-on.

Gradually, step by step, we heaped up chains around him and sent him back down into the oubliette of Rafi's soul. He went smiling, enjoying his joke, but he went. I took the whistle from my lips, flexed my stiff fingers, and listened to the silence that was descending on the room.

'Where am I?' Bic demanded groggily, sitting up. 'Where's Mum?'

'You're with friends,' I assured him, surprised by my own cracked voice. 'Imelda, thanks for everything. I owe you, and I'll find a way to pay you back.'

She didn't move, but her head came up slowly and she stared at me.

'You let yourselves out,' she said stonily, not acknowledging the thanks. 'I'm staying here until I'm sure.'

'He's asleep,' Rafi said, sounding even more wrecked than I felt. 'I'd feel him if he was still awake.'

'He fooled us once,' Imelda reminded him. 'When he kept a little piece of himself inside your hand. There's nothing to stop him doing the same thing again, so I'm not taking anything on trust here.'

She walked with us to the door. Trudie made to take Bic's hand but I got there first and handed her the helmet instead. 'Sorry,' I said. 'Rules are rules.'

She took it, giving me a slightly hurt frown, and slid it over her head again without a word.

Imelda confronted me squarely. 'When you're done tonight,' she said, 'you come back and take your friend out of here. I've got nothing against Rafael, and Pamela is as sweet a child as ever I saw, but I got my own child to think about, too. Enough is enough, Castor. This is your notice to quit.'

'Could you give me a week?' I asked her. I just didn't feel like I could deal with this right now, on top of everything else. 'A week or a fortnight, to scout out another place? Seriously, Imelda, I don't know if I can find anywhere at this kind of notice. And you know what will happen if—'

She cut me off coldly and bluntly, swiping her hand horizontally between us in a *no pasaran* gesture. 'It's your problem,' she said. 'It's not mine. Not after tonight.'

I nodded, giving up the point. She went down to tell Cheadle we were through while I trussed Trudie up like a BDSM turkey again and Bic watched me with big, bemused eyes.

'It'll all make sense when we get you home,' I promised him. And then, as he opened his mouth to ask a question, I silenced him with a cowardly 'Your mum will explain.'

Cheadle appeared at my elbow. 'All done?' he asked cheerfully. 'Right, let's get off, then. I've got another job on.'

I almost asked him what it was, and whether he took everything as completely in his stride as he had this scary, weird circus; but I knew I wouldn't get any kind of an answer I could actually use.

We led Trudie down the stairs between us, Imelda following with Bic. He got to sit up front this time, a blanket of Imelda's draped over his shoulders, but Trudie was once again locked in the back of the van after Cheadle had checked the adequacy of her restraints.

'Soon be done,' he said, slamming the doors on her. This seemed to be addressed to Bic, who nodded silently. He'd barely spoken a dozen words since he'd woken up, but it wasn't because he was groggy or disoriented. On the contrary, he seemed entirely alert and even thoughtful: but whatever was in his thoughts he didn't seem to want to share.

When we got to Walworth Road and saw the orange glow colouring the night sky ahead of us, I realised that the night was far from over. It was many hours past sunset, and many months before Bonfire Night, so there was no good explanation for that redecoration of the heavens.

'Someone's having a fry-up,' Cheadle remarked dryly.

Someone was. A few blocks further on we came to a gap between buildings where some old shops had been levelled, and we could see the Salisbury a scant mile away. One of the towers was burning, flame pouring out of the windows on the top three storeys.

'It's not Weston,' I said to Bic. 'It's too far over.'

'And anyway, it's not . . .' The boy faltered, but he ran out of words. He showed me his hand instead, and I nodded. No wounds involved. The demon loved wounds: it had no interest in fire. So the fire was just a by-product of something else.

At the Salisbury there were police cars and fire engines parked three-deep on the road and a crowd of uniformed constables hid the front steps like a flock of crows that had all descended at once on some particularly tasty bit of road-kill. Cheadle swore when he saw them. Carefully and slowly, giving a copper in the road a smile and a respectful nod, he wove his way through the thicket of paddy wagons and kept on going.

'Let us out here,' I said.

Cheadle scowled and shook his head. 'We're parking around the corner,' he muttered. 'In Balfour Street. Use your loaf, eh? If they see what we've got in the back of the van, we're none of us going anywhere besides a holding cell tonight.'

He was right, of course: the combination of Trudie in her bondage rig and Bic in his pyjamas would be enough to make even the most laissez-faire of plods reach for his handcuffs.

We took the next left and pulled in to the kerb. Then I followed Cheadle around to the back of the van and – as soon as he'd unlocked the doors – untied Trudie for the last time that night.

'I'm sorry you had to go through this,' I said.

'I didn't have to go through it,' she said, rubbing her wrists. 'Not if you'd taken my word in the first place.' Our eyes met for a moment, and there was something in hers that looked like reproach. 'What is it you've got against us, Castor? Our intel on you says you were raised Catholic yourself.'

'It's not Catholics I've got a problem with,' I said. 'It's paramilitaries.'

'You can drop the *para*. This is a real war. And you know what's at stake better than anyone.'

'Nothing is at stake.' My voice sounded harsh even to me, but then it had been a long night. 'Not in the way you mean it. *Loup-garous*, ghosts, zombies . . . Most of what I deal with as an exorcist is just human souls in different flavours. The demons are different, but they're not an army. So you're not at war. Unless every farmer who picks up a shotgun and stomps off towards the henhouse because he's heard squawks and flutters in the middle of the night is at war.'

Trudie looked past me, out through the open doors of the van towards the burning tower. The taste of smoke was in the air and it hurt a little to breathe. She didn't need to speak to make her point. Somehow, I felt like I did.

'Yeah,' I said. 'I'll give you the demons. Like I said, they're different. But that's the point, isn't it? You people treat the dead – all the dead – as the enemy. I may be an exorcist but at least I've got a bit more discrimination than a hand grenade lobbed into a crowded room.'

Trudie seemed disposed to carry on the argument, and maybe ramp it up a few notches, but Cheadle was tapping his feet and the night was on fire.

'Skip it,' I suggested. 'We can have the big political debate some time when London isn't burning.'

'Castor—'

But I was already stepping down out of the van. 'Come on,' I said to Bic, 'let's get you home. Mister Cheadle, it's been a pleasure to watch you work.'

'Thanks.' Cheadle gave me a nod that conveyed the thinnest possible sliver of civility as he climbed back into the driver's seat. 'You know where to find me if you need me. Prices as per scale. Unsociable hours a bloody speciality.'

Trudie barely had time to jump clear: Cheadle drove away with a squeal of tyres, braking sharply after ten yards so that momentum would slam the tailgate closed for him. Then he put the van into gear again and disappeared into the night at a speed you seldom see clocked in the centre of London.

I led Bic around to the main road and the steps up to

the estate's front entrance. Trudie fell in beside us, but she didn't try to open up the conversation again.

Before we got to the steps, a constable stopped us with an upraised hand. 'Sorry, sir,' he said. 'There's a fire in progress and we've had to close the street at this point.'

'He lives in there,' I said, putting my hand on Bic's shoulder.

The cop looked away, squinting. 'There's some community support people,' he said, 'with yellow tabards. They've got a van set up. You find them, they can look after him.'

'I need to get inside,' I said.

He gave me an old-fashioned look. 'We've got the bloody Third World War going on in here,' he said. 'Just move along, okay?'

But even while he was saying it, I caught sight of a familiar figure as she tacked between the parked police cars behind him. 'Basquiat!' I yelled. 'Over here!'

She turned and saw me, and a whole range of emotions crossed her face one after another. For a moment I thought she was going to turn again, like Dick Whittington, and keep right on going. But she said something brief and to the point to a uniformed officer hovering at her elbow, and then as he ran off to do her bidding she crossed over to join us. She didn't look very happy, though: and bearing in mind the outcome of our previous conversation, neither was I.

'It's a demon,' I said, getting my version in first before she could open her mouth.

Basquiat scowled, looking from me down to Bic and then back up at Trudie. 'We're thinking it's a gang war,' she said, 'on account of the gangs. And the warfare. Castor, I thought I told you to stay where I could find you.'

'You did,' I agreed.

'And yet you went away. I sent someone to collect you from the address you gave, and I get told you're up north finding your fucking roots.'

'I found something else too, Ruth. I found out what you're dealing with here. I think it was responsible for Kenny Seddon's death. I think it's killed a lot of people since. And I think it's going to keep right on trucking if you don't let me go in there and stitch it. *Now* would be good.'

Basquiat's eyes narrowed. 'Your brother killed Kenny Seddon,' she said. 'And if you call me Ruth again, I'll break all your fingers. I bet that'll limit your musical repertoire for a while.'

'What's going on in there?' I demanded, pointing at the nearest towers. 'Just teenagers rumbling on the walkways? You've got twenty cars on the street and a fire you can't get in close enough to put out. It's getting out of hand – sergeant.'

'It's already out of hand,' Basquiat growled. 'The gangs have barricaded the walkways two-thirds of the way along. The only towers we can get into are Barratt, Marston and Longley. The fire's in Carlisle, way over at the south end of the estate.'

'What about getting in at ground level?'

She shot me an exasperated glare. 'You think I'm an idiot, Castor? The fire's on the fourteenth floor, and they've dragged all the furniture out and dumped it in the stairwells. I'm not having my officers climbing over that mess with bricks and bottles raining down on their heads – let alone the poor bloody fire crews.'

'Then what are you doing?' I demanded.

'We've got two anti-riot units coming down from Colindale,' she said. 'When they get here, we go in. And in the meantime, you keep out of my way.'

'No. Castor is with us.' The dissenting voice was Gwillam's, although I didn't see him for a moment or two after he spoke. I could only see Feld, clearing a path for his boss through the cops and firefighters just by strolling unstoppably through their midst.

Basquiat turned as Gwillam hove into view, Feld clearing the last obstacles by courteously stepping aside and sweeping a couple of unwary firemen off the pavement into the street.

'You remember me, Sergeant,' Gwillam said – a statement rather than a question. 'We met yesterday, and again earlier this evening. And I believe you saw the letter of introduction that the chief commissioner was kind enough to send.'

He was taking a folded sheet of paper from his pocket and offering it to Basquiat as he spoke, but she made no move to take it. 'I saw it,' she agreed. 'But I don't remember it giving you any right to walk around inside our perimeters or make up tour parties of uninvolved civilians.'

Gwillam was still holding out the paper. 'That would be paragraph three,' he said coldly. Basquiat snatched it out of his hand, read it and tossed it back against his chest. It fell to the ground, from where Feld retrieved it, grunting as he bent from the waist.

'There are people dying in there,' Basquiat said, her voice tight.

Gwillam nodded. 'We're working on it,' he said. 'And consulting –' he nodded towards me '– widely.'

Basquiat shook her head in sombre wonder. 'Just don't

get in my way,' she snarled. 'Just do not get in my fucking way.' She stalked off, her shoulder whacking hard against Feld's as she passed him. The big man didn't react: he probably didn't even feel it.

'So how did your expedition fare?' Gwillam asked. He was speaking to Trudie, and she nodded in confirmation. 'I've got the goods,' I said. 'Glad you were holding up your end.'

Ignoring the cheap shot, Gwillam became all clipped efficiency. 'Trudie,' he said, 'report in to Sallis. We're still working to stop the demon's influence from spreading any further. If it manages to infect the minds of the police or fire crews, the situation could escalate very quickly. Feld, take the boy back to his family.'

'You can't do that,' I pointed out. 'He lives in Weston, which is one of the blocks that's on the far side of the barricades. And Gwillam — that's where I have to go.'

'One of the policemen said that there's a relief van somewhere nearby,' Trudie said, putting a hand on Bic's shoulder. 'I'll take Bic there and then rejoin you.'

Bic looked at me, and I nodded. 'Go with her,' I said. 'I'll make sure your folks are okay, and I'll bring them to you as soon as this is over.'

Reluctantly the boy allowed himself to be led away. I turned to Gwillam, who was looking at me with something like mistrust. 'Why is the location important?' he demanded. 'Why can't you do the exorcism from here?'

'Because I fucking can't, okay?' I snapped. 'If you think you can, go ahead. You'll be trying to reel in a whale from a rowboat. It's too big, Gwillam. It's not like a ghost you can just summon to wherever you happen to be. When I tried something like that at the Royal London, I ended up in a place that looked like Hell's sub-basement. And you saw what happened to your own people when they took the thing on. It's camping out in a thousand different places – every piece of wounded or broken flesh on the entire estate. But it has a focus – the place where it first broke through onto this plane – and I'm going to take a wild guess and try Kenny's flat.'

'Why there?' Gwillam demanded.

A wave of weariness swept over me. I felt like I'd explained this a hundred times already. 'Because Mark Seddon was a self-harmer, and this demon has a hard-on for incised wounds. You figure it out.'

'The boy's activities summoned something. An unintentional invocation.'

'Exactly. If I'm wrong, we shift ground and we try again. But either way, this thing isn't coming to us. We've got to go doorstepping if we want to have a chance.'

Gwillam looked at Feld, who – impossible though it seemed – stood an inch or so taller as he prepared to take his orders. 'Get the others,' he said. 'All of them. Meet us on the eighth floor of Marston Block.'

Feld nodded once and strode away, the crowd parting for him like the Red Sea parted for Moses, only with a lot more swearing.

'What do you need from me?' Gwillam asked.

'As much back-up as I can get,' I admitted. 'The demon is going to fight back – hard – and it's outside my weight class. Your people will have to anchor me and – if they can – run interference while I play so I can stay focused on the tune and not have to worry about getting my frontal lobe fried.'

Gwillam nodded. 'All right.'

'I'll probably need some physical protection as well. Best-case scenario — the guys on the walkways are just running wild. Worst case, the demon's got some measure of control over them. Either way, I could get sliced and diced before I get a single note out.'

'I'll do my best to ensure that doesn't happen,' Gwillam said. 'And Castor . . .'

I paused as I was about to walk up the steps. 'What?'

He seemed to be choosing his words with some care. 'In the organisation I have the privilege of serving,' he said, 'someone with your background and your very consid-erable skills could rise further and faster than you'd imagine.'

'Well, how about that,' I mused. 'We're up on a moun-tain top in South London, Gwillam, and you're showing me all the kingdoms of the world. Now guess what I have to say to you?'

'I'm serious.'

'*Retro me, Satanas.*'

'I said—'

'You're serious. So am I. Get your hand out of my pants, you God-bothering bastard. I'm on your side for as long as this takes, but don't think for a moment that I won't beat the living shit out of you the next time I meet you without your muscle.'

He touched his bruised cheek. 'Well,' he said calmly, 'I had to try. Keep your friends close . . .'

'You think disciples are the same thing as friends?' I demanded. 'Try asking Jesus.'

* * *

The walkway ahead of us was eerily silent, but the rubble and broken glass that littered it made it clear that the silence was a relatively recent development. Dark, irregular splashes and streaks on the walkway's cracked concrete showed black in the actinic glare of the police spotlights, but from closer up, I was willing to bet, would turn out to be the rust-brown of dried blood.

Facing us was Boateng Tower, and beyond that was Weston. Maybe fifty yards, across no man's land and into the valley of death.

We'd had it easy up until now. Gwillam's magic paper and the police escort it conjured up had got us up the stairs at Marston Tower and through the police barricade – passing along the way a very large number of tense young constables waiting for the riot squad to arrive and scared shitless that they were going to have to go back into the breach before that happened.

But now here we were, on the front line. Behind the smashed windows overhead, vague shadows moved: and between us and Boateng, rearing up to precarious heights as though someone was trying to rebuild the Tower of Babel out of smashed furniture, was the rioters' barricade. Nobody was manning it that I could see: but a couple of hours' attrition would have removed the thrill-seekers who were prepared to stick their heads up for a look around and take a rubber bullet or a tear-gas canister in the chops. The ones who were left on the far side of the barricade would be the ones who had a bit more going on upstairs, and therefore by definition they'd be more dangerous.

'You can leave us,' Gwillam told the uniformed sergeant who'd been our escort up to this point. 'My people can handle it from here.' His people included flat-faced Feld, scarred but cuddly Speight, the man in black whose name I couldn't even remember, and a couple more exorcists from the Anathemata typing pool – a very young man and an elderly woman – who nobody had bothered to introduce me to.

'Wait,' I said. 'Do you have anything we can use as cover when we go out there? Mobile shields, that kind of thing?'

The sergeant, who was in Kevlar and sweating like a horse, shook his head emphatically. 'Not until the riot units get here,' he said. 'We're expecting them inside of twenty minutes, but then they've got to deploy. And you'd have to talk to their chief about commandeering any of their gear. I wouldn't hold my breath if I was you.'

'We'll handle it,' Gwillam repeated, gesturing towards the stairs to indicate that the sergeant's presence was no longer required. He gave us a sour nod and withdrew.

'Feld,' Gwillam said. 'And Speight.'

The big man appeared at his left shoulder, the scarred Father Christmas at his right. They both inclined their heads, awaiting orders.

'I'm going to let you off the leash,' Gwillam said. 'I want you to clear us a path – ideally without killing anyone. This is a police operation, and we have to stay within their rules as far as possible.'

'What about bones and soft tissue?' Speight asked. Somehow the question sounded worse in his mild upper-crust voice than it would have done in Feld's guttural growl.

'All flesh is grass,' Gwillam observed. 'It withers, and its flower fades. Do what you need to do, my sons, and take my blessing with you.'

Very matter-of-factly, Feld and Speight stepped out of their shoes and took off their coats. Then they removed the rest of their clothes, stacking them neatly at the foot of the wall.

Father Gwillam bowed his own head as though in prayer, but the resemblance was only superficial. When Gwillam quotes from the Bible, his power flows through the words the same way mine does through music: he was performing an unbinding.

'Hast thou not read that which was spoken by God? He stirreth up the sea with His power, and by His understanding breaketh up the storm. For my thoughts are not your thoughts, nor my ways your ways. The fruit of the righteous is a tree of life . . .'

As Gwillam spoke, something truly obnoxious and unsettling began to happen to the two men who flanked him. Feld's shoulders broadened and his flat face folded down from the neck, so that – while still flat – it was angled forward, the eyes shifting to the front. Speight, already short, became shorter and dropped down onto all fours, his lower jaw elongating both across and down until it was as big as a bear trap. Hair sprouted on his back in ragged clumps that flowed and merged, while the hair on his head lengthened into a spiked mane that looked as though it would cut your hand like a razor if you touched it.

Both men were *loup-garous*, as I'd more than half suspected already: human souls that had forced their way into animal flesh for a messy, compromised rebirth. I had no idea in this case, though, what animals had been party to the deal. There was something about the increased mass of Feld's shoulders that suggested a gorilla, but his fanged face and clawed hands looked like someone had crossed a weasel with a leopard and fucked up the vertical hold in the process. Speight mostly looked like a big dog, but the quills of his mane recalled a porcupine – and surely that mouth had never been seen before on anything that walked, crawled or did the can-can.

'Write in a book thyself,' Gwillam intoned, 'all the words that He hath spoken unto thee. The sun to rule by day, the moon and stars by night, for His mercy endures for ever.' Feld stretched his elongated body full length on the ground and a ripple ran through his flesh, his spine arching like a bow. Speight's terrifying jaws clashed, making a sound like a hundred spears on a hundred shields.

Gwillam looked to the left, then to the right, and it seemed that he was satisfied. 'Go,' he said.

Feld and Speight hit the ground running – so fast that they became liquescent blurs and you found yourself staring at their after-images without quite knowing how. Bricks and bottles and even steel window frames rained down around them as the watchers in the windows higher up reacted to the assault on the barricade, but the missiles landed where the two *loup-garous* had been, never where they were. In less than two seconds they were across the rubble-strewn walkway and swarming up the barricades.

Then they were gone from our sight, and we could only track them by sound. For the most part, they were sounds I'd prefer to forget, if that were an option: the scuffles, the thuds and even the screams were innocuous enough, but there were more insinuating sounds in the mix, too: choked gurgles, liquid pops and splats, and in one case the shudder-some impact of what could only have been a skull on the unyielding and unforgiving concrete.

A second later, Feld's streamlined head appeared atop the barricade and he signalled to us with a hand whose scimitared claws were dark with blood.

'After you,' said Gwillam.

We ran hell-for-leather, but the bombardment we received was both more sporadic and less accurate: the watchers in the windows were able to see what had happened on the far side of the barricade, and clearly shock and awe weren't even the half of it.

All the same, a lobbed brick came way too close to my head for comfort as I crested the top of the shifting, treacherous mound: and as I half-slid, half-fell down the other side, a flatscreen TV set hit the ground and shattered explosively two feet to my right, showering me with a million shards of high-impact plastic.

But the door was open ahead of me, and on the far side of the door was a safe haven. Never mind what I was treading on, or what unforgivable acts the two were-beasts were still committing up ahead of us as they cleared our path. I ran along in their wake, feeling something thump against my shoulder but without really hurting all that much. I realised why when I glanced down: it wasn't a bottle or a piece of masonry but somebody's severed thumb.

'Jesus Christ!' I yelled involuntarily. Speight's head snapped around and he bellowed, opening those horrendous jaws right in my face. The man in black – Eddings, that was his name – pushed me forward through the doors, interposing himself at the same time between me and the *loup-garou*. 'No, Speight!' he snapped out. 'Leave him!'

Touchy Catholic werewolves: you have to remember to watch your language around them.

I slumped against the wall, getting my breath back. Speight and Feld were at our backs, facing the doors we'd just come through. Of course: the stairs were on the outside of the building, so nothing could come at us so long as the doors held.

Unless they used the lift.

It pinged at that moment, with perfect ironic timing. Eddings turned to stare at it. The illuminated displays above the three lift doors weren't working, so there was no way of telling which lift was in operation or whether it was heading for our floor. I chose the middle one and stood squarely in front of it, waiting to see what would emerge, but Eddings touched my shoulder and shook his head sharply.

'Go inside,' he said tersely, pointing to Kenny's door. 'You complete the exorcism, this all stops. Until then, we're just racking up the body count.'

'What about Gwillam?' I asked. 'Don't we wait for him?'

Eddings looked out towards the barricade we'd just scaled. I did too. There was no sign of movement out there now. 'No,' Eddings said. 'Father Gwillam will join us when he can. The three of you should be enough to make a fist of it. If not – get word out to me and I'll send Speight in to you.'

I looked at the hideous thing hunkered down by the right-hand lift doors, like Frankenstein's cat at the world's biggest mousehole. 'Speight?' I echoed.

'He's an exorcist,' Eddings reminded me. 'When he's in human form. Go. We'll deal with whatever comes through here.'

To put the matter beyond argument, he kicked in the boarded-up door of Kenny's flat. It wasn't hard: the council do that sort of job in the perfect knowledge that it's not going to last more than a day or two.

I went inside and down Kenny's stairs, followed by the woman and the boy. I heard Eddings levering the particle board back into place behind us, sealing us in as best he could.

The living room was a shambles, which I was more or less expecting. The most likely reason for the place being boarded up was because it had already been broken into: a familiar pattern that almost made me nostalgic for the Walton of my youth. Our feet crunched over fractured photo frames and shards of porcelain.

Mark's bedroom, though, hadn't been touched: possibly because there hadn't been anything there to steal or despoil. I settled myself on the edge of the bed and gestured to the other two to take up their stations. 'You got names?' I demanded.

'Star of Renewed Being Phillips,' said the old woman.

'Caryl Langford,' said the boy. 'With a 'y'. Like Caryl Chessman.'

Well, *that* was a fucking great omen. I took my whistle out and shrugged off my coat. It was feeling oppressively hot, all of a sudden. 'Okay,' I said. 'Caryl. Ms Phillips. If this was a firing squad, you'd both be shooting blanks today. I'm the one who's going to kill this thing. All I want you to do is to weave stay-nots around me so it can't tear my soul into confetti while I'm working.'

The woman nodded but Caryl with a 'y' didn't look too happy. 'What if it turns on us?' he asked.

'It won't,' I promised. 'Once I start playing, it'll only have eyes for me. Okay, get your kit out and get ready.'

I watched them with half an eye as I went over in my mind the tune Asmodeus had given me, like a tailor poring over a swatch of cloth before starting to cut. It had to be good quality, and it had to be all of a piece. If there was a dropped stitch somewhere, we were all going to die in this room, probably with most of our insides on the outside.

Star of Renewed Being's method of performing an exorcism seemed to rely on jacks – the children's game in which you throw knuckle-bones up in the air and catch them again in more and more complicated ways. Of course, most kids these days use little plastic nubbins with six rounded points, whose resemblance to knuckle-bones is purely accidental. The old lady had the real thing: ten of them, well worn and shiny, off-white with brown flecks like the colour of clotted cream that's been allowed to grow a proper crust.

The boy had a book, and I assumed for a moment that he'd learned his craft from Gwillam – that this would be another bloody Bible-reading. But the pages of the book were blank, and he took a stick of charcoal from his trouser pocket, choosing a page and smoothing it flat with nervous fingers.

There was no point prolonging the agony. This would either work or it wouldn't. I started in to play, with none of my usual exploratory tuning-up because the tune was present in my head already, a finished thing. It started high and fast but plummeted precipitately into a doleful decelerando: abandon hope, all ye who riff on this one.

Nothing much seemed to happen at first. Because I was playing quite low, I was able to hear from outside the sounds – shouted order, shouted response, boots in lockstep – of serious men moving into position. The riot squad were here, and incredibly things were about to get even uglier than they already were.

But we had our window, and within it we made music. I did, anyway: the old woman threw bones and the boy sketched obsessive angular lines, turning the paper into a fractal landscape.

The air thickened and roiled. Something huge and diffuse turned its attention towards us.

Darkness fell like a curtain, but it was darkness shot through with light: a curtain flapping in a strong wind, allowing me to glimpse through its folds a silver, saturated light like the luminosity of a coming storm. Everything was working beautifully: Star of Renewed Being and Caryl with a 'y' had my back, and the demon couldn't drag me down into its black-on-black Hell the way it had at the Royal London. It could only bring a piece of that Hell along with it as it came into the room; as it coalesced around us like gritty shadows, angry and confused.

Got you now, you bastard. Your turf, but my rules. Now let's put you on the griddle and see what colour your juices run.

I shifted my fingers on the stops and pushed the tune into a higher gear, raising the volume because the volume was the delivery system for the pain: and the demon *was* hurting now. Its rush on me had got it nowhere, because charcoal and knuckle-bones encompassed me like the arms of the Lord. Now it tried to withdraw, but it was too late for that. It was in a barbed-wire entanglement of music, a thicket of thorns like the devil's briar patch. Unable to advance, unable to retreat, it thrashed and gored itself on the tune.

And I saw it.

Only for a moment, but I saw it. It stared at me through the shredded layers of its own protective darkness, as it had stared at me in the lightless abyss when I had met it by Kenny's hospital bed. Not that our eyes met, exactly: in this synaesthetic maelstrom, seeing and hearing were metaphors for something else.

Say, I *knew* it.

It was just one synapse closing in my mind: making the last link in a chain of connections that I'd probably assembled subconsciously but not allowed myself to see until now.

A door opening, Asmodeus had said. *An eggshell breaking across. Call it metamorphosis. Call it transformation.*

Juliet, reading *The Very Hungry Caterpillar*: *the little caterpillar pushed his nose out of the cocoon, and looked around in wonder . . .*

Kenny's ghost, wailing, '*He's too big now, and he made me—*'

One note, one beat, one breath away from the mercy stroke, and I knew the demonic presence for what it was. Knew, what's more, Asmodeus's treachery and the depth of his hatred for me. How perfectly he'd set me up and how many layers of perverse sadism his little plan had wrapped up in it.

The whistle fell from my hands. It scattered the old lady's knuckle-bones and she yelled in alarm and fear, but she was a second behind the times because the sudden silence had opened a hole in the net: the demon rushed through it and was gone, too intent on its own survival even to hit out at us as it left.

'What are you doing?' Caryl screamed.

'Shut up.' My voice was so thick that he probably couldn't even make out the words. I lurched to my feet, made it as far as the door before my legs buckled under me. My knees hit the floor first, my hands a second later. I could hardly breathe. My chest was heaving but no oxygen was making its way through to my brain.

'Mister Castor.' Something cold touched my throat: the barrel of a tiny pistol. A Jesus gun. The old lady had a Jesus gun, hidden up her sleeve. How funny was that? 'Finish the exorcism.'

'Go – fuck – yourself!' I panted.

'Finish the exorcism, or I'll have to shoot you. A bullet this small probably won't kill you, but if I aim it straight at your spine I can almost guarantee it will leave you quadriplegic.'

I didn't answer.

'It's your call, Mister Castor. What do you want me to do?' There was cold steel in the old lady's voice. She'd have made a good nun: might even have been one, at some point, before she'd heard Gwillam's call.

'Pray,' I suggested, with a bitter, choking laugh. 'Pray for him.'

The gun stayed where it was for a moment longer, then withdrew.

The next time I looked up, I was alone. But not really: you're never really alone in a big city. The screams and scuffles and the sounds of ruinous impact as the riot squad met the people of the Salisbury Estate right outside my window were more than enough to drive that fact well and truly home.

22

From the comfort of Mark's bedroom, I watched the world end. Or at least, that was how it felt. Melodramatic, I know, but it's not easy to keep a sense of proportion when the wind gusts with the bitter reeks of burnt flesh and half-spent tear gas, and ignorant armies are clashing by night right in front of your sleep-deprived eyes.

The riot cops had a hard time of it when they made their first charge. They got past the barricades at ground level and on the third-floor walkways, but they couldn't penetrate on the eighth and twelfth floors – so the further they advanced, the tougher the going got. A plexiglass riot shield is a fine defence against a lobbed brick or a Molotov cocktail, but it's not much use when an armchair drops on you out of the skies. They pulled back at last, leaving a few sprawled bodies – some in uniform, some civilians – behind them.

The second time was better coordinated, and they seemed to have larger numbers on their side too. Using the towers at the north end of the estate as staging points, they swept the upper walkways first, blasting away the barricades and the opposition with water cannons before venturing out themselves. The top-to-bottom sweep meant they weren't exposed to attack from above, and they made good headway, moving on past me towards the southern towers which they hadn't been able to crack the first time around.

But by then they themselves were visibly slowing as they felt the effects of the demon's touch. One by one they started to take an interest in the broken glass on the walkways, jabbing shards of it experimentally into their own palms or seeking out rioters or former colleagues for impromptu knife fights.

With so many wounds in which to root itself, so much sliced and broken flesh, the demon's power was increasing exponentially. My own palms were itching almost unbearably, and the cutting kit that had been in Kenny's wardrobe kept coming into the forefront of my mind. It would be a useful thing to have to hand, in case I felt the need to . . .

No! I whistled the first few bars of the tune over and over again to keep the demon's insidious tendrils from anchoring in my mind. And I tried not to think about blood. The blood that beats in the tell-tale heart of every one of us. The blood that's thicker than water.

I couldn't collect my thoughts: couldn't get my mind through the minefield of sick despair to the point where I could start thinking of a way out of this. There didn't have to be one. Maybe I'd really hit the wall this time, because I couldn't complete the exorcism and we were way past the point where nailing up a few wards over people's doorways was going to have any effect.

But it goes against the grain to give up just because you're outnumbered, outgunned, painted into a corner and running a quarter of a tank past empty. I forced my numbed, sluggish brain to connect one thought to another, and I came up with three ideas which – together – made a kind of sense.

Matty. Juliet. Gary Coldwood.

Coldwood first. I fished my cellphone out of my pocket, tried vainly to remember his number before I finally found it in the calls-received list.

It's a wonderful and awe-inspiring facet of modern technology that you can call out from the heart of Armageddon to share the experience and chat with like-minded friends.

Nothing the first time around: the phone rang for the best part of a minute before kicking me through to the voicemail service. No time to piss around with that: something told me it might be a while before Gary had a chance to catch up with his messages.

I tried again. Hung up again. A third time . . .

'Hello?' Coldwood's voice, with a babel of other voices, movements, sirens behind him. They were the same sirens I was hearing, away out there in the red night, but slightly out of phase because radio and sound waves don't march in lockstep.

'Hello, Gary.'

'Castor? Bloody hell, where are you? Basquiat said you—'

'Weston Block, flat 137,' I said.

'Jesus fucking wept! You're still in there!'

'And you're somewhere out on the edge, yeah? New Kent Road?'

'Other side. Henshaw Street. Listen, if you want a rescue, you can forget it. We can't get close. The riot boys have taken over, and their OCO doesn't play well with others. They're making a right pig's breakfast of it, but there isn't a bastard thing we can do. He's got us running escorts for the paramedics and evacuating people out of the north end.'

'I don't want a rescue, Gary. I want Matt. I need you to bring him here.'

Silence at the other end of the line, apart from the sirens and shouted commands.

'Did you hear me, Gary?'

'No. I'm not sure I did. I thought you said you wanted me to bring your brother in to you.'

'Yeah. That's right.'

The next sound I heard was an incredulous laugh. 'Did you fall on your head at some point, Fix? I told you, I can't get in. And your brother's on remand for fucking murder.'

'Which he didn't do. But that's beside the point. He's the only person alive who can stop this.'

'Why?' Coldwood's voice was strained. 'Explain the logic. No, on second thoughts don't bother because this is not fucking happening.'

He hung up on me. I dialled again. There was nothing else to do except keep hitting at the one point and hope that something gave way. If it didn't, I was going to sit here until the demon crept past my defences: and then I was probably going to do pretty much what everyone else was doing.

'Fix, piss off out of it,' Gary yelled down the phone.

'I'd love to, Gary. Sincerely. But if I do, a lot more people are going to die tonight – including a lot of *your* people, unless you pull back and let every man, woman and child who lives on the Salisbury cut themselves to ribbons. I mean it. Get Matt and we can do something.'

There was another silence, but I took it to be a positive sign. I was still hearing the background noises, so he hadn't hung up.

'Give me a reason,' Coldwood said. But I didn't feel I could do that. Not yet.

'I'm giving you all I can,' I said. 'Matt's the key to this. What does it cost you to get him out of his cell and bring him in here? You can handcuff yourself to him if you're worried. Or you can sit back and watch while half of South London goes to hell.'

'It's not half of South London. It's one estate. A thousand people.'

'For now,' I agreed. 'For now that's all it is.'

'Fuck!' Gary exploded. 'Even if I wanted to get him in there, how would I do it?'

'You want an escort, you call an escort service,' I told him.

'Is that meant to be clever?'

'Juliet.'

Gary laughed again, even less convincingly than before. 'Juliet. Right. Because what this situation needs is another demon.'

'Juliet will meet you at the station,' I said. 'She'll bring Matt here. You can come too, if you want to.'

'And then what? You wave your magic wand?'

'No,' I admitted. 'This probably isn't going to do a blind bit of good. But it's a racing certainty that nothing else will. You want to end this, Gary, you get my fucking brother up here. We'll talk about sin, because priests are experts at that stuff, and he'll lead us in a few prayers. And maybe we'll all still be alive when the sun comes up. Or alternatively, make sure you've got enough body bags.'

I waited to see if he was going to come back with any

more smart-ass questions. When he didn't, I hung up and called Juliet.

'Felix,' she said, with a warning rumble in back of the usual cat's-purr roughness of her voice. 'I'm busy.'

'Doing what?' I asked.

'Making love.'

'Well, call me back when you get to the cigarette stage. I hate to be a gooseberry, but this won't wait while you get your rocks off.'

'I'm coming *now*, Castor. Succubi can sustain an orgasm for days. It's our tempers that are short. Tell me what you want.'

'I figured it out,' I told her. 'About the thing at the Salisbury, and why you got so coy all of a sudden. It's kind of a revelation, Juliet – that there are things that make a sex-demon blush.'

She didn't bother with fencing or denials. 'Do you really know what's happening,' she demanded, 'or are you just bluffing me to see what I let fall by accident?' So I told her the truth, as I saw it, in three bald sentences. I managed to keep my voice steady, but my hand was trembling as though I was in the last stages of malaria.

'Very well,' Juliet said. 'What now?'

'Just tell me – is that it? Is that how it happened?'

'Yes. I think so. In broad terms, it must be. Why are you calling me, Castor?'

'Because you said you'd tried to exorcise this thing. Was that just bullshit, Juliet, or do you really want to help?'

'I don't have time for bullshit,' she reminded me with some asperity. 'So please, stick to the point. I'm in the process of satisfying my lover – my other vocation. But this is a bad thing, and the forerunner of things a whole lot worse, so yes, I'll help if I can.'

'Just not with information.'

'You know why I was silent, Castor. And I still have to decide whether I can trust *your* discretion. Tell me what you want from me.'

'When you're sure that Susan is fully satisfied, go to the Uxbridge Road nick and pick up my brother. Gary Coldwood will hand him over to you. Or he may want to come along too. Either way you'll have to get Matt in here, through Hell and high water and maybe the occasional Catholic werewolf.'

'Here being—?'

'The Salisbury. Flat 137, Weston Block.'

'I'll be there as soon as I can.'

'Juliet—'

A pause. 'Yes, Castor?'

'Nicky said you're the youngest in your family. '*She is of Baphomet the sister and the youngest of her line*, yada yada.'

'So?'

'So who did you . . . ?' I let the question linger, because I had no idea how to finish it.

'It was a long time ago, Castor,' Juliet said coldly. 'I don't remember.' She hung up on me.

Nothing to do now but wait. And watch the show.

23

It took them close on two hours, but under the circumstances I think that was pretty impressive. Then again, the cross-London cop-demon-and-priest six-legged race is never going to become an Olympic event, so I don't have anything to base a comparison on.

Now that I'd put my head back together again at least partially after the botched exorcism, I'd come to the realisation that I wasn't completely helpless. Whistle in hand, I stood at the window and played – the first part of the exorcism ritual, the summoning: drawing the demon in towards me again and again, and then letting it off the hook at the last moment.

It was draining, and in the long run it wasn't going to get me anywhere. It did tie up some of the monster's psychic resources, though, so that the riot police mostly woke up from their trance, wiped the blood off their hands and retreated at a stumbling, undignified run. Only a few remained: presumably those in whom the demon had been able to embed itself most deeply and most quickly. Maybe they were guys who already had a tendency towards self-harm, or at any rate a fetish thing about wounds and pain.

Inside the flats of the estate, though, nothing moved. There was no general exodus: no chorus of screams as people woke up to the full horror of what they'd done during the night. The demon's hold was unbreakable there because he had too much of a head start on me. Some of them were never going to wake up at all.

The sky off to the left, behind Guy's Hospital, had started to lighten just a little but then stalled: the sun stayed stubbornly below the horizon and the zenith was as black as a lecher's heart. Maybe sunrise had been cancelled.

Then a commotion below me told me that the riot police were back. Only a small contingent of them, coming in from the north in a packed huddle that was vaguely reminiscent of the ancient Roman 'tortoise' manoeuvre.

There was a stirring on the barricades and behind the windows. The demon gathered itself – a single entity looking out through a thousand eyes. I put the whistle to my lips and played again, but I was weak and spacey from lack of sleep and my fingers kept fumbling on the stops. I'm not sure if I made any difference at all.

Missiles started to sail down and crash onto the concrete around the tight cluster of Kevlar-clad cops. A couple of bottles and something bigger and heavier found their mark, hitting raised riot shields with thunderous reports that echoed through the eerie silence enveloping the rest of the estate. One of the bottles was a Molotov cocktail, and spilled flame spread across the topmost shields in neon traceries.

One of the riot cops who'd stayed behind when the rest had left appeared now from somewhere and sprinted across towards his colleagues. I thought – and they probably thought, too – that he was trying to rejoin them: but then his hand came up with something jagged clutched in it and he uttered a scream that was more like a torture victim's dying agonies than like a battle cry. A rubber bullet felled him at about ten yards out from the tortoise: his legs shot out from under him and he went down hard. He lay twitching, trying to rise, his hands fluttering like dying birds.

More bricks and bottles came down, but the tortoise headed on, straight towards me – then passed out of my sight under the walkways directly beneath my window. I had to judge what was happening now from the percussive sounds that came up to my ears. More screams, and a couple more rounds discharged. The smashing and rending of something heavy being moved.

Then the tortoise retreated the way it had come, moving at the same sluggish pace as before because of the need to keep the shields locked together.

Like I said, my mind wasn't working all that well by this point. It took me a while to realise what payload the tortoise had delivered. I went out of the bedroom, up the stairs, and eased my way cautiously through Kenny's boarded-up door out into the hallway.

The stairwell below me was in heaving commotion. Presumably the cops had lost their hold on the third-floor walkways and the blood-crazed trancers had ventured north to reclaim the territory. Now they were wishing they hadn't, because Juliet was passing through them in much the same way that a scythe passes through corn.

I didn't go down to join them: moving as slowly and clumsily as I was now, I could only have got in the way and most likely ended up with a bottle broken over my head or a knife in my ribs. But I played the summoning again, drawing some of the demon's attention my way in the hope that it might have to loosen its hold momentarily on its possessed servants.

The mismatched threesome came fully into view now,

Coldwood coming first with Matt right behind him casting terrified glances to left and right; Juliet bringing up the rear and polishing off a last few attackers without haste or passion: she saved her passion for other things. One man stabbed her in the shoulder: she grasped his arm in an unbreakable grip, removed the blade from her own flesh and gave it back to him, hilt-first. He slumped against the wall, blood gouting from his broken nose. I was amazed – and grateful – that she hadn't killed him. One of the hardest lessons for Ajulutsikael to learn, when she made the decision to live among men and so became Juliet, was to pull her punches.

'In here,' I shouted. Gary looked up and saw me. A few moments later, he and Matt were making their way up the last few steps. I led the way into Kenny's flat and down to his gutted living room.

'That was bloody blue murder,' Gary complained. I ignored him and looked at Matt. He'd sustained a certain amount of damage in getting to this point – a bruised cheek, and a jagged cut on the back of one hand – but clearly he hadn't been seriously wounded.

Yet.

'Why am I here?' he asked me, looking around in something like terror. 'Why have you brought me here, Felix? Is this where—?'

'This is where he lived,' I said. 'Yeah. Sit down, Matt. Pull up a broken-off bit of furniture and park your arse on it, because you're not getting out of here until you've heard the truth.'

Juliet entered the room, rubbing her hands together.

'It's worse than I would have expected,' she said.

I shrugged. 'Well, you'd know,' I said.

'Get to the point,' Coldwood suggested. He was leaning against the wall just next to the door, arms folded. His lip was thickened and his voice was slightly slurred, but he too seemed to have got away lightly. Juliet's flawless white skin, by contrast, was criss-crossed with new wounds, none of which would last: she healed fast, and she would have deliberately put herself between the others and the worst of the violence.

'The point,' I said. 'Right. Matt, you didn't sit down yet.'

'I don't want to sit down,' Matt said. 'Not in this place.' He looked around him with a mixture of fear and hatred.

'Fine,' I said. 'Then stand. Okay, we'll start with the obvious. You have a son. Or at least you did have one. He's dead now. And there – right there – is our fucking problem.'

Matt made a strangled noise and staggered backwards, one step and then a second. Slowly he sank down onto his knees. Probably it sounds as though I was being unnecessarily brutal: but there was so much worse to come, there seemed no point in beating about the bush with the relatively straightforward stuff.

'Oh God!' Matt whimpered. 'Oh God!'

'But you knew that,' I said. 'You had to know that. I mean, Anita didn't want to be too obvious, but she named him after the next evangelist along. And how else could Kenny have got you to come out here and meet him, Matt?'

'He said – but I wasn't—' Matt looked up at me with horrified, pleading eyes. 'I couldn't be sure. I didn't – I didn't want it to be true. If it was true, then—'

'Then you left your kid to be brought up by a psychopathic bully,' I finished. 'I did wonder about that one.

Working backwards from Mark's age, it must have been when you came back from the seminary. Before you went to your first ministry. Is that right?'

Matt was still staring at me, unable to look away, unable to speak.

'Is that right?' I repeated. The details were going to matter. I couldn't let him off the hook, even though I could see how much this was hurting him. I had to hurt him a lot more yet.

'That was – the last time,' Matt said. 'We'd already—I loved her, Felix. I almost gave up the Church for her. As it was, I just gave up my conscience. Did what any cowardly philanderer does – taking the easy solace and postponing the hard decision. But I swear to you, Felix, I never knew she'd had a child. My child. If I'd known that, I would have gone to her. I would have been with her, whatever it took.'

'And you never saw her again?'

He shook his head, tears now chasing each other down his cheeks. 'I – I only – only heard—' He fell silent for a while, folding in on his pain. Juliet looked at me inquiringly: she was probably wondering whether there was any point to this beyond pure sadism. Coldwood was watching me too, wary and truculent. He'd been dragged into this against his will and now he knew it bore on his murder case as well as on the current mayhem. He wasn't happy, but he was letting me play my hand.

A hand in which razor blades counted as aces.

'Kenny didn't get in touch with me until after Anita disappeared,' Matt said, his voice barely audible because he was speaking into his own chest, his upper body bowed now almost to the floor. 'He said – he said she'd had my child, a long time before. He said he knew all the details. Names. Addresses. If I met him – on the Borough Road overpass – he'd tell me. He'd tell me everything.'

'And did he?' Gary chipped in.

Matt looked up, startled. He seemed to have forgotten that we weren't alone.

'No,' he admitted. 'He just – he said he'd lied to me. There wasn't a child. Then he said there was, but he was already dead. He'd killed himself with a – a straight razor.'

'And he showed you the razor,' I said. 'He made you touch it.'

Matt nodded.

'None of this will ever stand up in court,' Coldwood said distantly, as though to himself. 'Okay, I buy Kenny hating his kid's real father: feeling like he had something to prove, maybe. But tenderising yourself with a straight razor and making it look like it was the other bloke? It's a plan with a fair few holes in it, isn't it?'

'It's a plan that might seem irresistible,' Juliet said, 'if a wound-demon was whispering in your ear. Blood and pain must have started to feel like desirable things in themselves. Kenny Seddon just tried to harness them to a different end.'

'But it doesn't work,' Gary pointed out bluntly. 'There's still the angle of the wounds. Some of them were self-inflicted, but some of them couldn't have been. A fit-up doesn't explain the facts.'

'It doesn't matter any more,' I said.

'Oh really?' Gary's tone was savagely sardonic. 'I thought

it did. Your fucking brother is facing a murder charge, you self-satisfied tosspot!'

'My fucking brother,' I snarled back at him, my temper fraying right through, 'thinks his biggest sin was a fucking bunk-up with Anita Yeats eighteen fucking years ago. When in point of fucking fact, it's *this*.' I threw out my arms, indicating with a sweeping gesture not just the room, the flat, the tower, but the whole of the Salisbury Estate in all its singed, shattered, punctured, incised and blood-smeared horror.

'This is your biggest sin, Matty. How long has it been since your last confession?'

In spring we used to walk to the Seven Sisters – the bomb craters on the Walton Triangle that had turned into lakes – and go fishing for frogspawn. You'd bring it home in a jam jar, transfer it to a plastic bowl or bucket, stick it in a secluded part of the garden shed or, if you had a death wish or an indulgent mum, your bedroom, and wait for the little black dots at the heart of the translucent jelly to turn into tadpoles. Then the tadpoles would grow legs and turn over the space of weeks into microminia-turised frogs. It was enthralling in a way that cut right across more macho pursuits. You could watch it for hours and feel like you were plugged into some kind of primal magic.

I was thinking about that now as I looked from Juliet to Matt and then back again.

'Do you want to tell him?' I asked her. 'Or is this one down to me?'

Juliet arched an eyebrow. 'This is your decision, Castor,'

she said. 'What you're about to say can't make anyone who hears it any happier. If I've kept the secret this long, it's not because I'm afraid of what you'll do with the knowledge. It's because it can't do you – any of you – one iota of good.'

'Mark was into self-harm,' I told my brother, who was coming out of his foetal crouch and staring at me with aggressive unease. 'He cut himself for pleasure. Mostly with razor blades, occasionally with other sharp objects that he picked up here and there and saved for the purpose.'

'Why are you telling me this, Felix?' Matt demanded.

'Because you need to know. He saw the whole process as kind of erotic somehow. I've read some of his poetry, and that was pretty much all it was about. How beautiful wounds are: how they're like flowers and fertile river valleys and mouths that speak in a language more eloquent than words. He never said they were like vaginas but it was sort of implied.

'It was his upbringing, Matt. Kenny was a sadistic bastard – you knew that – and Anita had convinced herself that she was a worthless speck of dirt who deserved no better than the abuse she got. The only thing in all of this fucking mess that I don't understand is how the strongest, most capable, most alive girl we ever knew turned into this . . . this *doormat*, but she did. Maybe because the one man she really loved got her up the stick and then walked away whistling "Jesus wants me for a sunbeam". Or maybe it was something else. I don't know. I wasn't there.

'But however it played, Mark had this thing in his life that was halfway between a hobby and a love affair. Blades. Wounds. Blood. And then he died. And his soul stayed here like so many souls do – stuck in the mire, too wrapped up in all the unfinished business to let go. I've never thought about it before, but there should be more young ghosts than there are old ones. Dead at seventeen? How could you go gentle into that last sod-off? How could you think it was your time?'

Matt uttered an unlovely sound, compounded of grief and pain and protest. He didn't want to hear any more. But I had to tell him. I had to make him understand what was coming next.

'I thought he summoned the demon by accident, Matt. I was certain that was how it must have happened. Like, his obsession opened a door wide enough for a creature that loved and lived in wounds to enter by. Like he made a trail it could follow. Like his soul had a scent.

'But I was kidding myself. First of all because the truth was too insane to be believed, and then because it was too hard. It hurt too much. Juliet refusing to tell me what was going on over here rang alarm bells, but I didn't know what to make of it. Then I met Bic – the kid next door. The closest thing Mark had to a friend, and the first soul the demon chose to anchor itself in. For months that was all it did. It lodged there, in that one small soul, until it was strong enough to try its luck elsewhere. Why him? No scars on him anywhere, so he's never cut himself. And the demon didn't cut him either. It cut everyone else, or made them cut themselves, but with Bic it was really gentle. It had to have the blood: couldn't do without that. But it made Bic bleed without breaking his skin.'

Matt was looking at me in pure horror now, and Coldwood, two steps behind but catching on, swore obscenely.

'Then I actually met the thing,' I said. 'And it spoke to me. Just the one word. "Mark". I thought it was telling me who it was after, but it wasn't.

'No, Felix,' Matt pleaded. 'No.'

'It was telling me its name. Mark didn't summon the demon. Mark *is* the demon. That's your son's metastasised soul out there, feeding on innocents and driving them to their own destruction.'

Matt's pleas turned into a wordless bellow of anguish and he started to hammer his head against the floor of the room. Coldwood and I lunged forward at the same time but Juliet's lithe body isn't subject to the same limitations as mere human flesh, and she got there almost before we started to move. She clasped Matt in her unbreakable grip and he slumped against her, moaning unintelligible syllables.

'I think you've made your point,' she said to me in a calm, detached tone.

'Is this how all demons are made?' I asked her, my mouth too dry to swallow. 'Is this what you are?'

'It's none of your business what I am, Castor. If you pry into that subject again, I won't take it kindly.'

'I can't believe I never saw it,' I continued, because the words kept spilling out of me whether I wanted them to or not. It was as though none of this had been real until I said it, or until she confirmed it. Now I had to live with this knowledge and I didn't think I could. *We have met the enemy and he is us.* The newest monster in town was my fucking nephew. 'I mean, it ought to have been obvious. Zombies are people. Werewolves are people. Why shouldn't demons be people too? It's Occam's fucking razor: it's the one common factor that makes sense out of everything. But how can it be so big, Juliet? How can it be so fucking big and so fucking powerful if it's –' the word had a sour, almost obscene taste to it as I shaped my mouth around it '– newborn?'

Juliet stared at me for long enough that I was sure she wasn't going to answer. But then she made a gesture that conveyed very succinctly the impression that in talking to me about this she was trying to pour a major ocean into a pint pot. 'Many of us start out . . . large and diffuse,' she said. 'Bodiless emotion. Pure power, but not concentrated. Like a vapour that fills any space it finds itself in. We condense gradually, over a long time. We find our form.'

'But you come from souls?' This from Matt, who was staring at her in utter horror. 'From human souls?'

Juliet made another gesture: something close to a shrug.

'Dear God!' Matt whispered. 'Oh dear God!'

'Tell me if I'm missing something,' Coldwood growled, 'but fascinating as all this is from a religious standpoint, is it not also totally fucking irrelevant? Either you can sort this out or you can't, Fix. Which is it?'

'The first ghost I ever exorcised was my own sister, Gary,' I answered, shaking my head with ferocious emphasis. 'I'm not going back there. Today it's Matt's turn.'

'Mine?' Matt's voice trembled as he raised his red, tear-stained face to stare at me.

'I think it's our only chance,' I said. 'He's kin to you and he'll feel the connection. He may listen to you where he wouldn't listen to anyone else. Most ghosts – they hang around because they can't get it into their heads that their life is over. They're tied to all the stuff they didn't do, or wish they hadn't done. You have to tell him it's okay. Make your peace with him. You have to ask him to leave, of his own free will. It's the only way.'

At least, I added mentally, it's the only way that doesn't involve me doing an encore for *my* biggest sin. For Katie. And I marvelled again at how big a bastard Asmodeus was: how nearly perfectly he'd led me to this massacre of the innocents. Because that's what Mark was, however deadly his infatuation with wounds had become. His real father literally didn't know he was alive, his stepfather was a vicious sadist and his mother was probably already broken before he was born. His cards had been well and truly marked. And then when he did finally break out of the ghetto, by metamorphosing into something big and powerful and scary, along came Uncle Felix with his magic equaliser.

No. Sorry. We are not at home to Mister Kin-slayer. Not today, at any rate.

'They've never met,' Juliet pointed out. 'There's no reason why the demon should recognise Matthew as its father.'

'No,' I admitted. 'That could be just wishful thinking on my part. But it's the only shot we've got left in the locker, because I'm telling you I can't do this. I'm empty.'

Matt got himself under some kind of control and climbed to his feet. Amazingly, Juliet's embrace didn't seem to have left him aroused at all: maybe it was because of the welter of other emotions running through him – or maybe she put out different pheromones when she was being maternal.

'I'll do it,' Matt said, bleakly but calmly. 'I— Obviously. Yes. I have to do it. I can see why it has to be me.'

He looked at me, trying to keep the fear out of his face. Fear of going up against a demon, or fear of meeting his son for the first time in these less than auspicious circumstances? Maybe it was a little of both. 'So what happens?' he asked. 'You play your whistle and I . . . call his name?'

'The whistle's the last thing we need,' I said. 'I play that tune, it's like I put his arm up behind his back and jam his face into a wall. And he's had a lot of that tonight already. No, I think we need a different approach.'

I went through into the other bedroom. Like the living room it had seen a bit of ransacking, but it didn't seem to have been very thorough in this case. Some drawers pulled out, a few clothes strewn around, but that was about the extent of it. Whoever the looters were, they hadn't put their backs into it: and by providential chance, they'd run out of steam before they'd got to the wardrobe.

I went back through into Mark's room, holding his cutting kit in my hands. Once again, just from holding the box, I felt the deep, insistent pulse of long-gone feelings that Mark had left there: the echo of his excitement and his joy. I put it down on the floor in the centre of the room where everyone could see it.

'If Mark had an emotional focus, it was this,' I said.

'What is it?' Juliet asked.

'His works. A box full of razor blades, essentially, with a few more sharp objects for the sake of variety, and a bit of disinfectant. This is what he used to cut himself.' Matt winced, but he seemed to know what was expected of him.

He knelt down and touched his hand to the lid of the box. Closing his eyes he spoke Mark's name.

Nothing happened. With my psychic antenna fully extended, I listened to the eerie silence beyond the windows. It was still dark out there. I looked at my watch and it was way past seven o'clock. There ought to be some light in the sky by now.

Matt called again, a little louder. Still nothing. No sense of movement, either on the psychic plane or in the world of brute, inarguable flesh.

A minute or two passed like this, with Matt calling Mark's name and nobody answering.

'Okay,' I said at last. 'It seemed like a good idea. Sorry to waste your time.'

'Where did he die?' Juliet asked. We all looked at her. 'The boy,' she clarified unnecessarily. 'Where did he die? Was it in this room?'

'No,' Coldwood said, pointing. 'It was out there. He threw himself off the walkway.'

'Then that's where we should be.'

It was clutching at straws, but it was worth a shot. I nodded and went to retrieve the cutting kit from the floor, but Matt had already picked it up and seemed unwilling to hand it over.

'Let's go,' I said.

The hallway was completely still. We pulled open the swing doors – with some difficulty because of the broken glass and débris littering the floor – and stepped out into the darkness. Automatically I looked towards the east. The sliver of light I'd seen there before had gone now: the sky was unrelieved black from horizon to zenith. Except that there wasn't any horizon, to speak of. The nearer towers loomed out of the dark like black cliff faces, pitted with darker holes like caves where the broken windows stared down at us. Beyond that, there was nothing.

Matt was in the lead as we spread out across the walkway. He cleared a space with his foot, knelt and set the cutting kit down between his knees. He looked up into the blind, black sky.

'Mark,' he said again. 'This is Matthew, your –' he choked on the word but he got it out '– your father. Please stop this. Please let these people—'

He didn't even get to finish the sentence. A wind from nowhere ripped the breath from his mouth. It hit us full-on, sending Coldwood and me slip-sliding backwards on the treacherous footing of broken glass and powdered brick. Juliet leaned into it and kept her footing.

A second later, we realised that the dust and débris on the walkway hadn't stirred. This was a wind that had no quarrel with matter: just with us.

'Mark—' Matt yelled, and the darkness swallowed the sound so that, standing a scant few feet away from him, I could barely hear it.

I heard an answering bellow, though, equally muted but many-throated. It came from the windows above, where the pale blobs of faces could now be seen looking down at us.

Okay. That probably wasn't good. Juliet was staring at Matt. I touched her shoulder and, as she turned towards me, pointed up. She nodded. She was aware of the watchers already: she didn't need to see them to know they were there.

Matt was still speaking, speaking continuously now, but the words were torn up and scattered by the void-wind so they never reached me. Seeing Juliet walk past Matt to guard the further end of the walkway, I turned with Gary beside me to watch the nearer end.

They came on us from both sides at once, with the terrifying, utterly focused madness of the possessed. There were a couple of dozen of them, and I realised with a shock that I actually knew some of the ones at our end: they were the gang that Bic's older brother belonged to. They had jagged shards of glass in their hands, and blood coursed down over their wrists unheeded as they ran at us. Gary faced them with his bare fists, but I had my whistle out and I blew the first skirling notes of the wound-demon's exorcism in their faces like pepper spray. They slowed and faltered, which saved Gary from being julienned in the first couple of seconds. After that, even though they moved like sleepwalkers, he was fighting for his life. The narrowness of the walkway worked in our favour, but there were so many of them: and a single lucky thrust might be all it took. Coldwood ducked and punched, spun and kicked, used every dirty trick they teach in cop school. I dropped the whistle and joined him, humming the exorcism tune between dry lips as I fought.

For a packed and frantic minute I held my own: then an actual knife rather than a glass one, thrown through a gap between the nearest attackers, caught me in the left shoulder, close to the throat. It must have been wickedly sharp: the thick cloth of my paletot would have kept a dull blade from penetrating too deep. Or perhaps the demon's magic worked like a blessing on knives and caltrops. In any case it went in hilt-deep, and I screamed with the shock and the pain.

I threw another punch, right-handed, but being a southpaw I threw it without any real conviction. The plukey teenager I was facing took it squarely on the chin and then rushed me, his clutching fingers closing around my throat as he raised his jagged-edged shank to plunge it into my face.

Someone hit him from behind, making him sprawl on top of me. I got a handful of his hair, levered his head up away from me and slammed my forehead into the bridge of his nose, giving him something else to think about. He jerked and went limp and I rolled him – with an awkward, one-handed heave – to the side.

I barely glimpsed my rescuer as he jumped right over me and charged on towards Matt. I saw him dive on a guy who'd got past our little Horatio-at-the-bridge last stand and was about to slit Matt's throat from behind. Further away, Juliet dipped and pirouetted in an elaborate ballet of carnage, inert and damaged bodies flying and falling away from her as her hands and feet wove their skein of graceful violence.

Then I returned my attention to the last few stragglers who were still trying to gut Coldwood. A half-brick to the back of the neck discouraged two of them, even in my weaker hand, and Gary took out the last man with his knee and his elbow.

We stared at each other, panting, taking a full three seconds to register the lull. It wouldn't last. The demon had hurled the nearest tools it could find at us. It had a thousand more lying ready to hand, and it wouldn't take more than a moment to hurl them into the breach. It could empty the whole estate on our heads. And then what? Even if we survived, what would we do when the damned thing started to look further afield?

Juliet walked towards us, heedless of the bodies that she stepped on. She was staring at the newcomer, who was facing Matt head-on as Matt came slowly upright. They seemed unable to look away from each other.

I knew this guy too, I realised without surprise. It was the dead man who I'd met here on the first day, and then again on the footbridge at Love Walk. The man who'd talked in a woman's voice and apologised as he'd tried to throw me off the bridge to my death.

I took a step towards him, and his gaze flicked momentarily to me. He nodded an acknowledgement, but his eyes narrowed as if the sight of me raised unpleasant memories.

'I hope that makes us even,' he said.

That voice again: *trompe l'oeil* for the ear. The wrong sex, the wrong age, the wrong – what? The wrong end of the map, is what. London, instead of Liverpool. Now instead of then. Drowned instead of waving.

'I wasn't sure what you were going to do,' he went on. 'If you'd tried to do an exorcism – I was going to kill you.' There was a knife in his hand – a heavy, brutal thing, double-edged, that looked as though you could use it to gut and skin rhinoceroses. He held it up by way of illustration. 'I would have had to, Fix. I'd already made up my mind. I know what you are. What you can do. You told me all about it a long time ago. But – you didn't try to hurt him. You talked to him.'

His gaze went to Matt again. Slowly and hesitantly, his

hand came out as though to touch Matt's cheek, but he stopped short and then withdrew it again.

'It didn't work,' Matt said. 'He won't answer me. But perhaps if we both try—?'

The pale man drew in a breath. Or at least, his chest worked as though he was *trying* to draw in a breath. There was no accompanying sound, and for a moment he seemed unable to speak. His fists clenched, and his face twisted into something like a grimace. It took me a while to realise that he was trying to cry, as well as to breathe. Zombies can't do either.

Finally he nodded. But at the same time he turned to me.

'Alone,' he said. 'The two of us. Fix, you can't be in on this. You, especially, can't be in on this.'

I threw up my hands, palms out. 'I'm good,' I said, the raggedness of my voice betraying me. I was anything but good. I was exhausted and hurting. Blood from my shoulder had found its way down the inside of my sleeve and was now running the length of my fingers before pattering to the ground in a continuous drip-drip-drip that sounded unnaturally loud in the surrounding stillness. I felt the pressure of the demon's attention, drawn by the blood. And then I felt its heavy, invisible gaze pass beyond me to the two figures at the centre of the walkway.

I backed away, one step at a time. Juliet and Coldwood came with me, Gary throwing a curious glance at the man who'd come out of nowhere to help us.

'Okay,' he said. 'Was he part of the programme?'

'No,' I said. 'Pure serendipity. It has to work on our side every once in a while.'

'What's his name?'

I shook my head. It was a long story, I was ignorant of more than half of it, and I was too tired to explain the parts I did know.

'The body belonged to a man named Roman,' I said. 'But that was a while back. I think he probably answers to Anita these days.'

Coldwood blinked. 'Anita, as in—?'

'Yeah. As in Anita Yeats. Kenny's – whatever you want to call it. She died, and she came back.'

'And she's what, cross-dressing?' Gary sounded pained.

'More or less. Ninety-nine times out a of a hundred, a zombie clings to their own flesh: Anita chose the flesh of the bloke she was knocking off. Maybe if you ask her she'll tell you why.'

I turned away from him to end the conversation, because it was scraping on a raw nerve right then. From behind us on the walkway, I heard Matt's voice and then Anita's. And then Matt's again, broken as he spoke by what sounded like sobs. I needed to get further away. I might hear some of the words, and I didn't feel strong enough for that. I pushed the swing doors open and stepped back into Weston Block. For a moment the floor under me seemed to lurch and shift. I slumped against the wall, waiting for the dizziness to pass. It intensified instead. It was costing me a lot of effort just to stay on my feet.

'Christ,' I muttered. 'I need a Band-Aid and some TCP.'

Gary inspected the knife that was still jutting out of my shoulder. 'You need a hospital,' he said. 'If we take this out you'll bleed like a stuck pig.'

By way of answer, I held up my blood-boltered hand.

Coldwood was unimpressed. 'That's nothing compared to the Niagara you're going to see when that knife comes out,' he said. 'Stay there, Fix. Do not fucking move.'

He got out his phone, dialled and started talking rapidly into it. But I couldn't follow the words. Juliet was talking too, looking back the way we'd come, out onto the walkway. I turned my head – actually, turned my body because my neck didn't seem able to move independently any more – and followed her gaze.

Matt was talking to the sky. Anita in her borrowed flesh stood beside him with her hands clenched into fists, her neck craned right back, her pale flesh almost luminous in the surrounding darkness. Something blacker than the darkness hovered above them, almost close enough to touch. Its voice was a soundless pulse inside my head: diastole followed by systole, the tide of my own blood given voice. Anita raised her hands – Roman's hands – above her head, not in surrender but as if she was trying to reach something that hung in the air above her, to lift it down. Matt had his hands on her shoulders now, offering her strength or comfort or maybe just clinging to her to keep from falling down onto his knees.

I thought of the two of them in the nativity play: *Come, Joseph. I am close to my time and we must reach Bethlehem before our baby is born.* It was too much. I closed my eyes and looked away.

But the darkness was still there, behind my eyes. It filled the space around me, so big and so vast that it became to all intents and purposes the landscape in which I stood. And I remembered that I'd stood here before, in this self-same black-on-black void: conversing with the genius loci,

which had named itself and then asked me – pleaded with
me – to stay.

not leave this place.

Which I'd read as a threat instead of what it was: the
lost boy asking not to be left alone in the dark.

The lightless immensity gathered itself and began to
shrink: receded from me by concentrating its terrible
essence into a smaller and smaller space. Soon it was almost
invisible: a distant point of anti-light, impossibly small,
painfully vivid. Then it winked out altogether, like the
dot in the centre of the screen when you turn off an old
CRT television set. What it left behind in the place where
it had been was an absence, almost equally dark but empty
of being, drained of purpose.

A metallic clatter from somewhere nearby made my
eyes snap open. The knife had fallen from my shoulder,
and Coldwood, still on the phone, was staring at it with
a bemused look on his face.

I put my finger in through the hole in the neck of my
paletot, searching for the wound. It had gone. My skin
was completely unbroken.

The demon – my kinsman, my brother's only son – had
withdrawn itself from me, and this was the mark of its
disfavour. A moment later, the rising sun peered out from
behind Boateng Tower and – finding no substantial opposition – threw its radiant weight around the suddenly clear
sky.

Bethlehem. That's where we're all heading for. The
rough beasts and the messiahs and the poor bloody infantry,
all slouching along together to the place where we'll finally
be counted.

24

Anita started to deteriorate almost as soon as Mark's spirit left us.

I'd seen this before. It wasn't physical decay: it was a more subtle and inexorable surrender, a failure of the motive force, the driving will-power that allows something as tenuous and fragile as a ghost to bludgeon something as solid as a body into submission. Her farewell to her son and her reconciliation with Matt had shifted some crucial point of balance within her, and her hold over her borrowed flesh was faltering moment by moment. She was slowing to a final halt.

We sat with her amidst the rubble of the walkway, keeping her company while she died for the second time. She told us about the first time: about how Kenny had found her and Roman in flagrante, in the climactic phase of a hastily snatched knee-trembler in the flat's poky kitchen.

She'd been doing the ironing before the sex got under way, and it was the iron that Kenny used to kill her. She was still turning, trying to disengage herself from Roman's embrace when it hit her, and that was the last she knew. But Kenny carried on hitting her for a long time after she was dead. She knew that because . . . well, because she'd seen the results. Later.

She woke in the ground: a burning splinter of consciousness filled with fear and urgency, not knowing why it had no eyes to see with and no hands to claw its way free from the undefined place where it was caught.

She did the zombie thing, but the zombie thing didn't work. Her own body was mostly pulp, bones broken in so many places her insides were like the kids' game of Pick-Up Sticks.

But Roman's body was right next to her, and Roman had been killed with a single stab wound to the neck. She didn't know why Kenny had dropped the iron and used a knife: maybe it was a kitchen knife that Roman had picked up to defend himself and Kenny had turned against him. It didn't matter, anyway. Roman's spirit had gone on to its eternal reward, and his flesh was lying there with a TO LET, UNFURNISHED sign figuratively pinned to his chest.

Anita moved in, and sat up. Kenny had buried them in his allotment, and he hadn't troubled to bury them deep because he was the only one who ever went there. She carefully replaced the soil so there was no sign of what had happened, and went off to settle accounts with her bastard husband.

But she wasn't sure how exactly she should go about it. She didn't feel she could go to the police because she had no way of proving who she was. She didn't even know whether the born-again could give evidence in court, or whether she'd be allowed to walk free again once she'd brought herself to the authorities' notice. Was taking Roman's body actually a crime? Would she be dispossessed and kicked out into nothingness? She couldn't let that happen.

And she'd spent longer underground than she thought

she had: almost a full year, in fact, which was why there was no change in the weather to warn her. When she got back to the Salisbury, it was to find Mark already dead. The shock and pain of it almost made her release her hold on life right then and there, but she held on by main force, determined to stay in the world long enough to see that Kenny got his come-uppance.

So while Kenny stalked Matt, she stalked Kenny. And when Kenny finally baited his sick, over-elaborate little trap, she was watching from a little way off. She saw Matt keep the rendezvous. She saw him walk away. She saw Kenny cut his own arms, his own face, squeezing out enough blood so that he could write Matt's name on his windshield. He was crazed, she said, revelling in it. There was no doubt at all that the wound-demon was inside him by this time, influencing his thoughts and actions. It wasn't responsible for Kenny's hatred of Matt: that had always been there, for as long as he'd known that Matt was Mark's father. But it was certainly the demon that made Kenny's revenge take the shape it did.

Anita watched the parked car for more than an hour. When she was certain that Kenny had passed out from blood loss, she moved in and finished the job with Roman's Swiss army penknife. It had just come to her, as she stared down at him, that she was never going to have a better chance: that her zombie body was too slow and uncoordinated for her to fight him when he was awake and alert. The temptation had grown in her, and suddenly she'd had the knife in her hand and she was working it backwards and forwards in Kenny's neck. The wound-demon again, maybe, although God knows she had reason enough on her own account to want Kenny dead. 'Cutting that bastard's throat was the best thing I ever did,' she said, through lips that were now a cyanotic blue. 'I just wish – I'd done it back when we were all – kids. I wish—'

She shook her head, unable to put the waste and the wistfulness into words.

'The penknife,' Coldwood said, ever the consummate cop. 'The one you used to finish Seddon off. Is there any chance you—'

'It was in my jacket,' Anita said. 'The pocket of my jacket. And the jacket was covered in blood. I couldn't bear the feel of it on my skin. I took it off and I – I threw it away. I don't know where.'

'I do,' I said to Coldwood. 'There's a car park underneath that underpass. I looked over the edge when you first called me to the crime scene, and I saw a jacket there behind some wheelie bins. You probably can't see it at all from the ground, so it may still be there.'

Coldwood went away to make another phone call, and Anita lapsed into silence. Then another thought occurred to her, and she cast her gaze around until she saw me.

'Fix,' she mumbled. 'I'm sorry I hurt you. I knew – I knew by then what Mark had turned into, and I thought you'd come to send him away. I was so scared, when I first saw you – I wasn't thinking straight. I wasn't – myself.' Her eyes rolled weakly as she saw the ironic sense of the words.

'Nobody on the Salisbury was, by that time,' I reminded her. 'It's okay, Anita. In a bizarre way you actually helped me. It was while I was in hospital that I saw Mark for the first time, and started fitting the pieces together.'

'Nita,' Matt said, his voice cracking, 'I'm so sorry. I'm so sorry I left you. If you'd told me – if I'd known that you were pregnant—'

Anita stared at him, perplexed. 'I knew you would have come,' she murmured. 'But – I didn't want to make you come, Matty. Not like that. What would it have meant – if you married me because I blackmailed you? And if you gave up – everything else you wanted – to be with me? You would have – hated me.'

He shook his head in denial or protest, sobbing aloud now. Anita put a hand up to touch his face.

'Don't cry,' she said. 'I don't want to see you cry. You ought to bless me. Now that you've heard my confession.'

Matt didn't bless her. I think I understood why he couldn't do that, even though he knew the words would have comforted her. To say a blessing would have been to turn back into a priest: it was too big a jump from where he was, and in a direction that he simply couldn't take right then.

He kissed her instead. The lips were rotting, because this was a body two years dead, and they weren't even hers in the first place. But then, this was a kiss that had been pending for a lot longer than two years: it probably didn't matter as much as you'd think.

Tired of waiting for me to get the hint on my own, Juliet grabbed my lapels and hauled me away, off the walkway into the ruins of Weston Block. It's coming to something when I have to take lessons in tact from a pit-spawned monster.

Although, it suddenly struck me, that was a phrase that needed to be scanned.

'Juliet,' I said tentatively.

'Yes, Castor?'

I picked my words carefully. 'I've always had – some fixed ideas about Hell. They seemed to make sense, in terms of the available evidence. It's kind of a point on a moral compass. It's where bad people go when they die, and the demons that live there have to be bad too, or they wouldn't be there in the first place.'

Juliet stared at me, deadpan. 'Yes. So?'

'So – how much of that is bullshit?'

There was a silence during which we could hear Coldwood on the floor below us chewing out one of his subordinates. 'Well, whichever corner is closest to the bloody underpass. Are you seeing wheelie bins? Well, right fucking there, then. Look behind them. I don't care how much fucking mess there is—'

'How many demons, Castor,' Juliet asked me, in a tone of long-suffering patience, 'have been summoned by how many necromancers and mages and scholars and hobbyists and enthusiastic imbeciles? Down the centuries, from the Middle Ages when the first grimoires were written, to the present day when the grimoires are almost irrelevant because you can raise a hell-hound with an incautious word? How many, would you say?'

I shrugged impatiently. 'I don't know. Hundreds? Thousands?'

'Or tens of thousands. And not one of them has ever discussed these matters with the ones who summoned them.'

'We don't know that.'

'Trust me,' said Juliet. 'It's the truth. Not one of them.

I told you a long time ago that there were certain things I wasn't prepared to discuss with you. I told you this was one of them. It still is.'

'What, because you're afraid?' I demanded, still hurting too much to be circumspect. 'Because you think I'll use the information against you in some way?'

'Not you, perhaps. And not against me. But someone, sometime. Against my kind.'

'Juliet, you're working as a fucking exorcist. You're already a class traitor, so what's to be coy about?'

She took a sudden step towards me, and the look on her face was so dark that I raised my fists, as if I had a hope in Hell against her if she wanted to take me out. But all she did was grasp my chin in her hand and hold my face in place as she brought her own up close. Mostly that only happens when I'm asleep and dreaming.

'Do you see a difference between the public execution of a criminal and an act of genocide?' she asked me, speaking very softly but very distinctly.

'I'm fort of oppoved to bofe,' I mumbled, unable to part my jaws.

'Whereas I'm perfectly happy with the first, but by and large prefer not to abet the second.' She let go of me, but she was still standing close enough that her achingly beautiful scent filled the air between us. 'Understand me, Castor. It occurred to me not to allow you — any of you — to walk away with what you've learned today. A few more deaths in the course of the riot wouldn't have raised any eyebrows or merited any special investigation. But I've gone native. I know that. I can't help thinking of you as a friend. Or to put it less sentimentally, having to murder you would make me unhappy.

'So you get to live. And you also get – at no additional cost – these three pieces of advice. Don't push this topic any further. Don't ask questions that you may not want to know the answers to. And don't assume for a moment that if you make me choose between you and my entire race, I'll choose you.'

I was about to answer her, but I wasn't able to because she pressed her lips to mine and kissed me, deeply and passionately.

This was our third kiss, and it was different from the other two. The first, way back when Gabriel McClennan had first summoned Juliet, had been part of a concerted attempt to devour my flesh and spirit in accordance with her brief: it had been an attack, which I'd only survived through dumb luck and fortuitous rescue. The second had lent me enough of her strength to survive the hardest and most gruelling exorcism of my entire life: it was a gift, and I'd never stopped being grateful for it.

This one was a warning. It was meant to remind me of her power, and of how little effort it would take her to destroy me.

When Juliet finally removed her lips from mine I sagged backwards and almost fell. But she kept me upright with one strong arm around my waist.

'I'd prefer,' she said, 'not to have to choose.'

She propped me up against the wall, not without care, and walked away.

Eventually I pulled myself together and became aware of the outside world again. Matt was still kneeling beside Anita on the walkway outside. I couldn't tell from this distance whether she was still moving and speaking, whether her spirit was still present, but either way I suspected that he wouldn't want to be disturbed. Coldwood was still talking on the phone on the landing below, directing his lackeys to take whatever they'd found down to the forensic lab on Lambeth Road and then stay with it until the results came through.

I stumbled across to the lift and pressed the call button. It came at once and didn't smell of piss, as befits an age of miracle and wonder. It made a scary grinding noise as it descended, though, and the floor shuddered and bucked under my feet as if some corner of the cage was scraping against the wall of the shaft. I was profoundly relieved when I got to the ground floor and the doors, after a few premonitory clicks and ratcheting sounds, slid open.

Outside on the concrete apron, paramedics were tacking between the other towers and the fleet of waiting ambulances, carrying bodies on stretchers: all alive, thank God, but then again they'd have left the dead where they were as a substantially lower priority. The police and fire crews were moving too, clearing barricades and locking off stairwells while they conducted shouted conversations on walkie-talkies.

I walked through the melee, unnoticed, and descended the steps to the New Kent Road. More ambulances here, and more cops. Also, away behind the barriers, the media crews and the disaster tourists.

I almost walked past Trudie Pax without seeing her. She was sitting at the edge of the kerb, her shoulders slumped, staring at the ground.

'Long night,' I said. 'How's Bic?'

She started at the sound of my voice, looked up at me as though for a moment she'd forgotten where she was.

'Castor—' She scrambled to her feet with a kind of urgency, but then didn't seem to know what to do when she'd got there. Her hands moved without purpose, and I suddenly realised that she'd been crying.

'What?' I asked. A horrible portent crashed into me from nowhere: like a contact on my death-sense, but with no ghost present. 'What's wrong? Did something happen to the kid?'

Trudie shook her head, but I read something else in her face: something like guilt, or maybe shame. I took a hold on her shoulders without even knowing I was doing it.

'Where is he?' I demanded. 'Where did you take him?'

Her gaze flicked left. I turned my head to see a light green tent where two or three nurses fussed around a huge water-heater while half a dozen others distributed the resultant hot horse-piss among the shell-shocked survivors: a comfort station.

'He's . . . in there,' she said.

And he was. I caught a sudden glimpse of him, still in his pyjamas, sitting next to his father while his mother knelt in front of him and wiped at his grimy face with a damp J-cloth, showing the same merciless assiduity that all mothers show when they decide that you need a public face-washing. And Bic was fighting back the way all kids do, by squirming and shifting around to make the task as hard as possible.

'He's fine,' Trudie blurted. And he was. It was plain to see.

'Then is there something else on your mind?' I began. 'Because you don't look—'

The penny started to drop as I was speaking, because my gaze had lingered on Bic and I finally saw what was staring me in the face. They were the wrong pyjamas: plain blue flannel rather than rampant superheroes. In a war zone? Someone had stopped to change him out of his old gear in the middle of all this? And not into outdoor clothes, but into another set of PJs?

'I didn't know,' Trudie was saying, her voice high and strained. 'They didn't tell me.'

I stared at her in sudden, near-incontinent horror. 'While – while Cheadle was making you change—'

'Father Gwillam had Sallis plant a GPS pip on the boy. He didn't tell me, Castor. When I said that you should trust me, I meant it. I never lied to you. I've told them I won't stay in the order—'

I was already running. I had to get out past the police roadblocks and out onto a road where there was some traffic running. The Walworth Road: there ought to be some cabs there. But the crowds of onlookers seemed to stretch out to the crack of doom, and short of bludgeoning them to the ground there was no way to get through them at anything faster than an arthritic shuffle.

Coldwood. I turned and headed back towards the steps, caught sight of him almost immediately coming down them. I headed towards him, but someone grabbed hold of my arm. Trudie again, her face red with crying.

'Let me come with you. Let me help.'

'When I need your help,' I snarled, 'I'll swallow a razor blade. It's quicker.' I pulled free with a savage wrench and yelled at Gary just as he was getting into the back of a big black cop-mobile. He saw me coming and stopped.

'I need to get to Peckham,' I panted.

'Try walking for once,' he told me coolly. 'I'm about to get your brother off a murder charge, and then I'm back here all day dealing with the fallout from this shit-fest.'

'Gary, I'm serious. I need to get to Peckham fucking now. It won't wait.'

He gave me a quizzical look and opened his mouth to argue the toss some more. With an agonised bellow of frustration, I grabbed his lapels and yelled into his face. 'Asmodeus! Fucking Asmodeus! You remember St Michael's church, in Acton? Abbie Torrington? The body bags at the Whiteleaf shopping mall?'

'Get in,' Gary said. And to the driver, 'Take him where he tells you. I'll scrape up an ARU and follow you.'

Amazingly, Trudie Pax was still with me. She got into the other side of the car at the same time as I got in myself. Kicking her out again would have scratched an itch, but it would have wasted ten or twenty seconds – longer if she'd fought – and I could always do it once the car was moving.

I told the driver Imelda Probert's address and waited in an agony of impatience as he threaded his way slowly and carefully through the interlaced armies of fire-fighters and nurses. Once we were clear, though, he put the siren on and hit the reheat, slamming us back into the leather upholstery.

Trudie was talking to me, but the words washed over me like whale-song. I was trying to decide which of the many appalling outcomes from this I was most afraid of.

And which I was actually hoping for.

25

The front door of Imelda's was broken in and hanging on a single hinge.

On the second-floor landing, Rafi's door seemed untouched, but closer inspection showed that someone had fired several bullets through the lock until the striking plate simply came away from the splintered door frame.

No sign of Rafi, but Sallis was there. He was staring at nothing. His hands were clasped across his lower abdomen, but they hadn't been able to halt the jack-in-the-box exuberance of bloody intestines that had spilled out through the huge hole in his lower torso. Feld was there, too: parts of him, anyway. Trudie was noisily sick in the corner of the room. I left her there, still sobbing and heaving.

A trail of bloody footprints led up the stairs from the second floor to the third. Imelda's door had been torn loose and thrown across the landing where it lay, in two separate pieces, on the floor.

I went inside with my heart hammering a hectic, unsustainable beat like a schoolgirl's skipping rope when she's high on adrenalin and pushing it too far: about to fall, all tangled up in her own misjudgement; about to hit the asphalt one last and lasting time.

Imelda was in her kitchen, which had become an abattoir. Her head was in Lisa's lap, and Lisa was in shock:

exhausted and bullied by grief into some private place from which she didn't stir when I came in.

But Imelda did stir. Amazingly, she wasn't quite dead, though how a body could take so much damage, so much insult, and still not yield up the spirit it contained was a mystery beyond my fathoming.

She couldn't speak. Judging from the blood that covered her lower face like a painted-on beard, Asmodeus had torn out her tongue. But she could move her right arm, just barely. She lifted it, like Atlas hefting the weight of the world. It trembled, but it stayed aloft while her chest rose and fell three times. Three last, agonising breaths.

She pointed at me.

And I nodded, accepting both the accusation and the challenge in those tortured, furious eyes.

You did this.

You talked to him, and he wound his lies around you.

You gave him to eat, and he grew stronger.

You let fools follow you here, and the fools set him free. Whatever they thought to do — whether to destroy him or to bind him faster — in their blind arrogance they set him free.

You killed me, Castor.

And now you have to kill your best friend.

extras

www.orbitbooks.net

about the author

Mike Carey is the acclaimed writer of *Lucifer* and *Hellblazer* (now filmed as *Constantine*). He has also written extended runs for Marvel's fan-favourite titles *X-Men* and *Ultimate Fantastic Four*, the comic book adaptation of Neil Gaiman's *Neverwhere*, and a movie screenplay, *Frost Flowers*, soon to be produced by Hadaly/Bluestar Pictures. He lives in London with his wife, Linda, also a novelist and screenwriter, their three children and a cat named Tasha.

For more information about Mike Carey visit www.mike-carey.co.uk

Find out more about Mike and other Orbit authors by registering for the free monthly newsletter at www.orbitbooks.net

interview

This is your fourth Felix Castor novel. Have you found the story branching off in areas you didn't expect when you started or has everything gone exactly to plan?

The plan is crucial, and everything conforms to the plan right up to the point where you start writing – then it instantly becomes irrelevant. No, I'm exaggerating for effect there. In terms of the big issues, the overall structure of the series, I've mostly stuck very close to what I originally had in mind. But a lot of the grace notes, incidentals, supporting cast and their arcs, came to me as I was writing and then were built into the whole. To take the most obvious example, Nicky Heath wasn't dead in the original Castor pitch: I just had this great idea when I got to that part of *The Devil You Know*, that he'd be much more interesting as a zombie.

There's a bit from Mervyn Peake's journal where he talks about sticking to the plan for Gormenghast while 'staying on the *qui vive* for a better idea'. That's what you find yourself doing: if you've built it right, the plan is the structural skeleton that gives you the luxury of improvising without falling apart.

Did the idea for the Castor books come to you fully realised or did you have one particular starting point from which it grew?

The starting point was Castor himself: the idea of a Chandler-style private eye who's actually a private exorcist. Then I had a subsidiary idea for the mechanics of the story – for how the various undead beings could be explained and connected to each other. Throwing those two ideas against each other gave me a rough vision of how the first three novels would play out, and the big reveal we might play towards in the longer term – if there was a longer term.

Like you, Felix Castor hails from Liverpool but makes his home in London. The advantages to this 'write what you know' approach are obvious, but have you found any pitfalls to writing Castor's history so much in line with your own?

Yes! In *Thicker Than Water*, the fourth novel, I take Castor back to Liverpool. There's a lot about his parents there, a lot about his brother Matthew, a lot about his relationships with other kids he knew in Walton. Without going into detail, there were whole chapters there that I wrote and then cut out because I realised after I'd written them that they were (a) confessional and (b) cathartic. They were there for me, not for the reader, and they just had to go. I also had to change some details for more mundane reasons, to avoid getting punched in the face the next time I see some of my friends and relatives.

Your take on the supernatural is almost scientific in its logic. Do you think there is a scientific explanation for everything or do you have some belief in the supernatural?

I'm an atheist when it comes to God, but an agnostic when it comes to most supernatural phenomena. Don't get me wrong, I come at these things from a rationalist perspective – and I'm dead set against the way the rationalist consensus is now under attack by extremists in pretty much every organised religion. But I don't necessarily see a fixed and unwavering line between the things that science can explain and the things that it can't. Quantum physics, if you see it from one point of view, looks very much like superstition and mumbo jumbo. I'm a rationalist but not a materialist: I believe in spirit, in a sort of animistic essence that outlives the body, whether or not it can be seen and measured. So I don't see any reason why the existence of ghosts, for example, offers any kind of affront to a scientific world view. The world is energies as well as objects, and we're constantly realising that there are some beans we haven't counted yet. You know, I'd better stop while there are still some metaphors I haven't mixed.

What advantages and disadvantages do you see in using fantasy as the vehicle for your stories?

I never really had any choice. I don't think I could write totally realistic fiction, although I'd be curious to try. For me, the spectrum that extends from horror through fantasy to science fiction is where I feel most comfortable and where I wanted to pitch my tent as a writer. Coming back to the previous question, not believing in Heaven doesn't reconcile me any better to Earth. I'm happiest when I'm cutting off at an odd angle, playing with counter-factual worlds.

It almost feels to me as though fantasy is a dimension – I mean, in the same way that length and height and breadth are dimensions. My step-father-in-law, Eric, finds it hard to read any fantastic literature because he can't take that first step of investing belief in the fiction – of accepting its premises. I said to him once 'so you're like a guy who loves ice cream, but only ever eats vanilla'. It was a really unfair comparison, but I feel that strongly about the pleasures and experiences that fantasy has to offer. I'd feel like I was living in Flatland if I tried to write something that was wholly realistic.

Do you find it frustrating that so much excellent work is currently being produced in SF and fantasy but that by and large it is still ignored by the literati?
I did, once. I think Philip Pullman and J. K. Rowling between them have done a lot to kick those doors down.

Do you have any particular favourite authors who have influenced your work?
Mervyn Peake. Ursula LeGuin. China Mieville. And in comics, Alan Moore, Neil Gaiman, Grant Morrison. I love and seek out two things: outrageous ideas and a vivid, chewy or elegant written style. The writers I come back to again and again are the ones that seem to me to offer both of those things.

Do you have a set writing routine and if so, what is it?
I don't really have a routine in terms of how my working day is structured. I have a core working day, which is from 8.00 a.m. when the kids go to school to 4.00 in the afternoon when they usually come back. Most evenings, though, I'll go back and do a couple more hours after that. I work weekends – Saturday morning, Sunday afternoon. I discovered a long time ago how easy it is to throw yourself out of the working mood – the zone, whatever you want to call it – and how hard it is sometimes to find it again. But then I realised something else, which is that the times when you're not working are probably necessary, too: part of the process. I don't worry so much about taking breaks now, because I know I'll pay that time back sooner rather than later.

How extensively do you plot your novels before you start writing them? Do you plot the entire trilogy/series before you start writing or do you prefer to let the story roam where it will?

The first two Castor novels were plotted in obsessive detail. The third I left a bit looser, and it changed more as I was writing it. I prefer on the whole to work with a detailed plan for the reasons I mentioned above. The plan is very useful as an anchor, and paradoxically it frees you up to change your mind because you've got a clear idea in your head of how a change *here* will feed through to what happens way over *there*.

Is this a strategy that has served you well in your comics writing?

It came out of the comics writing, to a large extent. I had the good fortune to work over many years with Shelly Bond at DC's Vertigo imprint. Shelly is one of the best editors I've ever met, and she insists on very explicit scene breakdowns. At first I found that a bit of a bind, but I soon realised that when you've only got twenty-two pages to tell your story, you've more or less got to become a miser, counting out story beats one at a time from a grubby burlap bag that you hide under your mattress. I still tend to do those breakdowns, even when I'm working with editors who don't specifically ask for them. Again, you don't let them become strait-jackets: you launch from them and come back to them, again and again.

Some authors talk of their characters 'surprising' them by their actions; is this something that has happened to you?

You know, every time I hear someone say that, it sounds like a boast to me. Like, 'my process is really, really organic; my characters are so vivid, they get up off the page and jam with me. Sometimes we go to wild parties together'. I guess it's just a question of what you mean by that, though. It's possible to get to a certain point in your story and suddenly think 'yeah, but he wouldn't do that, he'd do this'. And it can *feel* surprising. But really it's your mind gradually getting a grasp of the character, and the details filling themselves out as you write. It happens gradually, but you can notice it suddenly. In that sense, I've been surprised.

Finally, if the Felix Castor books were ever filmed, who would you like to see directing and starring in the movies?

I just want to be there when they cast Juliet, that's all.

if you enjoyed
THICKER THAN WATER
look out for

ALREADY DEAD

by

Charlie Huston

I SMELL THEM BEFORE I SEE THEM. All the powders, perfumes and oils the half-smart ones smear on themselves. The stupid ones just stumble around reeking. The really smart ones take a Goddamn shower. The water doesn't help them in the long run, but the truth is, nothing is gonna help them in the long run. In the long run they're gonna die. Hell, in the long run they're already dead.

So this pack is half-smart. They've splashed themselves with Chanel No. 5, Old Spice, whatever. Most folks just think they have a heavy hand at the personal scent counter. I close my eyes and inhale deeper, because it could just be a group of bridge and tunnelers in from Jersey or Long Island. But it's not. I take that second breath and sure enough, there it is underneath: the sweet, subtle tang of something not quite dead. Something freshly rotting. I'm betting they're the ones I'm looking for. And why wouldn't they be? It's not like these things are thick on the ground. Not yet. I walk a little farther down Avenue A and stop at the sidewalk window of Nino's, the pizza joint on the corner of St Marks.

I rap on the counter with the ring on my middle finger and one of the Neapolitans comes over.

—Yeah?

—What's fresh?

He looks blank.

—The pizza, what's just out of the oven?

—Tomato and garlic.

—No way, no fucking garlic. How 'bout the broccoli, it been out all day?

He shrugs.

—Fine, give me the broccoli. Not too hot, I don't want to burn the roof of my mouth.

He cuts a slice and slides it into the oven to warm up. I could eat the tomato and garlic if I wanted to. It's not like the garlic would hurt me or anything. I just don't like the shit.

While I wait I lean on the counter and watch the customers inside the joint. The usual crowd for a Friday night: couple drunk NYU kids, couple drunk greasers, a drunk squatter, two drunk yuppics on an East Village adventure, a couple drunk hip-hoppers, and the ones I'm looking for. There are three of them standing around the far corner table: an old-school goth chick, and two rail-thin guys, with impossibly high cheekbones, that have fashion junkie written all over them. The kind of guys who live in a squat but make the fashion-week scene by virtue of the skag they bring to the parties. Just my favorite brand of shitdogs all in all.

—Broccoli.

The Neapolitan is back with my slice. I hand him three bucks. The goth and the fashion junkies watch the two NYU kids stumble out the door. They push their slices around for another minute, then follow. I sprinkle red pepper flakes on my slice and take a big bite, and sure enough it's too hot and I burn the roof of my mouth. The pizza jockey comes back and tosses my fifty cents change on the counter. I swallow, the molten cheese scorching my throat.

—I told you not too hot.

He shrugs. All the guy has to do all day is throw slices in the oven and take them out when they're ready. Ask for one not too hot and you might as well be requesting coq au vin. I grab my change, toss the slice back on the counter and take off after the junkies and the goth chick. Fucking thing had garlic in the sauce anyway.

The NYU kids have crossed the street to cut through Tompkins Square before the cops shut it down at midnight. The trio lags behind about eight yards back, walking past the old water fountain with *Faith, Hope, Temperance, Charity* carved in the stone above it. The kids reach the opposite side of the park and keep heading east on Ninth Street, deeper into Alphabet City. Great.

This block of 9th between Avenues B and C is barren, as in empty of everyone except the NYU kids, their trailers and me.

The junkies and the goth pick up the pace. I stroll. They're not going anywhere without my seeing it. What they want to do takes a bit of privacy. Better for me if they get settled someplace where they feel safe, before I move in.

They're right on the kids now. They move into a dark patch under a busted streetlamp and spread out, one on either side of the kids and one behind. There's a scuffle, movement and noise, and they all disappear. Fuck.

I jog up the street and take a look. On my left is an abandoned building. It used to be a Puerto Rican community center and performance space, before that it was a P.S. Now it's just condemned.

I follow the scent up the steps and across the small courtyard to the graffiti-covered doors. They've been chained shut for a few years, but tonight the chain is hanging loose below the hack-sawed hasp of a giant Master lock. Looks like they prepped this place in advance of their ambush. Looks like they may be a little more than half-smart.

I ease the door open and take a look. Hallway goes straight for about twelve yards then hits a T intersection. Dark. That's OK. I don't mind the dark. The dark is just fine. I slip in, close the door behind me and take a whiff. They're here, smells like they've been hanging out for a couple days. I hear the first scream and know where to go. Up to the intersection, down the hall to the right, and straight to the open classroom door.

One of the NYU kids is facedown on the floor with the goth chick kneeling on his back. She's already shoved her knife through the back of his neck, killing him. Now she's trying to jam the blade into his skull so she can split it open. The junkie guys stand by, waiting for the piñata to bust.

The other kid has jammed himself in a corner in the obligatory pool of his own fear-piss. His eyes are rolling around and he's making the high-pitched noise that people make when they're so scared they might die from it. I hate that noise.

I hear something crunchy.

The chick has the knife in. She gives it a wrenching twist and the dead kid's skull cracks open. She claws her fingers into the crack, gets a good grip and pulls, tearing the kid's head open like a piece of rotted fruit. A pomegranate. The junkies edge closer as she starts scooping out clumps of brain. Too late for that kid, so I wait a couple seconds more, watching them as they start to eat, and listening to the other kid's moaning go up another octave. Then I do my job.

It takes me three silent steps to reach the first one. My right arm loops over his right shoulder. I grab his face with my right hand while my left hand grips the back of his head. I jerk sharply clockwise, pulling up at the same time. I feel his spinal cord tear and drop him, grabbing the second one's hair before the first one hits the ground. The chick is getting up off the kid's corpse, coming at me with the knife. I punch the second junkie in the throat and let him drop. It won't kill him, but he'll stay down for a second. The chick whips the knife in a high arc and the tip rakes my forehead. Blood oozes from the cut and into my eyes.

Whatever she was before she got bit, she knew a little about using a knife, and still remembers some of it.

She's hanging back, waiting for her pal to get up so they can take me together. I measure the blank glaze in her eyes. Yeah, there's still a little of her at home. Enough to order pizza and pick out these kids as marks, enough to cut through a lock, but not enough to be dangerous. As long as I'm not stupid. I step in and she thrusts at me with the knife. I grab the blade.

She looks from me to the knife. I'm holding it tightly, blood spilling out between my clenched fingers. The dim light in her eyes gets minutely brighter as something gives her the word: she's fucked. I twist the knife out of her hand, toss it in the air and catch it by the handle. She turns to run. I grab the back of her leather jacket, step close and jam the knife into her neck at the base of her skull, chopping her medulla in half. I leave the knife there and let her drop to the floor. The second junkie is just getting back up. I kick him down, put my boot on his throat and stomp, twisting my foot back and forth until I hear his neck snap.

I kneel and wipe my hand on his shirt. My blood has already coagulated and the cuts in my hand have stopped bleeding, likewise the cut in my forehead. I check the bodies. One of the guys is missing a couple teeth and has some lacerations on his gums. Looks like he's been chewing someone's skull. Probably it belonged to the clown I took care of a couple days ago, the one with the hole in his head who tipped me off to this whole thing. Anyway, his teeth aren't what I'm interested in.

Both guys have small bites on the backs of their necks. The bite radius and size of the tooth marks make me take a look at the girl's mouth. Looks like a match. Figure she bit these two and infected them with the bacteria. Happens that way sometimes. Generally a person gets infected, the bacteria starts chewing on their brain and pretty soon they're reduced to the simple impulse to feed. But sometimes, before they reach that point, they infect a few others. They take a bite, but don't eat the whole meal if you get me. No one really knows why. Some sob sisters would tell you it's because they're lonely. But that's bullshit. It's the bacteria compelling them, spreading itself. It's fucking Darwin doing his thing.

I check the girl's neck. She infected the others, but something infected her first. The bite's been marred by the knife I stuck in her, but it's there. It's bigger than the others, more violent. In fact, there are little nips all over her neck. Fucking carrier that got her couldn't decide if it wanted to just infect her or eat her. Whatever, all the same to me. Except it means the job isn't done yet. Means there's a carrier still out there. I start to stand up. But something else; a smell on her. I kneel next to her and take a whiff. Something moves behind me.

The other NYU kid. Right, forgot about him. He's trying to dig his way through the wall. I walk over to him. I'm just about to pop him in the jaw when he does the job for me and passes out. I look him over. No bites.

Now normally I wouldn't do this, but I lost a little blood and I never got to eat my pizza, so I'm pretty hungry. I take out my works and hook the kid up. I'll only take a pint. Maybe two.

The phone wakes me in the morning. Why the hell someone is calling me in the morning I don't know, so I let the machine get it.

—*This is Joe Pitt. Leave a message.*

—Joe, it's Philip.

I don't pick up the phone, not for Philip Sax. I close my eyes and try to find my way back to sleep.

—Joe, I think maybe I got something if ya can pick up the phone.

I roll over in bed and pull the covers up to my chin. I try to remember what I was dreaming about so I can get myself back there.

—I don't wanna bug ya, Joe, but I figure ya gotta be in. It's ten in the morning, where ya gonna be?

Sleep crawls off into a corner where I can't find it and I pick up the damn phone.

—What do you want?

—Hey, Joe, busy last night?

—I was on a job, yeah. So what?

—I think ya made the news, is all. Shit.

—The papers?

—NY1.

Fucking NY1. Fucking cable. Can't do shit in this city without them poking a reporter into it.

—What'd they call it?

—Uh, *Gruesome quadruple homicide.*

—Shit.

—Looks pretty sloppy, Joe.

—Yeah, well, there weren't a lot of options.

—Uh-huh, sure, sure. What was it?

—This thing I'm working on, brain eaters.

—Zombies?

—Yeah, shamblers. I hate the Goddamn things.

—You get 'em all?

—There's a carrier.

—Carrier huh? Fucking shamblers, huh, Joe?

—Yeah.

I hang up.

It's not like I didn't know leaving the bodies over there could cause trouble, I just thought they'd sit till I could clean things up tonight. Now the neighborhood's gonna be crawling with cops. But that's the least of my worries just now, because the phone is ringing again, and I sure as shit know who it's gonna be this time.

Uptown. They want me to come uptown. Now. In broad daylight. I put on the gear.

In winter this is easy, just wrap up head to toe, pull on a ski mask and some sunglasses and go. I'm not saying it's comfortable, but it's easy and you stay inconspicuous. I'll be OK once I get to the subway, but it's four blocks from here to there, and once I get uptown it'll be another few blocks to their offices. It's those blocks between the subway stations and the front doors I worry about.

I know a guy wears a white delivery-boy outfit with white latex gloves, a big wide-brimmed white cowboy hat, and zinc oxide all over his face. It keeps him pretty well covered, but even in Manhattan he gets looks. Me, I use a burnoose.

I pull on the boots, baggy pants and shirt, then the robe. The headpiece always gives me fits and I have to relearn how it wraps every time I do this. Once it's on and feels like it won't unravel and fall off, I slip on white cotton gloves, draw the veil across my face, put on my shades and head out. Sure I get eyeballed a bit, but who gives a fuck, no one can see my face.

What I do care about is getting to First and 14th fast as I can. Even with all this cover, even with it being white and reflecting the sunlight, even though it's only four fucking blocks, I'm still getting the shit burned out of me by the short-wave UVs. And this isn't like the cuts I got last night that close right up and are gone in the morning. This hurts like hell and is gonna take days to heal. And if a patch of bare skin should happen to get hit by some direct rays? Well, I just need to be careful that doesn't happen. So I walk fast and think about aloe and ice-water baths while my skin gets roasted and my eyes tear up behind my shades and I make it to the station and rush down the steps to the sweltering, but dark platform.

The uptown guys are making a point. They could say what they need to say on the phone. They could wait for dark to rip me a new asshole, but they want to make me burn a little. They want to flex and teach me a lesson for getting sloppy. That's what's on the surface anyway. The real reason they're doing it this way is because I still haven't joined the Coalition. And the truth is, I haven't joined exactly because of shit like this. But I did get sloppy last night, and someone is gonna swing for it. So I'll fry a little to keep them happy and to keep myself alive. Because I don't want to die. Except, oh yeah, I'm already dead.